Gamrick had been looking for evidence that Seaman Paul Anderson orchestrated the killing of Gus Downs. Downs had died in the gun turret explosion, and left Anderson two million dollars in insurance money.

Now Gamrick had his evidence. Hard evidence —as hard as it could get.

It came in the mail. Four photographs. They were grainy color prints, but they were clear enough. Anderson and Downs were in them, along with Julie, the voluptuous young woman who called herself Anderson's fiancée. All were naked in positions that made passion seem a key motive in the spectacular mass murder.

The photos should have been the final nail in Anderson's legal coffin. But they turned out to be something else . . . as they opened up the ugliest can of worms a naval officer ever had to confront . . . and that a military establishment would do anything—and destroy anyone—to conceal. . . .

RUSH TO JUDGMENT

Irving A. Greenfield

RUSH
TO
JUDGMENT

A SIGNET BOOK

SIGNET
Published by the Penguin Group
Penguin Books USA Inc., 375 Hudson Street,
New York, New York 10014, U.S.A.
Penguin Books Ltd, 27 Wrights Lane,
London W8 5TZ, England
Penguin Books Australia Ltd, Ringwood,
Victoria, Australia
Penguin Books Canada Ltd, 10 Alcorn Avenue,
Toronto, Ontario, Canada M4V 3B2
Penguin Books (N.Z.) Ltd, 182–190 Wairau Road,
Auckland 10, New Zealand

Penguin Books Ltd, Registered Offices:
Harmondsworth, Middlesex, England

First published by Signet, an imprint of Dutton Signet,
a division of Penguin Books USA Inc.

First Printing, March, 1995
10 9 8 7 6 5 4 3 2 1

 REGISTERED TRADEMARK—MARCA REGISTRADA

Printed in the United States of America

PUBLISHER'S NOTE
This is a work of fiction. Names, characters, places, and incidents either are the
product of the author's imagination or are used fictitiously, and any resemblance
to actual persons, living or dead, events, or locales is entirely coincidental.

This book is respectfully dedicated to my Aunt Miriam and Uncle Mac, and to my colleagues in the English Department at Fort Hamilton High School who helped me weather a very serious illness.

Irving A. Greenfield
Staten Island, New York

NOTE TO THE READER

The author is aware of the liberties he has taken with the court-martial procedure.

Law is more than words that are put on the books;
law is more than any decisions that may be made
from it; law is more than the particular code of it
stated at any one time or in any one place or nation;
more than any man, lawyer or judge, sheriff or
jailer, who may represent it. True law, the code of
justice, the essence of our sensations of right and
wrong, is the conscience of society. It has taken
thousands of years to develop, and is the greatest,
the most distinguishing quality which has evolved
with mankind. None of man's temples, none of his
religions, none of his weapons, his tools, his arts,
his sciences, nothing else he had grown to, is so
great a thing as his justice.

—Walter Van Tilburg Clark
The Ox-Box Incident

Prologue

The *Utah-BB 64,* a World War II battleship that had been reconfigured in the nineties, furrowed the dark water of a calm sea whose depth dropped to five thousand feet. Two days out of Norfolk, she was on a routine training mission in the Atlantic between Puerto Rico and Cuba that would last another day. Then she'd steam up to New York for the Armed Forces Day celebration.

For the last two hours Seaman Third Class Donald Hawkins and the twenty-seven others had sweated in the confined space of turret number two. For the past hour he and another powder handler had loaded bag after bag of powder into the tray of the ship's gun number two in the number two turret.

The actual firing of each of the ship's sixteen-inch guns had been controlled from Central Fire Control, an environmentally secure space located several decks below the main deck. But a break in the firing sequence signaled to the gun crews of the ship's main turrets a change of firing orders. The skipper and the ship's gunnery officer would probably call for "local fire control."

Hawkins, a tall, slender man with dark blond hair, muddy brown eyes, and the pallid, thin face of an ascetic, had never traveled farther than the town of Cider Corners, five miles from the farm where he was born and raised until he'd joined the Navy three years before.

"Well, Preacher, you ready for those New York

women?" Amos Bin asked, grinning at Hawkins. Bin, a black man, came from Philadelphia, and eagerly anticipated the ship's visit to New York after the training exercise was completed.

Hawkins answered, "I'll keep God's word."

Bin said, "I'll keep it too, but I'll also take whatever a woman gives. I ain't proud."

Hawkins's attention shifted to another member of the gun crew, Gunner's Mate First Class Paul Anderson, who was talking to the gun captain.

"He's leaving the fucking gun," Bin commented, also looking at the two men. Then he added, "His damn friend Gus got sick at chow this morning."

Hawkins gave Bin a quick glance. "You sure?"

"Gus ain't fucking here, is he?" Bin challenged.

Hawkins didn't answer. Instead he turned and started for the turret door.

"Hey, man, where the fuck are you going?" Bin questioned.

"To do God's work," Hawkins answered.

"You're going to get yourself in deep shit, man. You just can't leave in the middle of a fucking firin' ..."

Hawkins ignored Bin, and before anyone else could stop him, he stepped out of the turret, closed its steel access door, and went down the ladder to the open deck. He paused for a moment to squint up at the intensely blue sky before he began to run aft on the ship's starboard side.

Breaking the silence of the surrounding sea, the ship's 1MC bleared, "All hands ... All hands ... Now hear this ... Turret number two, stand by to commence manual fire ... Stand by!"

Several moments later the 1MC came once again. "All hands ... All hands ... Now hear this ... Turret number two commence firing."

A thunderous explosion like a giant hammer slammed against the ship's starboard side, making her shudder. Flame and black smoke erupted from the muzzle of the sixty-eight-foot number one gun as

Hawkins reached the door to the ship's superstructure. Before opening it, he paused to gulp several deep breaths, but the caustic smoke of burnt powder choked him, bringing on a fit of violent coughing.

A second explosion threw him against the door.

He looked forward, toward the turret. The top of it was crowned with flames and dense black smoke.

The Klaxon began to scream.

Several secondary explosions sent the flames high above the ship's radar masts. The black smoke plumed out behind the ship, casting a shadow over a narrow ribbon of ocean.

The 1MC came on. "Battle stations . . . Battle stations . . . All hands, battle stations! Damage control, number two turret . . . Damage control, number two turret . . ."

Sailors were running toward the burning turret, pulling fire hoses with them.

"The wrath of God," Hawkins shouted, getting up on his feet.

"You, sailor, get on that hose over there," a chief shouted coming toward him.

He hesitated. He was doing God's work.

"Move your fucking ass, sailor," the chief bellowed into his face.

Hawkins ran to the nearest group of men and helped them pull a high-pressure fire hose toward the burning turret.

Chapter 1

"Please sit, Captain," Admiral Russo said, gesturing to the brown leather, high-back chair in front of his desk.

"Thank you, sir," Captain Gamrick answered. As he sat, Gamrick took in the admiral's office for the first time. With its deep pile blue wall-to-wall carpet, mahogany desk, and dark brown leather chairs, the furnishings were posh, even for a three-star admiral. There were the obligatory color photographs of the President, the Secretary of the Navy, and the Chief of Naval Operations. The American flag was on the admiral's right, and a flag indicating rank was on the left. The walls were decorated with color photographs of the various warships and two very large paintings: one of the *Bonhomme Richard* and the other of the *Constitution*. Both were under full sail with the wind on their starboard quarter. And at various intervals along the walls, models of sailing vessels rested on almost invisible shelves, giving the illusion that they were miraculously suspended between the floor and ceiling. The large window behind him framed a portion of the Potomac River.

Russo, deputy director of the Naval Criminal Investigative Service (NCIS), leaned back in his swivel chair and for several moments studied Gamrick. "Have you reached a conclusion, Captain?"

Completely relaxed, Gamrick answered, "I was waiting for you to give me yours, sir."

The fingers of Russo's right hand drummed lightly on the top of the desk.

Gamrick continued to look at Russo, who in his younger days had been a fighter pilot during the war in Vietnam. A bantam cock of a man with close-cropped red hair, bright amber-colored eyes, and a reputation for being a son of bitch, except with women. Married three times and divorced as many, at sixty he was on the loose, playing the field again.

"You're not impressed, are you?" Russo asked, breaking the silence.

"Sir?" Gamrick questioned.

"With this," Russo said. He stopped drumming on the desk and made a gesture with both hands to encompass the whole room. Then he added, "Or with me?"

Gamrick suppressed a smile. "The room matches the rank. But my own preference, if that's what you're asking—"

"By all means, Captain, your own preference."

"I prefer a polished hardwood floor to one covered with a blue wall-to-wall carpeting," Gamrick said.

"Look around. Is there anything else you'd change?"

This time Gamrick allowed himself to smile. "Sir, I'm not much of an interior decorator. I'm just a simple sub driver."

"Not so simple as you would have people think," Russo said somewhat stiffly.

Gamrick shrugged but said nothing.

"I noticed that you did not answer the second part of my question," Russo said.

"Again, sir, with all due respect, I'm a sub driver. I respect your rank and assume, from what little I know about you, that you've earned it."

Russo began to drum on the desktop again. But this time the sound was more pronounced. "According to the information in your service file, you were second in your class at Annapolis, where you earned a Bachelor of Science in nuclear engineering. You hold an M.A. in English literature from Columbia. You've been married for twenty-five years. You have two sons: Hal, who is a professor of history at New York Univer-

sity and has two children, and Jeff, one of our own jet
jockeys, who is also married and has two children."

Gamrick gave the obligatory nod when Russo
looked at him.

"And you were awarded the Navy Cross for having
hunted and killed a Russian attack submarine in the
Arctic during the height of the Cold War," Russo said.

"Yes, sir," Gamrick answered.

"And a law degree from—"

"Sir, that's from one of those California correspon-
dence schools. I took courses—"

With a wave of his left hand Russo stopped Gamrick
and asked, "You took and passed the California bar
exam with a ninety-two and the New York bar exam
with a ninety-five. Those are excellent grades, Captain."

Gamrick said, "They were better than I had expected."

"Then, you have some familiarity with the law?"

"Sir, I took those examinations fifteen years ago,"
Gamrick replied, moving slightly forward. "I thought—"

"Captain, your service record is excellent, and the
fact that you have a working knowledge of the law
might prove invaluable."

Gamrick eased back into the chair. He was tall and
leathery-looking with green eyes, high cheekbones,
pepper-and-salt hair, and the self-confident bearing of
a man who knows his own worth.

Russo stopped drumming on the table. "I want you
on my team," he said.

Gamrick raised his eyebrows but remained silent.

"Later today the Secretary of the Navy, John Howard, will announce my appointment as the chairman of
the court of inquiry formed to investigate the accident
aboard the *Utah*," Russo said.

"Congratulations, sir," Gamrick responded, aware
the proverbial second shoe was about to follow, and it
would land on him.

"You will be my chief investigating officer," Russo

said, smiling. After a momentary pause he asked, "How does that grab you?"

"I'm honored," Gamrick answered, unable to filter the sarcasm out of his voice.

Still smiling, Russo said, "You're the only officer on staff available now with a legal background."

Gamrick wasn't pleased with this new assignment. He wasn't even pleased about having been assigned to the NCIS. He would have much preferred to be teaching at the submarine school. There he would have been able to give young submarine officers the benefit of his years of experience in every sort of boat from the World War II Tang class to latest nuclear attack type. But NCIS was a necessary stop on his way to flag rank, at least as far as the Bureau of Personnel was concerned.

"Sir, with all due respect to you for having chosen me, I must tell you that I have never been inside a courtroom in any legal capacity," Gamrick said.

Angered, Russo drummed his desktop harder. "You're like all of your ilk—especially the good ones—a persistent son of a bitch."

"Sir, I'm much more valuable doing what I'm doing."

"Any submarine skipper could evaluate the kind of technical information you handle on foreign submarines. There's really nothing new happening. The Russians don't have the money to build any more boats of any type, and what they have is rapidly becoming obsolete. And as for the Chinese—well, they're a long way from causing us to worry, at least as far as their submarines go, and that's not very far." Russo laughed at his own joke.

Gamrick remained stone-faced.

"Even admirals have a sense of humor," Russo said.

Gamrick could feel a flush come into his cheeks. "I thought my expertise gave the evaluations a validity that they would otherwise lack," he said in a low voice tight with suppressed anger.

Russo stopped tapping. "Your work is excellent, and valuable. But the investigation of the accident aboard the *Utah* needs a man like yourself to head the team, to evaluate, check, and recheck every bit of evidence before I write my report and submit it to the Secretary of the Navy and the Chief of Naval Operations, and they take it to the President. Twenty-seven men were killed in that explosion and another sixty were injured, some so seriously that they will be invalids for the rest of their lives."

Gamrick nodded. There wasn't any use in trying to buck Russo. The admiral, for reasons known only to himself, had made his decision.

"Sir, I will do the best I can," Gamrick said.

"I'm sure you will," Russo responded. "As my chief investigator, you will have the opportunity to rub shoulders with members of Congress, the Senate, and the media. You'll be coming up for flag rank in another couple of years, and getting to know some politicians on a first-name basis can't hurt you."

"Luckily, the media has nothing to do with the selection process," Gamrick commented.

"No, it doesn't. But the media can chew a man up and spit him out because it just happens to be Tuesday, or any other day when there isn't much real news and it has to make its own. To be on the safe side, don't make any statement to the newspaper or TV people until you check with me, and I'll clear it with our people before I give you the go-ahead."

"That much of a problem?" Gamrick questioned.

"More, much more if they get on to something and decide to ride it awhile. You see how they're riding the accident aboard the *Utah*. For chrissakes, they have even put the weeping grandmothers of three of the casualties on the TV screen."

"I saw that," Gamrick said, disgust in his voice. "Something similar to that happened about ten years ago when I skippered the *Shark*. An explosion in the generator room that killed three men and injured a dozen more. They interviewed the girlfriends of the dead men on TV."

"Well," Russo said, "I've invited the TV anchorwoman Kate Bannon to join me for cocktails at the officers' club. Maybe I can persuade her to change the kind of coverage. Make it less emotional."

"I hope you can," Gamrick answered.

"Tomorrow at oh-eight-hundred you'll meet the three men who will be your team. Two commanders—Bob Folsim and Steve Wright—and a lieutenant named Harry Cool. Folsim and Wright are fighter jocks doing a tour of duty here, like yourself. They will be reassigned to fighter squadrons when it is completed. Lieutenant Cool is NCIS all the way."

"Perhaps adding an officer with battleship experience would help the rest of the team understand—"

"That can be done later if you still think you need that kind of input," Russo said. "We want to limit the number of oars in the water."

"Yes, sir," Gamrick answered.

Russo stood.

Gamrick immediately got to his feet.

"Good to have you aboard, Gamrick," Russo said, coming around to the front of the desk and offering his hand to Gamrick.

"Thank you, sir," Gamrick answered, shaking the admiral's hand.

"There's an office down the hall from mine large enough for you and your team to use. You can requisition anything you need. Desks and phones have already been installed. My secretary—Lieutenant Martins—will help you with anything you need. Better install yourself this morning. I want you with me when my appointment is announced to the press."

Gamrick asked, "Sir, is that absolutely necessary?"

"You're my point man. You'll have to speak to the press," Russo said.

"Yes, sir," Gamrick responded.

"During the course of the investigation you have the

authority to use the full power of this department at your disposal, and I can assure you, in situations like this one it is considerable."

Gamrick nodded. He was fully aware of the NCIS's power. Everyone in the Navy was.

They walked to the door together, and after Russo had opened it, he put his hand on Gamrick's shoulder. "If you play your cards right, Captain, this assignment can go a long way toward putting you in the position of decorating your own office."

Gamrick laughed. "I certainly would like to try my hand at it," he said.

"I'm sure you would," Russo responded.

By 1030, Gamrick and his staff had moved into their new office. Gamrick's desk was alongside the window, which overlooked the parking lot and a nearby highway. Bob Folsim and Steve Wright placed their desks along one wall, giving Harry Cool, the only black on the team, three other walls to choose from. But he placed his desk in the center of the room.

To Gamrick it became immediately apparent that Bob and Steve considered themselves united and that Harry was odd man out. Bob was built much like Admiral Russo with black hair and eyes. Steve was taller and more angular. Both Bob and Steve were North Carolinians—Bob born and raised in Raleigh, and Steve from Rocky Mountain. Cool, a New Yorker, was easily six foot four, thin, and looked very strong.

Earlier, Gamrick had given their personnel files a quick read. All of them had excellent ratings by their former superior officers and probably would be able to conduct a thorough investigation of the accident aboard the *Utah*. But Gamrick still thought they needed a team member with battleship experience, or even someone with something in his background akin to criminal investigation.

Gamrick sat at his desk thinking about the men now

under his command when he suddenly realized that Bob was standing in front of him.

"Sorry," Gamrick said, "I was thinking."

"Ah, you had that faraway look of a man thinking lovely thoughts," Bob joked, winking broadly.

Gamrick ignored the obvious sexual reference and said, "I want to set up a modus operandi that will get us started."

Bob nodded his head approvingly. "Steve and I talked about that the other day when we found out that we were going to be assigned to the investigation. If you let us loose, you can just sit back and relax."

"I suppose you included Lieutenant Cool in your operational plans?" Gamrick asked, wondering if the two fly boys were taking their cue from Russo or winging it on their own?

"Sure, sure. He can arrange all the data into report form," Bob said.

Gamrick smiled at him. "I'll give it some thought," he said. Then he stood and called out, "Steve, Harry, pull up a couple of chairs. I want to have our first official, unofficial meeting." He looked at Bob. "You're part of the team too. Pull up a chair."

He waited until the three of them were seated before perching on his desk. "The first thing I want to make clear to each of you is that I will appreciate and consider every suggestion you make, but I am not here for the free ride. I will direct this investigation to the best of my abilities. Each of you will follow my orders to the proverbial letter." For dramatic effect he paused several moments. "Starting tomorrow morning, each of you will begin questioning the men in number one and number three turrets. I will question the two men—Anderson and Hawkins—who were out of number two turret at the time of the explosion. Is that clear?"

The three men nodded and chorused, "Yes, sir."

"The *Utah,* as you know, is in Norfolk. We'll go down by chopper tomorrow morning at oh-eight-hundred. There are twenty-eight men in a turret. Bob,

you will question the men in turret number one—
Steve, do the same for turret number three. Harry, the
survivors from turret number two.

"Your basic task is to find out if there was anything
unusual about the men in number two turret, anything
unusual in the way they operated. Obviously, the men
in turret number one and three were at their stations
when the explosion occurred; therefore, they could not
have been directly involved."

"Sir, are we assuming that the explosion was acci-
dently caused—?" Harry began.

"Certainly. A mechanical malfunction, or some kind
of human error," Bob said.

"We are not assuming anything," Gamrick answered. He looked straight at Bob. "If we make any
sort of assumptions, it could blind us to the real cause
of the explosion."

"Can we quote you, sir?" Steve questioned.

Gamrick shifted his eyes from Bob to Steve. The
pair of them were playing a game that he didn't care
for, and he intended to stop it before it got in the way
of what he was assigned to do. "I'm glad you asked
that, Steve, because it brings up the matter of security.
To answer your question, no. But a simple no will not
carry the message. Therefore, I will spell it out. Nothing—absolutely nothing—that you hear, or read, or
discuss is open for discussion outside of this office.
Consider it top secret."

"Sir, you do have the authorization to declare the
material top secret?" Bob asked.

"I have the authorization to do exactly what I have
to do to complete this investigation, Commander,"
Gamrick answered.

"Yes, sir," Bob snapped.

"No one on this team speaks to any members of the
press or TV without authorization from me or from
Admiral Russo," Gamrick said. "And to reinforce the
kind of security blanket I want wrapped around this in-

vestigation, it's not a subject for 'pillow talk' either. Is all of this understood?"

"Yes, sir," the men answered in unison.

"The last item on my agenda is simply to welcome all of you aboard, and to tell you that we will have an informal-formal meeting at least once a day to brief one another, and discuss progress we are making. Any questions?"

"Sir, does the matter of security extend to Admiral Russo?" Bob asked.

The question caught Gamrick by surprise, and it was several moments before he answered. "The admiral is privy to all that we do."

"Yes, sir," Bob answered, casting a quick look at Steve.

Gamrick wasn't about to let this slip away, and he said, "With one caveat, Commander."

"Sir?"

"Answer only if you are asked a direct question, and only answer the question. Do not volunteer any information or state your opinion on any given aspect of the investigation. The final report will be our statement."

Again Bob glanced at Steve.

"Have I made myself clear, gentlemen?" Gamrick asked.

Each man snapped out a "Yes, sir."

"That's it for today. I'll see all of you tomorrow at oh-eight-hundred at the helicopter," Gamrick said, leaving the top of the desk.

The men withdrew to their own desks.

Gamrick made a half circle on the swivel chair and looked out of the window. There wasn't any doubt in his mind that Bob and Steve would play his game until the opportunity came for them to play theirs. They were hot-shot pilots, and everything they did, they did as if they were in the cockpit of a fighter plane and going in for the kill. Nothing subtle about either of them. Probably just as hard with their women as with anything else ... His thoughts shifted to Russo's press

conference, which was called for 1400. That was sure
to be a real experience.

Gamrick turned around. None of the men were there.
He looked at his watch. It was 12:15. "Time for
lunch," he said aloud, and taking his cap from the
desk, he left the office.

"I can assure the families of the men who lost their
lives in this tragic accident that the Navy will do everything in its power to find out why it happened, and
make sure it will never happen again," Russo said,
speaking to an auditorium filled with press and TV
people.

Gamrick was on Russo's left, and John Howard, the
Secretary of the Navy, was on his right. Just before the
conference, Russo had introduced him to Howard, who
had a big smile and firm handshake, and had said, "I
heard good things about you, Captain. We need to nail
this down as quickly as we can." And Gamrick had answered that he would do the best he could. Then all of
them had been ushered on to the stage by a public information officer.

Russo was still talking about the "responsibility of
the Navy to the men whose lives have been taken from
them, and to see this investigation through I have appointed Captain Clark Gamrick to head the investigation team. He not only has served brilliantly—I might
add, in this nation's 'Silent Service,' which all of you
know as our Submarine Service—but he also has the
necessary legal expertise to insure that the investigation is thorough, and follows the stipulations in the
Navy legal code. Ladies and gentlemen, it gives me
great pleasure to introduce Captain Clark Gamrick."

Flushed and already sweating, despite the air condi-
tioning, from the heat of the TV lights, Gamrick
stepped forward, nodded, and quickly stepped back.

"Captain Gamrick, can you give us any indication of
what direction your investigation will take?" one of the
reporters shouted.

Gamrick glanced at Russo, who gave him a quick nod. "Anything I would say at this time would be less than useful," he answered.

"Have you done any preliminary investigatory work?" another reporter asked.

"None."

"Could the explosion be the work of a saboteur?" a third reporter asked.

"That possibility will be investigated," Gamrick answered.

Russo suddenly held up his hands. "Please, ladies and gentlemen, we really don't have any concrete information for you at this time. But as soon as we do, we'll release it immediately. Thank you very much for coming here, and for your patience."

The press conference was over, and Gamrick followed Howard through an opened door into an area behind the auditorium stage. Now he was sweating profusely and used a handkerchief to wipe his face and the back of his neck.

"You did very well, Captain, the first time out," Howard said.

"I felt as if I were talking nonsense," Gamrick answered.

"They bought it, and that's what matters," Russo said.

Howard agreed.

"Well, we'll be doing this more than any of us likes to. But it's all in a day's work," Russo said. Then he shook hands with Howard, and Howard shook hands with Gamrick.

"Let's meet for lunch, or drinks—whichever is more convenient for you—and talk," Howard said.

"It would be my pleasure," Gamrick answered.

"Admiral, give him my private number," Howard said as he departed.

"Certainly, Mr. Secretary," Russo answered, and turning to Gamrick, he said, "We're going in the same direction, aren't we?"

"Yes, sir," Gamrick said. An order was an order even if it was stated as a question.

"I hear you run a tight ship," Russo commented as they rode the elevator up to the third floor, where their offices were located.

Gamrick smiled. "Word travels with the speed of light," he said.

"It does that," Russo responded.

The elevator stopped. Its door slid open and Gamrick followed Russo out of the car.

"I have a special interest in Folsim and Wright," Russo said.

Gamrick said nothing.

"Each is the son of a friend."

"They're good men," Gamrick finally said.

"I'm glad you see it that way," Russo responded.

Furious, Gamrick stopped abruptly.

Russo was forced to stop, turn, and actually retreat two steps.

"Sir, if either Folsim or Wright have any complaints about the way I operate, those complaints should be brought to my attention, not yours. You are much too busy with really important matters to bother with such an insignificant matter."

Russo stared at him.

"I'll see that it doesn't happen again, sir," Gamrick said and started to walk on.

Russo immediately caught up with him.

They reached Gamrick's office first.

"I will be down in Norfolk for the next couple of days," Gamrick said. He had not only outmaneuvered him, but he also had skillfully reprimanded him.

"Have you made the necessary arrangements?" Russo asked.

"Your Lieutenant Martins was kind enough to do it for me."

"Good luck," Russo said.

"Thank you, sir," Gamrick answered, saluting.

Russo returned the courtesy.

On the way home, Gamrick stopped at the Sea Sands, a weather-beaten low-roofed building—with a large apron of gravel in front of it for parking—set back in the trees some distance from the road and several miles from the main highway. There was sawdust on the raw wood floor. The bar was long, the room in half-light, and the scent of beer was heavy in the air.

The owner and barkeep, Peter Shenk, a man slightly younger than Gamrick and a former Marine who had done two tours in Vietnam before a large piece of shrapnel from an NVA mortar tore part of his stomach out, served him a Stoli on the rocks. Pete had a tattoo on his muscular right forearm of an orange heart with the words IT BELONGS TO LUCY done in blue. But when Gamrick had once asked him if he was married to Lucy, Pete laughed and said, "I can't remember who the hell she was."

Gamrick sat at the bar drinking Stolichnaya. The day had been a wild one. If he had had any real choice, he would have avoided it altogether. He swallowed more of his drink. But he didn't have the choice. Russo wanted him, and that was the end of the discussion. Well, at least he had told him what he thought of his two favorite fighter jocks. Thinking about that brought a smile to Gamrick's face. It had been the only pleasure in what otherwise had been a pleasureless day. He drained the glass. Time to go home at tell Iris about the new developments in his life—their lives.

Chapter 2

Gamrick lived on a cove in a large white house, three miles south of Galesville, along the upper reaches of Chesapeake Bay. There were three other houses on the cove. According to Iris, two were owned by local industrialists and the third by a New York banker who seldom used it.

The cove gave Iris and him a private beach and place to moor the *Snark,* a forty-foot ocean-going sloop that he had built from the keel up. It slept six but could be sailed by one. Twice he had crossed the Atlantic: once—alone—to England, and a second time—with Iris and another couple aboard—to the Azores. The house was surrounded on three sides by two acres of woods, mainly scrub pine, and a variety of bushes that thrived in the sandy soil.

Gamrick turned his Jeep into the black-topped driveway, and as he parked it next to Iris's white Lincoln, he suddenly remembered that Iris's brother Wayne and his wife, Monique, were driving down from Philadelphia to spend a few days with them before they continued on to Hilton Head, where they owned a condominium.

He switched off the ignition, set the emergency brake, and, reaching into the rear of the Jeep, he picked up an old, battered briefcase embossed with the Submarine Service's insignia. He left the Jeep, and even before he started for the side entrance of the house, Iris came out from behind the screen door and Dimitri, a very large mongrel doberman with shepherd and wolf in him, ran to Gamrick.

"You were on the five o'clock news," she said excitedly, running toward him. "You should have called and told me." She threw her arms around him.

Gamrick embraced her. "It all happened so fast that there wasn't any time." He petted Dimitri on the head, acknowledging him.

"That's all right. I'm so excited. I can't wait to tell Wayne and Monique."

Gamrick laughed. "Their Rolls has a TV, remember, and a very fine sound system. And if I know Monique, she will either be watching the TV or listening to the radio."

Iris hung on his arm as they made their way into the house. "How did all of this happen?" she asked, pressing herself against him. She wore a pair of white short shorts, a blue silk blouse—with the top three button open and no bra—tied around her bare midriff, and thongs on her bare feet. She was nut brown—even her breasts were brown. Their secluded home gave her the privacy to sunbathe nude. At forty-five she managed to keep her body svelte, and was still a beautiful woman with lovely blue eyes and long blond hair, which she had to touch up every so often to maintain its corn silk color.

"Luck of the draw," he answered.

"Oh, Clark, tell me."

They entered the house, and she let go of him.

"When do our guests arrive?" he asked, heading for the den to deposit his briefcase. Before he had left his office, he had BuShips fax him detailed plans of the *Utah*'s main batteries, and he had brought them home to study later in the evening, or at night when everyone else would be asleep.

"By six," she answered, stopping at the doorway to the den. "Wayne called me when they were just this side of Baltimore."

Gamrick looked at the chronometer on the wall over

the stone fireplace. It was 1630. "I still have time to go
for a swim and relax before they arrive. Knowing
them, six will be more like six-thirty or seven, if we're
lucky."

She stepped in front of him, and said, "You're not
going anywhere until you tell me exactly what happened."

"Admiral Russo somehow got the idea into his head
that I'm some sort of legal eagle because I have a degree in law and I passed the bar examinations in California and New York. Now, before I say anything else,
I need something to drink."

"Your command is my pleasure," Iris answered. "I'll
mix the best martinis—"

"A cold beer will do nicely, thank you," he said. He
didn't want her to start drinking early on his account.
She would certainly drink more than she should when
her brother and his wife arrived.

"Come on, Clark, this is really a cause for a celebration. It's not often that a wife gets to see her husband
on TV," Iris said.

He had a way out, and he took it. She drank too
much. And lately because she didn't get the part she
had wanted in the play given by the local theater, she
always seemed to have a glass in her hand. Pointing at
his briefcase, which he'd deposited on the floor next to
the very large rolltop desk, he said, "I have some
homework to do, and I will need a very clear head
when I do it."

"Oh, Clark, you're not just going to walk out on my
brother and his wife," she complained.

He shook his head. "I'll wait until everyone is
asleep."

"Clark—"

"Tomorrow morning I have to be in Norfolk," he
said.

She worked her face into a childish pout.

"It comes with the assignment," he said, putting his
hand on her shoulders and drawing her close to him.

"I'll be home in the evening and will take Wayne and Monique out to one of the local seafood restaurants."

"Promise?" she questioned, looking up at him.

"Yes," he answered and kissed her.

Iris took hold of his hand and, pressing it against her breasts, she whispered, "Let's go upstairs and celebrate the way we used to when we were younger and something good happened."

. He smiled. "I'll buy that, but then I want that beer."

"I don't care about 'then.' I feel sexy now. Now I want you to make love to me."

Gamrick led her out of the den and upstairs to their room.

Physically sated, Gamrick showered and redressed in red shorts and a green polo shirt, while Iris still lay naked in their large, authentic eighteenth-century white canopy bed. Her eyes were mere slits. Making love to her was still very good when it happened, but it didn't happen that often. She would give him her body. Sometimes she'd even have an orgasm. But she'd lost interest in the physical aspect of marriage. She—

"A dollar for your thoughts," she said.

"That's a pretty high price," he answered.

"When your brow furrows, I know you're thinking serious thoughts."

"Was it really furrowed?" he asked, sitting on the bed and stroking her naked thigh.

"Furrowed as any plowed field," she said.

His first inclination was to tell her that he was thinking about his new assignment, but that, he knew, would open a box he would prefer to keep closed, at least for now.

"Now the wheels are spinning," she said, opening her eyes.

"I was thinking about us," he told her.

"Oh?" She pushed herself up and rested against the headboard.

"We should do this more often—make love, I

mean," Gamrick said, looking straight at her. "It was good, Iris. Real good."

She flushed, looked at the white antique clock on the night table, and said, "My goodness, I didn't realize it was so late." A moment later she moved to the opposite side of the bed, and standing, she slipped into a teal blue silk negligee. "I want to have a quick shower," she told him, starting for the bathroom.

"Sooner or later we are going to have to talk about it," he said, now standing.

"There's nothing to talk about," she answered. "Nothing."

He pursed his lips.

"If you wouldn't talk about it, maybe it wouldn't be such of a damn problem."

"That's just the 'damn problem,' as you put it. There's nothing to talk about, as far as you're concerned."

She stopped and faced him. "What's that supposed to mean?"

Gamrick threw up his hands. His intent had gone off track.

"The next thing you'll tell me is that I drink too much," she said fiercely.

He shook his head. "I was trying to tell you how much I enjoyed—"

"Fucking me," she said harshly. "And that you want it to be that good all the time."

He flushed.

"Well, 'all the time' I don't feel it," she said. "I don't feel a thing."

"I'm sorry for you," he said quietly.

"No, you're not. You're sorry for yourself."

"I am sorry for the two of us," he answered in the same quiet voice.

"You even have to spoil the times that I do feel something, the times when I want to be fucked."

"I better go and get things ready for our company," he said and left the room.

* * *

Surprisingly, Wayne and Monique arrived only ten minutes late. Wayne, like Iris, had blond hair and blue eyes. But there the resemblance ended. He favored his father, Vice Admiral William (Bill) Tagget, a bull of a man who had retired from the Navy at the age of sixty and before his death, ten years later, had gone on to build a multimillion-dollar company, Deep Dive, Incorporated, which manufactured deep-water rescue devices for the Navy.

Wayne had graduated from Annapolis two years before Gamrick, had done the four-year obligatory stint of active service in various submarines before he resigned and became the vice president of his father's company a year before the admiral died. That had happened twenty years ago. Between then and now Mrs. Tagget—Louise—had also died, leaving Wayne and Iris co-owners of the company, of which Wayne was now the president and Iris, the board's chairperson.

Wayne bounded out of the Rolls, came running over to where Gamrick and Iris stood, and gave his sister a huge bear hug, lifting her off the ground and shouting, "I'm starved, absolutely starved." He put Iris down and shook Gamrick's hand. "So you've become a TV personality," he said, still pumping his brother-in-law's hand. "Not much of a delivery, but it's a start."

All of this happened before Monique got out of the car and started toward them. Younger than Wayne by twenty years, Monique was his third wife. He'd met her a year ago in Las Vegas, where she had been a dealer at the Sands casino. She was a black-haired, sloe-eyed beauty with an exquisite body and a lovely, high-cheekboned face. Before she'd married Wayne and before Las Vegas, she'd tried to get work in Hollywood as an actress, but could only land bit parts and never enough of them to make it worthwhile.

"Iris, you look wonderful!" she said, embracing her sister-in-law and kissing her on both cheeks. Next she

embraced Gamrick and said, "I had to see you on TV
to see you in your uniform."

Wayne clapped his hands together and said, "I
brought a couple of cases of champagne down. Not the
ordinary stuff you buy. I had them flown in for me
from a chateau in France that I am thinking of
buying—kind of a fun business and a good tax loss."

"Well, let's try a bottle or two," Iris said.

"Now, that's my kind of woman," Wayne answered,
circling his sister's waist with his arm. He guided her
toward the Rolls, where a casually dressed chauffeur
leaned against the side of the car.

"We'll be dining on the rear deck," Gamrick said to
Monique.

"Is that an invitation to follow you?"

"It's more than that," he said, taking hold of her
arm. "I'll personally escort you there."

"My pleasure," she answered, allowing him to
gently move her.

They walked through the house and into the kitchen,
where Gamrick opened a sliding glass door, then a
screen, and said, "Dinner will be served shortly. You
relax and enjoy the good, clean salt air while I do the
yeoman's work here at the grill."

Monique dropped down on a chaise. She wore a pair
of white short shorts and a see-through floral design
silk scarf over her breasts. "If you need help—"

"No, I'm good at what I do," he said.

"I bet you are," she commented.

He gave her a quick glance over his right shoulder.

"Just an observation," Monique said.

He gave his attention back to the steaks and frankfurters on the grill. The filet mignons marinated in
Beck's dark beer were Iris's choice. He had chosen the
frankfurters, much to her chagrin. But he knew that almost everyone, including Wayne and Monique, enjoyed a hot dog on a toasted bun.

"You looked and sounded good," she said, referring
to his brief TV appearance.

"That's not the way I felt about it," he answered.

"Felt about what?" Wayne asked, managing to open the screen door with his left hand even though he held a bottle of champagne by its neck in it and two more in his right hand.

"Uncomfortable about his TV debut," Monique said.

Iris came out onto the deck. She held two more bottles of her brother's champagne. "I'll get a couple of coolers."

"Need any help?" Monique asked.

"You had a difficult drive down here," she chided. "I wouldn't think of asking you to do any work."

"Terribly difficult to let your chauffeur do the driving," Monique answered.

"Do you want to freshen up a bit before dinner?" Iris asked, looking at her brother, then at his wife.

"What I'd like to do is have a swim in that wonderful-looking water," Wayne answered. "What about you, Mone?"

"Only if we don't have to change for dinner. What say you, Admiral, will we be permitted to dine in our—?"

"I don't care if you dine in your altogether," Gamrick said, rolling over several of the frankfurters. "But—"

"Ah, with some men there is always a 'but,' " Monique replied. "Sir, explain the but that applies to this situation." She was on her feet now, at attention.

Gamrick faced her. She was a stunningly beautiful women, and she wanted him to be aware of it—no, she wanted him to want her. Amused, he smiled and said, "The but that applies to this situation requires that everyone be out of the water and ready to eat by the time the hot dogs are done."

"Aye, aye, sir," Monique answered, highballing him.

Everyone laughed, and Iris ushered Wayne and Monique up to their room, leaving Gamrick to continue working the grill. He was glad to be alone, even for a few minutes. The events of the day had piled up on him, and the unexpected argument with Iris only increased the weight he felt.

Admiral Russo knew his personal and professional background. Unlike Iris, Clark had not come from a monied family. His father, a failed lawyer, had driven a cab to supplement the family income, and his mother had worked as a seamstress in one of the thousands of small factories that occupied the loft buildings off Seventh Avenue, the heart of the garment industry in New York City.

When Clark met and fell in love with Iris and they married, her father was still in the Navy. But later, after inheriting her share of her father's company, Clark had become one of the wealthiest men on active duty in any branch of the service, if not the wealthiest. But the reality of the situation was completely different from the rumor. Iris had the wealth, and she used it as she saw fit. He had his salary, and that was all he had.

Clark moved away from the grill and looked out toward the opening of the cove, where the ocean began. Maybe, if the weather held, he'd take the *Snark* out for a weekend sail and—

Wearing a ridiculous pair of denim shorts, Wayne came barreling through the door.

"You're not going to swim in those, are you?" Gamrick asked.

"Hey, man, these are the latest style," he answered, flinging himself off the deck and creating a huge splash. "Wonderful," he shouted as soon as he surfaced. "Wonderful!"

"Watch out for crabs," Gamrick warned, going back to the grill.

"Sure, sure," Wayne answered.

Gamrick turned the steaks and the frankfurters again. "Five more minutes and I begin to serve," he called out.

"It smells delicious," Monique said, stepping out onto the deck and taking several deep breaths.

Gamrick looked at her. The patch of red cloth she

wore over her crotch barely covered it, and the top of
red chiffon left most of her breasts bare, except for the
nipples, and they were completely visible. "Not much
left to the imagination," he commented.

"Not much," she answered with a sly smile. Going
to the edge of the deck, she paused before diving into
the water.

"Come on in," Wayne shouted. "The water is
warm."

Gamrick was almost tempted to turn around to see
what Monique looked like from the rear, but Iris came
out on the deck. She too wore a bikini, but hers seemed
almost priggish in comparison to Monique's. "Just
time for a dip," he said.

She nodded but didn't speak.

"Is this the way it's going to be all evening?" he
asked, looking straight at her.

"I'm coming," she shouted, running to the edge of
the deck and diving off.

Gamrick uttered a weary sigh. Sooner or later they
would have to make a decision about the marriage, and
he wasn't at all sure he wanted to remain in it.

"Hey, how's the food coming?" Wayne called out.

"Ready," Gamrick answered as he started to put the
frankfurters on toasted rolls.

A soft summer twilight settled over the cove. The
water turned black while overhead stars began to pop
out of the dark blue sky.

"This was the best barbecue I've had in years,"
Wayne commented. He, Monique, and Iris wore white
terry cloth robes, which both had dried them when they
had come out of the water and protected them against
the evening chill. "By the way, I had lunch with Hal
last Wednesday. He certainly has some liberal ideas,
including a strong view on letting gays serve in the
military."

Gamrick shrugged and said, "Both my sons are free
to hold whatever views they feel comfortable with."

"I'd be willing to bet that Jeff doesn't agree with his brother on the subject of gays in the military," Wayne replied.

"You might be surprised," Gamrick answered.

"Is he still on Flight-Ops?"

"The carrier is somewhere in the Antarctic Ocean."

"Just thinking about it gives me goose bumps, and I'm not his parents," Wayne commented.

"He's probably enjoying every minute of it," Iris said.

Suddenly Monique complained, "Clark, you still haven't told us anything about your new assignment."

"You heard it all on TV," Gamrick answered.

"Could it have been sabotage?" Wayne questioned.

Gamrick shrugged. "Nothing has been ruled out. We just don't know."

"And you will be the one who finds out what happened?"

"I have a team of men—"

"But it will be you who makes the final determination," Monique pressed.

"You won't get him to tell you anything," Iris said, her speech slightly slurred. "Remember, he's a member of the Silent Service." She crossed her lips with a finger and made a shushing sound. "Not a word," she commented. "Not a word."

Wayne glanced at his sister, then looked at Gamrick. "I admire a man who knows how to keep silent about certain things."

"Even if I knew something that you people don't, I couldn't tell you. Everything that happens during the investigation is considered top secret until the information is officially released."

Monique reached over to where Gamrick was sitting and patted his hand. "We understand, Clark. We really do."

"Would you believe that I have had to understand for thirty-five years—more, if you count the time my father was in the service," Iris said. She looked at her brother and smiled. "I only had to understand four years with you. That's because you got out of the fucking Navy and entered the real world."

"I think my sister overdid it a bit," Wayne said. "Come on, Monique, give me a hand with Iris. We'll put the lady to bed and in the morning, after a couple of cups of strong coffee, she'll be able to face the world."

Monique helped Wayne ease Iris out of her chair and toward the door.

"We'll be back to help you tidy up," Wayne called.

"It's all right. I'll just take care of the things that the raccoons can get at. Everything else is either thrown out or put into the dishwasher," Gamrick said as he began to clear the plates of whatever food had been left on them.

Just as Gamrick finished putting the deck in order, Wayne rejoined him and said, "You shouldn't let her drink so much, Clark. She isn't doing herself any good."

"Ever try stopping her?" Gamrick asked, moving to the railing and sitting down on it. "Mention her drinking and she goes into orbit. She hasn't got a drinking problem."

Wayne nodded sympathetically. "I'll try while I'm here," he said.

Gamrick didn't answer.

"You plan to do any sailing this summer, or what's left of it?" Wayne asked.

"I was thinking about going out this weekend."

"Overnight?"

Gamrick shrugged. "I'd like to. Maybe go down to one of the Outer Bank islands."

Monique opened the screen door and stepped out onto the deck. "Iris is asleep," she announced, walking over to the chaise and settling on it again.

"Clark was thinking about taking the *Snark* out this weekend," Wayne told his wife. Then, to Gamrick, he said, "Go south a few more miles and you could stop at Hilton Head."

"A few hundred miles," Gamrick corrected.

"What's a few hundred miles between members of a family?" Wayne said.

"Oh, that would be wonderful!" Monique exclaimed, leaping to her feet and taking hold of her brother-in-law's arm.

"A few hundred miles is a few hundred miles," Gamrick answered.

"I've never been aboard your boat," Monique said. "And Wayne says you're an expert sailor. Did you really build the boat yourself?"

Gamrick wanted to shake her off. She pressed so close to him he could feel the softness of her breasts through the terry cloth robe. "Yes."

"He did everything himself from laying the keel to decorating the interior," Wayne explained.

"Please, sail down," she pleaded.

"You know, I could call down to Hilton Head, change our date of arrival."

Gamrick stepped forward, breaking Monique's hold. "Wait a minute, Wayne. I'm suddenly getting a different message. You want me to sail you and Monique down to Hilton Head on Saturday."

"No, we start tomorrow evening," Wayne said, smiling.

"I'd love that," Monique added.

"That would give me more time to speak to Iris. Clark says she has a drinking problem," Wayne explained to Monique. "I said I would talk to her. Maybe I could convince her to go for help."

"Iris isn't the type to go for help, at least not until she has nowhere else to go," Monique responded.

Gamrick raised his eyebrows questioningly. It was the first time he had heard Monique say something substantive.

"Trust me. I know," she said in a low, throaty voice.

Gamrick accepted what she said without comment. He guessed she spoke from personal experience.

"Will you do it?" Wayne asked with boyish anticipation.

"What the hell, why not?" Gamrick answered.

Monique threw her arms around him and kissed him on the lips. "That's for being a hell of a good brother-in-law, an excellent cook, and just a nice guy."

This time her whole body was against him.

"That's not bad coming from a woman who's mighty careful who she praises," Wayne said.

"I'm honored," Gamrick responded, gently extricating himself from her embrace.

"Well, now that our travel plans have been settled, I think I'll watch the late news, then go up to bed," Wayne said, leaving his chair.

"I have some papers that I must go over," Gamrick said.

"Don't let us stop you," Wayne answered. "Come on, Mone, we'll watch the eleven o'clock news. See you tomorrow."

"See you," Gamrick responded, watching them leave the deck. A few moments later, stepping into the kitchen, he switched off the deck lights, closed the sliding door and locked it, then made his way to the den.

The diagrams of the *Utah*'s main batteries came from OP-769, a five-hundred-page manual covering every phase of the turret's operation. Gamrick had never had any reason to be interested in how a turret functioned. His only experience with a gun of any size had been thirty years ago when he had been assigned to the *Barracuda*—a World War II boat that mounted a five-incher fore and aft.

Slowly, diagram by diagram, he began to understand how the turret functioned mechanically. Later he would learn how the gun crews operated. But now it was important for him to know what the turret looked like inside: it was composed of several levels, the last of which went down practically to the bottom of the ship.

The three guns were separated from one another by steel bulkheads so that damage to one would not stop the others from firing. Each turret had a door—located between the outer shell of armor plate and the skin of the turret—that opened either directly onto the main deck or, in the case of number two turret, onto a ladder leading directly to the main deck.

Closing his eyes for several moments, Gamrick was able to form a mental picture of the inside of the *Utah*'s number two turret. Satisfied, he decided to call it a night. He was tired, more tired than he'd realized.

"Ah, I thought you'd still be working," Monique said, opening the door and stepping into the room.

The only light in the room came from the lamp on the desk, but the light coming from the hallway silhouetted her body, covered only by a gossamer white nightgown.

Gamrick stood up.

"I was having trouble falling asleep, so I came down to the kitchen for a glass of milk," she explained.

"Well, I'm finished for the night," he said, walking out from behind the desk.

"Don't I even get an invitation—"

Gamrick shook his head. "I'm too tired to be social, and I have a hard day ahead of me."

"I thought we could sit and talk for a while," she said, moving closer to him. "If you think about it, we have a lot in common. Both of us are married to lushes; me to the brother lush and you to the sister lush. The only difference between the two, as far as their drinking goes, is that Wayne can drink more before he gets zonked out."

"I guess that does give us something in common," he answered sadly. He'd always known Wayne to be a heavy drinker and frankly admired his capacity.

"The other women in his life must have had one hell of a time trying to handle his problem," she commented.

Suddenly Gamrick became even more intensely

aware of her than he had been. Maybe it was the floral scent of the perfume she wore, or her visibly erect nipples. "And you've learned to handle it?" he asked, trying to keep the tone of his voice steady.

"Well, in a manner of speaking. I let him handle it. I handle my life and he handles his."

"Meaning that you lead separate lives?" Gamrick questioned.

"I give him his space, he gives me mine."

"Is that why you're here?" he asked her directly. "Because if it is—"

The phone on his desk rang. "Christ, it's almost midnight!" he exclaimed.

It rang again.

"Aren't you going to answer it?" she asked.

He went back to the desk and picked up the phone. "Gamrick here," he snapped.

No one answered.

But he could hear the heavy breathing on the other end.

Monique came alongside him. "Who is it?" she questioned.

He put his hand over the mouthpiece, and moving the phone to her ear, he said, "Listen."

A moment passed. Then she grinned. "All that heavy breathing and here we are doing nothing."

Gamrick put the phone back in its cradle. "I'm not a prude, Monique."

"Well, I never thought you were, even if you do look rather stiff in your dress whites."

"I'll be frank—"

"By all means be frank," she said.

"You're my sister-in-law. That's where it begins and that's where it ends."

"And if I wasn't your sister-in-law?" she questioned.

"Then you would not be here, and we would not be having this conversation," Gamrick answered.

The phone rang again.

Gamrick picked it up before the ringing stopped.

"Love God," a muffled voice gasped. Then the line went dead.

Gamrick lowered the phone and stared at it.

"What—"

"Some freak just told me to love God," he explained, setting the phone back in its cradle a second time.

Monique shrugged and her breasts rolled provocatively. "Kind of weird," she said.

"I'd say so," Gamrick answered, switching off the desk lamp. "Damn weird," he added, leaving the den with Monique trailing behind him.

Chapter 3

Gamrick's court of inquiry took place in the main building of the Norfolk naval base. The command furnished him with two bare white-walled offices. Each had two standard gray desks with chairs, a phone on each desk, and a second chair.

Before they began to requisition everything from paper clips to ballpoint pens, Gamrick called his staff together.

"This is informal meeting number two," he said, sitting on the edge of one of the desks. "Folsim, you will share an office with me." He waited a moment, almost hoping that either Folsim or Wright would come up with an objection of some sort that would give him a reason to jump all over them. But they didn't. "There will be two changes in the procedure I outlined yesterday: first, to expedite the questioning, we will divide the men of the two remaining gun crews between the four of us. That means I will be doing exactly what each of you will be doing. Second, we will question the ship's captain, the XO, and anyone else on the bridge who had a view of the forward deck at the time of the explosion. Any questions?"

"None, sir," Cool said.

"No questions," Folsim answered.

"None, sir," Wright responded and sat on a chair off to the right.

Gamrick nodded. "Every interview will be recorded," he said.

"Videoed?" Wright asked.

Gamrick considered the question for a moment before answering. "That would be better than just taping the man, wouldn't it? We could review the video and take a good look at the reactions of each man. Damn good idea, Wright. See that we have the necessary equipment."

"Yes, sir."

"Does anyone else have an idea about how we should operate?" Gamrick asked.

"Knowing there's a camera pointed at him, the man will be more nervous than he would be if he were just being questioned," Cool said from where he stood close to the wall.

"Wright, make sure you get some camouflage for the cameras," Gamrick ordered.

"Yes, sir," Wright responded.

"When is all this supposed be in place?" Folsim asked. He was seated on the edge of the other desk facing Gamrick.

"Yesterday," Gamrick answered. "We'll be operational by 1300 this afternoon."

Wright nodded.

"Mr. Cool, you and Wright get our taping setup going. If you have any difficulty getting the equipment, let me know immediately."

"Yes, sir," Cool responded.

"Folsim, bring a chair over to my desk. We're going to develop a simple set of questions that each interviewee will answer."

Together they worked out a questionnaire: the man would be asked his name, rank, and serial number, his present assignment, and to describe the events as he had experienced them on the day of the explosion; then he would be asked if he had been aware of anything unusual about the gun crew in number two turret.

To "window dress," a dozen more questions were added. Then they reworded the questions concerned with events that had occurred at the time of the explosion to detect any noticeable difference between the gun crew of number one turret and the gun crew of number three turret. Finally Gamrick was satisfied with the wording of each.

By 1130, Cool reported that voice-activated video cameras had been installed in a corner of the room. Each camera was pointed directly at the chair next to the desk. The cameras were flange-mounted to ceiling and camouflaged to look like an elbow joint in the piping. For a man to realize that it was a video camera, he would have to study it awhile, and Gamrick counted on the fact that the men would be too nervous to do that, or even look anywhere but at the officer in front of them.

At 1130, Gamrick called the base security officer, a Marine major, and told him that he would begin interviewing the men at 1300. "I want them here on the hour," he said.

"Yes, sir," the major snapped.

At 1145, Gamrick and his staff went to the officers' club for lunch. He wasn't new to the base. Three times during his career it had been his home port.

Almost as soon as he entered the building, he was greeted by other submarine officers, including Admiral John Dawson, commander of the North Atlantic Submarine Command, who asked after his wife and two sons, shook his hand, and said, "You'll be back with us when you finish your present assignment."

"I hope so, sir," Gamrick answered.

Turning his attention to Gamrick's three-man team, Dawson said, "You're being skippered by one of the best."

Gamrick flushed.

"Good hunting," Dawson said.

"Thank you, sir," Gamrick answered, saluting him.

Dawson returned the courtesy.

As Gamrick and his men found a table, Folsim said, "Sir, it's not every day that an admiral makes it a point of greeting—"

"He was my skipper and I was his XO," Gamrick explained. "We're submariners."

"I heard something about you guys being tight," Wright commented.

Gamrick didn't bother answering. He picked up a tray and joined the line that moved slowly along the hot food counter.

At 1630 they called it a day.

Gamrick said, "Pass the word, we'll pick it up tomorrow morning at oh-nine-hundred."

"Yes, sir," Folsim answered and left the office to relay Gamrick's order to Wright and Cool.

Before Gamrick left, he secured the videotapes from all of the cameras in a steel file cabinet and locked it.

"Are we going to view the tapes as a group, or will each of us view a tape?" Cool asked as they left the building and headed for the jeep waiting to drive them to the airport.

"I haven't decided that yet," Gamrick answered.

"So far I've come up with zilch," Wright commented.

"I think we all have," Gamrick said. "But tomorrow is another day."

"Maybe nothing is something," Cool offered in a quiet voice.

"Run that by us again," Folsim said.

"There's just too much of nothing. After a while the men I interviewed sounded as if they were all the same," Cool explained.

"That's true," Folsim agreed.

"As if they knew what the questions would be and had memorized the answers to them," Wright said.

"Mine weren't any different," Gamrick said, rubbing his chin. "If we get the same response tomorrow, then we can reasonably assume that the men are either covering up something, protecting someone, or just plain afraid to tell us what they really know."

They reached the pad and there a helicopter was

waiting for them. Fifteen minutes later, they landed in Washington.

Gamrick thanked the pilot.

"Glad to set this bird down. There's a line of very heavy thunderstorms moving in from the west," the pilot said.

Gamrick looked to the west. The sky was dark blue, almost black, and every so often jagged streaks of lightning slashed across the roiling, dark mass of clouds.

"I'm on my way," Folsim called, waving as he hurried toward the parking lot.

Wright waved and ran too.

"I guess we're the only ones left," Gamrick said as the two of them headed in the direction of the parking lot.

"Sir, fighter jocks aren't quite as bad as they seem," Cool said.

"I know. They have to be mean and lean to live up to the image," Gamrick answered. "I know. My son Jeff is one."

"Yes, sir. Just the way some of us have to be silent," he said, flashing a big smile.

Gamrick glanced at him, laughed, and said, "You certainly are cool, Mr. Cool."

The storm broke while Gamrick was driving home. The rain struck the car with such tremendous force that he couldn't see more than a few feet in front of him even though his headlights were on. Once he left the highway, the road conditions were worse. Sections of the road were covered with water, in spots forming miniature rapids, and wind tore away large branches from the trees on either side of the road. One struck the roof of the car and bounced off it.

Several times Gamrick considered pulling off to the side and waiting until the storm's fury abated, but he continued to drive, although at no more than five miles per hour.

Luckily, he told himself, he was driving a vehicle that sat high off the road. An ordinary car, even his wife's Lincoln, would not have been able to go through some of the water that he had without stalling.

After an hour the storm lost most of its fury. The sky lightened, and though the rain continued, now it was a cold summer rain. The heat wave that had scorched the entire East Coast for more than a week had been broken.

Gamrick turned off the air conditioner and rolled down his windows. It was actually cool and the air had a wonderfully clean, salty scent. He increased his speed, though from time to time he slowed to go through the flooded parts of the road. He was close enough to the tavern to think about stopping and phoning Iris to assure her that he was all right, and then taking time to have a cup of coffee.

"What the hell, why not?" he said aloud when the low building came into view, and signaling a right turn, he looked up into the rearview mirror. There was a blue pickup behind him. An instant later he started to turn into the gravel parking area, and the pickup accelerated, swung in a Ω around him though he was no longer on the road, and shot past.

"Goddamn fool!" Gamrick yelled after him. Then suddenly he realized that he hadn't seen anyone at the wheel. "Of all the dumb ass things to do," he growled, bringing his Jeep to a stop at the side of the tavern, where there were several others cars parked.

As soon as Gamrick was inside, he went to the phone on the far side of the bar room.

"It's dead," Pete called out. "The phone lines are down all over the place."

Gamrick approached the bar, sat on a stool, and asked for a cup of coffee.

"One cup of coffee," Pete ordered from the cook through a small window behind him. "Cream and sugar?" he asked, looking at Gamrick.

"Black, please."

"Black it is," Pete said, and within moments he placed a cup of steaming coffee down on the bar.

Gamrick nodded.

"One hell of a storm," Pete commented.

"A lot of water is on the road and tree limbs," Gamrick told him as he lifted the cup. Then he said, because it was still fresh in his memory, "Some wiseass kid driving a pickup shot past me as I was turning into the parking area and was so low behind the wheel I couldn't see him. The son of a bitch was driving blind."

"Kids nowadays have some strange ideas about what's funny," Pete answered. "I get some wild ones in here on Friday and Saturday nights."

"I bet you do," Gamrick answered before taking another sip of coffee.

"I saw you on the eleven o'clock news," Pete said. "I told my wife, Loli—she's the brunette who sometimes is behind the bar—that's one of our customers. You find the bastards that blew that fuckin' turret. Find them and throw the fuckin' book at them," Pete said vehemently. "I wouldn't even bother with a court-martial. I'd shoot the cocksuckers."

Gamrick answered, "Come on, Pete, you know that's not the way it's done."

"Sure. Sure, I know. But that's the way it should be done, even out here. If it were done that way, you wouldn't have some shithead in a pickup playing games with you, and I wouldn't need a fuckin' baseball bat and a bouncer to keep things normal around here on Friday and Saturday nights."

"If we don't go by the book, we don't go by anything, and if we don't go by anything, we wind up being nothing," Gamrick said.

Pete considered that for several moments, looked at Gamrick's almost empty cup, and said, "Have another on the house." Then he took Gamrick's cup, pushed it through the window, and asked for a refill. When he replaced the cup on the bar he said, "Get the bastard.

Go by the book, but make sure he doesn't wiggle away."

"I'll make sure," Gamrick answered.

Suddenly a woman behind him asked, "Aren't you Captain Gamrick?"

The question surprised him,. He was so involved in his conversation with Pete that he hadn't seen her come up behind him, even though he could have noticed her in the bar mirror in front of him. He didn't recognize her.

"I was sure it was you!" she exclaimed, extending her hand.

Shaking her hand, Gamrick asked, "Am I supposed to know you?"

She laughed. "You would if you watched the five o'clock news. I'm Kate Bannon. I was with the group of media people—"

"Yesterday . . . you asked me a question, didn't you?" Gamrick recalled.

"Yes," she answered with a smile. "But I know it was difficult to see· particular individuals because of the bright lights."

"If that's what stage actors experience, they can have it with my blessings," Gamrick said. Then he asked what she was doing at the bar.

"Covering the storm," Kate answered. "The town of Galesville lost all its power, some of the fishing boats were sunk, and the bridge over the Galesville creek was washed away. You'll see it all on the eleven o'clock news."

Gamrick looked at his watch. "Don't you have a news—"

"Done live from Galesville," she said. "What about you?"

"What about me?" he repeated, looking at her as if seeing her for the first time. She had red hair, even her eyebrows were red, and her eyes were blue. There were freckles on her face and her neck. He guessed they were on her breasts too. She wore a light green pantsuit. Gamrick guessed her to be in her late thirties—at least twenty years younger than himself.

"Do I pass inspection, Captain?" Kate asked with an unmistakable edge in her voice.

Gamrick ignored it. "I asked a question first," he said, keeping his eyes engaged with hers.

"What brings *you* here?" she asked.

"I live close by, not far from Galesville," he explained.

She looked over to the bar. "Coffee?"

"Now . . . Sometimes I stop for something with more of a kick," he said.

"Will you join us?" Kate asked, waving toward a table around which were seated eight people. "They're my crew."

"Thanks, some other time. Now I better start home. My wife is probably worried about me," he said.

"If I were her, I'd worry too," Kate responded.

He looked at her questioningly.

She didn't miss a beat. "You wouldn't have anything to say about the inquiry—"

"Nothing," Gamrick snapped, feeling that she'd been playing him just to ask him that question.

Kate threw up her hands, palms out. "My God, that answer had a crackle to it."

Gamrick took a five-dollar bill out of his pocket.

"Put his coffee on my tab," she told Pete, who had been standing within earshot throughout the conversation.

"Your tab is on the house, Miss Bannon," Pete answered. "It's a real pleasure to have you here."

"Why, thank you—"

"Pete Shenk," he said, basking in the warmth of her smile. Then, looking at Gamrick, he added, "My missus isn't going to believe that you and Kate Bannon were here."

"Would our autographs convince her?" Kate asked.

Pete quickly produced two matchbooks. "Write on the inside," he said, handing her a ballpoint pen.

"What's your wife's name?" she asked.

"Loli."

"To Loli, you've got a good man—Kate Bannon," she read as she wrote the words. Then, handing the pen to Gamrick, she said, smiling, "Your turn, Captain."

Following her example, Gamrick also spoke the words aloud as he wrote them. "To Loli, I am one of your customers—Captain Clark Gamrick."

"Thanks a million," Pete said, taking the two matchbooks. "After I show them to Loli, I'm going to put them on the mirror behind the bar." He moved down the bar to serve a new arrival.

"That was a nice thing to do," Gamrick said in a quiet voice.

"Thank you, but it was nice of you too."

"Honestly, it would not have occurred to me," Gamrick said, getting off the stool and starting for the door.

Kate walked with him. "But once you saw the opportunity, you took it," she responded with a smile. "Are you sure you won't join us?"

"Sure," Gamrick said and called to Pete, "See you." Then to Kate he commented, "I guess I will be seeing you again or, more accurately, you'll be seeing me."

Tilting her face up toward his, Kate looked straight into his eyes and said, "I'd much prefer it if we saw one another."

He flushed. She was close enough to him to feel her breath. "I was thinking the same thing," he responded in a low voice.

They stared at each other for a moment before she said, "See you, Captain."

"See you," he echoed, turned, and opening the door, stepped out into a cool sun-splashed evening.

The years at sea had turned Gamrick into a very light sleeper. Often a visiting raccoon or deer would wake him. But now Dimitri was barking.

Gamrick was up and out of bed.

"What is it?" Iris asked sleepily.

Gamrick slipped into a bathrobe and quickly padded downstairs.

"What's going on?" Wayne called from the opened door of the guest room.

"That's what I'm going to find out," Gamrick answered.

Dimitri was at the front door, growling ominously.

"Easy, boy," Gamrick said, stroking the dog's head. "Easy."

In his bathrobe, Wayne came down the stairs, followed by Monique. "You got a gun?" he asked.

Gamrick looked at him. "What the hell would I need—"

"You're not going to open the door without one, are you?" Wayne questioned.

"I sure don't need a gun to open the door," Gamrick answered.

"Monique, run upstairs and get mine," Wayne said.

Gamrick shook his head, switched on the outside lights, and unlocked the door.

"Jesus, can't you wait a fucking couple minutes before you open that door?" Wayne asked angrily. "You don't know who the hell might be out there."

Monique ran down the steps with a snub-nose .38 in her right hand.

Wayne took the gun from her and said, "Okay, open the door."

Gamrick unlocked the door with one hand and held Dimitri by his collar with the other.

"He's certainly angry," Wayne commented.

Gamrick pushed the door open. At the far end of the driveway, where the trees overhung and formed a living archway, there was a vehicle.

"Who the hell would be out there?" Wayne asked.

Gamrick was having difficulty holding Dimitri, who was barking furiously and straining to break away.

"I can't see what the hell kind of car it is," Wayne complained.

Gamrick could; it was a pickup.

"Can you make it out, Mone?" Wayne asked.

"A truck, maybe."

"Give me the gun," Gamrick said.

"Wha—"

"Give me the gun and get a hold of Dimitri," Gamrick ordered.

Wayne handed the .38 to him.

"Hold Dimitri by the collar and don't let go."

"What you doing to do?"

"Play a little hardball," Gamrick answered and walked through the open doorway.

"You're crazy!" Wayne called after him.

Gamrick headed straight for the pickup. Because it was under the arch of the trees, he couldn't make out its color. But he was sure it was blue. The son of a bitch had followed him after he'd left the tavern, and because of what had happened between him and Kate, he would not have been aware of it. If an elephant had followed him, he would not have known it. He had driven home in a kind of haze. When he had reached the house, he hadn't any recollection of how he got there.

Suddenly Iris shouted from the open door. "Clark, the police are on their way. Come back."

He continued to move toward the truck. He was halfway between it and the house when the truck's brights flashed on. He dropped to a shooting position and squeezed off two rounds, moving the gun slightly from right to left.

The right headlight went dark.

Gamrick squeezed off another round, but the truck was already in motion. Backing out of the driveway, it turned onto the roadway. Then, burning rubber in a screaming getaway, it raced down the road.

Gamrick stood up and started back toward the house.

Dimitri clawed the air, broke free, and ran to Gamrick. "Easy, boy," he said, stroking the animal, who jumped on him and licked his hands. "Good boy ... easy."

Iris, Wayne, and Monique were close behind Dimitri.

"My God, man, that was the coolest damn thing I have seen in a long time," Wayne said with obvious admiration.

"You might have been killed," Iris commented in a choked whisper.

Gamrick put his arm around her shoulder. "But I wasn't. Might have been doesn't count," he said.

A police car with its blue and red lights flashing, pulled into the driveway and stopped in front of the house. Two officers got out, and when one of them saw a gun in Gamrick's hand, he went for his.

"No need for that, Officer Lance," Wayne quickly said, reading the man's name tag and holding up his hand. "Captain Gamrick used it to scare off an intruder."

The other officer was named Richie. Lance was older and heavier than his partner by at least a score of years and thirty pounds.

Gamrick invited the two officers into the house and led them into the living room, richly carpeted with a rare Persian rug and furnished with authentic Colonial American chairs, tables, and a very large sofa. Various period paintings and prints were on the walls, and a large crystal chandelier hung from the ceiling.

"Please, gentlemen, sit," Wayne said as he sat on a high-back chair.

Gamrick parked himself on the sofa, and gesturing to two chairs across from him, he said, "Please."

Lance nodded.

"Would you care for something cold to drink?" Iris asked.

Almost in unison both men declined.

As Gamrick explained what had happened, Richie wrote in a small black loose-leaf notebook.

"I'm sure it's some local character, a teenager who

probably should be institutionalized," Gamrick said, finishing his statement.

Lance responded, "We have a few of those around here . . . We'll be on the lookout for a blue pickup with the left headlight shot out."

"Thanks for coming out here," Gamrick said.

"Would you men like a drink?" Wayne asked.

"We would, but we won't," Lance answered. "Not when we're on duty. But thanks anyway. If that truck comes back, or if you see it around, give us a call."

He stood up and Richie followed suit.

"Will do," Gamrick answered, shaking Lance's hand first, then Richie's. He walked them to the door and was just about to bid them good night when Richie said, "Now I recognize you! You were on TV last night. I knew I saw you before."

Gamrick smiled. "Comes with the job," he said.

"You think it was an accident?" Richie asked.

"I'm sorry, I can't comment," Gamrick answered.

"Listen, if somebody wasted all those guys and you get him, make sure the bastard gets his," Lance said.

"It will not be up to me."

"Yeah, yeah, I know," Lance said. "But just imagine, if the cocksucker gets off, the kind of message that would send to other psychos. Only a psycho would do something like that."

Eager to end the conversation, Gamrick said, "I really can't say anything about it without violating security."

"Oh, we understand," Lance replied.

"Sure we do," Richie seconded.

Gamrick shook each of their hands again, bade them good night, and waited until they pulled out of the driveway before he went back inside the house.

When he returned to the living room, Wayne greeted him with "Jesus, Clark, you never said a word about this blue pickup."

"Didn't think it was important," he said quietly, adding, "Why don't all of you go back to bed?"

"I mean, you're carrying this shit about the Silent Service just too far," Wayne continued.

"I need a drink," Monique announced. "Maybe more than one before I could fall asleep again."

"I'll join you," Iris said.

The women left the room together.

"You should have some kind of gun around just for situations like the one just happened," Wayne said.

To put an end to the conversation, Gamrick said, "I'll think about it. Now, why don't we join the ladies for a drink?"

"You really will?" Wayne pressed.

"I told you I will, and I will," Gamrick said, turning off the lights in the living room and calling to Dimitri to follow him.

Even after two straight vodkas, Gamrick couldn't sleep. He stood at the window and, looking out at the moon-silvered waters of the cove, he wondered why he'd been singled out by the driver of the blue pickup. Had he inadvertently done something that set the man off? He wasn't even sure it was a man. It could have been a woman. But that didn't seem likely. Maybe the driver had seen him on TV?

The possible connection between his TV appearance and the driver of the blue pickup startled him. His mind again wandered from the blue pickup to Kate Bannon . . . She was a beautiful woman. Not the same way that either Iris or Monique were. Her beauty had a kind of fire, a kind of glow that made a man want to be close to it and—he stopped himself and laughed softly at his circuitous way of admitting he was physically attracted to her. Had they lingered another moment, he would have taken her in his arms and kissed her.

Gamrick pursed his lips and shook his head. At this stage of his life, he didn't need any emotional entanglements. He wanted to keep away from anything that might take his career off track. Though he couldn't deny what he had felt about her, he certainly could keep her at arm's distance. More, if necessary. . . .

Chapter 4

Despite the previous night's incident, Gamrick was up at five and on his way to Washington by six. He met his team at the heliport. Neither he nor the other men spoke much, except to mention the storm.

Gamrick's morning began with questioning the *Utah*'s skipper, Captain John D. Eckers, who said that he had seen two men run aft immediately before the explosion.

Eckers was a tall, broad-shouldered man with crow's feet around his eyes. He'd been in the Navy for thirty years and had been put on the list for flag rank. He was very tense.

"Your XO saw the men too?" Gamrick asked.

"Yes."

"Then he commented on them?"

"Yes. Two men on the deck during a firing exercise is not a normal condition."

"Did you initiate any specific action with regard to those two men?"

Eckers rubbed his hands together. "I'm not sure. I think I asked the OD to find out why they were out there."

"Did he?"

Eckers shook his head. "I really can't answer that. There wasn't much time between the appearance of the first man and the second."

"Were they on deck at the same time—in sight of one another?"

"I don't know. I was occupied with the firing mission. We switched from automatic control to local."

"Would you explain that, please?" Gamrick asked.

"Local control? Well, ordinarily the guns are aimed and fired from the CIC—Combat Information Center. But they have the capability of being fired locally from the turret. We were in that firing mode when the explosion took place."

"Had there been any mechanical malfunction on the ammunition-transfer machinery in either the upper or lower barbette portions of the turret prior to the exercise, during routine inspections or during the mission?"

Eckers shook his head. "None," he said.

"Do you have any ideas about what caused the explosion?"

"None."

The interview was over, and Gamrick stood up and, shaking Eckers's hand, he said, "I'm sorry I had to put you through this." Though the room was air-conditioned, the man was sweating profusely.

"You're only doing what you were assigned to do," Eckers answered generously.

"Thank you," Gamrick said.

"Good luck to you," Eckers responded and left.

Gamrick walked out of the office, found a water cooler, and helped himself to a cold drink. The hallway was a busy place. There was a constant flow of men and women in and out of the various offices on either side of it.

Gamrick thought about Eckers. He was sorry for him. The captain would be questioned by many different individuals and, given the magnitude of the disaster, probably by a congressional committee as well, whose members would be out to score points with their constituents and find a scapegoat. Gamrick was standing at the cooler, ruminating on the justice of the ancient law that holds the captain of a vessel responsible for everything that happens on the vessel under his command, when he realized Wright was coming toward him.

"I needed a break," Wright said. "I just finished with the OD. He said that two men left the turret prior to the explosion. The first, the turret's communications man, he knew about. Gunner's Mate First Class, Paul Anderson, the talker on gun number two. Got sick, and was headed for sick bay."

"Did he ever get there?"

Folsim nodded. "Just as the explosion occurred. According to the record, the man was suffering from a severe sinus attack. But as soon as the explosion occurred, every corpsman and doctor rushed topside."

"And the other man?" Gamrick questioned.

"*Nada* on Hawkins," Wright answered. "His name doesn't show in the sick bay log."

"Let's see what we come up with when he's questioned," Gamrick commented, helping himself to another cup of water.

"How's old Folsim doing?" Wright asked.

"Making a name for himself as lean, mean interrogator," Gamrick answered.

Wright laughed, wagged a finger at Gamrick, and said, "I told everyone they were wrong about you. You do have a sense of humor."

"On that note, we better quit while we're ahead," Gamrick responded.

"Ah, that's the not so subtle call to go back to the grindstone."

"Once we're finished with all of this, I promise to be subtle," Gamrick said as they walked back to their offices together.

Gamrick returned to his desk and began interviewing the men again. Their answers were more or less carbon copies of the answers that had been given both by the men whom he had interviewed the previous afternoon and by those who had preceded Captain Eckers. Then a man said, "Donald Hawkins, Gunner's

Mate Third Class, reporting as ordered, sir." Hawkins
stood at attention in front of Gamrick's desk.

"Please sit."

"Yes, sir."

For several moments Gamrick studied the young
man in front of him. Good-looking, the kind of man
some women would take great pleasure mothering.
"All right, let's begin. This won't take long."

"Aye, aye, sir," Hawkins responded softly.

"State your present assignment," Gamrick said.

"Powder handler, middle gun, turret number two,
BB-46, the battleship *Utah*," Hawkins answered.

"Where were you at the time of the explosion in turret number two?" Gamrick questioned, guessing from
the man's accent that he probably had been raised
somewhere in the Midwest—Kansas or Nebraska.
Corn country.

"Main deck, starboard side. Just about to enter the
ship's superstructure."

"You were away from your station?"

"Yes, sir."

"Why?"

Hawkins flushed. "Bad case of the runs."

"You had permission to leave your station?"
Gamrick asked.

"Yes, sir."

Gamrick leaned slightly forward, rested his elbows
on the desk, and pressed the balls of his fingers together, forming a triangle. "You know there isn't any
way for me to verify that statement. I have to take your
word."

"Yes, sir."

Gamrick was silent for a few moments. The man's
answer was direct, and his gaze never wavered.

"To your knowledge, was anyone else absent from
their station at the time of the firing exercise?"

Hawkins stiffened. "My partner—" He cleared his
throat several times, but still couldn't get the words
out.

"Take your time, son," Gamrick said gently.

"Bin, sir, Amos Bin was my partner," Hawkins croaked.

"Was he absent?"

Hawkins shook his head. "Give me a minute, sir, and I'll be all right."

Gamrick nodded.

"Thank you, sir . . . No one, sir."

"Tell me about your friend Amos," Gamrick said, dropping his hands to the desk and moving back in his chair.

"He wasn't really my friend."

"A shipmate?"

"Yes, sir. We worked the powder together."

"Why wasn't he your friend?"

Hawkins flushed again. "A drinking, whoring black man."

Gamrick almost shrugged, but instead he asked, "What bothered you more: the color of his skin or the fact that he drank and went after women?"

"I don't take kindly to blacks, at least not in the way of them being my friend, sir," Hawkins said.

"Then you didn't really care about his drinking and woman-chasing?" Gamrick questioned.

"Sir, he was what he was. I try not to meddle in other people's business."

"But you liked him enough to become upset a few minutes ago when you started to tell me about him."

"Sir, he was a man. Just because he was black, that didn't mean I wanted him dead."

"Of course not," Gamrick answered. Then he said, "Now, you do know there is another survivor?"

"Yes, sir."

"But when you were at your station, you did not know that another man, Paul Anderson, left the turret?"

"No, sir."

"This is a diagram of turret number two. Will you please look at it and mark with a red circle where your station was?" Gamrick said, passing the paper, then a red crayon pencil, across the desk.

Hawkins studied the diagram for several moments. "Here, sir," he said, drawing a small red circle.

"Thank you. Now, will you tell me exactly what happened after you left the turret," Gamrick said as he retrieved the diagram and the crayon pencil from Hawkins.

"I ran to get to a head. There's one not far from the bulkhead door. Just as I reached the door, the first explosion happened. It knocked me down. Maybe there were a half-dozen more explosions."

"What did you do when battle station sounded?"

Hawkins looked at him blankly.

"I know you couldn't go to yours," Gamrick said. "But you just didn't stand there, did you?"

"No, sir."

"Tell me what you did," Gamrick pressed.

"I helped man the hose on the starboard side."

"You were with a damage-control unit?" Gamrick asked.

"Sir, I never asked who they were. There was so much fire and smoke."

"You're a lucky man, Hawkins," Gamrick said.

"Yes, sir."

Gamrick dismissed him, but just as Hawkins was about to stand up, he said, "Just one more question. Would you say that gun crew of turret number two was in any way different from the gun crews of the other turrets?"

Hawkins remained in the chair. "I don't think I know what you're driving at, sir," he said.

"I'm not driving at anything in particular," Gamrick answered.

"No, sir, there wasn't anything different about them," Hawkins said.

Gamrick nodded and said, "Thank you, Hawkins, you're dismissed."

Hawkins stood up and saluted.

Gamrick returned the salute and waited for the next man to come in.

Gamrick, Folsim, Cool, and Wright sat at a table in the officers' club. None of them would venture to speak about the inquiry in such a public place, but Wright said, "The skipper tells me, Bob, that you're getting a reputation."

"Doesn't count, unless it's a rep with the ladies," Folsim answered.

"He doesn't want to be known as a lean, mean interrogator," Wright said. "A man of his size would prefer to have the sobriquet Big Stick. It's an ego thing with him."

"Something of an 'ego thing' with all of us," Cool commented.

"I only like—no, I relish—what I do with expert attention to detail," Folsim answered before he speared the last piece of roast beef on his plate. "Some guys fish, some hunt. I go after the only real game there is."

Everyone laughed.

Folsim continued, "For me, it's the only game in town."

"That because you never tried surf casting," Wright said with a straight face.

Cool added, "Or spelunking."

"The only tunnel I'm interested in is some beautiful woman's love tunnel, and as far as surf casting goes, it could never equal experiencing that wonderful, miraculous, fantastic pleasure that only a woman can give a man."

An image of Kate flashed in Gamrick's mind. The next instant he'd stripped her naked. . . .

Then Cool said, "What do you gentlemen think about gays in the military?"

Instantly Gamrick came out of his fantasy. A sudden tension stretched like thick, ugly rubber bands on the table. This was a subject that drew sharp adversarial lines in and out of the military.

Irving Greenfield

Wright said quietly, "They've always been with us.
I don't see what this fuss is about. It's as if someone
has made the big discovery that some men prefer
blondes and some brunettes."

"What's your opinion, Skipper?" Cool asked.

Gamrick made a show of easing back in his chair
before he answered, but the movement was absolutely
necessary to ease the sudden pain in his right lateral
muscles.

Then, before he could answer, Folsim asked, "Ever
have one under your command?"

"Yes, I have," Gamrick answered. "Good men, all of
them."

"Then, if you could vote to have them in or out,
you'd vote to have them in," Cool said.

"No, I didn't say that."

"Correct me if I'm wrong, Skipper, but your position is the same as, or close to, Steve's," Folsim said.

"Yes, pretty much so," Gamrick replied.

"Me, I'm strictly a cunt man," Folsim announced.

"We got that impression," Gamrick commented
wryly. Then, looking at Cool, he said, "I'd like to hear
what you think about the subject."

"They might be good men, in the sense that they are
good sailors, but—and it's a big but—they're like a
compass that points west or east instead of north."

"But they're not steering a ship," Folsim objected.

"They might, and that possibility gives me trouble,"
Cool said.

"Then, based on 'that possibility,' you'd get rid of
those we have, not let others in?" Wright questioned.

"I have a problem with that too," Cool answered. "I
don't think laws or a presidential edict will make a bit
of difference to the situation. Both will be political
window dressing."

"As far as you're concerned, there isn't a solution
we can live with," Gamrick commented.

"No, sir, I don't believe that either," Cool responded.

Exasperated, Folsim asked, "Holy shit, Harry, what do you believe?"

"Individual case by individual case," he said quietly, looking down at his empty plate.

"That would leave things pretty much as they are, wouldn't it?" Gamrick questioned.

"Yes, sir."

"No changes?" Folsim asked.

"Two, sir. I'd eliminate the question of an individual's sexual orientation when he joins the service, or any time during his time in the service unless charges are brought against him for homosexual behavior.

"Second, I put the burden of proof on the accuser and not on the accused. This would make it very difficult for an individual to use the charge as a weapon against another individual."

"But not impossible," Gamrick said.

"Not impossible," Cool agreed.

"Well, this has been one hell of a lunch hour," Folsim commented. "A few more like it, and I'll really have to get the old brain oiled up and working again. What say you, Steve?"

"If I don't get indigestion, then I don't mind it."

"That's why I like that guy. He thinks with his stomach," Folsim said. "My daddy told me you can always trust a man who thinks with his stomach."

"Your daddy told you good," Gamrick said.

"Ah, but remember, gentlemen, the old song that says the head bone is connected to the neck bone and the neck bone is connected to the stomach bone, and—"

"We have the general idea," Wright said.

Laughing, the four of them left the table, and walked slowly back to the main building. Gamrick was beginning to feel very comfortable with the members of his staff. That's the way it happens in the military once a commanding officer establishes his authority, and he had done it with these men.

* * *

As soon as Iris opened the screen door, Dimitri bounded out to greet him even before he was out of the car.

"There's a message for you from Lance, the policeman who was here last night," Iris told him. She'd followed Dimitri out of the house.

"Did he say what it's about?" Gamrick asked, reaching back into the car for his briefcase.

"Something about the vehicle," she said, taking hold of his free hand.

They walked toward the house together with Dimitri running circles around them.

"Any plans for dinner tonight?" Gamrick asked as he let go of Iris's hand and stepped aside to allow her to go through the open door first.

"I made reservations for seven o'clock at the Lobster Box," she answered.

Gamrick followed her into the house just as Monique came down the steps wrapped in a white terry cloth robe. " 'Home is the sailor, home from the sea,' " she said with a broad smile.

"Hardly the sea," Gamrick answered.

"I'm going for a quick swim. Wayne is already out there playing whale," she said.

"I better call Lance," Gamrick said, starting for the den.

"Want anything to drink, or eat?" Iris asked.

"A cold beer would be nice and whatever to munch on," he answered.

"My God, you're an easy man to please," Monique said.

"Not all that easy," he answered, going into the den before she could answer.

A few moments after Gamrick dialed the number Iris had put down on a piece of yellow self-stick paper, he was connected to the Galesville police station.

"This is Captain Gamrick. Officer Lance—"

"Yes, yes, Captain, I'm Sergeant Coombs. I have Lance's report right here in front of me. He and Officer

Richie found a blue pickup abandoned ten miles south of here. Its left headlight had been shot out. The slug was buried in the metal of the headlight casing. The vehicle has a Virginia plate. We checked the plate number and its VIN. It was reported stolen yesterday afternoon from a Mr. Sidney Carpet, of Norfolk. We're trying to get some prints off it.

"Does any of this mean anything to you?" Coombs questioned.

"Not a thing," Gamrick answered.

"Lance said you thought the intruder was a local kid."

"Might still be," Gamrick replied, though it did seem less likely now that it was known where the pickup had come from.

"If we find out anything more, we'll let you know," Coombs said.

"Thanks, and thank officers Lance and Richie for me."

"Sure will, Captain. Good-bye."

"Good-bye," Gamrick responded and replaced the handset in its cradle. Then he rubbed his chin, which already had the bristly feel of five o'clock shadow, the nemesis of a well-groomed man. When Gamrick was at sea, he grew a beard. Most of the officers and enlisted men did.

He shook his head.

"What's that for?" Iris asked, coming into the den.

"I was thinking about growing a beard and discarded the idea."

"Thank God," Iris said.

"I'm going to go in for a swim before I dress for dinner," he said.

She followed him out of the room. "What did Lance have to say?" she asked.

"Tell everyone all about it when I come down," Gamrick answered from the head of the stairs.

"I brought beer and some munchies out to the deck," she called up to him.

"Good!" Gamrick answered. "Very good."

* * *

Gamrick swam toward the mouth of the cove, some two miles from the dock at the rear of his house. The cool water refreshed him. He was a powerful swimmer, and he alternated his stroke from overhead, to crawl, to side kick, and back to overhead. He loved swimming almost as much as he loved sailing. Both relaxed him, seemed to blow his brain clear of any clouds of confusion that hovered in it.

The closer he got to the mouth of the cove, the colder the water became. Like all submarine skippers, Gamrick had used the temperature differentials that occur under water in the open sea to elude detection by enemy sonar. Using thermal barriers for protection, he'd once spent three days playing cat and mouse with a pair of Russian destroyers just a few miles outside of Vladivostok.

Gamrick reached the mouth of the cove and turned around. Going back, he slowed his pace and even indulged in a few minutes of floating, which gave him time to think about the question Cool had asked at lunch. Cool might have chosen it because it was controversial. Or was he genuinely interested in the others' opinions? Or did he have a more personal reason? Or he was trying to sort out his own feelings about the subject . . . ?

Gamrick turned onto his stomach and began to swim slowly. He had had homosexuals under his command, but never had to take any disciplinary action against any of them. Although if he had really followed regulations, he should have brought them up on charges that would have had them dishonorably discharged from the Navy. None of them, to his knowledge, had been involved with men aboard the boat. That was his territory, and what happened in it was his concern. What happened outside of it was none of his business. . . .

"Hey, that was a long swim," Monique called from the dock.

He answered, "Good for what ails you." A few moments later he was at dockside and climbed out of the water.

"I'm ready for that beer and those munchies," he said, throwing a blue terry cloth robe across his shoulders. He went up the steps to the deck.

Iris handed him a beer, and he reached down to the platter for a piece of salami speared on a toothpick.

"Now, tell us what Lance told you about the pickup," Monique said.

Gamrick dropped onto a wicker chair with a soft seat cushion on it. "Stolen," he said and took a long pull on the bottle of beer.

"From where?" Iris asked.

"Norfolk. Sometime that afternoon."

"So the driver wasn't a local," Wayne commented.

"Don't know that yet," Gamrick answered, popping the salami into his mouth, chewing it, and drinking more of the beer.

"Local or not why the hell would he do what he did?" Wayne asked.

"I sure as hell can't answer that. But maybe there will be more answers if the cops find some prints on the pickup," Gamrick said.

"Imagine, all the way from Norfolk!" Iris exclaimed.

"How long would it take to drive from Norfolk to Washington?" Wayne asked rhetorically, then answered with, "Say about two hours, three at the most."

"That's about right," Gamrick said, taking yet another pull at the beer.

"Jesus, don't you see it?" Wayne asked, lifting himself out of the chair.

"If you mean someone followed me—"

"I mean, someone stole a pickup, drove up to D.C., waited for you—"

"Come on, Wayne, aren't you pushing it?" Gamrick laughed.

"Not if that someone wanted to scare you. Jesus, Clark, you're heading a team of investigators."

Gamrick set the nearly empty bottle on a small table next to him. "Well, at least whoever it was knows now that I don't scare."

"Is that all you're going to say?" Iris asked, alarmed by the possibility spelled out by Wayne.

"Every day thousands of vehicles are stolen in one place and abandoned in another."

"But how many of those vehicles were used to follow someone and then showed up in a particular person's driveway?" Wayne asked.

"Not many. I'll give you that."

"One?"

"So?" Gamrick challenged.

"So, maybe, just maybe it's connected to what you're doing," Wayne said.

"Even if you're right, there's not a damn thing I can do about it."

Wayne threw up his hands. "You can be thick at times, very thick. It could mean that the accident wasn't an accident—"

"That's exactly what my team hopes to determine," Gamrick answered icily, becoming annoyed at the way Wayne was acting—playing Sherlock Holmes would be more accurate.

"Jesus, Clark, someone is sending you a message."

Gamrick shook his head. "You don't know that. I don't know that. None of us here knows that. Just because you say it doesn't make it so."

"But—"

"I don't want to continue the discussion," Gamrick said.

"Well, I'm damn glad I did what I did," Wayne told him. "Iris, show him what I bought for him."

She hesitated.

"All right, what did you buy? If it's—"

"A double-action, double-load shotgun and a 9mm automatic," Wayne said defiantly. "Just remember, Clark, out here your nearest neighbor is too damn far to hear a damn shot, let alone someone yelling for help."

For several moments Gamrick remained silent and thought about what Wayne had said. "Okay, you made a point," Gamrick told him.

"Well, at least he's got some common sense, sis," Wayne said.

"All right, enough of this. I'm bored to tears by it," Monique complained. "Tell me, Iris, this place we're going to, is it formal or informal?"

"Coastal rustic would be an accurate description," Gamrick said, helping himself to another beer.

Monique raised her eyebrows.

"The only way you might attract attention there would be to walk in *au naturel,*" Gamrick explained.

"Don't give her any ideas," Wayne said.

The four of them laughed.

"Anyone for a nightcap?" Wayne asked as soon as they entered the house. "What about you, Clark?"

"One and only one," Gamrick answered.

"Sis?"

She glanced at Gamrick, then declined the offer.

"Count me out also," Monique said. "I'm bushed. Too much sun this afternoon, I think."

Wayne laughed. "She was *au naturel* on the deck of your boat trying to get a tan all over."

"You'll fry before you tan," Gamrick commented.

"I'm almost well fried now," Monique said, starting up the stairs.

Gamrick and Wayne went into the family room on the east side of the house. It had sliding glass doors that opened out on the deck, a very large color TV, a good wet bar, and occasional furniture that Iris had bought at yard sales, flea markets, and assorted local auctions.

"What's your pleasure?" Wayne asked.

"Bourbon. It's the bottle without a label. It's locally made."

"I'll have one too," Wayne said.

With drinks in their hands, the two men sat: Gamrick on a rocking chair and Wayne on the couch.

"From my sources I hear you have a good chance for flag rank," Wayne commented.

"That's pretty much what I hear. Russo—"

"Never heard of him until I saw him on TV," Wayne said.

"Take my word for it, he's been around and has a lot of political pull."

"Say, this local stuff is damn good."

"Illegal," Gamrick said.

"Who cares?"

Gamrick smiled.

"You know, once you make flag, you can put your papers in and come aboard the family business. Maybe you can convince one of your sons to come aboard also. Hell, Clark, I don't have any children, and it's not likely that Monique will give me any."

"As for the boys joining the business, you'll have to discuss that with them. But—"

"You'll stay in the Navy, right?"

"Right."

"I knew that would be your answer. But I thought I'd give it a whirl anyway."

"I understand," Gamrick said, finishing his drink.

"You're not angry with me for buying the guns?" Wayne asked.

"No. Amused. In all my years in the Navy, I've never had a weapon in the house," Gamrick said. "Never felt the need for one."

Wayne pointed at the empty glass. "One more?"

"No, thank you. I haven't finished going over the OP diagrams of the turret. I knew it was a complex piece of machinery, but I never really understood how complex."

"That's your problem, brother-in-law," Wayne answered.

Gamrick agreed, told Wayne to put his glass in the sink, and said good night.

"See you tomorrow," Wayne answered.

Gamrick made a quick stop in the kitchen, placed his glass in the sink, and went into his den. The answering machine's red signal light flickered.

He rewound the tape and pressed the Play key. "Admiral Russo here. You should have a beeper. I will visit your operation 1100 tomorrow morning. Important information has surfaced concerning one of the survivors."

Gamrick stopped the machine, sat, and rubbed his chin. Russo was certainly wily enough to use several investigating teams. One for show and the others for himself. What the hell—if Russo was doing that, there wasn't anything he could do about . . .

Reaching over to the answering machine, Gamrick hit the Play button again. " 'And there were also Sodomites in the land . . . which the Lord cast,' " a muffled voice said. Then, nothing.

Gamrick stopped the tape, rewound it, fast-forwarded Russo's message, and listened to the muffled voice again. "Christ!" he exclaimed, resetting the machine, and he began to pace.

"Is anything wrong?" Wayne asked, poking his head into the den. Before Gamrick could answer, he said, "I heard you swear."

"Listen to this fucking thing," Gamrick said.

Wayne walked up to the desk.

"The first one is Russo," Gamrick explained, fast-forwarding the tape. "But listen to this guy."

"A nut job," Wayne said even before the message was finished.

Gamrick reset the machine again. "If I get more calls like that one, I'll have to have my number changed, or get one that's unlisted."

"Yeah, you're fair game for all the nuts now," Wayne said.

"That makes me feel better," Gamrick responded with sarcasm that was lost on Wayne.

"Those guns should make you feel better. At least if any crazy comes around here, you will scare the bejesus out of him."

"That even makes me feel a lot better. Go to sleep, Wayne, before you make me feel so good, I just might want to get as drunk as you are."

"Half drunk."

"Half drunk. Go to sleep."

"I'm going, but if the protection of this house was left up to you, it would be a fucking disaster," Wayne said, hiccupped loudly, and stumbled out of the room.

Gamrick went to the window and looked out at the cove. A picture postcard view. Then suddenly he realized he was thinking about Kate—an absolutely idiotic thing to do. By now she had forgotten about him. He shook his head and went back to his desk.

"Nuts or no nuts, I still have work to do," he said, and opening his briefcase, he removed the diagrams of *Utah*'s main batteries.

Chapter 5

Admiral Russo arrived precisely at 1100 flanked by two aides—by their name tags: Captain Louis and Commander Phelps. Both were former surface men.

Gamrick, busy interrogating a gun captain from number one turret, did not know Russo was there until Folsim called, "Attention!"

Gamrick, Folsim, and their interviewees leaped to their feet.

"Carry on," Russo said.

Gamrick remained standing.

"Finish what you were doing, Captain," Russo said.

"Yes, sir," Gamrick answered.

In an attempt to be inconspicuous, Russo and his aides moved off to the corner of the room. But the admiral and his aides became as invisible as a naked woman in a room full of horny men.

Gamrick dismissed the gun captain and immediately joined Russo, who said, "Let's take a walk."

"Yes, sir," Gamrick responded.

Russo looked at his watch and said to his aides. "Meet me at the officers' club at twelve-hundred. We'll lunch here. I have a thirteen-thirty meeting with the CNO."

"Yes, sir," the captain responded. "Twelve-hundred at the officers' club. Shall I have the table ready for you, sir?"

"A salad would do fine and a small bottle of white wine," Russo answered.

"Yes, sir," the aide responded.

Russo beckoned to Gamrick, and together they left the office. Gamrick opened and held the door for Russo, then followed him into the corridor.

Russo didn't speak until they were out of the main building. "Get yourself a beeper," he said. "I want to be able to call you when I need to."

"Yes, sir."

Then Russo said, "Anderson—one of the two men who were not in the fucking turret at the time of the accident—has filed a claim for a two-million-dollar insurance policy with Metro Life."

Gamrick stopped short.

"That grabbed you, didn't it?" Russo said, still walking.

"Yes, sir, it grabbed me."

"One of my friends—retired Admiral John Malone —is CO for Metro life. He called me because the claim was sent to him for his signature. The insured is Seaman First Class Gus Downs." Russo stopped, took off his peaked cap and wiped his brow. "It's hot and the air feels like a sponge soaked with warm water."

"Boomers are in the forecast for this evening," Gamrick said.

Russo replaced his cap and began to walk again. "Downs—we can't even identify who the fuck he was. Now, some son of a bitch comes along and is going to collect two mil? What about this guy Anderson?"

"He's scheduled to be interrogated tomorrow morning," Gamrick answered.

"I want to know every fucking thing about that man, understand?"

"Yes, sir."

"Did Downs have any family?"

"None."

"When was the claim sent?" Gamrick asked.

"According to the postmark, the day the *Utah* made port. Anderson didn't waste any time."

"What is the company going to do?"

"What can they do? They're going to pay. But I asked them to stall for a while."

"Will they?"

"They must pay the claim within ninety days of its receipt," Russo answered. "That's the law in this state."

"I'll question Anderson this afternoon," Gamrick said.

"No. Keep to the schedule, but give me a call later in the day. I want your first impressions."

"Yes, sir."

"If this guy Anderson killed his shipmates to collect the insurance money, I want him nailed to the fucking ship's bow."

Gamrick felt the same way, but he did not voice his feelings. This was Russo's show.

"And I'll tell you this, Captain, from now on I am holding you personally responsible for what happens during the course of the investigation. I want the man, or men, responsible for killing twenty-seven of their shipmates." Russo's anger turned his face red and made him quicken his pace. "I don't have to tell you what the media will do as soon as they find out about the insurance policy, do I?"

"No, sir."

Russo uttered a grunt-like sound, then he complained, "If this fucking thing with the insurance policy isn't enough, this morning I had some crazy message on my answering machine."

Gamrick said, "A muffled voice talking—"

Russo squinted at him. "On your machine too?"

"At home. The call came in sometime last night. I was out with my wife, brother-in-law, and his wife."

"Let's start back. Why don't you have lunch with me?" Russo asked.

"It would be a pleasure," Gamrick replied.

"There's not much that we can do about crank calls," Russo said. "The women—" He stopped himself.

Gamrick immediately filled the breach. "My wife doesn't know about them yet," he said.

"You had more than one?"

Gamrick nodded. "The first one told me to love God, and the second was a quote from the Bible."

"I got that much. I even got the idea it had something to do with Sodomites. To use an expression, what the hell does that have to do with the price of beans in Shanghai on a cold winter's night?"

"Sir, the people who make those kinds of calls function with a different set of values."

"That's for sure," Russo answered.

They were close to the officers' club, and the conversation between them lapsed until Russo asked, "Isn't a Sodomite a homosexual?"

"That's one definition. But it could also mean a person who deviates from normal sex, whatever that means," Gamrick said.

"Normal means a man and a woman," Russo responded.

"Not according to the dictionary."

Russo was silent for a few moments, then he said, "Getting good head, or doing it the Greek way is—"

"Sodomy."

Russo suddenly guffawed. "Live and fucking learn," he laughed. "You know I didn't know that?"

"I didn't either," Gamrick admitted. "I checked the dictionary just before I left the house this morning."

Russo nodded approvingly. Then stopping immediately inside the club, he asked, "How are my two guys doing?"

"Since they've learned, as the expression goes, the rules of engagement, fine."

Russo raised his eyebrows.

"We've quickly become a team," Gamrick explained.

"Glad to hear it," Russo said, continuing toward the dining room.

* * *

Lunch was a breezy affair, with Russo showing that he was a man of many parts—the social part was witty, knowledgeable about world events, the theater, and even about various cuisines.

Gamrick learned that Captain Louis had been commander of a destroyer flotilla and had skippered several different ships from frigates to light cruisers; and Phelps had commanded several different frigates.

When the conversation lagged slightly, Russo said, "The President intends to release his recommendations for gays serving in the military by Friday."

Gamrick couldn't tell whether Russo was testing the waters, or wanted to have a discussion on the subject. Certainly the topic was on everyone's mind. Even Wayne and Monique had said something about it at dinner the previous evening. Wayne, surprisingly, said he had had several very good officers whom he had suspected were homosexual, and in his opinion the entire matter was a brouhaha over something that couldn't be changed. Monique was rabidly against allowing homosexuals to serve, saying that it could create situations that could destroy the ability of a superior to make logical judgements.

The table was quiet.

Then Russo said, "Gamrick, of the four us, you're the only one who has experienced living in very tight quarters. What's your opinion?"

"Sir, I will abide by whatever decision is given by the President," Gamrick answered evasively.

"No doubt you will," Louis said. "But—"

Russo cut him off. "Did you ever have the occasion to discipline a man because of his homosexual conduct?"

"Yes, sir, I did."

"What was your reaction at the time?"

"In each situation the man involved was a good sailor. But the regs are regs."

"You had no personal feelings on the matter?" Phelps asked.

"Only that I was losing a good man because of a foolish indiscretion. Submariners are highly trained men, and a boat's crew is a tightly knit group. The loss of a man and the subsequent introduction of a new man has an effect on the crew and its efficiency. My concern was always about my men and my boat."

"In that order?" Louis asked.

"Yes, in that order," Gamrick answered. He didn't dislike Louis and Phelps, but he didn't particularly like them either. Maybe they had to play the role of lackey to Russo, but they were playing with too much enthusiasm to suit him.

"Well, I have it on very good authority that in the President's decision there will be something for everyone," Russo said.

"A typical political settlement," Louis laughed.

Everyone joined him.

Russo changed the subject. "Clark, you and your wife must come to one of my famous barbecues. We're about due for one any time, now that summer is here."

"It would be a pleasure," Gamrick answered, aware that Russo had used his given name for the first time.

"Louis here," he said, looking at the captain, "says I have the best barbecue east of the Mississippi."

"You certainly do," he answered, mimicking a Texas drawl.

It was Russo who signaled that lunch was over by announcing that he had to go back to Washington.

Later that afternoon, Gamrick went aboard the *Utah* to examine Anderson's service jacket. Anderson had been born and raised in Chicago. He had enlisted when he was eighteen and now was twenty-one. He'd served on the heavy cruiser *Normandy*, whose home port was Staten Island, New York. He had graduated from high school and had taken self-study courses in English, history, and French. He had received excellent ratings by his superiors. Two months ago he had turned down the opportunity to attend a fire-control school. Nothing in the file tagged him as different from tens of thousand of other sailors.

Though Gamrick had been aboard the *Utah* with the other members of the team the first day they came down to Norfolk, he took another look at the turret. This time, because he'd studied the diagrams from the ops manual, he had a very clear picture in his mind of what the inside of the turret looked like. But what he saw was a twisted mass of metal, some of which had melted, even though it was steel, from the intense fire that had roared through it. The breech block of each gun was fused to the gun's barrel, and there was an enormous hole, now lit by electric lights dangling from wires, that went down to the upper barbette. There were specialists working in various places in the turret and the barbette. Had the explosion or the flames penetrated to the lower barbette, where the powder had been stored, the ship would have been blown apart.

Gamrick returned to the office a few minutes before he would leave for D.C.

"The admiral have anything interesting to say?" Folsim asked on the way to the heliport.

Gamrick hesitated.

"Come on, Skipper, we're all in the same club," Folsim chided.

"I'll tell you what I was told only on condition that we do not discuss it and you do not discuss it either among yourselves or with anyone else," Gamrick said.

Each of them nodded.

"Paul Anderson is the beneficiary of a two-million-dollar life insurance policy that had been bought by one of the casualties—Gus Downs."

Wright let go a long whistle. "That's really—"

"No discussion," Gamrick said. "We'll deal with it tomorrow after I interrogate Anderson."

Gamrick turned into the parking area adjacent to the Sea Sands tavern, went up to the bar, and settled on a stool.

"News is coming on," Pete said, looking up at the color screen to his left.

"Coffee," Gamrick said.

Pete ordered through the small window. Then he pointed at the matchbook covers taped to the mirror behind the bar. "Wife was thrilled when I showed them to her," he said.

"Coffee," a voice on the other side of the window announced.

Pete placed the cup on the bar in front of Gamrick. "Our favorite TV lady," he sad as the camera focused on Kate Bannon. "She's certainly a looker."

"She certainly is," Gamrick answered. She was wearing a red dress, with a green scarf around her neck. He hardly heard what she was saying. He just wanted to look at her. That was why he had stopped.

"And we have this information on the ongoing investigation about the cause of the disaster aboard the *Utah* that took the lives of twenty-seven men. We have learned late this afternoon that a member of the gun crew who survived the terrible explosion will become a millionaire because of it. The Navy is investigating this bizarre turn of events." Then she went on to other news.

Gamrick was stunned. That information was classified. How had she got it? Even if she had it, she should not have used it. Not until it had been officially released.

He left without finishing the coffee or waiting until the news was over. Angry, he drove faster than he should have. He was sure Russo had already called, and when he pulled into the driveway Dimitri and Iris were out of the door at almost the same time.

"Admiral Russo phoned. He wants you to call him as soon as you get home. He sounded steamed about something," she said.

"Did you watch Kate Bannon at five o'clock?" he asked, rubbing Dimitri's head as the three of them went into the house.

"No."

"I'll tell you about it, but now I have to call the admiral," he said, going directly into the den and closing the door behind him.

The admiral was in high dudgeon. "How the fuck did she come by that information?" he shouted.

"Sir, I haven't the remotest idea," Gamrick answered.

"Well, she got it from someone."

"Sir, newspeople have their sources."

"That particular piece of information is highly sensitive," Russo said. "The CNO, the Secretary of the Navy, and the President have been on my goddamn back since it was aired."

Gamrick remained silent.

"Are you still there?"

"Yes, sir."

"Did you tell anyone else about the insurance policy?" Russo asked.

"The members of my team."

Now Russo was silent except for his heavy breathing.

Gamrick felt very uneasy. He took a deep breath.

"Mister, when I tell you something, it's for your ears only, unless I tell you differently."

Slowly exhaling, Gamrick answered, "Yes, sir."

"If I find out it was one of those three men, I swear to Christ I'll make him wish he was out of the Navy," Russo growled.

"Sir, I warned them—"

"You should have kept your mouth shut, Captain."

Gamrick could feel the heat in his cheeks.

"Have a good night," Russo said.

Before Gamrick could answer, he heard the click of the phone on the other end. He put the handset back in its cradle and took several deep breaths to calm himself. Just as he was about to stand, the phone rang. He answered it.

Russo was back on the line. "Listen, Clark, I apologize for blowing off like that, but I've been on the receiving end because of that broadcast."

"Yes, sir, I'm sure you have," Gamrick answered.

"I just was told that the information came out of the insurance company," Russo explained. "It won't happen again."

"Thank you for calling," Gamrick said. Russo showed a sensitivity he hadn't expected him to have, let alone exhibit.

"Good night, Clark."

"Good night, sir," Gamrick answered, and this time when he put the phone down, he did not have to take any deep breaths. He was calm.

The next morning Paul Anderson, a chunkily built young man of twenty-one with muscles to spare, the obligatory crew cut, and black eyes, sat calmly in front of Gamrick's desk.

"I have a few questions to ask you," Gamrick said, changing the format that he had been using. "I know how painful this must be for you."

"I know it's necessary, sir," Anderson answered in a soft but steady voice.

"Before you left the turret, you received permission, didn't you?"

"Yes, sir. I had a very bad sinus attack."

"And you reported to sick bay?"

"Yes, sir. It's—"

"I have the record," Gamrick answered, paused a few moments, and then asked, "Describe exactly what you did after the explosion occurred."

"Well, sir, I ran topside with the corpsmen and doctors," Anderson answered.

"You made no attempt to return to your duty station?" Gamrick questioned, carefully scrutinizing the young man.

"Sir, my duty station didn't exist."

Gamrick leaned forward, resting his elbows on the desk. "How do you feel about that? I mean, you're alive because you had a sinus attack. Just how do you feel about it?"

"Well, sir, I feel—as the preacher would say—God had a reason for saving me."

"Was the preacher a member of the gun crew?" Gamrick asked.

"Donald Hawkins, sir. He's the preacher. God must have had a reason for saving him too."

"Are the two of you friends?" Gamrick questioned.

"Shipmates, sir. Hawkins keeps to himself."

"And you don't?"

"I like being with people," Anderson replied.

"Do you have a girlfriend, Paul?" Gamrick asked, purposefully using the man's given name to reinforce his feeling of well-being.

"Yes, sir."

"Here in Norfolk?"

"She lives in Staten Island, New York," Anderson said.

"Do you have a picture of her?"

Anderson produced a photograph of a young, black-haired, gypsy-looking woman in a bikini with LOVE AND KISSES, JULIE across the bottom of it in a childish handwriting.

"A foxy-looking lady," Gamrick commented, winking.

Anderson grinned. "She has her moments."

"I bet she does," Gamrick answered.

"If I can get liberty this weekend, I'm going up to see her," Anderson volunteered.

"Are the two of you planning to marry?"

"Yes."

"When?" Gamrick eased back into the chair.

"Her folks—well, she's Italian, and her folks—"

"Giving her a hard time?"

Anderson nodded. "They only see me as a sailor . . . someone with no future."

Gamrick slowly moved forward again. This time he didn't plant his elbows on the desk. Instead he placed his hands on the edge of the desk, palms down, as if he were seated at a piano and about to play it. "But all that will change, won't it, Paul, when you show Julie's parents a check for two million dollars?"

Anderson flushed.

"You really didn't think that could be kept a secret, did you?" Gamrick asked.

"Gus and I were friends," Anderson blurted out.

"Two million dollars' worth of friendship is a lot of friendship," Gamrick said.

"We were friends," Anderson said, his voice choked with emotion. "He was going to be my best man when Julie and I married."

Gamrick pressed the balls of his fingers together. He needed to know something about the dead man Gus Downs, and he needed to know a great deal more about the man sitting in front of him.

Without being asked, Anderson said, "Gus was my best friend. We were like brothers. He didn't have any family. My family became his family."

"What were his feelings about Julie?" Gamrick asked.

"Brotherly."

"I mean, did he resent her for taking you away from him?" Gamrick asked.

Anderson shook his head. "Gus wasn't like that. There wasn't a resentful bone in his body."

"Did he go home on leave with you?"

"Often."

"What about the times you were with Julie?" Gamrick questioned.

"Julie would find a date for him. Gus was a handsome man. A blond-haired, blue-eyed giant—he was six four without shoes."

Gamrick nodded.

Suddenly there were tears in Anderson's eyes. "He was my best friend and—"

"Tell me about the insurance policy," Gamrick said, handing him a tissue.

"One day—night, really—we were in the Horseshoe Crab bar, that's down on the main strip in Norfolk, drinking, and Gus said to me, 'You know, Paul, I got this strange feeling that I'm not going to be around much longer.' I told him he was nuts. But he said that he wanted to do something for me and Julie, something that would make life easier for us. He knew that Julie's folks were giving us a hard time. That's when he came up with the idea for the insurance policy."

"Did you suggest that you take out a policy on your life?" Gamrick asked.

"No, sir. I didn't feel the way he did," he answered.

"Understand, Paul, that the insurance policy throws a spotlight on you as far as the Navy is concerned," Gamrick said. "Every man in that turret was killed. You and Hawkins are the only survivors. Hawkins left the turret because he had the runs, and you left because you had a sinus attack."

"Accidents—"

"I know, accidents happen, if that's what you were going to say. But—and it's a very big but—they don't happen in the Navy so that an enlisted man or an officer becomes a millionaire as a result of the accident. That has never happened before."

Anderson shrugged and used another tissue.

"That two million is going to complicate your life," Gamrick said.

"You mean you think I did it?" he asked, his voice going up. He started to stand at the same time.

"Sit!" Gamrick snapped.

Anderson dropped into the chair. "Sorry, sir," he said.

"Pass the word to the OOD. You are restricted to the ship until further notice."

"Yes, sir," Anderson answered.

"Dismissed."

Anderson stood up and saluted.

Gamrick returned the salute, and when Anderson finally left the office, he sank back into his chair. Press-

ing the balls of his fingers together, he stared at them.
For that sailor this was just the beginning. . . .

"Close the door," Gamrick said to Cool. The team
had ended the day and was ready to return to Washington.

"I bet this is going to be another unofficial
meeting," Wright commented.

"You win," Gamrick said, settling on the top of his
desk. "We've come up with something."

"About Anderson?" Cool asked.

"Yes, about Anderson," Gamrick answered.

Then Cool said, "The only thing I came up with is
the fact that the men in the various divisions don't in-
termingle. Turret men stay with turret men, radar with
radar, and so on. Rarely do the men of one specialty
make friends with the men of another."

"Is it that way aboard a submarine?" Folsim asked.
He sat on the edge of the other desk.

Gamrick shook his head. "No. The men are too de-
pendent on one another for survival. A man belongs to
the boat."

"How about telling us what we came up with?"
Wright said. "Besides the fact that Anderson was all
but named by that cunt Kate Bannon on the five
o'clock news yesterday."

Gamrick let the comment about Kate glide past him.
Even if he wanted to defend her, he couldn't. There
wasn't any reason for him to take umbrage at Wright's
comment, other than it was in poor taste. And he
wasn't about to do that because there was a looseness
now between him and the other men that made it easier
for them to work together. "Forget about Kate Bannon.
Now we have to concentrate on Anderson."

Wright, who had been standing next to Cool, walked
over to one of the chairs and sat.

"Is that why the admiral paid a visit?" Folsim asked.

Gamrick nodded. "A friend of his is CO of Metro

Life and had to sign off on the claim before the check was cut."

"So, naturally he called the admiral," Cool said.

"That's the picture," Gamrick answered.

"That's a kill, if ever there was one," Wright said. "We can shut down and go back to doing whatever we were doing before."

"There's no law—" Cool began.

Interrupting, Folsim said, "Come on, look at the motivation."

"Oh, the motivation is there, but we would—the government—would have to explain to the court how it was done. The explosion occurred when he wasn't in the turret."

"A fucking time bomb could have been set," Wright argued.

"It would have to be proved," Cool maintained.

"Okay, Skipper, you call the shots. What do we do now?" Folsim asked.

"First, it will be Admiral Russo who calls the shots. I only see that they are fired in the right direction. Second, starting with tomorrow's interrogations, I want each of you to ask questions about the relationship between Paul Anderson and Gus Downs. I also want questions asked about 'the Preacher,' a.k.a. Donald Hawkins. Then on Thursday and Friday, each of you will reinterrogate Hawkins and Anderson. I'll arrange for individual rooms."

"Will interrogations be videotaped?" Cool asked.

"Yes. Wright, as soon as I get the rooms, you make sure the taping equipment is there and invisible."

"Yes, sir," Wright answered.

"Any questions?" Gamrick asked.

"Just a comment," Folsim said. "I don't think Anderson will ever get to enjoy his two million."

"Probably not," Gamrick replied. Then he added, "But we'd really be able to wrap this up if we could get a confession from him."

"Sweet dreams," Cool responded.

"Okay, that's it for today. I'll join you in a few minutes. I have to give the admiral a rundown on what happened."

"The officers' club?" Wright asked.

"I'll be there as soon as I can," Gamrick said. He waited until he was alone before he picked up his phone and dialed Russo's number.

Russo's office was not where Gamrick wanted to be. As soon as he had made the mistake of saying Anderson might be guilty, Russo had demanded to see the tape and he had no choice but to deliver it.

"Cigar?" Russo asked, taking one from the humidor on his desk.

Gamrick politely declined. He wanted to be out of there as soon as possible, but he was sure that Russo was operating with a completely different time frame. Slow ahead. . . .

"Well, now that you've viewed the tape, what do you think? Do we have our man or don't we?" Russo asked, blowing smoke toward the ceiling.

"Sir—"

"Did you see the way he looked when you told him that the two mil would complicate his life?" Russo asked.

"Sir, the only crime Anderson has committed was that he didn't die with the others," Gamrick said.

Russo was on his feet. "You're joking, Captain," he practically roared. "That's one hell of a fucking thing to say."

"Sir, we don't even know whether he coerced—"

Russo pointed the burning end of the cigar at Gamrick. "You questioned him. You just reviewed the tape, and you can still tell me that we don't have our man?"

"We have a very strong motivation for—"

"A two-million-dollar motivation," Russo growled, taking a position in back of his chair and leaning his forearms on it. "Tell me this, do you believe that bullshit about their friendship? I mean, Gamrick, he's trying to pull our chain."

"Sir, the man was visibly upset when he spoke about Downs."

"Alligator tears."

Gamrick uttered a deep sigh. He knew Russo needed a quick solution to the mystery.

Russo returned to his chair. "I know that you want to do a thorough job and you should, but you've given us someone we can ride with, someone—"

"Someone to take the fall," Gamrick said harshly.

Russo leaned back and looked hard at the man. "You just continue to do what you're doing, Captain, and I'll decide what to do with the information you give me."

"Yes, sir," Gamrick snapped.

Neither one spoke.

Then Russo stopped puffing on the cigar and said, "Between men there's friendship and there's friendship. The friendship between Anderson and Downs was sick. Probably sicker than you or I could possibly imagine."

"Yes, sir," Gamrick answered.

"The bottom line is we have our man," Russo said. "We have the motivation, and—"

"Nothing else, sir," Gamrick responded forcefully. "Give me a few more days, a week, and maybe I'll have what we need to really nail him."

Russo remained silent.

But Gamrick could tell the man was listening. He took an even more aggressive approach. "Suppose you are right. Suppose their friendship was more than just friendship between men."

"Homos?"

Gamrick nodded. "Suppose that was the case and suppose they had a falling-out and Downs, who was—as you heard—a very handsome man, dropped Anderson and took another lover. That would strengthen our case, wouldn't it?"

Russo nodded.

"I need more time, Admiral, to find out what really happened. We have two men, Anderson and Hawkins, who left the turret just before the explosion. Both of them have valid reasons for having left. But one had permission. There is a record of him having gone to sick bay. The other says he had permission, but we have nothing to prove it. Both men were involved in fighting the fire that occurred after the explosion. The answers to our questions have to come from these two men. They are the only ones who know the truth."

Russo stared at him and shook his head. "Didn't you tell me that you never had courtroom experience?"

"Yes, sir."

"After what I just heard, I don't believe you."

Gamrick allowed a small smile to race across his lips.

"You have more time but not much more. I have people breathing down my neck."

"Yes, sir, I understand that," Gamrick said.

"That invitation to my barbecue still stands," Russo told him. "I'll tell you when."

"Yes, sir."

"All right. Get out of here and keep me wired in," Russo said.

"Yes, sir," Gamrick answered, stood up, and saluted.

Russo returned the salute. "When there's just the two of us, you don't have to do that," he said.

"I'll remember," Gamrick answered with a smile.

Chapter 6

For several moments Gamrick deliberately looked at Hawkins without speaking. But Hawkins' eyes never wavered from his. This was the third interrogation session. The second had taken place in the morning, and it had been almost a rerun of the first. But during lunch, Folsim had suggested that he have another round with him.

"There's something spooky about him," Folsim said.

Wright agreed, but Cool put it another way. "He's too composed, even more composed than Anderson."

"Maybe he has nothing troubling him," Gamrick suggested.

"Listen, he may be young and stupid—I don't really think he has much more than feathers between his ears—but he is one of two men who escaped being killed. That has to ring a bell somewhere in all those feathers, and as far as I can tell, it doesn't."

Gamrick agreed to have another go at Hawkins.

"Smoke, Donald, if you want to," he finally said.

"Don't smoke, sir," Hawkins answered.

"What do you like to do most?" Gamrick asked, leaning back in the chair.

"Things."

"I like sailing," Gamrick said. "Ever been sailing?"

"No, sir."

"Isn't there something special that you like to do?"

"Hunting."

"Deer?"

"Some. But mainly duck during the season. Bird calling. I can do a couple of dozen birds."

Gamrick placed his hands together. "Did you graduate from high school?" he asked.

"Yes, sir. It's in my service jacket."

Gamrick nodded. Then he asked, "Do you go to church on Sundays?"

"Yes, sir."

"Is that why the men nicknamed you the Preacher?" Gamrick hadn't asked that question, though he knew the other members of his team had.

"Sir, I told the two commanders and the lieutenant that Anderson was the only one who called me Preacher."

"Not Downs."

"Sometimes."

Gamrick leaned forward. The answer was exactly the same Hawkins had given to Folsim, Wright, and Cool. "You don't like Anderson, do you?" he asked.

"He and Gus were tight. They didn't have any other friends."

"Did you have many friends?"

"No, sir."

"Did you want to be friends with Anderson and Downs?"

Hawkins changed his position for the first time since he had sat down.

"Well, Donald, did you want to be their friend?" Gamrick pressed.

Hawkins shook his head.

"Yes or no."

"Yes, sir—I mean, no, sir," Hawkins said.

"Which is it: yes or no?"

"No, sir."

To ease the tension inside his own body, Gamrick stood up and took several steps to the right, where a wall stopped him. The room was small and windowless.

"Why didn't you want to be their friend?" Gamrick

asked, stopping behind the desk chair and placing his hands on the back of it.

Hawkins shrugged.

"Come on, Donald, I want an answer."

"They had their own thing going. Know what I mean?"

"No. I want you to tell me what you mean," Gamrick pushed.

Hawkins looked straight at him. "They did it together, sir. Everyone knew it."

Gamrick wanted to utter a deep sigh of relief. He'd finally gotten something meaningful out of Hawkins. Now he would dog that for all it was worth. "Did what?" he asked, assuming complete innocence. "You have to be more specific, Donald."

Hawkins' face became beet red. "Did it," he said, his voice going higher. "Did it!"

"Tell me what they did."

"Fucked!" Hawkins shouted, wringing his white cap in his hands. "They fucked."

"They were lovers."

"They fucked."

Gamrick sat. Though the room was air-conditioned, he could see that Hawkins was sweating. "Take it easy, Donald. That would have come out sooner or later."

"I'm all right, sir," Hawkins answered.

"Would you like a drink of water?" Gamrick asked.

"No, sir."

Gamrick was going to ask Hawkins what he thought about the presidential decision regarding gays in the military, but decided not to. Instead he asked, "So, Anderson and Downs were lovers."

Hawkins' face turned red again.

"Donald, have you ever made love to a woman?" Gamrick asked.

"I ain't no damn queer, sir," Hawkins flared.

"Does that mean yes or no?"

"Means yes, sir."

Gamrick nodded and asked, "Have you a girlfriend now?"

"No, sir."

"Oh, one or two more questions, Donald, and then we're done," Gamrick said.

"Yes, sir."

"Tell me, Donald, just before the explosion—I mean, before the ship left port on the training mission—was there anything different going on between Anderson and Downs? Think hard before you answer."

"Don't have to think. All the guys knew it. They weren't tight the way they were before."

Gamrick forced himself not to show any emotional change. But a sudden rush of adrenaline made his heart race. "How do you know that?"

"Downs switched racks with another man," Hawkins said.

"Did they speak to each other?"

Hawkins shook his head. "No, sir."

"When did Downs change his rack?" Gamrick asked.

"Just before we left port," Hawkins said.

Gamrick stood up again, paced the width of the room, and finally stopping behind the chair, he asked, "Would you tell the members of a court-martial what you just told me?"

Hawkins looked at the floor.

"I need an answer, Donald," Gamrick said in a low but kind voice.

Hawkins looked up at Gamrick. "Yes, sir, if I have to."

Gamrick dismissed him, returned his salute, and let out a long pent-up sigh. He had gotten some of what he needed to make a case against Anderson. But even what he had didn't clinch it. In a court-martial it would come down to Hawkins' word against Anderson's.

* * *

"Anderson didn't waver one bit," Folsim told Gamrick during their unofficial meeting at the end of the day.

"I got the same story too," Cool said.

"Same," Wright added.

By now each of them occupied the same place in the room. Folsim sat on the edge of the other desk, Cool stood leaning against the wall, and Wright had a chair.

Gamrick modestly said, "I guess I was a lot luckier with Hawkins."

Folsim left the edge of the desk. "How lucky?" he asked.

"He told me that Anderson and Downs were lovers."

"That doesn't come as a big surprise," Cool said.

"He also said that they had a falling-out just before the ship left port," Gamrick explained.

"And he'll repeat all of that in front of a court-martial?" Folsim asked.

Gamrick nodded.

"Where do we go from here, Skipper?" Folsim asked.

"Sit tight and let the admiral decide," Gamrick answered. "It would still be Hawkins' word against Anderson's. And if Anderson got himself a good lawyer—well, Hawkins isn't an example of the Navy's brightest lights."

"I still think it calls for a celebration. These last few days we've been working our asses off," Wright said.

"Okay," Gamrick agreed. "But let's go somewhere off base. A place that's quiet."

"I know a bar, a quiet bar where the exotic dancing—"

"Quiet exotic dancing?" Cool questioned.

"Trust me."

"Hard to do," Cool answered with a broad smile.

"Bob, call our friendly air service back to D.C. and tell them we'll be delayed about two hours. And I better call my wife and tell her the same," Gamrick said.

"Don't forget to tell her where you'll be," Wright said.

Gamrick nodded. "There are some things wives just don't understand," he said, picking up the phone and punching out his home phone number.

The four of them piled into a cab, which they found just outside the base's main gate. Wright and Cool sat on jump seats in front of Gamrick and Folsim.

"You know the Pussy Willow?" Wright asked the driver, a man wearing an old, dirty sailor hat and mirror sunglasses.

"Yes, sir, I sure do," the driver said.

"Take us there."

The driver looked back at the four of them. "All white girls there," he said.

Gamrick felt the rush of heat in his cheeks.

"Listen, I'll catch a couple of drinks with you guys another time," Cool said, opening the door.

"Stay!" Gamrick snapped.

"Yes, sir," Cool responded, closing the door.

"Do you know a place where the four of us can sit down and have a couple of drinks?" Gamrick asked, his voice still tight with anger.

"A couple," the driver answered.

"Take us to one of them," Wright told him.

"With women—"

"I don't give a flying fuck if there are women or not," Gamrick exploded. "Just fucking take us."

"Yes, sir," the driver answered, facing front and turning the ignition.

Furious, Gamrick faced the window.

"Skipper, it's not worth it," Folsim said in a low voice. "It's just the way things are. There are rules—"

Gamrick faced him and shook his head. "We make the rules by not breaking them. Cool is a human being and officer in the United States Navy, and he can't go where we go because his skin is darker than ours. Hell, he serves just as we serve."

"Bob is right, Skipper," Cool said. "The laws that Congress passes are one thing, and most people obey them, like it or not. But then there are the rules that people live by, and they're not the same as the laws."

"I say we drop this discussion," Wright commented. "Remember, we're going out to celebrate, not to remake society."

"Wright is right," Gamrick responded with a forced smile. "We're not going to talk shop; we're just going to have a good time."

"If this spirit of camaraderie keeps up, we might get the reputation for being the Navy's four musketeers," Folsim commented.

"Worse things than that could happen," Wright said.

"Sure they could, and that's looking at the bright side," Cool responded with a straight face.

Just as four of them were about to guffaw, the driver shouted, "Oh, Jesus!" The next instant a large dump truck slammed into the front of the cab, spinning it around a full one hundred and eighty degrees into the opposite lane, where it was struck head on and thrown to the right side and sideswiped two other cars before crashing into a telephone pole and coming to a jolting stop halfway into a drainage ditch.

Gamrick was pinned under Folsim. He willed himself to move. "Bob, Steve, Harry?" he croaked.

Cool answered.

Gamrick pushed against Folsim and finally climbed over him.

Suddenly someone pulled the door open, reached in, and grabbed hold of Cool. Other hands got Gamrick out. "The driver and two more in the rear," he said, hearing the wail of sirens. He struggled to free himself. "Other men!" he shouted. "Other men."

"Take it easy," a voice said. "Take it easy."

Gamrick was set down on the grass next to Cool. "Got to get—" A man in a white jacket bent over him. He felt the prick of a needle, and before the growing grayness covered him, he heard a huge explosion and saw orange flames leap into the nearby trees.

* * *

Gamrick called Iris from Dr. Breen's office in Norfolk General Hospital and explained what had happened. She wanted to drive to Norfolk to pick him up,
but he convinced her not to. "I'm fine," he assured her.
"I have a few bruises externally and internally, but otherwise I'm fine."

She asked about the other men.

He paused, took a deep breath, and when he finished
exhaling, he said, "The driver never got out and Steve
is paralyzed from the waist down. Bob is okay. He was
knocked unconscious by the impact, but he'll be all
right. So will Harry. He had a compound fracture of
his left hand."

"You're a lucky man," she said.

He agreed and said, "I'll be home as soon as I can."
Then he put the phone down and thanked the doctor
for letting him use it.

Gamrick had already spoken to the police and told
them he had seen the dump truck a moment before it
struck the cab. He couldn't even tell them what color
it was.

The man in charge of the investigation—Lieutenant
Tass—told him that witnesses at the scene had said that
truck was black, that it ran a red light, that it didn't
seem to have a license plate, and that the driver made
no attempt to stop. And one man said that it didn't begin to move until the light had changed to red.

Gamrick couldn't give him any information that
would help ID the truck, but Tass gave him his card
and had asked him to call if he thought of anything.

Dr. Breen handed a small bottle to Gamrick and
said, "These are for pain. You might have some in the
next few days. If I were you, I'd take it easy for a couple of days."

"I was going to sail down to—"

"Easy," the doctor said. "Sailing, depending on the
weather, can be a whole lot less than easy."

Gamrick nodded and, reaching across the desk, he
shook the doctor's hand. Then he left the office. His

legs felt a bit wobbly, and he stopped to steady himself. It took him several minutes to walk from the doctor's office to the cab station immediately outside the hospital.

Less than an hour later, he was in his own car driving slowly home. To be sure that other cars gave him a wide berth, he switched on the car's blinkers. He was beginning to feel the pain now. Especially along the back of his neck and up into the back of his skull.

Gamrick concentrated on driving, but when he saw the Sea Sands tavern he realized that he had to stop. He had pushed himself as far as he could. Now he needed a break—an hour or so to pull himself together. He looked at his watch. It was 2030, and the light, especially in the wooded areas along the road, was rapidly graying to the darker twilight tone.

There were several cars pulled up close to the building when he turned into the parking area. He chose a spot as close to the door as possible, and leaving the car, he made his way slowly into the tavern.

Suddenly Pete was at his side holding him up. "Holy shit, what happened to you?" he asked.

"Accident."

"Car wreck?"

Gamrick shook his head. "Better get me to a table," he said. "I'm not going to make the bar."

Pete brought him to a table and eased him down into a chair. "Kate Bannon called just two minutes ago. She wanted to know if you were here. I told her you weren't. And she said she was in the neighborhood and would stop by in about ten minutes."

Gamrick closed his eyes. "I don't want to be interviewed," he said. "I need a few minutes to rest." And he put his arms on the table and cradled his head in them. . . . *Small galactic circles spin in his head. The face of his father whirls in front of him. A man stretched out in a hospital bed with IVs in both arms, eyes closed and breathing noisily. He reaches down and smoothes his father's white hair. "I'm home,*

Dad," he says. No response. "Dad, I love you." No response. He clasps his father's hands and holds them tightly as if he could pull him back. But he can't. He can't heal the breach between them. Can't heal his father's disappointment and his own resentment. "Become a lawyer. Be someone," his father told him. But he followed his own calling. His father never forgave him, and he never forgave his father for not forgiving him. Now it was too late. He could only hold back the tears and grip his father's childlike hands. . . .

"Captain . . . Captain Gamrick?"

He heard the voice. It floated on the scent of jasmine.

"Damn hardass, man. He should have checked into the base—"

"Pete, get him something to eat. Soup, if you have it," the woman said.

"Fresh beef barley," Pete answered.

"Ms. Bannon, do you want a drink?" the man asked.

"No, thank you, Admiral."

Gamrick could clearly hear the conversation now.

"Pete, bring me a Jack Daniels on the rocks," the man said.

Gamrick was sure he recognized the voice, but he couldn't attach a name to it.

"Captain?" the woman softly called.

Gamrick forced his head up. His blurred vision took several moments to clear.

"My God, I can't believe you were let out of the hospital," she said.

"Kate? Kate Bannon?" he asked, focusing on her.

She smiled at him. "In the flesh, and Admiral Russo," she said, gesturing to Russo, who was seated across from her.

Gamrick moved his eyes from her to his boss.

"We've been chasing you since you left the hospital. I went there as soon as I was told about the accident," Russo told him.

"Steve—Commander Wright is in bad shape," he said.

Russo nodded. "He's been moved to Bethesda."

Gamrick pulled himself up. "I guess the driving was more than I should have tackled." He looked back at Kate. "I can't give you an interview or—"

"Not to worry," she answered. "I met the admiral at the hospital," she explained, her eyes darting to Russo.

"Yes, we met at the hospital," he said.

"I went out to the hospital with my crew to get the story," she explained. "But no one would give us any information, including the police."

"I told them to black it out," he responded.

"Good thinking," Russo commented. "We'll handle this the right way."

"I would have called you—" Gamrick began.

"Whatever it is, it can wait a day or two," Russo said. "Ah, here comes my drink, and your soup."

"Soup?"

"I ordered it for you," Kate explained.

Gamrick smiled, but didn't object.

"The police said it was a hit-and-run accident," Russo said.

"The driver was killed."

"I didn't know that," Russo said, lifting his drink. "To the speedy recovery of all my men," he toasted.

"You finish your soup and we will drive you home," Kate said in a take-charge voice.

"Admiral, there's no need—" Gamrick started to say, but Russo quickly cut in with "There's every need, and let's not have any more discussion about it."

"Yes, sir," Gamrick answered.

"You're a difficult man to catch," Kate commented.

"Imagine what he'd be like if he were well," Russo added.

Gamrick didn't answer. The soup was hot and tasty, and he was hungrier than he had realized.

Russo ordered another drink.

And Kate asked, "Tell me, Captain, have you always been lucky?"

"Please, not so formal. My name is Clark."

She nodded. "Well, Clark, have you always been so lucky?"

Gamrick smiled. "I don't feel very lucky, though of course I know that I am. But that's a question I'll have to give some thought to."

She laughed.

Gamrick finished his soup, and Russo called for the check.

"Another one on the house," Pete answered.

"Okay, Gamrick, you go slow and easy," Russo said, coming alongside him as he stood up.

Kate placed herself on his other side, and he wrapped his arm around hers. "Do you want to drive him, or shall I?" she asked across Gamrick as the three of them made their way to the door.

"Choice is yours," Russo answered.

"Okay, I'll drive him home in his car, and you follow in mine," she said.

Gamrick suddenly stopped.

"This is not the time," she whispered tightly to him.

"Anything wrong?" Russo questioned.

"Needed a quick rest," Gamrick said.

They reached his car.

"Front or back?" Russo asked.

"Front," Gamrick said. "I have to be her navigator."

They eased him into a bucket seat, and Kate buckled the safety belt, then came around to the other side. Settling into the driver's seat, she asked him for the keys.

Gamrick dug them out of his pocket and handed them to her.

"See you at the house," she called out to Russo.

"Just remember, I'm behind you," he called back.

Gamrick wasn't sure whether Russo meant it to caution her against driving too fast and losing him, or he was reminding her of something more significant between them.

Kate pulled up to the road and waited until Russo positioned himself behind her before she drove on.

"It's about twenty minutes from here," Gamrick said, working himself into the corner, next to the door, so that he could look at her. She wore a red headband, a white blouse with the top three buttons open, a loose, flimsy white bra that didn't prevent him from seeing her nipples, and a blue skirt, which she'd hiked up as far as it would go when she entered the car.

"Handles easy," she said, referring to the Jeep.

Gamrick took a deep breath and when he exhaled, he asked, "Do you handle easy, Kate?"

She glanced at him.

"You didn't meet him at the hospital, did you?"

"That's a question you don't have a right to ask and one that I will not answer," she said, reaching for the knob to turn on the radio.

Gamrick stopped her hand and before he could engage his fingers with hers, she pulled it away.

"I've thought about you," he told her.

"You're putting something together that doesn't exist," she said.

"Turn right at the next intersection," Gamrick directed. He waited until she made the turn, then he said, "You wouldn't be here if it didn't exist."

She glanced up into the rearview mirror for a moment. "We were having cocktails when his beeper went off."

"You didn't have to—"

"Yes, for what it's worth, Clark, I had to make sure you were all right," she said. "There, now, are you satisfied?"

Gamrick cleared his throat. "It's going to take a lot more than that to satisfy me," he told her in a hoarse voice.

"It's not going to happen," she said resolutely.

He reached out and placed his hand on her bare thigh.

"No," she protested.

He slowly moved his hand down between her thighs. "You're not listening to me."

Gamrick didn't answer. He watched the heave of her breasts.

Slowly Kate opened her thighs. "You're going to get us killed," she said.

"I won't if you tell me."

"Okay, I had to see you because—"

"No, tell me."

"What? What do you want me to tell you that you don't already know?"

Gamrick removed his hand, leaned back into the corner, and closing his eyes, he said, "It's been a long time since I've wanted a woman the way I want you. A long, long time, Kate."

She touched the side of his face with the back of her fingers.

Iris insisted that Kate and Russo come into the house, though Russo appeared to be eager to leave. She ushered them into the living room and quickly assumed the role of hostess, telling Wayne, "Take Clark upstairs and get him into bed."

Gamrick said, "I'm not in the least bit tired. The very least I can do is give Admiral Russo and Ms. Bannon drinks. Wayne will do the honors."

"Certainly," Wayne answered.

Russo and Kate sat in chairs opposite each other. Gamrick occupied one side of the couch and Monique the other.

Small talk buzzed. Wayne and Russo found they knew several of the same people. And Monique told Kate how much she enjoyed her TV news show.

Wayne added, "You have a real feeling for the underdog, Miss Bannon."

Kate smiled. "That's because I wasn't always what you see." But she didn't not elaborate.

Iris returned from the kitchen with a platter of cheese, dips, crackers, and fresh vegetables which she placed on a coffee table. "Please, everyone help themselves," she said.

Wayne made sure everyone had the drink of their choice.

"To Clark, may he always be as lucky as he was today," Russo toasted.

Everyone agreed.

"I hate to bring this up, Admiral, but I know my brother-in-law well enough to know that he would never mention—"

"Come on, Wayne, you're making assumptions," Gamrick said, knowing that he was going to tell Russo about the intruder.

"Clark took several shots at an intruder the other night," Wayne said.

Russo's eyebrows went up.

"Not at the man, at the headlights of the vehicle he was driving," Gamrick said, looking down at the carpet.

Wayne said, "That damn truck was stolen from a man in Norfolk and was abandoned just a few miles from here."

"Clark, you never mentioned this," Russo said.

"Sir, I saw no reason to. One incident—"

Kate entered the conversation: "You were followed from D.C.?"

Gamrick nodded. "He or she almost hit the rear of my car outside of the Sea Sands," he said, conscious of the slight tremor in her voice and also aware of Monique's interest in Kate.

Russo's brow furrowed. "Fingerprints?" he asked.

"What the local police force picked up has been sent to the FBI," Gamrick answered. "But I understand that it takes up to two months to get a reading of them."

"Well, I might be able to speed that along," Russo said.

Wayne walked over to Gamrick and put his hand on Gamrick's shoulder. "This guy went out there with a .38 and shot out one headlight, and the guy didn't hang around until the other light was shot out. He was out of here."

"It was just like watching a western when the hero goes after the bad guy," Monique commented, looking at Kate and smiling at her. "He doesn't look the type, but Clark, deep down inside that Silent Service sailor, is a wild cowboy."

Kate smiled back and said, "Less wild and more calculating, from what little I know about him."

"An interesting observation," Monique responded.

"Well, we'll be on our way," Russo said, getting out of the chair. "Mrs. Gamrick, did Clark mention that I invited the two of you to a barbecue?"

"Not a word," she said with a smile.

"I was going to this evening," Gamrick said defensively.

"Make it next Saturday night. I'll give Clark the necessary directions."

Everyone moved toward the door.

"Well, thank you for the drinks and munchies," Russo said, shaking Iris's hand, then Monique's, and finally Wayne's. "Clark, take the day off tomorrow."

"But, sir—"

"That will give you a long weekend. That's an order," Russo said.

"Yes, sir," Gamrick answered.

It was Kate's turn to say good-bye to everyone, and she did it graciously. She left Gamrick for the last and to him she said, "Take care of yourself, Captain. I don't doubt that we'll meet again."

Their eyes met, lingered in each other's gaze for a moment as they shook hands, and separated when their hands parted.

"That's certainly an odd couple," Monique commented as soon as Russo's car was out of the driveway.

Gamrick started for the steps. He was interested in Monique's analysis of the relationship between Russo and Kate.

"She's not quite young enough to be his daughter," she continued.

Iris said, "Many young women find older men attractive."

"That's true," Monique answered. "But the admiral looks so—so puffed up with himself."

"I'm going up to bed," Gamrick announced.

"But we haven't had dinner," Iris complained. "We waited dinner for you."

Gamrick apologized. "I should have told you to go ahead without me. I really can't eat a thing."

"You sure? I could fix a tray and bring it up to you," Iris offered.

Gamrick declined the offer and made his way upstairs.

"Can you manage?" Wayne called after him.

"Yes. Yes. I'm doing just fine," he answered, but every part of his body ached, especially the back of his neck and head.

Gamrick porpoised in and out of sleep, then he finally surfaced. The room was dark, but not so dark that he couldn't see anything and moonlight coated the window. The green numbers of the digital clock on the night table read 03:30:23 when he looked at it. He'd been asleep for several hours, a deep, restful sleep, except for the last few minutes when he had wanted to remain asleep but was pulled into wakefulness.

He felt the back of his neck and head. The pain was still there, but not as fierce as it had been earlier. Suddenly he found himself thinking about the accident and broke into a cold sweat as he replayed it in his head. . . . *Out of the corner of his right eye he caught sight of the truck barreling down on them, and before he could shout a warning it struck. Then everything whirled until the cab dropped on its side into the ditch. . . .*

Gamrick suddenly realized that Russo had never said whether or not he thought there was a connection between his encounter with the blue pickup and today's—yesterday's accident and his role in the investigation. Probably because the conversation had taken that odd turn, almost a confrontation between Monique and Kate. More of a cat fight than a confrontation.

He pulled himself up into a sitting position, propped his pillows against the headboard, and leaned against them.

Iris too changed her position, rolling from her right side on to her back.

Gamrick was wide awake now, thinking about Hawkins' statement. There must be more proof that Downs and Anderson were lovers than Hawkins' word. The tape might convince a court-martial, but as Bob had pointed out, a good defense lawyer would be able to take Hawkins' testimony apart. Obviously Hawkins didn't like either of them—that dislike would play a major role in discrediting his testimony.

"I need something more," Gamrick said and quickly looked at Iris to make sure he hadn't awakened her. She did not stir.

The pain in his neck and head became more difficult to deny. He quietly left the bed, padded into the bathroom, and with the aid of some water, he swallowed a painkiller and a sleeping pill. Then he padded back to the bed, and before climbing into it, he rearranged the pillows for sleeping.

Just before his eyes closed, he thought about Kate— the warm smoothness that he had felt inside her thigh. The touch of her fingers on his face. The scent of jasmine . . .

Then he slept.

Chapter 7

Gamrick slept until eight-thirty the following morning and found he was all aches and pains in more parts of his body than he could name.

When he joined the others for breakfast on the deck, Iris told him, "Sailing down to Hilton Head is now out of the question."

"You convinced me," he said, pouring coffee into a cup from a carafe. "I'm black and blue on parts of me that I didn't know existed."

Dimitri settled down next to him.

Wayne said, "Monique and I will stay the weekend to make sure you're all right, and then we'll go down by car."

Gamrick was about to object, but then he realized they were trying to be helpful and said, "Thanks. We'll spend a calm weekend here."

"I want you to rest," Iris said.

"That's about as much as I feel like doing," Gamrick said with a slight laugh. Then, helping himself to several slices of bacon, two sausages, and two pancakes, he added, "I'm hungry."

"You should be. You didn't eat dinner last night," Iris said.

"That will do it every time," he answered, reaching down to run his hand over Dimitri's head.

"That Ms. Bannon is even more lovely off the screen than she is on," Iris commented. "With her freckles she almost looks like a young girl."

"Don't let the freckles fool you. That's a woman there, if there ever was one," Monique commented.

Gamrick took a piece of sausage and fed it to Dimitri.

"What do you think, Clark?" Monique asked, adding, "You seem to know her."

He answered, "She's good at what she does."

"I bet she is," Monique quickly snapped.

"Professionally," Gamrick responded, annoyed with himself for giving her the opening which she so deftly exploited.

"That too, I'm sure," Monique spat out.

"Hey, what's this: hate Ms. Bannon day?" Wayne asked, looking at his wife.

Monique smiled. "*Au contraire,* my darling, I admire any woman who can do what I can't."

As Gamrick helped himself to another pancake, he said, "Wayne, what do you think about driving over to one of the beaches on the ocean side this afternoon?"

"Only if you let me do the driving," Wayne answered.

"You have a deal," Gamrick said. He poured more coffee into his cup and studied the sky for a few moments. "It's really a wonderful morning."

"On the morning news the announcer said that it would be in the high nineties this afternoon," Iris commented.

"Good reason to go to the ocean side, then. It will be cooler there. We'll take Dimitri. He loves the water," Gamrick said, starting to stand, but immediately checked his action. "I forgot to do everything in 'Slow ahead,' " he commented with a laugh.

Dimitri stood up.

"Come on, boy," Gamrick called to Dimitri, "we're going for a walk."

"Wait, I'll join you," Wayne said.

"Don't overdo it, Clark," Iris cautioned.

Gamrick assured her that he wouldn't, and with

Dimitri in front of him and Wayne at his side he went down the steps and along the side of the house.

"Monique thinks there's something going on between the admiral and the anchorwoman," Wayne said as they moved onto a pathway that followed the edge of the cove.

Gamrick's cheeks flushed. "I wouldn't know. I just work for Russo; I'm not his bosom buddy, and Ms. Bannon certainly wouldn't tell me who she's fucking."

"I told Monique she's all wet. Russo is almost twice Bannon's age. Jesus, she's young enough to be your daughter. And he's got you spotted by at least ten years."

"At least," Gamrick answered. He didn't want to think about Kate and Russo. Thinking about Kate was pleasant and exquisitely erotic, but joining her to Russo changed her into another man's woman, though he realized how foolish it was to think of her as his. There wasn't even a bond—

"Russo seems to be amiable enough," Wayne commented.

"He has his moments," Gamrick replied as he stopped to watch an osprey take a fish out of the cove.

"As the son of an admiral, I can tell you they all do. My mother used to say, 'Your father has his normal voice, his charming voice, and then he has his admiral's voice. When you hear that one, as the expression goes, batten down the hatches and run for cover.'"

Gamrick laughed. "A wise woman."

"A saint to have put up with Dad. He was a tough old bird. What about your father? I don't think I ever remember having heard you mention him."

Gamrick broke a cattail and ran it through his hand. "Oh, we never managed to square it away between us. He wanted me to go one way, and I went my own way."

"What did he do?"

"A failed lawyer," Gamrick answered. "He never really got a practice off the ground. He worked for a small firm in New York preparing briefs and drove a cab to make ends meet."

"Tough for a man not to make it," Wayne said.

"Tougher for his family," Gamrick replied. Though he knew Wayne waited for more, he didn't elaborate. There wasn't any point going on about the past. You live with it the best way you can.

They walked a bit farther, then Wayne suggested they turn back.

Gamrick had no objection, and he whistled for Dimitri, who came running to him. There wasn't any conversation between him and Wayne on the way back to the house.

The walk tired Gamrick more than he had thought it would. The coolness of the morning had given way to heat and humidity.

"I guess the women are inside," Wayne said as they climbed the steps to the deck and found it empty.

Gamrick opened the sliding door and entered the air-conditioned kitchen, where their housekeeper was busy at the sink.

Wayne went straight to the refrigerator and helped himself to a bottle of beer. "What?" he asked, looking at Gamrick.

"I'll settle for a soda," Gamrick said, going to the table where the morning's mail lay. He went through it.

"Root beer?" Wayne asked, bringing a large bottle to the table and glass.

Gamrick shrugged and pulled a small package—a white envelope folded in half—addressed to him. He hefted it and said, "There isn't a return address on it. My address is where the return address should be."

"Whoever sent it wanted to make doubly sure that you would get it. Where was it mailed?"

"Virginia Beach, I think. Here, you look at it," Gamrick said, giving the package to Wayne, then pouring root beer for himself.

"Open it."

Gamrick took a small knife from the rack near the

sink and slit the Scotch Tape seal. "Couple of pieces of cardboard and photographs—Jesus Christ!" The first photograph showed Anderson and another man— Downs, Gamrick guessed—naked, kissing and holding each other's erect penises. The second showed Downs on top of Anderson and a third showed Julie between them. Each had a hand on a breast. Downs had his other hand on her ass, and Anderson had his on her crotch, while she held the erect penis of each in her hands. And the fourth was of Anderson having inter-course with Julie. All were grainy color photographs and looked as if they had been shot from a long dis-tance.

Wayne reached for the photographs.

Gamrick stepped back. "Sorry, I can't. They—"

"Something to do with the investigation?"

Gamrick nodded. "Excuse me, I have to speak to Russo."

"But—"

"No buts," Gamrick snapped and headed for the den.

"Couldn't get the admiral," Gamrick said, walking into the kitchen, where everyone was gathered. "He's away until Monday—out of the damn country."

"Wonder if ol' Kate is with him," Monique ques-tioned archly.

Wayne threw her a dark look.

"My, my, I didn't know that certain topics were off limits," she jibed.

Gamrick moved to the sliding glass door and looked out on the cove.

"Wayne told us that someone sent you photo-graphs," Iris said.

"Yes."

"I bet they were really wild," Monique said.

Gamrick turned slowly around, and in a low voice he answered, "Wild enough, as you put it, to cost a man his life."

For a moment Monique looked as if she was about

to answer, but Wayne said, "Can't you see it's serious, Monique?"

She nodded. Helping herself to an apple from the bowl of fruit in the center of the table, and began eating it.

Gamrick faced the cove again and clasped his hands behind him. It was going to be one of those interminable weekends and he knew that there was nothing that he could do about it. "I'm going up to rest for a while," he announced, facing Iris. "If I sleep more than an hour, wake me. I want to get to the beach this afternoon."

"Are you sure you're up to it?"

"Yes," he said, forcing a smile. "I'm just a bit off my stride."

"Are you going up to the bedroom?" Iris asked.

"No, I'll be in the den. The couch there will be fine," he said, starting across the room. "Besides, I left word for the admiral to call me—that is, if he can be located."

"I wouldn't count on it if I were you," Monique cautioned.

Gamrick ignored her, and with Dimitri following, he went directly into the den, where he stretched out on the couch and placed a fluffy pillow under his head.

Over the years Gamrick had trained himself to sleep whenever he needed to. He slept lightly, for the most part on the edge of sleep, where he could be aware of sounds and smells normal to an operating submarine, and whether he was aboard a submarine or at home, he was always aware of the normal sounds and smells in the environment around him.

The instant the door opened, Gamrick awoke.

"You've been sleeping for more than hour," Iris said. "I didn't want to wake you, but—"

Wincing, Gamrick sat up and planted his feet on the floor. "I needed that nap."

"Wayne said he'd try his hand at surf casting," Iris told him.

"Good idea. Maybe he'll catch our dinner," Gamrick said, getting to his feet. "Come on, Dimi, we're all going to the beach."

Dimitri dashed for the door.

"That is one smart dog," Gamrick commented, taking hold of Iris's arm and escorting her out of the den.

"You always say that," she laughed.

"I probably do."

Wayne greeted them with "We're ready. Iris tell you I'm going to do a bit of surf casting?"

"Yes," Gamrick said.

The three of them went outside with Dimitri running back and forth between them and the Jeep, where Monique was ensconced in the seat next to the driver.

Gamrick got Dimitri into the Jeep, helped Iris get into the rear, then climbing in himself, he said, "Shove off, sailor."

"Aye, aye, sir," Wayne laughed, turning the ignition on and easing the Jeep on to the road.

It was a white sand beach with several rock jetties stretching a hundred yards or more into the water. The tide was in, and the combination of it and a strong easterly wind brought huge breakers crashing down high up on the sand.

Gamrick and Wayne set up the beach chairs a short distance above the wet sand, while Iris and Monique spread out a large blanket.

The men quickly stripped down to their trunks, and Gamrick, with Dimitri running in front of him, went into the water but didn't try to swim in the heavy surf. Ordinarily he would have dived into a breaking wave and come up behind it, or let it carry him in. But now he was too badly bruised to risk it. He played with Dimitri, who enjoyed charging into the white water as it rushed up the beach.

Wayne swam a bit, going as far out as the end of the jetty, then came back to set up his rig for serious surf casting.

While the women swam parallel to the shore, Gamrick stretched out on a beach chair and tried to relax. But his thoughts centered on the photographs. They gave the Navy a clear-cut case against Anderson. The photographs and Hawkins' testimony would do it. The defense might be able to discredit some of Hawkins' testimony, but it couldn't discredit the photographs.

"Are you hungry?" Iris asked.

For a moment Gamrick hadn't realized she was standing directly in front of him. She had come out of the water and now was drying herself with a very large green beach towel. "I could go for something," he said.

"There's one of those lunch wagons in the parking lot," she said. "I don't know what it has."

"Probably hot dogs, soda, and ice cream," Monique chimed in. She was wearing the same bikini she'd worn the day she went swimming in the cove. She too was drying herself, but her towel was yellow. "I'll go—"

Wayne said, "Hey, Mone and I will go if you watch my rod, Clark."

"Deal. If they have hot dogs, get two for me, well done with mustard, onions, relish, and whatever else they have to put on it."

"Iron stomach man," Iris said. "I don't know how he can tolerate the spicy food he likes." She settled into another beach chair and put a kerchief on her head, pirate style.

Gamrick lifted himself out of the chair and ambled over to the rod, held at a sixty-degree angle by a plastic sleeve with its spiked end driven into the sand. He looked back at Iris and waved.

She waved back. "Anything on the other end?" she called above the roar of the surf.

"Not even his bait, I'd bet," Gamrick answered with a laugh. Looking at her made him think of Kate. He loved Iris, at least he did when she wasn't drunk. She was a good wife and had been a very good mother, especially during the times when he had been at sea.

But—there was always a but—a man or a woman could become attracted to someone else. And attracted he was, like some adolescent who had never been in love before and—

The fishing reel's drag suddenly screamed, the rod bent.

Gamrick grabbed the rod, let out some line, then pulled hard up on the rod. It then flexed again.

"You have something," Iris shouted, running to him.

"I have a fucking whale on the end of the line," he answered, working the rod and at the same time slowly reeling in.

"My God, look at the rod!" Iris squealed.

The carbon rod was practically bent into a Ω.

"Whoa, hold it ... Hold it, I'm coming," Wayne shouted.

Gamrick glanced over his shoulder. Wayne was running toward him. Monique ran after him. Both were carrying paper plates loaded with hot dogs and cans of soda in brown paper bags.

"Take the food from Wayne," Gamrick told Iris.

She met Wayne a few yards up the beach.

"Okay, take it easy," Wayne said.

"He's solidly hooked," Gamrick answered.

"Let me take the rod."

"It's yours," Gamrick answered, deftly handing his brother-in-law the rod.

"It's a big one," Wayne said, beginning to play it.

Panting, Monique reached them. "This damn beach is wider than I thought," she gasped.

"Which dog is mine?" Gamrick asked.

"The one with everything on it," Monique answered.

"Here it is, honey," Iris said.

Gamrick picked it off the plate, examined it, smiled happily, and bit into it. "Kind of like being a kid again," he laughed. "Soda?"

"In the bag," Wayne said.

Monique held a hot dog while Wayne took a bite at a time. "If this isn't enough for dinner, then—"

"I just saw it!" Monique exclaimed, jumping up and down. "It almost jumped out of the water."

"It's going to be a while before I bring this guy in," Wayne said. "It's got plenty of fight in it."

Gamrick finished his first hot dog and started on the second.

In a few minutes Iris and Monique lost interest in Wayne's struggle with the fish and ambled back to the beach chairs.

"Want me to spell you?" Gamrick asked.

"Long enough to get a beer?"

"Sure."

Gamrick took the rod and immediately took in some of the slack. The fish fought back, bringing memories of the first time he had read Hemingway's *The Old Man and the Sea. Life* magazine had devoted a complete issue to the book. He was not exactly the old man, but the thrill of landing a big fish was there. Even if Wayne brought it in, he actually had caught it.

"You okay?" Wayne asked, returning with a can of beer.

"Okay," Gamrick lied. The strain of the fish pulling on the line made his shoulders and arms throb with pain.

Wayne set the can down in the sand. "I'll take over," he said.

Gamrick relinquished the rod, stepped away, and said, "He's slowed down a bit."

"He has," Wayne agreed. "He's at least twenty pounds, maybe more."

Gamrick said, "I think the *more* is probably a better guess." He took a pull on the soda. Dimitri came over and brushed against his legs, then walked back to the shade of Iris's beach chair and lay down again.

"Those photographs were pretty bad, weren't they?" Wayne asked without looking at Gamrick.

"Gives the Navy what it needs."

Wayne said, "Then you'll go back to what you were doing?"

"Probably. The one thing I don't want is more of what I'm doing now. I don't like it."

"I wouldn't either," Wayne responded, reeling in a substantial amount of line. "I think I could bring him in now, but I'll play him a bit more."

"Better bring him in soon. There's a squall line moving off shore," Gamrick said, pointing to the south east. I've been watching for the last few minutes. It's become more defined."

"You sure as hell don't miss much."

"Comes with the turf."

"Yeah, my old man used to say the same thing," Wayne replied.

"Those hot dogs were really good," Gamrick commented.

Wayne laughed. "You know, you really are an unpretentious son of a bitch."

"I'm sure I have my moments just like anyone else." Wayne shook his head.

"To get a real honest evaluation you'd have to ask your sister, your nephews, and my men."

Wayne reached down and picked up the can of beer, took a long pull, and set it down again. Suddenly he exclaimed, "I'm going to take this sucker in. He's just about stopped fighting."

"Iris, Monique, Wayne's bringing him in," Gamrick called.

The women came running down to the water's edge. Dimitri ran along with them.

Wayne reeled in line.

"There she blows!" Monique shouted, jumping up and down.

"Look at the size of it," Gamrick said.

Wayne stuck the rod back into the plastic sleeve, ran to where the fish was beached, and picked it up by its left gill.

"What kind of fish is it?"

"Striped bass," Wayne said proudly.

Dimitri celebrated the occasion by running around Wayne barking.

"That's enough for a week of dinners," Iris remarked.

"Now, when I need a camera, I haven't got one. No one is going to believe me when I tell them about it," Wayne lamented.

"Don't worry, darling, I'll back you up," Monique assured him.

"Okay, people, better get everything together before the rains come," Gamrick said.

"What rain?" Monique challenged. "There was nothing about rain in the forecast."

"That rain," Wayne answered, pointing at the very dark clouds. "Don't argue with him about the weather. He's an expert. He can smell a change coming."

Monique shrugged but said nothing.

They picked up the beach chairs and whatever other paraphernalia they had brought with them and trooped back to the Jeep.

"A nice afternoon," Wayne said as he began to drive.

"Who's going to clean and fillet that sucker?" Monique asked. She looked back at Gamrick.

"Me," Wayne answered gleefully. "Me and the guy in the first fish store we pass. And I know we pass at least two because I saw them on the way out."

Monique looked at her husband and wagged her forefinger at him. "That was your plan all the time. Catch a big fish, then have everyone else do the work."

"Absolutely," Wayne laughed. "I even paid a diver to go down, attach the fish to the hook, and then pull on the line to make it seem as if the fish was doing it."

Gamrick smiled. Though he still ached, he was pleasantly tired. He closed his eyes and rested his head on Iris's shoulder. She smelled pleasantly of salt and suntan oil. It really had been a good summer's afternoon. If Wayne hadn't mentioned the photographs, he wouldn't have thought about them again. . . .

* * *

The rain caught up with them almost as soon as they left the fish store with several pounds of fish fillets wrapped and iced. The clouds darkened the sky, the air turned cold, and the rain slashed down.

Wayne switched on the headlights and slowed down.

A streak of lightning tendriled in front of them. A crash of thunder followed.

"That seemed right on top of us," Iris said.

"Close, but not on top of us," Wayne commented.

"Maybe it would be a good idea to pull over and wait a few minutes," Iris suggested.

"Too many trees around."

"Clark, you think it's a good idea to stop?" Iris asked.

"No. Not here. Besides, the storm is moving fast. It will be gone before we reach the house," Gamrick answered, and even as he spoke the cloud cover began to move farther inland and the sky became lighter.

"The question is whether we grill the fillets or fry them?" Wayne asked.

"Grill them," Monique answered.

"I think so too," Iris said. "Frying them will make a mess in the kitchen."

"Then grill them we will. Clark—"

"I'll supervise while you do the work," Gamrick answered.

"I accept the challenge," Wayne replied with exaggerated dignity in his voice. Then he switched on the radio and told Monique, "Find some easy music."

Gamrick suddenly felt unaccountably depressed. One moment he was as bright and cheerful as the sun which was now shining, and the next he was in a mood, a dark one. He moved away from Iris and took hold of the rooftop brace.

"Are you all right?" Iris asked.

Gamrick managed a smile. "Sure, I'm fine," he told her. "I just ache a bit."

She looked as if she were about to say something

else, but instead she took hold of his hand and kissed the back of it.

"The boo-boo doesn't go away that easily," he said sotto voce.

She wiggled closer to him, put her arm halfway around his shoulders, and ran her fingers lightly over the back of his neck. "There are other things that would make you feel better," she whispered.

Gamrick faced her, winked, and whispered back, "Here in the Jeep with those two present?"

Iris's face seemed to crack, and she began to laugh.

Gamrick laughed too, though he hurt when he did.

"Well, whatever it is that's tickling you guys, share it with us," Monique said, looking back at them. "Wayne isn't much fun when he's driving."

"An in-joke," Gamrick answered.

"With me it's either drive and talk, or drive and listen to music. I don't like to do three things at the same time," Wayne explained.

Letting go of Iris's hand, Gamrick shifted a bit. Kate was responsible for at least part of his mood. She was there in his thoughts, had been practically all day—

"Clark, are you with us?" Wayne asked.

"Sorry," Gamrick apologized. "I was thinking about something else." He caught Wayne looking at him in the rearview mirror.

"You certainly were somewhere else as well," Monique said.

"In the 'land where lollipops grow on peppermint trees,' " Gamrick responded flippantly.

"This for you, Captain Gamrick," Monique said, giving him the finger.

Gamrick and Iris laughed until tears started to flow out of their eyes.

Monique remonstrated, "I'm glad you guys are having a good time. I'm bored to death."

"Make the next right turn," Gamrick told Wayne, still laughing.

In moments they were on blacktop.

"Jesus, look at the heat waves come off of that!" Wayne exclaimed. "I don't think it rained here, or if it did, it wasn't nearly what we had."

"I could go for a nice cold martini," Monique said. "A shower, or maybe a good soak in the tub. Then a cold, really cold martini with an onion in it and some munchies before dinner."

"Clark and I will take care of the fixings and the martini; the rest is up to you," Wayne said.

A few minutes later, they reached the house.

"I'll take care of the fish," Gamrick said. "I'll give some to Cora, marinate what we'll use tonight, and freeze what's left." He left the Jeep, and Dimitri jumped after him. When he reached the kitchen, Cora was getting ready to leave for the day. He told her to take as many fillets as she wanted, and asked if there had been any phone calls.

"No calls for you or the missus," she said. "But the phone company came."

"Phone company?"

"Man said you called service a couple weeks back."

Iris came into the kitchen.

"A couple of weeks ago, did you call the phone company and ask them to send someone out here?" Gamrick asked.

She shook her head. "I don't remember."

"Damn it, Iris, did you or didn't you?" Gamrick flared. "They were here today."

Iris glanced at Cora.

"When did they come?" Gamrick asked.

"A couple minutes after you left."

Gamrick ran his hand over his chin. "Try to remember," he urged.

"I can't. I can't, Clark."

Gamrick ground his teeth.

"What's so important? The phone company came. Cora, how long were they here?" Iris asked.

"Half hour maybe. Dey work on all the phones."

"They?" Gamrick asked.

"Two mens came," Cora answered. "One tell the other there be problems from the big storm da other night."

"Did they fix whatever was wrong?" Iris asked.

Cora nodded. "Dey wuz real polite."

Gamrick shook his head. "Iris, it's important. Try to remember if you called."

"Can't we discuss this later?" Iris asked, again glancing at Cora.

Gamrick said, "Take what you want, Cora." Then he went out on the deck. He was too angry to go upstairs.

Iris stepped onto the deck. "Will you please tell me why it's suddenly so important what I did a couple of weeks ago?" she questioned, trying to keep her voice normal.

He wheeled around. "Because you drink, and when you drink too much, which is frequently, you don't know what the fuck you're doing. Is that a good enough reason?"

"Oh, Clark!" she cried.

"Men come into the house and no one knows why the hell they're here," he said.

"They came to fix the phones."

"That's what they told Cora, but suppose they came for something else. Suppose they came to find out what was inside the house or—"

"I don't want to hear," Iris cried. "I don't want to hear any more. You've said enough, Clark. You said enough." And clapping her hands over her ears, she ran back into the house.

Angry at himself and everyone else, Gamrick faced the mouth of the cove, pursed his lips, and thought about Kate.

Chapter 8

By Monday morning Gamrick was eager to return to work. He had phoned Bob and Harry late Sunday afternoon and had told them to go to Norfolk without him. Though he hadn't given either of them specifics, he had indicated that he had "something for the admiral."

The remaining two days moved with incredible slowness. And to make it worse, another commentator had sat in for Kate and explained, "Kate Bannon had taken a short vacation and would be back on Monday evening." But he had patched things up with Iris, or she had by coming down for dinner later Friday evening and behaving as if nothing had happened between them. For her to have done that, he realized, had taken a great deal of courage.

Gamrick arrived at Russo's office at 0830. Russo was already at his desk his secretary said, "But he had a meeting schedule for oh-nine-hundred."

"Tell him Captain Gamrick is here," Gamrick said. "Tell him I must see him before he goes to that meeting." Then he moved away from the desk to allow her to speak to Russo in relative privacy.

Several moments passed before she said, "He'll be with you shortly, Captain. Would you like a cup of coffee while you wait?"

Gamrick considered the offer, was about to decline it, then changed his mind. "Yes, Lieutenant, I would, thank you."

"A Danish with it?" she asked, smiling.

"Just coffee black, no sugar."

She left her desk and in less than two minutes—three at the most—she was back with a styrofoam cup of hot black coffee and a napkin.

Gamrick thanked her, sat down, and slowly drank the coffee.

"I was sorry to hear that Commander Wright—"

Gamrick raised his eyebrows. "What about Commander Wright?"

"Sir, I thought you knew."

"I don't know."

"He died early this morning," she said softly.

Gamrick's hand shook, then steadied. Swallowing hard, he said, "I didn't know."

"I am sorry," she responded. "I really did think—"

The door to the admiral's office opened, and Russo said, "I tried calling you early this morning, but you had already left."

Gamrick put the coffee down on the table near him and stood. "The lieutenant just told me about Steve," he said.

Russo waved him into the office. "There's more," he said, closing the door after Gamrick entered the room. Then he added, "The truck could have been one of ours."

Gamrick stopped short of the chair in front of Russo's desk.

"The police have someone who said it looked like one of our dumptrucks," Russo explained, moving to the other side of the desk and motioning Gamrick to sit. "It's being checked out by the police and by our people too."

"Steve has family," Gamrick said.

"They will be notified early today. His mother and sister were already here. They arrived Thursday night."

"Funeral arrangements?" Gamrick asked.

"We've left that to the family," Russo answered.

Gamrick ran his hand over his chin. "If it's one of our trucks—"

"Then we have another problem," Russo said. "But

I don't want to think about it—and I don't want you to think about it—until we are absolutely sure it was one of our trucks."

"Have you any idea when we might know?" Gamrick asked, shifting to ease the sudden burst of pain in his right side.

"None," Russo answered. "But I did do some pushing at the FBI. By the end of the week we should have information on the prints that were lifted from the blue truck by your local police."

Gamrick nodded.

"But if you didn't know about Wright, why are you here?" Russo suddenly asked.

"I left several messages for you, sir. I even called your home."

"I haven't check my message box yet, and my wife—well, I had no idea that you phoned."

Gamrick opened his attaché case and took out the small package that had been sent to him. "There are photographs inside," he said, putting the envelope down on Russo's desk.

Several moments passed before Russo had the four pictures in front of him. "What the fuck is this all about?" he roared, momentarily getting out of the chair and then sitting again. "Who the fuck are these people?"

"The short dark-haired man is Seaman First Class Paul Anderson and the second man is—or rather was—Seaman First Class Gus Downs. The woman is Julie Giodono, Anderson's girlfriend."

Russo pushed himself back in the chair. "These were sent to you?"

"Yes. From Virginia Beach, according to the postmark," Gamrick answered.

Russo put his forefinger down on the photographs of Anderson's head. "I want this cocksucker's ass nailed," he growled. "He's our man."

"I think so too, sir, but—"

"You got him. These photographs and the testimony that—what the hell is his name?"

"Hawkins, sir."

"That Hawkins gave will get Anderson the death sentence from any court-martial," Russo said. "I already told you, I'm getting a lot of pressure. The President wants this settled. He's under pressure too. Twenty-seven men were killed. You got the man who murdered them."

"Sir, I have one man's word, which will turn out to be his word against the accused, and I have a set of photographs that show—not necessarily prove—that the accused engaged in homosexual activity with one of the men who died in the explosion."

"These photographs are enough to get a guilty verdict."

"Sir, we could have a much stronger case against Anderson if his prints show up on the blue pickup, or if in some way he's tied to the accident."

Suddenly red in the face, Russo wagged his finger at him. "If that son of bitch is responsible for Steve's death, I'll—I want him, Captain, and I want him now!"

"Sir, I want him to. But I also want to be fair."

Russo leaped to his feet. "Fair? Fair . . . ? Was that cocksucker fair to the men he killed? Fair would be letting that fag bastard rot in hell. That would be fair." Breathing hard, he dropped into the chair. "Captain, you have done an excellent job, and today at fourteen-thirty you will hold another press conference and tell the people of this country that you and your men have the man who murdered his fellow shipmates."

Gamrick stood. "Sir—"

"Fourteen-thirty, Captain. Dismissed."

"Yes, sir," Gamrick answered.

The press conference was held in the same auditorium. Russo and the Secretary of the Navy, John Howard, were there. Howard stepped up to the podium and said, "Ladies and gentlemen, it gives great pleasure to introduce Captain Gamrick, who will brief you on the results of the ongoing investigation into the causes of the explosion in number two turret on the battleship *Utah*. Captain, please." He gestured to Gamrick to take his place at the podium.

The lights seemed even brighter and hotter this time. Gamrick cleared his throat and said, "We are investigating various possibilities, one of which involves a member of the crew."

"Are you telling us that the cause was sabotage?" a woman asked.

Gamrick recognized Kate's voice, though he couldn't see her because of the lights. "I'm sorry, I am unable to comment on that any further."

"You mean you won't," Kate challenged.

"I guess you've read that right, lady," Gamrick answered, suddenly furious at her badgering.

"Then, are we to understand that you have a man in custody?" Kate asked.

"No comment," Gamrick answered and stepped away from the podium.

Russo took his place. "Ladies and gentlemen, please give your attention . . . Thank you . . . Captain Gamrick has been all too shy about his accomplishment. A former member of the Silent Service, he is unaccustomed to our world openness." He was interrupted by laughter and waited a few moments before it subsided. "Captain, will you please give these members of our fourth estate the information that we have as of this morning?" He put his hand on the microphone, and when Gamrick stepped back to the podium, he whispered tightly, "Do it, Captain. That's an order."

Gamrick nodded and spoke into the microphone, "The Navy has reason to suspect Seaman First Class Paul Anderson and Seaman First Class Gus Downs were responsible for the explosion in turret number two aboard the *Utah*."

In an instant every reporter shouted questions at Gamrick. He waited until the auditorium was quiet be-

fore he said, "We have testimony that these two men
were involved in a very close relationship that fell
apart shortly before the *Utah* left for its training exercises."

"You mean the two were lovers," one of the reporters shouted.

"That possibility is being investigated."

"Where are these men now?" someone else asked.

"Gus Downs is missing and presumed dead, and
Paul Anderson has been confined to the ship."

"When will Anderson be placed under arrest and
taken from the ship?" another reporter asked.

Gamrick looked at Russo, who stepped up to the podium and said, "He was removed from the ship and
placed in the brig in Norfolk." Then he moved back to
where he had been standing.

"Has Downs's body been found?" Kate asked.

"There are several bodies that still have not been
identified. His is presumed to be among them."

"Will Anderson be charged and face a court-
martial?" a reporter asked.

"The Navy will respond appropriately," Gamrick answered, attempting to see Kate through the glare of the
lights.

"Will you give us some idea of what 'appropriately'
means?" Kate asked.

"I'm not in the position to answer that," Gamrick responded.

Russo was immediately at his side. "Ladies and gentlemen, as soon as we have more information we will
pass it on to you. Thank you for coming."

The lights were switched off.

Gamrick saw Kate. He waited a few moments, then
walked to where she stood speaking to another reporter, and said, "Excuse me, Ms. Bannon, I want to
see you."

She smiled at him.

"The Sea Sands about eighteen hundred—that's six
this evening," he said tightly.

"Sorry," she answered.

"I'll be there."

"Sorry," she repeated.

Russo called him.

"Six," he said and hurried to Russo's side.

"Well, you gave a good account," Russo said, putting his hand on Gamrick's shoulder. "A bit stiff. But considering it was a fast bailout, a good account. Come on, there's someone I want you to meet."

Gamrick returned to Russo's office, where Russo introduced him to Senator Jason Dobbs from Illinois. Dobbs looked his role: paunchy, a florid face, and cow-like brown eyes. As chairperson of the Armed Service Committee he was one of the most powerful men in the Senate.

"I watched you on TV," Dobbs said to Gamrick. "You hesitated."

"Sir?"

"Russo kind of pulled your chestnuts out of the fire," Dobbs said.

Russo laughed, invited them to sit down, and explained, "That was Clark's second time in front of the cameras."

"My grand-nephew was an ensign in that turret," Dobbs said.

"I'm sorry," Gamrick responded in a low voice.

"You got the bastard; now hang the cocksucker," Dobbs said forcefully. "There are dozens of people who lost a husband, son, or boyfriend in that explosion, and they want to see justice done. Hell, man, the country wants to see justice done."

"Sir, my job was—"

"You did part of your job, Captain. The other part is to put your heart and soul into the rest of it. To make sure that fucking queer doesn't get off the hook. There are people in this great country of ours who see nothing wrong with an alternate lifestyle. Well, sir, what happened aboard the *Utah* because of it could just be the thing to change all that, if you get my drift."

"I do, sir," Gamrick answered, remembering that Dobbs had been a very vocal opponent of the President's plan to permit homosexuals in the military.

"Nothing is written in stone, not even a presidential decree," Dobbs commented, smiling slyly.

Gamrick remained silent.

"Well, Captain, I was anxious to meet you," Dobbs said, still smiling, but now the slyness was gone.

Russo said, "Steve's family will take his body home for burial. The funeral is the day after tomorrow. He will be given a military funeral, and of course we will be there. I have made arrangements for an aircraft to fly us down."

"I'll notify the other men," Gamrick said.

"Good," Russo commented, then said, "remember Saturday night."

"Looking forward to it, sir," Gamrick answered. He wanted to leave, but couldn't until he was dismissed.

"That's a good-looking woman out at the desk," Dobbs commented.

"Clark, on your way out, will you please tell the lieutenant to report to me?" Russo said.

"Yes, sir," Gamrick answered, immediately standing.

Dobbs lifted himself to his feet. "It has been a pleasure to meet you, Captain," he said.

Gamrick shook his hand. "The pleasure has been mine," he answered, then faced Russo and saluted.

Kate did not come to the Sea Sands.

Gamrick waited until seven-thirty before he left the tavern and drove home a disconsolate, frustrated, and angry man. He knew that his feelings for Kate were getting out of control. He wanted her and from her response to him, he was certain she wanted him. But he did not understand why she did not show up, why she had tried to take advantage of his feelings for her at the press conference.

Gamrick said aloud, "Cool it . . . Cool it, Clark. You're making a fool of yourself." And he drove the rest of the way home feeling better about himself.

As soon as Gamrick stopped, the door opened and Dimitri ran to meet him.

"Well, my TV star, you did wonderfully well," Iris said, greeting him with a kiss and a hug as soon as he entered the house.

"Oh, there's talk of putting me on a late-night show," he answered.

"Wayne called from Hilton Head. He saw you too," she told him.

Gamrick suddenly felt tired and achy. He walked into the kitchen, sniffed the air, and said, "Smells good."

"Cora made a wonderful fish stew," Iris said, already uncovering the pot. "Full of veggies."

"I'm starved," he said. "But before I do anything else, I want to change into something more comfortable."

"I won't serve until you're back."

"Won't take long," Gamrick answered, leaving the kitchen and hurrying upstairs to the bedroom, where he went into the bathroom and ran cold water over his face and head and swallowed one of the pain pills the doctor at the hospital had given him. He felt as if his brain were trying to smash its way out of his skull.

A few minutes later, he returned to the kitchen and sat at the table. When he and Iris were the only ones in the house, they had their meals in the kitchen. But if they had guests, especially when the weather prevented them from serving out of doors or if the occasion was formal, they used the large dining room.

Iris ladled out the fish stew over warm, garlicky french bread. Then she sat down.

"Very good," Gamrick commented.

"You know, Wayne says that this investigation can be your ladder to flag rank," Iris said. "If only you had more stage presence, you'd really be—"

"Listen, when this is over, I don't even know if I'll be in the Navy, let alone make flag rank."

"I don't understand," Iris said.

Gamrick put his fork down and pushed the plate away.

"I thought you said it was very good," Iris said.

"It is. I've had a very hard day, and I have a gigantic headache. And—"

"And what?" Iris questioned.

"One of my men—Steve Wright—died from injuries he received in the crash."

"Oh, my God!"

"I'm afraid He wasn't there when the truck hit," he said bitterly.

"Why don't you go out on the deck and relax?" Iris suggested. "You'll feel better outside than in here."

Gamrick nodded, left the table, and walked out onto the deck. The air was cool and had a delicious salty tang. He placed his hands on the railing and looked out toward the mouth of the cove. A small white boat was anchored off shore.

Iris came up behind him and put her arms around him. "You want to tell me what's really bothering you?" she asked softly.

"Maybe I've been in the Navy too long," he said quietly, voicing his innermost thoughts. "Maybe I've become too used to being told what to do, how to do it, and how to think about it."

"Clark, you're almost where you've always dreamed of being," she answered, pressing herself against him.

"Russo is out for blood. The Navy wants this out of the way as quickly as possible. And now Senator Dobbs is involved. He's going to use it for his own agenda, whatever it is."

Iris let go of him and stepped away. "You're not responsible for what happens to Anderson."

Gamrick faced her. "If he's found guilty, it won't be because of the evidence. It will be because he's a homosexual, or at least appears to be."

"Appears to be?"

"I can't tell you any more."

"Well, whatever happens, I am sure you will do the right thing," she said.

Gamrick dropped into a nearby chair. "The right thing has more than one meaning, a lot of gray area."

"I don't understand. Something is either right or it's wrong."

Gamrick shrugged, and in a low, bitter voice he said, "I will do the right thing because I have always done the right thing, at least as far as the Navy is concerned."

"What's that supposed to mean?" Iris asked.

"It means . . ." He left the chair and went to the railing again. The white boat was no longer at the mouth of the cove.

"Well, tell me," Iris demanded.

He looked over his shoulder at her. "The truth is, I don't know what the hell it means." Then, in a lower voice he added, "Maybe I do and won't admit it."

"I don't understand circles within circles," she said. "Another man would take advantage of—"

Gamrick faced her. "I don't want to take advantage of another man's death. I don't want to be part of the cabal that puts him to death for the wrong reason if he's innocent."

She studied him for several moments. "You're not trying to tell me that you're a closet homosexual, are you?" she asked in a voice that was almost a whisper.

"No!" Gamrick exclaimed, throwing up his hands and dropping them. "I'm trying to tell you that the Navy doesn't have a case against Anderson. That's what I'm trying to tell you."

"I was afraid—"

"Don't be," Gamrick said, grinning broadly. "I'm as heterosexual as man can be."

The next instant Iris put her arms around his neck and kissed him on the lips. "As I told you before, I know you will do the right thing."

* * *

The phone rang.

Gamrick heard the ring and answered it.

A muffled voice spoke.

"Who is this?" he asked.

The line went dead.

Gamrick put the phone down. The voice had been deeper than the other callers. The words sounded like gibberish, maybe, or possibly another language. He looked at the digital clock. Just five minutes before the alarm would have gone off.

"A hell of a way to start the day," he told himself and left the bed to shower and shave.

Forty-five minutes later, he was on his way to D.C. The morning was cool and the sun was behind him. Early morning and the twilight hours were his favorite times of the day. Each had a unique quietness. The morning was full of bright colors, almost sounds themselves, while the twilight muted the colors and sounds, readying them for the night.

As soon as Gamrick was on the main highway to D.C., he ran into traffic. The closer he got, the slower he was forced to drive. Finally he pulled into the parking lot and joined Folsim and Cool at the heliport. Both were bandaged, and both were reserved.

"I saw Steve's family last night. They're over at the Marriott," Folsim said. "His fiancée was there too."

"I had no idea he had one," Gamrick commented.

"A former high school sweetheart," Folsim answered.

"Do you think they would mind if I visited this evening?" Gamrick asked.

Folsim shook his head. "No, sir. I'm sure they would appreciate it. I'll be with them."

Gamrick glanced at Cool. "We'll go together," he said.

"Yes, sir."

"I would guess that we'll get orders to shut down

operations in a few days," Gamrick said as they boarded the chopper.

"Figured that would happen as soon as I saw you on the tube last evening," Folsim said. "But what the hell happened?"

Gamrick told them about the photographs, and when he finished, Cool gave a long, low whistle and said, "Those pictures are enough to burn his chestnuts."

"But who took them?" Folsim asked.

"Don't know. I don't even know who sent them. There wasn't a return address on the envelope."

"Jesus, someone wants to get Anderson real bad," Cool said.

Folsim agreed and said, "But how does that connect him to causing the explosion? All it does is offer proof that he's a homosexual, or bisexual."

Gamrick didn't answer, but Cool did. "All the charges and specifications will relate to the explosion, but once those photographs are given in evidence to the court, he will be convicted as charged."

"There's Hawkins' testimony also," Folsim said.

"The two of them had a falling-out, and to collect the two-mil insurance on his erstwhile lover's life, Anderson murdered twenty-seven men," Cool added.

"That's it," Gamrick told them.

"Couple that with the photographs, and the Navy has its man," Folsim said.

"Scapegoat," Cool responded.

Suddenly the chopper pilot announced, "Captain Gamrick, you and your men are ordered back to D.C. and to report to Admiral Russo immediately upon your return."

"I guess we'll be closing shop sooner than I expected," Gamrick said.

Russo was waiting for them on the pad when they landed. "At noon, Clark, there will be another press conference," he said as he led them back into the building. "We'll work out the details beforehand. Now

I want all of you to see what those photographs—
Clark, did you tell them about the photographs?"

"Yes, sir," Gamrick answered. He was alongside
Russo, while Folsim and Cool followed in step directly
behind them.

"I turned the photographs over to the photo lab ge-
niuses," Russo said. "It's just absolutely amazing what
they're capable of doing."

Gamrick nodded but said nothing. From his own experience, he knew what miracles could be accom-
plished by photographic specialists. He had taken
pictures through a periscope of Soviet missile launch-
ings from several of their Arctic bases, and he had seen
the results after they had been digitally reconstructed.
Although the boat had been fifteen miles away from
the actual launch sight, the photographs looked as if
they were taken within a few yards of the launch pad,
and sequentially they also gave a detailed picture of
the ignition process.

Russo slowed and stopped in front of a door marked:
RESTRICTED AREA—DO NOT ENTER WITHOUT THE PROPER
CLEARANCE OR AUTHORIZED ESCORT. He opened the door,
gestured to them to enter, and immediately followed.

Another door, guarded by an armed Marine, was in
front of them.

The Marine snapped to attention.

"Admiral Russo and party to see Dr. Jarvis," Russo
said.

"Aye, sir," the Marine answered, and unlocking the
door, he stepped aside and announced them.

Russo led the way through the door and was greeted
by a short, slender man with wispy brown hair and
half-lens eyeglasses perched on his nose.

"Captain Gamrick, our chief investigator, Commander Folsim, and Lieutenant Cool," Russo said in-
troducing them to Dr. Jarvis, who shook hands with all
of them.

"Gentlemen, please follow me," Jarvis said.

They did and wound up in another room in which

there were several large computer monitors and what appeared to Gamrick to be tape drives for two mainframe computers.

Jarvis said, "We were able to determine that the photographs were taken from a minimum distance of four hundred feet, using a telephoto lens of questionable quality." He paused. "The camera was hand-held and was shot from a thirty-degree angle."

Gamrick glanced at Russo, who smiled.

"From the pattern of sunlight and shadow we know the photographs were taken at two-thirty in the afternoon on July tenth at the latitude of North Truro, Massachusetts."

"That is something!" Folsim said.

"We also know from the kind of sand on the beach that they were taken on Truro Beach, Cape Cod. This would confirm our determination of latitude. Have you gentlemen any questions?"

"Doctor, can any of the characteristics you just described be faked?" Gamrick asked.

"Probably. But it would take very elaborate equipment and a great deal of knowledge to fake the information," Jarvis answered.

Russo asked, "Would you be willing to submit your analysis to another government laboratory for confirmation?"

"Certainly," Jarvis answered, leading them to a large computer monitor.

Gamrick glanced at Russo. He was smiling as if he had just been given a gift.

The Riverboat restaurant was moored on the Annapolis waterfront. It was a Mississippi riverboat that had been converted into a floating motel and a trendy, expensive dine and dance restaurant. Gamrick met Iris there for dinner at seven-thirty. She had called early that afternoon and had suggested they go to the Riverboat for dinner and dancing. "The change of scene will do us good," she had told him.

He had agreed and said that he definitely could use a change of scene.

Iris had reserved a table with a view of the harbor, and when Gamrick arrived, she was already there, looking very chic in a white lamé dress that accentuated her tan. She wore a simple gold heavy-link chain around her neck and a gold chain around her waist, creating a stunningly provocative effect, especially since a part of the chain around her waist hung directly in front of her crotch, as if it were pointing to it.

"You look bushed," she said after he'd greeted her with a kiss and sat across from her.

"I didn't do much today," Gamrick answered. The room was spacious with a highly polished dance floor at one end. Enormous crystal chandeliers with bulbs like glowing candles provided the light. The clientele was well heeled. From what he could see, he was the only man in uniform.

"I tried phoning you in Norfolk—"

"Never got there. Spent the day in D.C. Had another news conference."

"Oh, I didn't have the TV on," she said, taking hold of his hands.

"My end of the investigation will be over very soon," he said.

Iris nodded. "Well, at least you got to meet some very important people."

"That too," Gamrick answered.

Iris let go of his hands and looked around. "The owners, I read in a local newspaper, spent six million dollars on this restaurant area alone. Everything in it is as close to the way it was when the boat sailed the Mississippi from St. Louis to New Orleans, and the staterooms have been decorated the same way."

"I'm impressed," Gamrick answered.

"No, you're not."

He smiled. "Really, I am. I'll be more impressed if the food is as good as this place looks."

"You're an impossible cynic," she chided, smiling. "Or maybe just impossible."

A waiter dressed as a mid-nineteenth-century riverboat gambler came to the table and asked if they wanted something to drink.

"A Stoli on the rocks with a twist of lime, please," Iris said.

"Do you have a dark beer on tap?" Gamrick asked.

"Bass ale."

"That will be fine."

"And an order of Cajun-style chicken bits and calamari with medium sauce," Iris told the waiter. When he left, she explained, "I looked at the menu before you came."

A six-piece dance band began to play a slow foxtrot. Iris smiled at him.

"Okay, you talked me into it," Gamrick said, leading her onto the dance floor, where slowly revolving globes cast variegated splashes of color over the dancers.

Iris moved very close to him and closed her eyes. "I've always liked the way you danced," she said. "You lead without leading."

Gamrick laughed.

She opened her eyes and looked at him. "You know I love you, don't you?"

He looked down at her upturned face and kissed the tip of her nose. "Yes, I know," he answered, executing a break.

When she came back to him, she put her hands on his shoulders.

He held her hips.

"I wish we could get away for a few days. Maybe join Wayne and Monique," she said.

"I'd take the *Snark* out if I could get the time," he answered.

"By the way, what do you think of Monique? This is the first time I've had the opportunity to spend some time with her."

"A street kid with some trimmings," Gamrick answered.

She raised her eyebrows.

Gamrick whirled her around. "She's Wayne's problem and he's hers. As long as they have a workable solution, they'll stay married. When the solution ceases to be workable for one or the other, they will get a divorce."

"That doesn't answer my question," Iris complained. "After all, she is married to my brother."

"What do you think of her? No, more important, what does Wayne think of her?" Gamrick responded.

"Wayne said he loves her."

"Well, then, there you are. You have your answer."

"No, I don't," she protested mildly.

Gamrick laughed. "Wayne—" He saw Kate Bannon and at the same moment she saw him. An instant later, her partner eased her to the far side of the dance floor.

"You were saying," Iris said.

"Yes, how your brother feels about her is more important than how we feel," Gamrick answered, still looking at Kate, whose black cocktail dress bared the top of her breasts.

"Yes, but you must have an opinion about her."

"I already told you," he answered, aware of how close Kate's partner was holding her.

"Clark, the music has stopped," Iris said suddenly.

"Now, how did that happen without me knowing?" He laughed and as he escorted her back to the table, where their drinks were already waiting, he said, "What's that famous line? 'I could have danced all night.'"

"Well, I think she's very nice. Maybe a bit rough around the edges. But she seems to have a good heart."

Gamrick quickly drank his ale, summoned the waiter, and ordered a double bourbon on the rocks.

"Clark, how are you going to drive—"

"This time I will leave the driving to you," he said, taking hold of her hands. "I'll just sit back and enjoy."

A busboy put a basket of hot rolls on the table and a small dish with three different scoops of butter on it.

"Strawberry, raisin, and mint," Iris said, then explained, "It tells what they are on the menu."

Gamrick suddenly stood.

"What—" Iris began.

"Kate Bannon, my wife, Iris," Gamrick said, forgetting that they had already met.

"My pleasure again, Mrs. Gamrick," Kate said.

"Thank you," Iris answered.

"Captain and Mrs. Gamrick, William Bly, my agent," Kate said.

Gamrick and Iris shook hands with Bly, who said, "Bill will do fine." Bly was Gamrick's height but not as broad. Younger, perhaps, by five years. A self-assured man.

"Please join us," Iris said.

"I would not want to intrude," Kate answered.

"You would not be intruding," Iris said, looking at Gamrick for confirmation.

"Not in the least," he responded, and summoning the waiter, he asked for two additional settings.

"Captain, I was sorry to hear about Commander Wright," Bly said. "Are there any leads?"

"Clark would be fine," Gamrick said with a smile. Then he added, "There aren't leads, at least none that point to the person who drove the truck."

"It's too depressing to even think about," Iris commented.

Kate agreed.

The dance band resumed playing, and Bly asked Iris to dance.

"I'd love to," Iris answered.

"Sorry," Gamrick said, looking at Kate, "but I'll sit this one out."

"No problem," she answered, giving the words a Spanish accent.

Looking at her, Gamrick said, "I waited for you the other night."

"You shouldn't have," she answered. "I don't take orders."

He took a deep breath and slowly exhaled.

"Iris is a beautiful woman," Kate said. "You should be—"

"Listen to me, Kate," he said, starting to reach for her hands and stopping himself.

She looked straight at him. "You were annoyed because I wouldn't let you off the hook at the press conference."

"I was angry because you took advantage of what you know are my feelings for you," he said.

"If you really think that, then . . . listen, you do your job to the best of your abilities, and you better believe that I do mine."

Gamrick smiled.

"What the hell are you smiling at?" she demanded to know.

"Your face is flushed and your freckles have become—Kate, I can't get you out of mind," he said, his voice full of passion.

She dropped her eyes. "You're not easy to put aside either," she told him in a low voice. Then, looking straight at him again, "I don't want any entanglements."

"I can't promise you there won't be any," he said.

"That's the other reason why I didn't meet you the other night," she told him.

The music ended, and as Bly held the chair for her, Iris said, "The two of you looked as if you were discussing the fate of the world."

"The fate of Paul Anderson," Kate said.

Completely nonplussed by her answer, Gamrick said, "That's still to be determined by the court-martial."

"Don't you think the Navy is going a bit too swift on this one?" Bly questioned.

Before Gamrick could answer, Kate said, "For what it's worth, Clark, that young man doesn't stand a snowball's chance in hell of surviving this even if he's innocent."

Gamrick could feel the heat rush into his cheeks.

"I think what Kate—"

"I can speak for myself," Kate said. "Anderson is going to need someone who believes he's innocent and would be willing to take on the Navy to prove it. No one—excuse the vulgarity—who values his ass is going to defend that young man."

"The Navy will appoint—"

"Who will go through the motions," Kate said, "and give the Navy what it wants—Anderson's head on a silver platter."

"He has the right to retain an outside lawyer," Gamrick responded.

Kate shook her head. "He doesn't have the money, and his family doesn't have it. His father is a factory worker."

"What about the insurance money?" Bly asked.

"The company won't release a single sou until he is proved innocent."

"How do you know all of this?" Gamrick asked.

"It's my business to know," Kate answered. "I checked it out this afternoon."

Bly put his arm around Kate's shoulders and affectionately squeezed the top of her arm. "That's why she's one of the best in the business," he said possessively.

Despite the fact Gamrick had told Iris she would drive, he was behind the wheel when they drove home.

"I enjoyed myself," Iris said after they had been on the road for a few minutes.

Gamrick concentrated on the road.

"Did you enjoy yourself?" she asked.

"Yes."

"Kate is even more exciting in person than she is on the screen," Iris commented, pressing herself closer to him.

"Yes, she is," Gamrick said.

"And Bill is a very personable man."

Gamrick agreed.

"I didn't understand what point she was trying to make about Anderson, did you?" Iris asked. "She makes it sound as if the Navy is doing something wrong."

Gamrick shrugged. "She's right about no one wanting to defend him," he said.

"Well, I'm glad that's not our problem," she said.

Gamrick shrugged again, but remained silent.

Then Iris asked, "Do you think they're sleeping together?"

"I don't think about it," Gamrick answered, though the same question had been in and out of his thoughts from the moment he had seen them together.

"Not that she's the type, but I know from my own experience in theater, some women will sleep with almost anyone to get ahead."

"For Christ's sake, what business is it of yours or anyone's who she fucks?" he exploded.

"Pardon me for living," Iris answered, drawing away from him. "I really didn't know you cared."

Gamrick glared at her, then gave his full attention to the road.

"This is not the way to end a good evening," he said after a few moments.

"I'm not the one who overreacted," she answered from the far corner of her seat.

"I'm sorry. I'm just very tired ... Come on back here," Gamrick said, extending his arm to embrace her.

Iris hesitated.

"Come on," he urged. "Come on."

She slid into the crook of his arm.

"That's a lot better," he said, gently squeezing her breast. "A whole lot better!"

Chapter 9

On Wednesday morning Gamrick flew to Norfolk with
Folsim and Cool, who were going to begin the tedious
process of reviewing the videotapes, while he was going to question Anderson again.

"There doesn't seem to be much point in reviewing
the tapes now that Anderson has been tagged," Cool
said as the chopper was settling down on its pad at the
base.

Gamrick agreed, but added, "Who knows, you might
come up with something that will strengthen the
Navy's case."

"Or lessen it," Folsim commented.

None of them responded to that, and a few minutes
later Folsim and Cool left the chauffeur-driven staff car
at the headquarters building, and Gamrick continued
on to the base brig, where—after identifying himself—he was escorted by a Marine corporal to a small
room that was furnished with a table and two chairs.
On the table was a clean ashtray made out of the rear
portion of a five-inch shell.

"The prisoner will be brought here in a few minutes," the Marine said.

Gamrick thanked him.

"Sir, do you want the door open or closed now?" the
Marine asked.

"Open."

"Aye, aye, sir," the Marine answered.

Gamrick set up a small voice-activated tape recorder
and made sure it was operating before he switched it

off. Then he leaned against the metal back of the chair and tried to get a sense of what it was like to be a prisoner. The room was probably the same size as a cell. He looked up at the ceiling. Two long fluorescent tubes provided a hard white light. Suddenly he heard footsteps. He looked toward the door.

A Marine sergeant and Anderson came into view.

"Prisoner, halt," the sergeant ordered.

Anderson stopped and stood at attention.

"Corporal, Seaman First Class Paul Anderson is now in your custody," the sergeant said to the Marine standing guard in front of the open door.

Gamrick stood up.

"I accept the prisoner," the Marine guard said.

Anderson's escort left.

"The prisoner will proceed into the room," the Marine guard said.

"Aye, aye, Corporal," Anderson answered, saluting at the same time.

Anderson approached the table and halted behind the chair.

"You may sit," Gamrick said.

"Aye, aye, sir," Anderson responded and sat.

"Corporal, may we have coffee?" Gamrick asked.

"Sir, the prisoner is only permitted to have water," the corporal answered.

"Since that's a rule, have two cups of coffee brought for me," Gamrick said.

"Sir—"

"Two cups of coffee, black, no sugar, Corporal," Gamrick said, hardening his voice just enough to let the Marine know he had been given an order.

"Aye, aye, sir," the corporal snapped.

"And close the door," Gamrick added in the same tone.

A rapid "Aye, aye, sir" followed and the door was closed.

Gamrick sat and took out a pack of cigarettes he'd bought for Anderson. "Take them, they're yours," he said. In less than forty-eight hours a radical change had occurred in Anderson. Dressed in a prison uniform of dungarees and a short-sleeve denim shirt with a white X stenciled on the front and back, he looked smaller and sallower than previously. And there was something in his eyes—a combination, Gamrick thought, of fear and hopelessness—that had not been there before.

"Go ahead, smoke," Gamrick said, placing his lighter on the table halfway between them.

Anderson made no movement toward the cigarettes or the lighter.

"Do you know why I am here?" Gamrick asked, wondering now why he had bothered to come.

"To ask more questions," Anderson said.

"Yes."

"To get me to confess to something I didn't do," Anderson said.

Gamrick leaned forward. "The Navy has in its possession—"

Anderson shook his head. "I heard about the photographs on the TV news, but I don't know anything about them."

"They show you and Gus and a woman—"

"I don't know anything about them," Anderson said.

"They were taken from a distance," Gamrick explained. "You probably didn't know you were being photographed."

"Fakes. Photographs can be faked," Anderson responded.

A soft knock on the door brought Gamrick's attention to it. "Come in," he called out.

The door opened and the corporal said, "Two black coffees, no sugar."

Gamrick went to the door, took the two styrofoam cups, thanked the corporal, and returned to the table. He placed one cup in front of Anderson and took a sip from the other. "These photographs were not faked," he said, sitting down. Then he told Anderson exactly where, when, and how they were taken.

"Was that why I was arrested and placed in here?" Anderson asked.

Gamrick nodded.

Anderson started to reach for the coffee but stopped.

"Take it. I got it for you," Gamrick said.

Anderson shook his head and in a low voice he said, jerking his thumb toward the door, "When those guys say only water, they mean it. If they even thought I drank some coffee, they'd work me over."

"Work you over?"

"Sir, I'm not only a prisoner, I'm the guy who killed his shipmates, and worse than even that, I'm a fucking queer."

Gamrick was about to ask if he was a queer, but the photographs showed that he was, at the very least, bisexual.

"How did you get those photographs?" Anderson asked suddenly, going limp as if he no longer had the strength or the will to sit up straight.

"I can't tell you that," Gamrick answered.

Anderson bit his lower lip. Tears welled up in his eyes, and he used the back of his hands to wipe them away. Then he said, "I'm all right, sir."

"Tell me about Gus," Gamrick said.

"We even loved the same woman," Anderson whispered.

"Julie?"

"Yes," Anderson responded.

"And she, did she love each of you in the same way?"

Anderson hesitated.

The man's hesitation was enough to cause Gamrick to change the subject, and he asked, "Have you written to or phoned your folks?"

"It wouldn't matter if I did," Anderson said.

Gamrick took a deep breath and slowly exhaled.

"Gus—" Anderson began and, swallowing hard, he shook his head, but he couldn't speak.

Again Gamrick waited until the man composed himself before he decided to take a direct approach. "If you gave the court a signed confession and threw yourself on their mercy, you might save your life."

Anderson pulled back, again stiff. "I'm not guilty," he said. "I didn't kill anyone."

Gamrick rubbed his hand over his chin and summoned the guard. "I'm finished with—" He had difficulty saying the word *prisoner*. But he started again. "I'm finished with the prisoner," he said.

"Aye, aye, sir," the corporal answered.

Gamrick waited until Anderson was marched out of the room before he left. The moment he was outside, he took several deep breaths and looked up at the sky. It was blue and spotted with puffy white cumulus clouds that sailed gently over the Chesapeake. He remembered the lines from Oscar Wilde's *The Ballad of Reading Gaol:* "I never saw a man who looked / With such a wistful eye / Upon that little tent of blue / Which prisoners call the sky." Then lowering his gaze, Gamrick squared his shoulders and resolutely strode off.

"You look kind of peaked," Folsim commented, looking across the table at Gamrick. "Doesn't he, Harry?" The three of them were in the base OC having lunch.

Cool nodded and asked Gamrick if he felt ill.

"Tired," Gamrick answered. "I was up later than usual last night, and I have the beginnings of a headache, the throbbing kind." The meeting with Anderson had drained him emotionally, and he had spent the previous night turning and tossing about, trying not to think about Kate and at the same time wanting to.

"Why don't you take the rest of the day off?" Folsim said. "Harry and I can handle whatever comes up."

"Hitch a chopper ride back to D.C. and go home," Cool advised.

Gamrick thought about it for a few moments before he said, "All right. If the admiral calls—"

"He knows none of us are feeling our best," Folsim said. "Jesus, we're lucky to be walking around."

Gamrick had almost forgotten about Folsim's relationship to Russo. "All right, Bob, you take the conn," he said. "I'll leave as soon as we're finished here."

"How did your meeting go?" Cool asked, broaching the classified subject.

"No change," Gamrick answered.

Folsim shook his head and Cool said, "I want to view Hawkins' tape again."

"Any specific reason why?" Folsim asked.

"Other than Anderson, he's the only survivor."

"I have no objections," Gamrick said.

"You know he didn't show up for the memorial service that was held for the men who were killed," Folsim said.

Gamrick raised his eyebrows.

"It was held yesterday at the base chapel. I went there with a couple of the officers I know aboard the *Utah*," Folsim explained.

"You never mentioned that you knew anyone aboard the *Utah*," Cool said.

"Radar people and the chopper pilots," Folsim responded. "They went because they knew the turret's gunnery officer and his family."

"And you sure Hawkins wasn't there?"

"I'm sure. There were a lot of officers from the ship, including the skipper, XO, and its chief gunnery officer. A lot of brass, some Washington types—politicians and Department of Defense people—and the families and friends of the dead. Hawkins would have stood out had he been there."

"It just might have been too painful for him," Gamrick said. "I wouldn't want to carry his sack."

"I just thought his absence was interesting," Folsim commented. "It could be that you're right. It would have been too painful for him or it could be . . ."

"He didn't have a motive," Cool said, adding with an impish grin and a southern accent, "We start with another suspect, we're going to confuse the Navy for sure."

"But you're the guy who started this whole conversation," Folsim laughed, pointing at Cool. "You said—"

Cool threw up his hands. "All right, I won't review the tape. I'll let sleeping dogs lie."

Gamrick entered the conversation. "Review the tape if you want to," he said, "but now, unless either of you want something else to eat, I'd like to leave."

"To quote Admiral Russo, 'No problem,' " Folsim said, mimicking a Spanish accent.

Gamrick stiffened. Kate accented the words exactly the same way.

"Skipper?" Cool questioned.

"Just the headache," Gamrick lied.

Gamrick felt much better almost as soon as he turned off the highway and onto the secondary road that would take him past the Sea Sands. Out of Washington, the air was cleaner.

He switched the radio on and listened to a string quartet which he couldn't identify, though he was a devotee of chamber music. For him the interplay of a few instruments was not only more emotionally stimulating than a larger work, but it also possessed an intellectuality that pleased him and sometimes a calmness that he found intensely rewarding. Now there was a dialogue between the violin and viola; then the bass and cello entered. Sad, low tones . . . He gave himself up to the sound of the music. By the time the Sea Sands came into view, the news came on. Gamrick was just about to change stations when the newscaster said, "This just in. There has been an explosion at the Norfolk naval base. No word yet on whether or not there are any casualties. We will update the information as it comes in."

Gamrick swung into the Sea Sands parking area, stopped, and ran for the public phone.

"Trouble in Norfolk," Pete called from behind the bar the moment he saw him.

Gamrick dialed his Norfolk number. Nothing. Not even a busy signal. He dialed Russo's number. His secretary answered.

"This is Captain Gamrick—"

She interrupted. "Sir, there's been an accident in Norfolk. The admiral is on his way there now."

"What happened?"

"I don't know. Some kind of explosion where Commander Folsim and Lieutenant Cool were working."

"Thank you, Lieutenant," Gamrick said and hung up. He walked slowly toward the bar and looked up at the TV. The local TV people were already on the scene. The picture on the screen showed what had been part of the main building and was now rubble.

"You're looking at the left side of the building," the TV reporter said. "The car—apparently loaded with explosives—headed for the main entrance, then suddenly swerved to its right and struck the building's left side. The damage has been extensive. The area, as you can see, has been completely cordoned off. Firefighters and rescue teams are still working to put several small fires out and to find people who might be buried under the massive debris. So far we have not been told if there were any casualties, but it seems impossible that there would not be any given the intensity of the explosion. This is Alex Ross reporting live from the Norfolk Navy Base in Virginia. We switch you now to our parent station QVW, Washington."

The camera immediately zoomed in on Kate. "This is Kate Bannon in the QVW Channel Six newsroom. We've just learned that government experts on the scene view this situation as being similar to the one that devastated the Marine headquarters in Beirut, Lebanon, in 1986. That explosion took the lives of over two hundred Marines. We will update you as soon as we are given new information. Now we return to our regularly scheduled programing."

Gamrick sat.

"On the house, Skipper," Pete said, pushing an empty glass in front of him and pouring bourbon into it.

Gamrick nodded and managed to croak, "Thanks." And in two gulps he finished the drink.

"Listen, if you want to call anyone, use this," Pete said, placing a handset on the bar.

"I owe you a couple," Gamrick said, and picking up the phone, he stabbed at a sequence of buttons with his forefinger.

Iris answered.

"I'm okay," Gamrick said. "I wasn't there."

"Thank God," Iris cried. "Oh, Clark, I thought—"

"I'm all right," he assured her when the TV screen filled with Kate's picture. "I'll be home soon," he said and hung up.

"This just in. The cause of the explosion has definitely been identified as a car bomb. And we have our first report of casualties. We understand that there have been several people who have been killed. The Navy will not release their names until the next of kin have been notified. . . . This has just come in to us. A witness to the explosion has told investigators that the car carrying the explosives was not driven by anyone. We repeat, the car carrying the explosives, according to a witness, was not driven by anyone. Now, back to our regular programming."

"Can you beat that!" Pete exclaimed.

Gamrick phoned Russo's office again.

"Captain, Lieutenant Cool's body was found in the hallway," Lieutenant Martins said in a tight voice.

"Commander Folsim?" Gamrick questioned.

"He was on the other side of the building when the explosion occurred," she said.

Gamrick uttered a ragged sigh.

"Sir, most of the videotapes were destroyed, but we do have typescripts of them," she said.

He wanted to answer with something flip, but he couldn't find the words to even speak. He switched off the phone and put it down on the bar. "Pete," he said, pointing at the empty glass, "I could use another one."

On the eleven o'clock news Kate gave the names of the casualties. Cool's name was among them. "So far," she continued, "twenty people have been killed and forty injured. Some of the injured are listed in critical condition. Investigators have determined that the car was radio-controlled by someone within sight of the building. Unofficially, the word is that Arab terrorists are high on the list of suspects, and even now law enforcement agents are looking for a man—a civilian— who was seen by several witnesses not too far from the main building. According to one witness, 'he seemed to have some sort of gadget in his hand.' Our heartfelt condolences go out to those who suffered the loss of loved ones in this terrible tragedy.

"Now, the international news—"

Gamrick switched off the TV and went upstairs.

Iris was already in bed. She was asleep when he entered the bedroom. Earlier, she had cried when he had come home.

"I was so frightened," she had wept. "So very frightened."

Then to blunt the edge of her fear, she had several martinis and had gone up to bed early.

Gamrick sat down on the bed and suddenly realized, though he was very tired, he would not be able to sleep.

He moved to the sliding door, opened it, and with Dimitri at his side, he stepped out onto the deck. Gamrick had expected Russo to call and hoped that Kate would, but neither of them had.

The night was cool, full of night smells and sounds. He could hear the plopping sound made by fish as they fell back into the water after having leaped out of it.

That he missed being killed on two different occasions in less than a week gave him the odd feeling of either avoiding his fate or beating the odds. He had no way of knowing which.

"Much like Hawkins and Anderson," he said aloud, suddenly aware he and Folsim now had something in common with Hawkins and Anderson. Because he did not believe in God, he saw nothing providential in his experiences, but he couldn't help wondering whether he was missing his "Appointment in Samarra," so to speak.

Gamrick reached down and scratched the top of Dimitri's head. "Okay, Dim, you give me your answer," he said.

Dimitri raised his head.

"A good answer," Gamrick said, scratching under Dimitri's head and down his neck. "I should have thought of that myself."

The following morning Gamrick reported to Russo. His secretary became teary the moment she saw him and apologized profusely.

When he entered Russo's office, the admiral was on the phone. He motioned Gamrick into the chair in front of the desk.

The conversation continued for a few moments, with Russo doing more listening than talking. Finally he said, "I will call you later if I can. If I can't, good luck." Then he put the phone down and said, "We lost most of the fucking tapes but not the transcriptions."

"Lieutenant Martins told me," Gamrick answered.

"We still have Anderson. Bob told me you questioned him again yesterday morning," Russo said.

Gamrick nodded. "Still maintains his innocence."

"Innocent in a pig's ass," Russo responded. Then, drumming on the top of the desk, he said, "Our best guess is that the explosion was caused by a radio-controlled car bomb. The experts will know more about it in a few days."

"Arabs?"

Russo nodded. "That's the word unofficially. But

there are a lot of crazies out there, and the security at the base isn't the best."

"Did Harry have family?" Gamrick asked.

"Father and mother and three or four brothers and sisters. Harry was the shining light. You know what I mean. He was the one who became 'an officer and gentleman' despite his color."

"He was a good man," Gamrick said.

"If there were more like him instead of so many of the other kind—but that's a topic for a different day."

Gamrick remained silent. Russo's color sense was showing and it was not his place to comment on it.

"You and Bob must be doing something right to walk away twice from the *old boy,*" Russo said, opening another line of discussion.

"If we are, I sure as hell don't know what it is. How is Bob doing?"

"Shaken."

"And you, how are you doing?"

"Shaken, I guess."

"Well, what's the old saying, 'The Lord watches over fools and mad men,' or is it, 'fools and children'?"

"Something like that," Gamrick said.

"But you get the general idea, don't you?"

"Yes, sir."

Russo reached over to the humidor, flipped it open, and said, "This time you can take one," he said, pushing the humidor toward Gamrick.

"Very good," Gamrick commented a few moments later, letting the smoke out of his mouth.

"I want you to stay with the *Utah* case awhile longer," Russo said. "At least until the court-martial begins."

"Yes, sir," Gamrick responded, though he had hoped to return to the work he had been doing as soon as possible.

Smiling, Russo said, "Now we come to the icing on the cake. Once this *Utah* business is behind us, you will have new orders transferring you back to the Submarine Service and to your new command, the attack submarine *Orca*."

"But she's still in the design stage!" Gamrick exclaimed, suddenly filled with such heart-pounding excitement he broke into a fit of coughing and was forced to put the cigar in the ashtray.

"And your input will help make her even better than she would have been."

"But I still have two years—"

Russo waved his objection aside. "I told you good things can come from this. You will command a submarine squadron operating out of Norfolk, and after that you'll no doubt get your star."

Gamrick wanted to stand up and walk. Even shout! But instead he picked up the cigar and took a deep drag on it. He had heard of things like this happening, but never believed either the rumors or that it could happen to him.

"We take care of our own. That's the way things are done. You're one of us now. I wouldn't be a bit surprised if you got your star ahead of some of those men senior to yourself. There are always special circumstances for special people," Russo told him.

"Thank you, sir," Gamrick said, realizing Russo was his prime advocate.

"You earned it. Well, now that's out of the way, there is something I'd like to ask you to do for me," Russo said.

Gamrick nodded. "Sir?"

"Bob and I will go down to Steve's funeral on Friday, but as a special favor to me, will you go to Harry's on Saturday? The Navy will provide you with transportation and you'll be paid—"

"I'll go," Gamrick said. "He came from Brooklyn."

"Isn't that your old neighborhood?"

"Not for a long time, sir," Gamrick answered.

"Lieutenant Martins has all the information. She'll arrange whatever transportation you will need. I would suggest that you and the wife make a weekend of it, but I'm looking forward to having you at the barbecue Saturday evening."

"We're looking forward to being there," Gamrick replied.

"Unless you have something else that needs my attention, you're dismissed," Russo told him.

"Nothing else, sir." Gamrick stood up.

Russo got to his feet, and extending his hand across the desk, he said, "Congratulations on your new command."

They shook hands and Gamrick left the office. Outside, he stopped at Lieutenant Martins' desk and said, "I'm going up to New York on Sunday for Lieutenant Cool's funeral."

"You'll go from Washington to the Home Port on Staten Island by helicopter and by private limo to the church," she said, her voice tight with emotion. "I'll have all the necessary paperwork done by fourteen-hundred, sir."

"Thank you, Lieutenant," Gamrick responded, but because she looked as if she was about to cry, he did not move.

Then she said, "Sir, if—"

"Yes, Lieutenant?"

"Would it be possible—?"

Suddenly Gamrick realized what she was having so much difficulty saying, and he said, "Meet me at the heliport at takeoff time."

"Thank you, sir," she answered in a choked whisper.

Gamrick nodded and went directly to his office.

His first impulse was to phone Iris and share the good news with her. But as he swung his swivel chair toward the phone, he suddenly realized that she would not react to it as he had. Few Navy wives are overjoyed when their husbands return to sea duty. Some never make a good adjustment to the long separations. For those aboard surface vessels, it was six to seven months on a particular deployment. But for submariners in attack boats, it was never more than sixty days and often as short as forty-five. Luckily, Iris was always able to handle the times when he was at sea. She always had her acting to keep her busy. And she never seemed to mind the lack of sexual activity, probably because her drinking had taken its place. Even now he didn't have much—

The phone rang.

"Captain Gamrick here," he said, lifting the phone and speaking into the mouthpiece.

"Dad, it's Hal," the voice on the other end said.

"I know who it is," Gamrick laughed. "Don't you think I recognized your voice?"

"Dad, I'm sorry I haven't called. I've seen you on TV, though."

"Well, you're calling now. It's good to hear from you. How's Donna and the children?" Gamrick asked. He hadn't seen his daughter-in-law or his grandchildren since the spring break in April.

Hal said, "Listen, Dad, I'm coming down to see you for a few days. I'll be arriving tonight at Washington International at ten, shuttle flight number 900 out of LaGuardia."

Gamrick's brow furrowed. He knew that Hal had a heavy teaching schedule for the semester.

"Dad?"

"Yes, I'm here. Is anything wrong?" Gamrick asked.

"Nothing that can't wait," Hal responded.

"All right, I'll see you at ten," Gamrick said and put the phone down. For several moments he remained very still. Then he left the chair and went to the window. Another hot, steamy day. He returned to the desk. He tried to think of a time when Hal had interrupted his teaching—even a summer schedule—to come home, but he couldn't. Hal was one of those individuals who never mentioned whatever difficulties he might have been having until long after they were over and then only casually, as if they had happened to someone else.

Though Hal carried being closed-mouthed a bit too far, as far as Gamrick was concerned, he often wished that Jeff, his other son, would be less revelatory about his life. And with that thought slowly evaporating, he was about to call Iris and tell her that Jeff would be coming down for a few days when the phone rang.

Iris said, "I wanted to know if you're feeling sick."

"I'm fit as a fiddle," Gamrick answered.

"Clark, would you mind if I went out this evening? One of the actresses in our local group is suddenly unable to make tonight's performance, and I was asked to fill in."

He heard the excitement in her voice, and knowing that she wouldn't go if she knew that Hal was coming, he said, "That's a wonderful chance for you."

"You won't mind if I'm not home for dinner?"

"No, no, you go and enjoy yourself. What's that expression you always use, 'Break a leg.' "

Iris laughed. "You got it right. Thanks, darling. I'll be home sometime after midnight."

"Not to worry, I'll be fine," Gamrick said, adding, "and I'll have a surprise for you."

"Hint?"

"No way," he said and hung up. He had a double surprise for her, and he wasn't sure that she would be pleased by either one.

Chapter 10

Gamrick arrived at the shuttle gate a half hour before Hal was scheduled to land, and checking the TV monitor, he discovered that the flight's arrival time had been pushed back an hour.

With nothing to do for an hour and a half, Gamrick decided to go to the airport's cocktail lounge rather than remain in the almost deserted shuttle area. Without the hustle and bustle of travelers it was an eerie place, where the few people who were waiting for the next flight out to either New York or Boston could have been easily transformed from people to mythic characters—eternal wanderers whose likes he had seen in airports, bus and railroad stations, cities throughout the world. . . .

Smiling at his own thoughts, Gamrick headed directly for the cocktail lounge. Usually a busy place, it too was now quiet. There were three people at the bar, a couple in a booth, a waiter and the bartender who were watching a large-screen TV tuned to a late-night talk show.

Gamrick sat at a small round table against the wall and faced the front of the lounge, opening onto the passageway leading to the shuttle area. The waiter didn't seem to be in a hurry to serve him, and he was content to sit there, though he would have ordered a beer if the waiter had come to the table.

Gamrick was tired. The work over the last few days and the accident had drained him. Skippering an attack submarine had sometimes exhausted him physically, but not emotionally the way this investigation had.

The waiter finally detached himself from the TV and sauntered over to the table.

Gamrick asked for a dark beer.

"Don't have none," the waiter answered in a slow southern drawl.

"Give me whatever you have on tap," Gamrick said.

"Coors—"

"That will do fine," Gamrick replied.

The waiter nodded and walked slowly back to the bar, and when he returned with the beer, he said, "We close at midnight."

Gamrick acknowledged the information with a thank-you and took a sip of the beer. Alone again, he suddenly realized he was not only very tired, he was also very depressed. He wanted to share the news of his new assignment with someone. Very few skippers ever get the opportunity to be in on the design phase of the boat they command. They have to live with the finished boat, but he would have the opportunity to—

He suddenly realized Kate was outside the cocktail lounge looking in. He stood up and waved to her.

"We have to stop meeting like this," she laughed as she came close.

Gamrick flushed. "I'm waiting for my son Hal to come in. His shuttle flight from New York has been delayed. Please join me."

"That's an invitation I can't refuse," she said, sliding a shoulder bag off her shoulder and at the same time sitting. "I have a job interview in New York tomorrow morning at ten. My flight out has been delayed too. It's probably the return of the one your son is coming in on."

"Probably," Gamrick answered. "Do you want something to drink?"

"No, thank you."

"A job interview. I thought you were a fixture—I

mean, part of the Washington scene. Whatever that means."

Kate laughed. "I'm only a gal making an honest buck."

"You know, just before I saw you, I was sitting here feeling sorry for myself," Gamrick said.

"You, feel sorry for yourself? I can't believe that," she responded facetiously. "You're a very lucky man."

"Oh, I have my moods," he told her, hoping she wouldn't mention anything about the accident or the bombing. He wanted to get away from both of those calamities for a while—at least when he was with her.

"Do you want to share this one with me? I'm a good listener."

Gamrick told her about his new assignment.

Saluting him she said, "I am happy for you, Skipper."

"I'm now happy for me too," Gamrick answered.

The two of them laughed.

Gamrick liked the sound of her laughter. He liked looking at her, and he liked the apple scent of her perfume.

When they stopped laughing, she said, her voice now serious, "That young man doesn't stand a ghost of a chance."

The statement instantly tore Gamrick away from his sensual appreciation of her to the reality of what she had said. Up to that moment neither of them had alluded to the investigation, and he had pushed any thoughts about it as far away as he could. But he answered, "Not much of a chance if he's found guilty."

"Don't you think the Navy is rushing this judgment of Anderson?"

"You know I can't discuss the situation," he said.

The waiter came to the table and asked if Kate wanted a drink.

"No," Gamrick answered, and putting two one dollar bills on the table, he picked up Kate's shoulder bag and suggested they go back to the shuttle area.

"I know you can't discuss it," she said once they were out of the cocktail lounge.

"Then let's drop it."

She stopped and faced him. "But I would really like to know what you think."

Gamrick wanted to put his arms around her, to hold her tight against him.

"Tell me," Kate urged.

"Even if I agree with you, I can't do anything about it," he answered in a low voice.

"Do you agree that the Navy has found an easy answer?" she pressed.

Moved by the urgency in her voice, he said, "I would have continued the investigation. But that decision wasn't mine to make."

"Admiral Russo?"

Gamrick remained silent.

"Somehow, someway, I'm going to help that young man," she said passionately.

"He might be guilty," Gamrick offered.

Kate shook her head. "Not on the evidence the Navy has."

They reached the TV monitors.

"My plane is in and your son has landed," she said.

Gamrick walked with her to the checkpoint, and handing her the shoulder bag back, he said, "Good luck with your interview."

"Thanks," she answered.

Gamrick offered her his hand, but she moved close and kissed him. He put his arms around her and pressed her to him.

She smiled at him. "I'm glad we met."

"So am I." He let go of her and stepped back.

"See you," she said, turned, and walked past the security check.

Even as he watched her, he wondered what she would be like in bed. A sudden flash of heat traversed his groin.

She turned and waved to him.

He waved back, knowing that somehow she not only knew what he was thinking, but felt the same way about him.

"Dad?"

Gamrick made a half turn and saw his son—a younger, even taller version of himself coming toward him.

They embraced, patting each other on the back.

"Any luggage?" Gamrick asked as they started to walk.

"Just what you see: a shoulder bag and an attaché case," Hal answered. "I'll only be here until Sunday. I have to be home early because I have papers to mark for my Monday morning class."

Gamrick accepted Hal's explanation without comment. He still found it hard to imagine Hal in front of a class, much less a father of two children of his own: John, already a teenager in high school and Barbara, a ten-year-old. But he found it no less difficult to imagine Jeff at the controls of a jet fighter. Both boys had been difficult to raise. Jeff had been more of problem child. More defiant than Hal . . .

"Who was that woman I saw you with?" Hal suddenly asked.

The question almost stopped Gamrick.

Hal laughed. "Don't worry, Dad, I won't tell."

"Her name is Kate Bannon. She's a TV news commentator down here."

The automatic doors opened, and they walked out into the parking lot.

"You've become something of a TV personality yourself," Hal said.

"Not by choice," Gamrick answered.

As they approached the Jeep, Hal asked, "Isn't Mom here?"

"She's filling in for someone who is sick. I didn't want to spoil her evening."

"You didn't tell her I was coming?"

"No," Gamrick answered, unlocking the Jeep's door

and sliding behind the wheel. A moment later he unlocked the other door.

Hal put his shoulder bag and attaché case on the floor in front of him and buckled the safety belt.

Gamrick switched on the ignition, the lights, and releasing the emergency break, he drove slowly out of the parking lot.

"Well, Mom will be surprised," Hal said.

"She said she expected to be home by midnight, but you know how those theater people are."

"Yes, I know how they are," Hal responded wearily.

Gamrick glanced at his son. Of the two boys, he was the one who resented Iris's theatrical pretensions—as he sometimes referred to her involvement with the theater—more than Jeff. Hal seemed to need his mother more than Jeff did.

"Sorry, Dad, I'm just tired," Hal said.

"I know that feeling."

"Are you okay?" Hal asked.

"Tired, but otherwise just fine," he said, picking up speed as they entered the highway. "Tell me, how's Donna and the children?"

"In there pitching," Hal answered.

Gamrick assumed that Hal's answer was inclusive and didn't press him for further details. He concentrated on the road, enjoying the silence and taking the quiet time it gave him to think about Kate.

Then suddenly Hal said, "John is missing."

Gamrick braked, pulled off to the shoulder, and stopped. "Run that by me again," he said, forced to keep a tight rein on his emotions. He and John had a special relationship. He often saw in his grandson much more of himself than he had ever seen in either of his sons. . . .

"John is missing. The last time we saw him was seventy-two hours ago," Hal said in a tight whisper.

Gamrick snapped his fingers. "Gone, just like that?"

Hal nodded, then without warning, he buried his face in his hands and began to sob.

Gamrick put his arm around his son's shoulders and held him close. "The police—"

"They've been notified," Hal answered tearfully.

Gamrick took a deep breath and slowly exhaled. "Donna must be going crazy."

"It will be a miracle if our marriage survives this."

Gamrick blinked away the tears forming in his own eyes. "She doesn't blame you for this, does she?"

"Me, herself, bad genes, the stars . . . And I guess I do the same. It happens that way, I'm beginning to find out."

"My God, John is only fifteen," Gamrick whispered. "What the hell does he know about anything?"

Hal eased away from his father. "I'm okay," he said, using a handkerchief to wipe his face.

Gamrick turned the Jeep off the shoulder. "Is there anything I can do to help?" he asked.

"Nothing, at least for now. I came down to get away for a few days. Donna is home with Barbara."

"Have you spoken to Jeff?" Gamrick asked.

"No, but I will. I'll call him when he returns from flight ops."

For several minutes, neither of them spoke, then Gamrick said, "I did the same thing when I was his age—run away, I mean."

"Not the same thing, Dad. John has always been a problem, always. Just to keep him in school has taken a major effort. There's the real world, then there's John's world. Even his therapist has a difficult time with him. He's just that way."

Gamrick swallowed the knot in his throat and said, "I wasn't aware of how difficult John has been."

"I'm sorry, Dad, that I brought this to you. But I don't have anyone else to go to."

Gamrick reached over and squeezed Hal's shoulder. "I'd let the situation ride a bit before you told your mother. John just might get lonely and turn up home in the next few hours."

"Maybe," Hal answered without conviction.

After another period of silence, Gamrick asked, "Do you think John is trying to—to follow what I did?"

"I don't think so. It's not like John to follow anyone."

Gamrick pursed his lips. The darkness of the road accentuated his fear for John's safety. The boy could be picked up and killed. He shuddered and gripped the wheel with such fury that his knuckles turned white. Then he looked over at his son, who sat in the corner of the seat crumpled like a cast-away rag doll. He wanted to reassure him that John would be all right, but he couldn't even reassure himself.

The following morning Gamrick and Folsim met with their technical counterparts—the experts responsible for determining the cause and characteristics of the explosion. They met in a conference room located in a waterside building in the old Washington Navy Yard.

Folsim looked drawn and there were dark semicircles under his eyes. Gone was his jauntiness. During the brief ride to the navy yard he had said that he wasn't looking forward to the trip down to North Carolina or the admiral's barbecue Saturday evening.

Gamrick voiced the same feelings about his visit to Cool's family the next day, but said nothing about Russo's shindig, though he would have preferred not to go.

The conference room was very large with three huge arch windows overlooking the river. A highly polished teak wood table dated back to the nineteenth century, and the walls were decorated with paintings of famous American warships and their captains. Also, spotted around the room were glass-cased models of various ships including the *Bismarck* and the *Yamamoto*.

The technical staff was headed by Captain Roger D. Jewett, a man whose domain was the Navy's forensic laboratory. With him were two commanders: Louis Borke, former chief gunnery officer of the battleship

New Jersey, and Frank Geron, a structural expert from BuShips.

After the introductions, neither Gamrick nor Jewett opted for the head of the table but chose instead to sit opposite each other. Folsim sat at Gamrick's right. Borke sat on Jewett's right and Geron on his left.

"As you know, gentlemen, our investigation has been concerned with the cause of the initial explosion and its aftermath," Jewett said, opening the meeting.

"We understand that," Gamrick responded.

"Our best efforts indicate some sort of bombing device," Jewett said.

"Conclusively?" Folsim asked.

"In an explosion of that magnitude it is often impossible to recover evidence that would prove—"

"Excuse me, Captain," Gamrick said, "but the situation here involves a man's life, and the bottom line has to be whether or not you have absolute proof that a bomb was used to set off the secondary explosions."

"Our best efforts indicate that it was," Jewett replied.

"Will you state that to a court-martial?" Folsim asked.

Jewett hesitated.

Commander Borke said, "The ship's log and the maintenance records for turret number two indicate that the middle gun was in operating order immediately prior to the firing exercises."

"The primary explosion occurred in the turret; then the resulting fire set off the other explosions. Commander Geron, will you please explain your findings?"

"From the burn marks in the turret we know that the force of the primary explosion traveled outward, destroying the steel separations between it and the other two guns in the turret. At the same time it moved downward into upper and lower barbettes where the powder-handling flat and the projectile ring are located. Had it reached the storage area, the results

would have been catastrophic. The resulting explosion
could have broken the *Utah* in half."

"If, as you theorize, the first explosion was caused
by a bomb, how large a charge would have been
used?" Gamrick asked.

"Perhaps a pound. A pound of RDX can do a great
deal of damage, especially in such a confined space,"
Captain Jewett said. "Even a smaller amount could
wreak havoc."

Gamrick sat back in his chair and rubbed his chin.
"Are you sure RDX was used?" he asked.

"RDX or a similar type explosive," Jewett said.

"Your lab's spectrographic analysis wasn't able to
detect what it was?"

Jewett raised his eyebrows.

"I did a bit of reading on the use of spectrography in
criminal cases, Captain, long before I was assigned to
this board of inquiry."

"The resulting fire destroyed much of the residue,
and the water from the fire hoses probably washed
away the rest of it," Jewett said.

"Interesting," Folsim commented.

"What Commander Folsim means," Gamrick said,
"is that you have come up with a probable cause, and
that's not good enough."

"At this stage in the investigation, it is the best we
can do, and I would have to add that the chances of
doing better are very slim."

Gamrick nodded.

"Have you any questions, Captain?" Jewett asked.

"None."

"Commander?"

"None," Folsim answered.

When they were on the way back to their office,
Folsim asked, "What was all that about?"

"Not much, I'm afraid," Gamrick replied.

"It won't wash in front of a court-martial."

Gamrick rubbed his chin and said, "That would depend on how good Anderson's defense counsel will be."

Folsim lapsed into silence, and Gamrick began thinking more about the dangers that his grandson might be exposed to than Anderson's fate. . . .

"You know, I'd much rather go one on one with an Iraqi jet jockey than be part of this inquiry, or for that matter, any other damn inquiry in the future," Folsim said.

"I won't be sorry to leave it either," Gamrick replied.

Almost as soon as they returned to their office, the phone rang.

Folsim answered it, listened, and said, "We're on our way."

"The admiral?" Gamrick questioned.

"That was Lieutenant Martins. He's waiting for us," Folsim said.

Russo greeted them warmly and invited them to sit down at the coffee table rather than in front of the desk. "Well, gentlemen, we seem to be making progress on all fronts. Tell me, Captain, how did your meeting this morning go?"

Gamrick said, "Sir, the laboratory has come up with a probable cause."

"No doubt some kind of a bomb," Russo answered.

"Yes, sir. But—"

"Once Anderson is in that courtroom and the prosecution gets to work on him, I have no doubt he'll tell the court everything it wants to know about the bomb and a great deal more besides."

"Sir, that laboratory can't even make a positive identification of the kind of explosive that was used," Gamrick said.

Russo's brow furrowed momentarily, then he smiled and said, "The truck that hit the cab you were in has been found and identified. It belongs to the 245 Sea Bee battalion."

"The driver?" Gamrick asked.

"We know it was driven by a civilian named Richard Cassado, but the civilian authorities have not been able to locate him," Russo said.

"At least it's not one of our men," Folsim said.

Russo agreed, then said, "According to the dispatcher, that truck was supposed to be at the Little Creek Naval Air Station."

"What was it doing in Norfolk?" Gamrick asked.

"We won't know the answer to that until the police get Cassado," Russo said. "But my guess is he was working some kind of scam and your cab got in the way. A classic case of being in the wrong place at the wrong time."

"Sir, then you might say Commander Cool was in the wrong place at the wrong time," Gamrick commented.

Russo's brow wrinkled again. "Are you suggesting that two incidents are connected?"

"Sir—"

"Each is a separate entity, though both had tragic results," Russo said.

"Sir, each took the life of a member of a board of inquiry," Folsim said, looking straight at Russo.

Russo, who occupied the club chair, leaned back. "I've never known you to be gunshy before, Steve," he said, using Folsim's given name for the first time in Gamrick's presence.

"Sir, not gunshy. I'm just wondering if someone is out there—"

"You're not asking me to give you a bodyguard, are you?"

Folsim flushed. "No, sir. I'm not."

Russo made a slight turn to the left to face Gamrick, who was sitting opposite Folsim on the couch. "Well, you brought the matter up. Do you think there's any connection between the truck that struck the cab and the car bomb in the navy yard?"

"Sir—"

"Our people are sure that the car bomb can be connected to Arab terrorists," Russo said.

"Then obviously there isn't any connection other than the fact—as Commander Folsim has just pointed out—that a member of a board of inquiry have been killed by each of the events," Gamrick answered. "But if the car bomb cannot be definitively tied to Arab terrorists or some other terrorist group, our people will have to reexamine the events for a possible connection."

Russo answered, "Yes. But it will never come to pass." Then smiling, he said, "Now, to a matter less grave. Remember, gentlemen, that Saturday night is barbecue night at the admiral's house. And Clark, Chief of Submarine Warfare Admiral Rice will be there. I know the two of you will have a lot to talk about, especially with your new assignment coming up."

For a moment Gamrick considered telling him that he and Iris would not be able to attend because of a family problem, but because he knew Iris would be disappointed if they didn't attend, he said, "My wife and I are looking forward to it, sir."

"I'll be there," Folsim added.

"Good," Russo said, standing.

The meeting was over.

Russo walked to the door with them, shook their hands, and then they left the office.

"You're a sly old dog," Folsim commented once they were in the corridor. "You never said a word about your new assignment."

"I just found out about it the other day," Gamrick answered, entering their office.

"When?" Folsim asked, following Gamrick and closing the door behind him.

Gamrick sat behind the desk. "No specific time. I'll be here a while longer, probably until Anderson is tried."

"New command?" Folsim asked, putting his feet on the desk and leaning back in the swivel chair.

"She's still being designed. I'll be her first skipper."

Folsim gave a long, low whistle before he said, "That's one hell of a payoff. I wonder what mine will be?"

Gamrick didn't want to think of it as a payoff, but that's what it really was.

"Being on the inside is always a hell of a lot better than being anywhere else," Folsim commented.

"I can't argue with that," Gamrick said.

Folsim nodded, pushed himself away from the desk, and dropping his feet to the floor, he stood up. "You know, if I were you, I'd let the powers that be have their way with Anderson."

"I understand what you said, but I'm not sure I understand why you said it," Gamrick responded.

Folsim said, "Anderson has already been tried and convicted. The court-martial will be a show. You know—"

"I don't know."

"Good versus evil and good will triumph," Folsim said. He went to the window. "You know, if there is a connection between the accident and the bombing, our lives aren't worth jackshit." Then he turned and faced Gamrick.

"The word *if* is the key word," Gamrick said. "We have three separate events: the explosion aboard the *Utah,* the hit-and-run driver, and the car bomb. So far our people say Arab terrorists were responsible for that one. And the explosion in number two turret was caused by a small bomb. Two bombings, each very different from the other, and if Anderson was responsible for the one aboard the *Utah,* he certainly couldn't have been responsible for the car bomb."

"But two of those events killed two men on a board of inquiry that is investigating the initial event—the explosion aboard the *Utah,*" Folsim answered. "Now, you're giving me a different version of what the admiral said, but it still comes down to saying that there is no connection between Harry's death and Steve's."

"Coincidence—"

"Not for my money," Folsim answered sharply.

"Suppose you're right. Suppose someone is gunning for us. There isn't really much we can do about it," Gamrick said.

"We can watch our backs; we can arm ourselves. The idea of going down without firing a shot sticks in my craw."

"You sound like my brother-in-law," Gamrick answered. "Just because some nut followed me home—"

"What the hell are you talking about?" Folsim asked, moving from the window back to his desk and sitting on the edge of it facing Gamrick. "Who followed you?"

Gamrick shook his head. "I don't know. But a pickup came into the driveway, and I shot out one of its headlights before he took off. The pickup, it turns out, was stolen from someone in Norfolk. I told the admiral about it after the accident. He said he'd push the FBI to see if they could get a match on any prints that were taken off it."

Folsim started to pace, stopped, and said, "Someone was dogging you and you never said a word about it? Hell, Captain—"

"Come on, Bob, that certainly hasn't any connection to anything else that has happened," Gamrick said, realizing that Folsim was rapidly becoming—or had already become—paranoid.

"You do what you want, but I'm going to carry a piece," Folsim said.

Gamrick shrugged and just as he was about to make an open gesture with his hands, his phone rang. He picked it up and said, "Captain Gamrick here."

"Hang the cocksucker," a woman on the other end screeched.

Then the line went dead.

Gamrick hesitated for a few moments before returning the phone to its cradle.

"Who is it?" Folsim asked.

"Wrong number," Gamrick lied. He wasn't about to give Folsim something else to worry about.

Folsim looked at his watch. "It's fourteen-hundred. We missed lunch."

"That's not going to hurt us," Gamrick said.

"Mind if I call it a day, Captain?"

"Go ahead. I intended to leave early myself. My son came home for a few days."

"Are you leaving now?" Folsim asked.

"Might as well," Gamrick said.

The two of them went out to the parking lot, and before they separated, Folsim said, "Give my condolences to Harry's family."

"I'll do that," Gamrick answered. "See you Saturday evening."

"Yes, sir," Folsim answered and saluted.

Gamrick returned the salute and then shook Folsim's hand. Minutes later, he threaded the Jeep through the street traffic and gained access to the highway, where he maintained a steady sixty. The voice on the phone came back to him. It had been high-pitched and clear. Gamrick took a deep breath and slowly exhaled. There were a lot of people who wanted Anderson dead.

Gamrick saw the Sea Sands tavern, and on the spur of the moment he decided to pull into the parking lot. A cup of coffee and a grilled cheese would do him fine. A short while later, he entered the tavern and waited a few moments until his eyes adjusted to the room's dim lighting.

"How's it going, Captain?" Pete asked familiarly as Gamrick settled on a bar stool.

"It could always be worse," Gamrick said.

Pete nodded and asked, "What's your pleasure?"

"Coffee and—"

"Homemade apple pie?"

"I'll have it," Gamrick answered with a smile.

Pete called the order into the kitchen and after a short wait returned with the coffee and pie.

"I was sorry to hear that one of your men was killed by the explosion in Norfolk," Pete said.

"A good man," Gamrick commented, taking a sip of the coffee. He looked at himself in the mirror behind the bar. Like Folsim, he looked tired and there were dark half-moons under his eyes too.

"What's that old saying, 'The good die young,' " Pete commented.

Gamrick nodded, tasted a piece of the pie, and nodded approvingly.

"Jesus, I almost forgot!" Pete exclaimed. "I got a message for you."

Gamrick put the fork down. "A message for me, here?" he questioned.

"Last night. The wife took it. Said it was a woman," Pete said. He opened the cash register, reached into the back of it, and pulled out a yellow slip of paper. "Here it is," he said, coming back to Gamrick and placing it on the bar. "The woman said to give it to you if you showed up in the next few days."

The number was not familiar.

"Want to try it?" Pete asked.

"Might as well."

Pete handed the portable phone to Gamrick, and he quickly punched out the number. Then a woman said, "I forgot to tell you how glad I am that you weren't hurt. This is a private line. You may leave a message if you want to. Just wait for the diddle-dee sound to stop."

Gamrick smiled, the diddle-dee sound making him chuckle. Then he said, "I'm glad you remembered. It's made my day." He pressed the off button and handed the phone back to Pete, who said, "That didn't seem painful at all."

"Wasn't," Gamrick replied, picking up his fork

again. "It was the best thing that's happened to me all day."

"Good. I was hoping that it wasn't something bad. As sure as God made little apples, you've had your share of bad luck lately," Pete said.

"Maybe this is a sign that my luck is about change," Gamrick said.

"My wife is big on signs, horoscopes—you name it, if it has to do with the future, she's big on it. But me, I take all that stuff with a grain of salt. I take one day at a time."

Gamrick said, "I guess when you get to the bottom line, one day at a time is about all most of us can handle anyway."

"That's what I tell my wife, but she doesn't believe me," Pete said, laughing. "She says the future was put there for us to know."

Gamrick laughed. "There are times when I'd like to know what the future holds," he said, specifically thinking about Kate.

Pete winked at him. "Yeah, there are times, Captain."

Gamrick flushed.

"Especially when a woman is involved. But even then it pays to take it one day at a time," Pete counseled, winking again—this time more broadly.

"You've given me something to think about," Gamrick said, finishing the pie and draining the last bit of coffee from the cup.

"Any time," Pete answered. "Drinks, food, and something to think about."

Gamrick put a five-dollar bill on the bar.

"Too much."

"Put what is left in my cash reserve account," Gamrick said, getting off the stool.

"You got it, Skipper."

Gamrick saluted him, left the bar, and returned to his Jeep. Kate's concern for him made him feel very good. "I could easily fall in love with a woman like her," he said aloud, and a moment later he admitted, "I damn well have. . . ."

When Gamrick arrived home, he was greeted by Cora and Dimitri.

Cora told him that Iris and Hal were napping and then asked if he wanted her to fix a sandwich for him.

He thanked her but declined the offer. Instead he decided to take Dimitri for a walk in the woods, along pathways that were there before he and Iris bought the house. As soon as he whistled, Dimitri ran to the door, eager to go.

To enter the woods, Gamrick chose the one nearest the house. Dimitri ran a distance ahead, then stopped to make sure that Gamrick was following.

Within a matter of moments the bright sunlight diminished and an overall grayness took its place. The air was filled with a combination of woodsy smells mixed with the sharp salty scent of the ocean, which was not far away.

Dimitri flushed out several pheasants, which took wing and landed out of sight in a small clearing. There were deer in the woods, raccoons, skunks, rabbits. More birds, snakes, frogs, and turtles than he could or would want to identify. It was pleasant to walk in the woods, especially with Dimitri, whose delight was so obvious.

The path curved away from the cove and, forming a Θ, ran close to the roadway until it ended at the beginning of the driveway. Gamrick followed Dimitri, who suddenly stopped in place just off the roadway, still in the woods. He began to dig furiously—something he often did during a walk in the woods.

"Hey, boy, what's there?" Gamrick questioned, coming up.

Dimitri began to bark.

Gamrick hunkered down and looked. Half buried, he saw a metal box. "Easy, Dimi," Gamrick said, and reaching into the hole, he was able to pull the box free.

"All right, boy, you found something. But what the hell is it?" The box opened. Inside were circuit boards, relays, and two AA batteries.

Gamrick stood up and looked around. The roadway was less than a dozen feet away and obscured from view by several bushes. The box had been buried alongside the path.

He scanned the ground but saw nothing unusual. But someone had taken the time to bury it. He examined its interior again. A group of numbers was pressed into the metal on left side, but he couldn't make them out.

"Well, Dimi, I don't know what the hell this is, but I'm sure if it's important someone will come back to claim it," Gamrick said, tucking the box under his arm. "We'll just hold it for him." And using his foot, he pushed the soil Dimitri had dug up back into the hole.

Because Gamrick was curious about what the circuits in the box did, he decided to have it examined by electronic specialists and put it in the back of the Jeep. He'd drop it off at the laboratory early the next morning before he left for the funeral and pick it up when he came back. "Okay, Dimi," he said, "let's go see who's awake now."

Even before he entered the house, Gamrick heard Hal shouting and Iris weeping. "I guess they're awake," he said, rubbing the top of Dimitri's head. He had hoped that Iris would not become hysterical when Hal told her about John.

Gamrick opened the screen door and let Dimitri enter first. He followed and found Iris and Hal in the living room.

Hal was holding a portable phone and shouting. "You just don't understand, do you, Donna. It's not your fault. It's not my fault. John is just that way." He listened for a few moments, then yelled, "You want to put yourself on a cross, put yourself but don't put me." Then he switched off. "That woman thinks—ah, fuck it!" he exclaimed and dropped into an easy chair.

Gamrick took the other chair. Iris was on the couch, still crying but more softly now.

"The only thing we can do is to keep ourselves on an even keel," Gamrick commented, looking at Hal.

"I better go back to New York," Hal said. "Donna can't handle it alone."

"For god's sakes, she's the boy's mother," Iris suddenly screamed. "You don't understand—"

"And I'm his father," Hal yelled.

"It's not the same," Iris shouted. "You're a man. You don't understand."

"Bullshit!" Hal exploded, leaping to his feet. "You think her feeling are any deeper than mine?"

"Hal, take it easy," Gamrick said, now standing.

"Goddamn it! It's about time she grew up," Hal yelled, pointing at his mother. "Tell me where her head is at. No, I'll tell you. It's on some fucking stage, where she can pretend—"

"That's enough, mister," Gamrick roared.

For a moment Hal looked questioningly at him. "I'm not 'mister' anything. I'm not one of your junior officers. I'm your son, remember?" Then he turned and left the room.

Shaken, Gamrick went to the bar, poured himself a double shot of vodka, and looking at Iris, he asked, "Do you want a drink?"

She shook her head. "He shouldn't have said those things," she wept. "I'm his mother."

Gamrick took a long swallow before he answered, "He was way out of line, way out . . . But he's carrying a heavy load. He's on edge."

"I never knew he thought that way about my acting," Iris sniffled.

Gamrick drank the rest of the vodka, sat down next to her, and said, "All of us are going to have to live with the situation no matter how it develops. It's not going to be easier or more difficult for anyone of us to—"

Hal reentered the living room carrying his shoulder bag and attaché case. "I'm sorry, Mom," he said, bend-

ing down and kissing the top of her head. Then, looking at his father, he said, "I didn't mean to put my
problem on you and Mom."

"Family—" Iris began.

"No. You raised me and my brother—you had your
problems with us. John is mine."

"He's our grandson," Gamrick said, standing again.

Hal pursed his lips and nodded. "I know the both of
you are concerned," he said.

"I'll drive you to the airport," Gamrick said.

"No need to. I've already phoned for a cab," he said
just as a cab's horn sounded outside the house.

Gamrick shook Hal's hand, then hugged him. "We'll
be in touch," he said.

"I'll call you as soon as I have any kind of news,"
Hal answered.

"Do that," Gamrick said.

Hal bent down and kissed his mother. "I love you,
Mom," he told her.

"I love you too," she answered fiercely, embracing
him.

The horn sounded again.

"I better go," Hal said, and a moment later he left
the room.

Gamrick listened to the sound of the cab pulling out
of the driveway before he poured himself another double vodka.

"I'll have a double scotch neat," Iris said.

Gamrick nodded and poured the drink. She needed
the drink even more than he did.

Chapter 11

It wasn't until Gamrick and Lieutenant Martins were in a chopper, seated next to each other, on their way to the Home Port in Staten Island, that Gamrick said, "Lieutenant, if you don't mind telling me, I'd like to know your first name?"

"Alice," she answered.

"Clark," he said.

She nodded. "I know. I processed your orders when you first came aboard."

Gamrick was tired and did not continue the conversation. After Hal's departure he had spent a ragged night. By dinnertime Iris had drunk herself into a stupor and had to be put to bed. Then Wayne had called, and though it was obvious he did not know John was missing, he had sensed something was wrong, or as he had put it, "I'm getting bad vibes from you. . . ."

"Is anything wrong, Captain?" Martins asked, looking at him.

Gamrick shook his head. "A sudden stitch in my shoulder," he lied. "The doc said I'd get them for a while from time to time."

She nodded solicitously and said, "Harry was a beautiful man." She choked up.

"There's no need to explain anything to me or anyone else," Gamrick said.

She nodded. "I know that, but if I don't tell someone that I loved him, I'll explode."

"You just told me," Gamrick said gently.

Her eyes watered and he handed her his handkerchief. "He said you were a good officer and knew what you were doing."

"Thank you for telling me that. I thought the same about him."

She returned his handkerchief and faced the window. Brooklyn was on their starboard side as they flew over the Raritan Bay, the Verrazano Bridge, then straight to the Home Port's landing pad on Staten Island. A limousine was waiting for them, and minutes after they landed they were on their way to the church in Brooklyn for the funeral services.

When they were on the bridge, Gamrick said, pointing into the borough, "I was born and raised down there—a place called Flatbush." A rush of memories suddenly filled his head: times he had bicycled in Prospect Park, or to Sheepshead Bay; walking with his father; going out with a girl on Saturday night. . . .

"I've been in Manhattan a few times," Martins responded. "To go to the theater and visit a few museums, but never for more than two or three days. Too crowded for my tastes. As the saying goes: a good place to visit but I wouldn't want to live there. I'm strictly a small-town girl."

They were off the bridge on the Brooklyn-Queens Expressway, and fifteen minutes later they were in front of a church in the heart of the notorious Bedford-Stuyvesant slum. A predominantly black and Hispanic section, its streets belonged to street gangs and drug pushers. A group of street toughs stood across the street gawking at the people who came to pay their last respects.

"Are you all right?" Gamrick asked just before he and Martins went inside.

She nodded.

The moment they entered, they became the center of attention, though several other officers and rates from section were there. Some Gamrick recognized—he had passed them in the corridor dozens of times.

"Harry had a lot of friends," Martins whispered.

A young black man came up the aisle to then and introduced himself. "I'm Harry's younger brother, Philip. My folks are up front."

Gamrick gave his name and rank, then said, "This is Lieutenant Martins, a colleague of Harry's."

Philip nodded and led the way to his parents. Harry's mother was a dignified gray-headed woman who shook his hand and said, "Harry told us about you, Captain. He said you were something special."

"He was the one who was special," Gamrick answered.

Harry's father, a tall, lean man with pepper-and-salt hair and sharp black eyes, also shook Gamrick's hand. "Thank you for coming," he said in a low, dignified voice.

Gamrick answered, "Harry was one of my men, a shipmate." Then he introduced them to Martins. They greeted her warmly, insisting she sit between them when the memorial service began.

Gamrick sat on Mr. Cool's right and Philip on his mother's left.

The choir sang "Rock of Ages" before the minister began to recite the Twenty-third Psalm.

Gamrick sat ramrod straight, and as he listened to the minister speak about Harry's all too brief life, he couldn't help but think of John. . . .

The choir sang "Meet Jesus at the Cross," and then the minister asked, "Does anyone want to say a few words about our beloved brother Lieutenant Harry Cool?"

For several moments no one moved, then Philip stood up, walked toward the podium, and took his position behind it. "Everyone here knows I'm Harry's brother. But what everyone here doesn't know is that Harry made me his brother. It's one thing for a man to have a brother because he was born to a family that already had a son. But I wasn't born into the Cool family."

Instantly there was a great deal of movement and whispering in the audience.

Philip waited until it stopped before he said, "Joshua Cool found me when I was few weeks old. He took me home to Elizabeth, and I became their second child, their second son. Harry was eight years old when this happened. To him I was a special gift—" His voice suddenly broke, but he held up his hand for a moment, and regaining his composure, he continued. "I became his younger brother. He never had something that he didn't share with me. I owe my life to Joshua, my father, and to Elizabeth, my mother. But I owe much, much more to Harry, who became my brother and made me his."

For a moment Philip stood very still. Then with his head bowed he sat beside his mother again.

Before the service was over, several other people spoke, but none were as moving as Philip.

At the graveside, a contingent of six sailors in dress whites fired six volleys. The two ranking sailors removed the flag from the casket, properly folded it before giving it to Gamrick, who presented it to Cool's father. Then "Taps" was played as the casket slowly descended into the open grave. The instant the first melancholy note sounded, Gamrick, Martins, and the sailors snapped to attention and saluted.

After the funeral, everyone went back to the Cools' house, a well-kept brownstone on Sterling Place, where a large buffet had been set up. All of the officers and several of the rates spoke with Martins and Gamrick, except two.

"Do you recognize either one of those officers?" Gamrick asked when they had a few moments alone.

"Which ones?"

"The two at the window?"

"No," she answered. "But they could be outside our section."

"Could be . . . I'm sure the taller one is assigned to the *Utah*. I may have even interviewed him. The other

I can't place. He looks uncomfortable, as if he's not used to wearing a uniform."

"Why don't you ask them?"

"This isn't the time or the place to ask someone to identify himself."

She agreed, adding, "They might be some of our agents."

"Agents?"

"Admiral Russo might have sent them."

He raised his eyebrows.

"I'm not sure that he did, and if he had, it would have been just a precautionary measure."

"But you don't know for certain."

"I don't know," she said.

Gamrick dropped the subject and mingled with the other mourners. At three o'clock he and Martins said good-bye to Cool's parents and brother.

On the way back to the Home Port, Gamrick asked if Martins knew that Philip wasn't Harry's real brother.

She shook her head and said, "I should have gotten up too. But I wasn't that brave."

"It took a great deal of courage to go there," Gamrick said. "Don't fault yourself on that score."

After another long silence, she said, "The night before he was killed, Harry asked me to marry him. I told him I'd think about it."

"Would you have married him?" Gamrick asked, facing her.

She whispered, "Yes." Then she began to sob quietly.

In the chopper on the way back to Washington, Martins fell asleep, leaving Gamrick with his thoughts. The presence of the two men that neither he nor Martins could identify disturbed him. If Russo had sent them, then he must have had second thoughts about the connection between the accident and the bombing. But he knew Russo well enough by now to know that even if he asked him, his answer would be evasive. What the admiral does, the admiral does.

Martins shifted her position, and her head wound up on his shoulder. He smiled and almost immediately he thought about Kate.

The sudden downward movement of the chopper awakened Gamrick. He had dozed, but hadn't remembered falling asleep.

Martins awoke too, embarrassed to find that her head had been on his shoulder.

He assured her that he didn't mind.

Minutes later, they were on the ground.

Gamrick offered her a lift.

"I have my own car," she said. "But thanks anyway."

They shook hands.

"No," she said. "Friends part this way." Leaning close to him, she kissed him gently on his lips.

He answered, "They do, indeed."

Gamrick waited until she was in her car before he went to his Jeep. Once he was on the highway, he accelerated to sixty-five. Suddenly he remembered the metal box in back of his Jeep. He had forgotten to drop off at the electronics laboratory. Now he'd have to wait until Monday to do it.

Admiral Russo's Texas-style barbecue took place in the backyard of his sister and brother-in-law's quarter-horse farm, Rolling Hills, near White's Ferry, Maryland. Most of the men and women wore jeans and either a plaid or denim shirt, boots, or very expensive sneakers. Several of the men sported the obligatory Stetson or some other western-style hat.

Russo wore a light-hued Stetson, jeans and plaid shirt, and tooled leather boots. He and Folsim were dressed somewhat alike, though Folsim's boots were not as elaborate as the admiral's.

Gamrick and Iris were greeted by Russo, who immediately introduced them to his sister, Helena, a tall, good-looking blond woman, and her husband, Bill, a large man with thinning blond hair and bulging blue eyes. But even as he was talking to them, he saw Kate and Bly. They were on the far side of the yard, where a temporary bar had been set up. But it was Russo who called his attention to Kate by exclaiming, "Look over there, my favorite anchor lady has arrived! Now, isn't she a sight for any man's eyes. Excuse me, folks, I just have to go over and tell that woman how good-looking she is."

"I have little doubt that she already knows," Helena commented.

"It's part of a man's duty to tell a woman that she's beautiful," Russo said, lapsing into a deep Western drawl, which suddenly made Gamrick think of the voice on the phone.

"Something wrong, dear?" Iris asked.

Gamrick shook his head, as if the physical movement would by itself remove the memory of the voice.

Then Helena said, "My brother and I were born and raised in El Paso."

"So that's where the horses and the accent originate." Gamrick laughed, having succeeded in pushing the attempt to identify the voice out of his consciousness.

"It comes back to Vincent whenever we have a barbecue," she answered, smiling.

"And you? When does it come back to you?" Iris asked.

"Whenever I get worked up about something," Helena answered.

"The horses—" Gamrick started to ask about the animals.

"A hobby and a business," she said. Then, excusing herself, she went back into the house.

"Captain and Mrs. Gamrick," a man said, approaching them.

"Yes, and who—" Gamrick started to ask, realizing the man was Chief of Submarine Warfare. He had seen

him many times, but always in uniform. The civilian
clothes—especially the western getup he wore—threw
him off track.

"Admiral Rice," the man said, smiling broadly and
extending his hand.

Gamrick shook his hand and introduced Iris.

"A pleasure," Rice said, kissing the back of her hand
with a courtly grace that few men possessed. But Rice,
a tall, lean man with white hair, looked, except for the
clothing, as if he had stepped out of a nineteenth-
century painting. "Well, Captain, I hear very good
things about you."

"Thank you, sir," Gamrick answered.

"We'll have an opportunity for conversation later,"
Rice said. "But now, if you will excuse me, I see some
people that I should greet."

"Certainly, Admiral," Iris answered, and when he
was out of earshot, she added, "What a gracious man."

"Yes, he is," Gamrick agreed. As he and Iris walked
away, he realized there were at least forty people there.
They were supplied with various kinds of Tex-Mex
hors d'oeuvres and drinks by a team of five waiters.
Under one tent were two buffet tables with various sal-
ads and cold cuts for those guests who found the Tex-
Mex food too hot. Tables and chairs were scattered
around the yard. And on one side was a very large barbecue pit tended by two chefs dressed the way the
guests were, except that each wore a white bib apron
and a very tall white chef's hat.

Iris said she wanted a drink.

"Go easy, please," Gamrick said, walking toward the
bar. She'd been drinking heavily since Hal left.

She gave him a pained look but didn't say anything.

They met Kate and Bly and exchanged small talk
with them. Bly was impressed by what he saw, and
looking up at the various colored paper lanterns strung
across the yard, he said, "This isn't going to be over
anytime soon."

"Not likely," Gamrick answered, looking at Kate,

who had the two ends of her denim blouse tied in a knot around her bare midriff and wore a wide-brimmed black gambler's hat on the back of her neck.

"See you people later. We're off to look at the horses," Bly told them.

"And, Clark, you were going to get me a drink. Remember?" Iris said.

"Drink it is!" Gamrick exclaimed.

They got their drinks at the bar, then Gamrick, taking her by the arm, lead her over to Folsim, who was talking to a good-looking brunette.

"Gloria Russo, my boss, Captain Gamrick and his wife, Iris, I believe it is," Folsim said.

"Are you related to the admiral?" Iris asked, shaking Gloria's hand.

"His niece," she answered. "He and my dad are brothers."

"And how are you feeling, Commander," Iris asked Folsim as she shook his hand.

"Bob, please. I feel about as good as I can," Folsim said, and suggested they go to see the quarter horses.

"No, thank you," Iris said. "But you may go if you want to, Clark."

"I'll pass this time," Gamrick said.

"See you, Skipper," Folsim answered, leading Gloria toward the stables.

Iris finished her drink, placed the empty glass on one of the nearby tables, and said, "I'd like another."

"Why not wait a bit?" Gamrick suggested.

"I tell you what—you get me another drink and I'll get us some munchies," Iris suggested. "I think that's a very fair exchange."

"If you say so," Gamrick answered tightly and walked toward the bar.

The dining table was shaped like a doughnut, and everyone was seated around the outside circumference. Kate and Bly sat next to Gamrick, while Russo, his sis-

ter, and brother-in-law sat between Gamrick and Iris.
Folsim and Gloria were on the right of Iris.

The waiters brought platters of barbecued ribs,
charcoal-broiled steaks, and grilled chicken for those
who eschewed the pork or red meat. Additional platters
of grilled and boiled corn, baked and french-fried pota-
toes were placed on the table. To complement the meat
and vegetables, there were pitchers of red and white
wine, light and dark beer, and sangria.

The conversation flowed easily and leap frogged
from topic to topic, most of the time without any logical segue.

At one point, Helena asked Kate why she had turned
down the New York job offer.

"I just put it on hold," Kate answered. Looking at
Gamrick, she added, "I have more important things to
do here now."

Gamrick felt the heat rise into his cheeks. To account for his change of color, he complained that he
was beginning to feel the effects of too much food and
drink. But in truth, he ate and drank very little. Though
very much aware of Kate, he watched Iris with mount-
ing concern.

She drank more than she ate, and from time to time
her voice became strident. She complained bitterly
about the ingratitude that children show toward their
parents.

Several times Gamrick tried unsuccessfully to move
her off the topic by beginning a new subject. She she
ignored him. Her speech became more and more
slurred.

Then in a loud voice she announced, "I'm going to
be sick!"

In an instant Gamrick was at her side.

"There's a chaise on the sun porch at the front of the
house," Helena told him.

He thanked and managed to get Iris into the bathroom before she upchucked.

"I want to go home," she whimpered.

"Take a nap first," Gamrick answered, maneuvering her to the chaise and settling her on it. Within a few moments she was asleep, and he returned to the table. Aware the other guests were embarrassed because they had been observers of a situation that revealed his relationship to Iris, Gamrick apologized and said, "Our grandson is missing. He has been gone a full week now, and Iris is having trouble coping." After a pause, he added, in a tight, low voice, "So am I."

The explanation had the desired effect. Everyone at the table expressed their sympathy and concern.

Bly said, "Give me a picture of your grandson, and I'll have it put on every TV station coast to coast."

Before Gamrick could thank him, Russo said, "I'll put some pressure on my friends in the Bureau."

Gamrick nodded, thanked them, and to put everyone at ease again, though he had no appetite at all, he began to eat again. But the feast was almost over, and after several of the guests abandoned the table, he left too and walked to the far edge of the farm, where a small tributary to the Potomac joins the river. There, he leaned against a tree and thought about John and his own wild adventures when he had run away from home. He had looked older than his fifteen years, and having been raised in a city slum, he had been street smart. A year earlier he had his first sexual experience with a woman in her twenties and—

"Can't keep away from the water, can you?" Kate joshed.

Gamrick turned.

"I followed you," she said, coming up to him. "I'm sorry about your grandson."

Gamrick fought down the desire to take her in his arms.

"Do you really want to be alone?" she asked.

"No," he said. "I just didn't want to be with all of those people for a while." Then he added, "I ran away from home when I was fifteen."

"It must be in the genes," Kate answered with a smile.

"God, I hope not," Gamrick answered, his voice almost a soft cry of despair.

Kate moved closer to him. "You've got to believe that he will come back safely."

"I know that," Gamrick answered. "But out there—" He shook his head.

Kate touched the side of his face.

"I'm all right," he told her.

"I know you are." Then she stepped back and said, "I know this is not the right time and probably not the right place, considering it's your boss's property, but I want to speak to you about Anderson."

Gamrick immediately stiffened. "I'm not at liberty to discuss the problem," he said, disappointed that she hadn't come because of her feelings for him.

"The Navy is taking the easy way out," she said. "That young man is—"

"A court-martial will decide whether he is guilty or innocent," Gamrick answered forcefully.

She ignored the anger in his voice and said, "He is only guilty of being indiscreet. The Navy has something they can use against the President's plan to allow gays to serve. Can't you see that? Those pictures of him and Downs—"

"They were enough to convince me to bring them to the attention of Admiral Russo."

"Doesn't the fact that Anderson is engaged to be married say anything to you about his sexuality?" she asked.

"Only that he might go either way."

Suddenly Kate put her hands on his arms. "Can't you see that it's too easy? The Navy wants to get rid of it as soon as it can."

Surprised by her intensity, he could feel the pressure of her fingers on his arm.

"The Navy will appoint an officer to be his defense counsel, and that will be that. Anderson won't stand a snowball's chance in hell of beating the rap. He could be sentenced to death for a crime he didn't commit. Clark, all he is guilty of is befriending a young man, who like himself, never melded with the other members of the gun crew. He will be tried on circumstantial evidence that he is gay. He could loose his freedom, if not his life, because of his relationship to Downs and not because of anything he did."

Gamrick rubbed his chin. "I can't do anything about it now. My role is over. I'm being assigned to sea duty."

"You can do something about it," she responded fiercely, tightening her hold on his arms at the same time.

Gamrick shook his head. "You're wrong. I have already done what I was supposed to do."

Kate let go of his arms and stepped closer. "First, tell me if you have any doubts about—"

"Certainly I have doubts. It is not an easy thing to accuse a man of a crime and know that if he is found guilty, he could very well be put to death."

"You didn't let me finish," Kate said.

"All right, finish."

"Do you believe that the Navy is making short work of the investigation?" she asked.

"You're asking—"

"I need an answer," Kate insisted.

"Yes," he answered, letting the word explode out of him.

"If that is so, isn't just possible that they don't want something uncovered?" Kate questioned.

"Yes. But there could be other reasons—namely, that it is capable of doing its own housecleaning, so to speak."

Kate grinned. "Not even the Navy can do that. But you will agree that the investigation was shallow?"

"I have already agreed it was."

"Then, on that basis can't you request it be reopened?"

"Kate, have you any idea—?"

"Or failing that, you could convince Anderson to let you defend him," Kate said.

Gamrick walked a short distance away from her and then came back. "First, it would be impossible. Second, it would certainly make Russo angry, and third, it would damn well put my career on the line. I have a good chance of getting flag rank in the very near future. That means I'll be a rear admiral and with still enough time to go higher, even to becoming the CNO or head of the Joint Chiefs of Staff. You're asking me to risk all of that. Kate, I'm not a civilian. I'm in the Navy, and I'm bound—"

Kate lowered her eyes. "I didn't figure you to be a lackey for anyone or anything, not even your own future." And she started to turn away from him.

"Don't go," Gamrick said, stopping her. "I—" He put his arms around and drawing her close, he kissed her passionately.

Her arms circled his neck and she opened her mouth.

His tongue met hers, touched the roof of her mouth, and finally, breathless, he separated his lips from hers. But he still held her close, delighting in the feel of her body against his. "I've wanted to do that from the very first moment I saw you," he whispered.

"Yes, I know. I could tell what you were thinking by the way you looked at me, the way you touched me when I drove you home."

"Everything?"

"Everything," she answered, touching his face.

He took hold of her hand and kissed the back of it.

"You still haven't given me an answer," she said.

"Kate, you're asking me to—"

"To do what must be done," she told him.

"I can't give you an answer this minute," Gamrick responded. "I need some time to think about it."

"Tomorrow. Call me tomorrow."

Gamrick nodded.

Kate put his arms around her waist. "I wanted you to kiss me," she admitted.

"Again?"

"Yes, again," she answered softly.

As he kissed her, he opened her blouse and gently caressed her breasts. He pressed his lips to the top of one and then the other while she moved her fingers through his hair.

"I think we had better go back," she whispered, kissing the top of his head.

"I want you, Kate," Gamrick said. "I want to make love to you."

"And I want you," she responded with equal fervor.

"Ah, so you're feeling better," Gamrick said, seeing Iris with several of the other women as he and Kate returned to the yard.

"Much," Iris answered.

Then turning to Kate, he said, "I'll have that answer for you in a day or so."

Kate smiled, thanked him, and to Iris she said, "I'm glad to see you're better." Then she sauntered off.

Iris whispered something under her breath.

There was more than a hint of the green-eyed monster in her voice. But Gamrick wasn't about to create the circumstances that could possibly turn into another embarrassing scene that might involve Kate. Besides, she had every reason to be jealous; he was in love with another woman. To change the focus of her attention, Gamrick said, "Looks like we only have half the complement of men."

"They're inside the rec room playing pool," Iris said. "Admiral Russo asked that you join them when you returned."

"The admiral's request," he laughed, "is really an order in disguise."

Iris answered, "Not all of us have the same power as he does."

Gamrick ignored her sarcasm and walked toward the house.

Iris came after him. "I want to go home soon."

"I'll leave after I play a few games," he told her.

She stopped. "Don't think I don't know what's going on."

Gamrick clamped his jaws together, went into the house, and following the sounds coming from the rec room, he was easily able to find it.

The room was very large, and a pool table occupied its center. Russo, Rice, Folsim, and a dozen other men were there.

"Just in time for a game," Russo said the moment he saw Gamrick.

"Ready, willing, and able," he answered. "Who do I play?"

"Me," Folsim said.

"Set it up. You can break."

Folsim managed to put away five balls before Gamrick took his first shot. In a few minutes he cleared the table.

Russo followed Folsim, and Gamrick put him down just as quickly.

"Where did you learn to play?" Rice asked.

Gamrick laughed. "Sir, I hustled pool when I was a teenager."

Rice puffed on his cigar. "I was champion at the Academy," he said. "Let's do it, Captain. You break."

Gamrick put a ball in the right corner pocket on a triangular shot. Broke a grouping of three and sent one of them into the left center pocket. And as he scanned the table for his next shot, Russo said, "Clark has done some fine work on this *Utah* board of inquiry."

The comment unnerved Gamrick, and he missed his next shot.

"Red two in the left corner," Rice said, shooting. And before his next shot he said, "The trial must be absolutely flawless." He called, "Black two, right center." The ball rolled to the edge and hung there.

"Has Anderson requested outside legal counsel?" one of the other men asked.

"No. If he doesn't do it soon, we will appoint a counselor for him," Russo answered.

"Anyone in mind?" Rice asked.

"One or two. But none of them heavyweights."

"Five red left corner," Rice said and as he shot, he asked, "Who will prosecute?"

"Captain Hugh McCafery."

Gamrick dropped his cue stick. McCafery's nickname was "Hard Assed McCafery."

Looking at Gamrick, Russo said in a sharp voice, "I want to see justice done. That man killed twenty-seven of his shipmates."

Gamrick remained motionless. Suddenly there was tension in the room.

"My thinking turns the same way that yours does," Rice said. He stopped playing. "But if he gets some damn civilian shyster. Well, with all due respect, your man may not be up to the task that you cut out for him."

Gamrick quickly bent down and picked up his cue stick.

"That faggot doesn't have the money to buy that kind of legal counsel. The insurance company isn't going to pay off until he is proven innocent, and that's not going to happen."

"Let's continue," Rice said, taking another shot and missing.

Gamrick forced himself to concentrate on the game. But it was clear to him that Russo wanted him out of the way and must have pulled a lot of strings to have him reassigned. And even more astonishing, Russo was, for some unaccountable reason, afraid of him.

"That was an easy one you missed, Captain," Rice said, and shifting the cigar from the right side of his mouth to the left, he began to clear the table.

* * *

Because a fog lay over the countryside, Gamrick drove slowly and listened to Iris talk about the women at the party. She liked most of them, especially Helena, who she said was a down-to-earth person.

Gamrick agreed.

"Her husband is into the mystic realities of life," Iris said.

"Whatever that means," Gamrick answered, watching his high beams slide off the trees along the road.

"Since we're talking about women, just what were you doing with that TV lady?" Iris asked.

"Oh, making love, of course," Gamrick said before he could stop himself.

After a momentary pause, Iris said, "She's not your type. Besides, she's too young for you."

Gamrick glanced at her. "I was only joking."

"More like wishful thinking, I would say," Iris answered petulantly.

Gamrick didn't answer.

"What, no denial?" she challenged.

"She's a very attractive woman and I'm a normal man," Gamrick said. He was going to say more, tell her how he felt when he saw her drunk, but that would be a low blow. Going on the offensive to put her on the defensive.

She responded with a wordless sound of disgust, then commented, "Normal, shit!"

Gamrick kept silent. It was too dangerous to argue while driving. After a few minutes he realized Iris had fallen asleep, and he was left with his own thoughts.

Kate was right: the Navy wanted the problem out of the way and wanted a scapegoat. He wanted to think about her, about how it would be to make love to her. But every time he thought about her, he also thought about Anderson. The two were melded in his thoughts, and he knew they shouldn't have been. Whatever he decided to do about Anderson had to be totally independent of his feeling for her.

Then his thoughts turned to his grandson. He was

sure John was doing what he had done at fifteen. But he had been tougher, a lot tougher than John.

When they arrived home, Iris awoke and went upstairs without saying a word to him.

Gamrick walked into the study and sat at the desk. Dimitri stretched out alongside him. "Well, Dimi, do I call Kate or don't I?" he asked, scratching the dog's head. "You're right, I'm acting like a lovesick teenager. Okay, call if you're going to call or go upstairs to bed. . . . I'll call."

The moment Gamrick heard the first ring on the other end, he cut the connection and put the phone down. The possibility that she was with Bly suddenly occurred to him, and if she was he didn't want to know about it. "Sorry, Dimi, there's even some chicken in me about certain things," he said. As he left the study he told himself, "It's not worth becoming involved with her. She's too young and you're too old."

Sleepless, Gamrick lay with his hands clasped behind his head. The clock's red numbers read 3:30.03. He'd be wiped out for the rest of the day even if he got a few hours' sleep. He glanced over at Iris. She was frowning in her sleep, as though she had to concentrate to do it.

Gamrick looked up at the ceiling again and just as he was beginning to remember the soft warmth of Kate's breasts, the phone rang.

" 'Vengeance is mine, saith the Lord,' and you have been chosen as his instrument," the man on the other end growled. " 'Vengeance is mine, saith the Lord,' and he has made you his instrument."

The line went dead.

"Who was that?" Iris asked, resting her head on her hand.

"A wrong number," Gamrick lied. "Nothing to worry about." He laid down and stared at the ceiling again. . . .

Chapter 12

Gamrick was up and about by eight. Iris remained asleep. She would not be up for hours and probably would remember very little of the conversation that had taken place between them during the drive home.

He went out to the front of the house for the Galesville Sunday newspaper. Later he'd drive up to Annapolis to pick up the Sunday edition of the *Washington Post.*

After he brewed coffee and toasted two slices of rye bread, which he coated with whipped cream cheese, he placed the folded newspaper, a mug of black coffee, the bread, and a glass of grapefruit juice on a Chinese red lacquered tray and went out to the rear deck to read the newspaper and eat breakfast. The cove was like a mirror except where a fish broke its surface to leap out of the water and splash back into it after a moment.

Gamrick drank the juice and scratched Dimitri gently on his neck. The day would be one of those rare August days that were sometimes sandwiched in between the hot, humid ones—a respite from very difficult summer weather. He unfolded the newspaper and scanned the front page.

MIDWEST HIT WITH RECORD FLOODING

The story headline caught his attention. The voice on the phone came back. "Bird calls," he said aloud and instantly matched the voices to a face-to-face of Gunner's Mate 1st Class Donald Hawkins. For several moments Gamrick did nothing, then he was out of the chair pacing. He stopped, made his decision, went back into the house, and picking up the portable phone, he took it out on the deck, where he punched out the number for the department's OD.

"Admiral Russo's office, Lieutenant Porter here," a man answered.

Gamrick identified himself and said, "I need to know the origin of two phone calls to 601-6640. The most recent was last night, and the other was a day or so ago. Both were made between midnight and four A.M."

"Sir, that will take some time to trace down," Porter said.

"It is urgent I have that information," Gamrick said.

"Sir, I will call you at your number as soon as I have it," Porter answered.

Gamrick thanked him, put the phone down, and went out on the deck again. This time he picked up the mug of black coffee, moved to the railing, and looked out at the ocean beyond the cove's mouth. Annoyed with himself for not connecting the phone calls with the "Preacher," he realized that he too had accepted Anderson's guilt regardless of his opinion about the lack of evidence. Somehow Hawkins was tied to the explosion. "Don't rush to judge this one too. You've got to be sure," he cautioned himself aloud. "Wait—"

The phone rang.

Gamrick had it in his hand before the ring ended.

"Lieutenant Porter, sir . . . Both calls were made from Norfolk. The first cam from a telephone booth. The second was made from a motel."

"Do you know the position of the phone booth?"

"Yes, sir. Pier twenty-three. I believe the *Utah* is berthed there."

"She is," Gamrick snapped. "Now, could you give me the phone number and the name and location of the motel."

"Yes, sir. I can even give you the room number."

"Very good!"

"The Ocean View Motel, on Ocean View Drive. The

phone number is 1-804-784-8900, extension 2. The extension and the room number are the same."

"Thank you, Lieutenant," Gamrick said. As soon as he clicked off, he punched out the motel's number.

The switchboard operator answered.

"Room two," Gamrick said, pacing back and forth with the portable phone in his hand.

The phone rang four times before a woman answered.

"Put Donald on the line," Gamrick told her. Then he heard her say, "I don't know who the fuck it is. You going to answer it? The guy is waiting."

Several moments passed before Hawkins asked, "Who is it?"

Imitating Hawkins' accent, Gamrick answered, "A friend." Then, smiling, he clicked off.

Gamrick wrote Iris a note, "Something has come up in Norfolk requiring my presence. I don't know how long it will take to deal with it. Don't wait dinner for me." And he signed it, *Clark*. For a moment he thought of adding *Love* just above his signature. But that was not what he felt for her. If he felt anything, it was pity, and that, he knew, was quicksand for any marriage. Without alerting the note, he placed it on the kitchen table where she could not miss seeing it. Then he called the OD again and ordered a helicopter to fly him down to Norfolk.

A half hour later—showered, shaved, and dressed in his whites—Gamrick was on his way to Washington. Traffic was light, and he held to seventy until he reached the city. It was difficult for him not to think that Hawkins was responsible for the explosion and was trying to frame Anderson. All they had was Hawkins' word that he had permission to leave the turret. But they had proof of Anderson's actions. There was an entry in the ship's log and in the sick bay's sign-in book. Hawkins could have easily set a timer that would have given him enough time to get out of the turret.

The helicopter was already on the pad, warming up when Gamrick went aboard. The fifteen-minute flight seemed too long. He was afraid he had spooked Hawkins and the man would run.

As soon as the chopper landed, Gamrick went to the base brig to question Anderson.

"I need to know if Hawkins did anything unusual," Gamrick said.

Anderson shrugged. "He didn't have much of anything going for him."

"I know he did bird calls," Gamrick said, exasperated by Anderson's lethargy.

"Yeah, he could really sound like a bird. He did voices too. Could make himself sound like a woman, or a foreigner. Between the bird calls and the voices, he drove us nuts. A few times a couple of the guys decked him because he wouldn't shut up."

"Did you deck him?"

Anderson flushed.

"Never mind, you don't have to answer that question," Gamrick said.

"What's Hawkins' bird calls have to do with me?" Anderson asked.

"Enough, I hope, to save your life," Gamrick said. Then he called the guard and told him he was finished with the prisoner.

As soon as Gamrick left the brig, he went directly to the base security building, identified himself, and told the OD, "I need the biggest and strongest Marine you have on duty. I want him armed and I need a jeep."

The OD, First Lieutenant Green, according to his name tag, answered, "Sir, I'll have to check—"

"There isn't time, Lieutenant. I'll sign for the Marine and the jeep. And I want the Marine armed. But there's no time for anything else."

Green studied him for a few moments. "Captain, aren't you heading the board of inquiry—"

"Yes and that's why I need one of your men and a jeep," Gamrick said. "Fill out whatever papers are necessary, and I'll sign them when I come back."

"I'm really not—"

"I'll take full responsibility," Gamrick said impatiently. "This is an urgent matter."

Green scratched his almost shaved head, nodded, and said, "I'll give you gunny Vincent Gorga. Around here we call him 'Gorilla.' "

Gamrick thanked him, and a few minutes later he was on his way to the Ocean View Motel with Gorga as his driver. The gunny, even with reflecting sunglasses, looked like a throwback to Neanderthal man. He even had the sloping brow and very little neck. But he also had a chest full of medals, including the Silver Star with two oak leaf clusters.

"Gunny—"

"Call me Gorilla, sir. Everyone does, even my wife," Gorga said with a smile.

Gamrick nodded. "I don't expect any problems, Gorilla. But if there are any, just put the man down. Try not to break any bones."

"I'll do it nice and easy, sir," Gorga answered.

The Ocean View Motel was one of several sleazy motels on the "Strip," as that section of Ocean View Drive was referred to by the sailors. A room for a night went for twenty dollars after midnight and fifteen dollars for three hours before. They drove past the office and pulled into a parking slot across from Room 2.

"If you don't have a woman, a place like this will supply one," Gorga commented.

"I'm sure it would," Gamrick answered. Walking toward the door and at the same time pointing at it, he said, "Our man is in there."

Gorga nodded.

Gamrick was about to knock when he suddenly heard the heavy thwack of something being struck, immediately followed by an agonizing groan. Then a woman said, "You've been punished enough for your wickedness."

"Say it right. Say it like you mean it," the man answered.

"Hawkins," Gamrick whispered. "Our man."

"What the hell is going on in there?" Gorga questioned.

Gamrick put his finger against his lips.

"You've been punished for your wickedness," the woman repeated. In a whiny voice she added, "I'm hungry. I want breakfast. It's almost time for lunch."

"Five more lashes, just five more," Hawkins pleaded. "Five more and I'll buy you two breakfasts."

Gamrick's breath changed to short gasps. He had read about S&M, had seen pictures in various magazines of couples engaged in it, and had even seen color videos of it at stag parties. But this was his first real encounter with it, and it disgusted him.

"Whatever you see in there remains with you," Gamrick said.

"Aye, aye, sir."

"Now break the door down."

Gorga took a dozen steps backward, stopped, and an instant later rushed the door, throwing his shoulder against it. The lock gave, the chain snapped, and the door burst open.

Gamrick rushed in.

Hawkins and the woman were naked.

Hawkins was prone on the floor, holding onto the legs of a chair. His back was crisscrossed with red welts, some of them oozing blood.

The woman had her arm raised. She screamed and dropped the belt.

"Gag her," Gamrick ordered.

Gorga threw one arm around the woman's waist and the other over her mouth.

Too surprised to move, Hawkins remained on the floor.

Gamrick looked at the woman, a skinny bleach

blonde with muddy brown eyes. "Get dressed and get out of here. This is Navy business." Then to Gorga he said, "Let her go."

"I want my money," the woman said.

"How much?" Gamrick asked.

"Fifty."

"Okay, fifty," Gamrick said, handing her two twenties and a ten. Then, looking down at Hawkins, "Get up and get dressed."

Hawkins remained motionless.

"Gorga, get him up," Gamrick snapped. "All right, now get yourself dressed, sailor."

"The woman—"

"I don't care how you fuck or what you do afterward," Gamrick said, looking at the bed.

"Sir—"

"Gorga, get the woman out," Gamrick ordered.

"Aye, aye, sir," the Marine answered.

Gamrick moved around the room. The mirror above the cigarette burn-scarred dresser was cracked. The carpet was filthy and full of burn holes. The walls were blotched with various kinds of stains. The bed sheet and pillowcase were gray. A single unshaded electric bulb was screwed into a dirt-encrusted ceiling fixture.

Hawkins was finally dressed.

"Check his gear for drugs," Gamrick said.

"Aye, aye, sir," Groga answered.

"He don't have to do that. I smoke some weed," Hawkins admitted. "I don't do the other stuff."

Gorga held a small plastic bag, opened it, and sniffed. "There's nothing else."

"Gunny, here's a fifty. Square the damage with the clerk," Gamrick said. "Then we'll go someplace where Hawkins and I can talk. We'll be at the jeep."

"Yes, sir," Gorga answered, saluting briskly.

Gamrick returned it.

Five minutes later, the three of them were tooling along on the state highway that ran parallel to the ocean. Gamrick told Gorga to go to Fort Story, inside the Seashore State Parks. In less than twenty minutes they reached the parking area behind the old fort.

"Follow us, Gunny," Gamrick said. "If Seaman First Class Hawkins makes a run for it, bring him down. Go for his legs."

"Yes, sir," Gorga snapped.

"Okay, sailor, let's walk," Gamrick said.

The three of them crossed the parking area, already spotted with a few cars even though it was the middle of the morning. Gamrick headed for the pathway closest to the water, and when they reached it, he said, "Start by telling me the real reason why you left your battle station."

"Sir, I wanted to protect the ship," Hawkins answered.

Gamrick stopped abruptly. "Bullshit, Hawkins. You left because you knew what was going to happen."

"Sir, they—"

Gamrick started to walk again. He was furious and having trouble controlling his temper. He wanted to grab hold of Hawkins and beat the truth out of him. "All right, start at the beginning. Tell me everything you know about the explosion in turret number two."

"Sir, they were Satanists."

"All of the men in the turret?"

"The men on gun number two, and Anderson and Downs were the worst."

"So you killed them," Gamrick said.

"No, sir."

"Tell me what you did."

"They tried to get me to join them, but I believe in Jesus Christ and He protected me. I slept with a cross in my hands."

Gamrick glanced back at Gorga, who made a circular motion with his finger at right side of his head.

"Sir, they sacrificed cats and rabbits and put the mark of the Devil all over the ship, especially in the bunk area."

"Why didn't you report this to your superiors?" Gamrick asked.

"Sir, some of the officers were Satanists too."

Gamrick stopped again, this time close to a rough-hewn wooden fence separating a beach area from the pathway and the beach vegetation. People were already on the beach enjoying the sun, and some were swimming. But there was an east wind and a slight haze off shore, which meant a change was in the offing. "Tell me about Anderson and Downs," Gamrick said.

"They were the worst. They were sodomites, abominations in the eyes of the Lord," Hawkins said, spitting the words out.

"Did you ever see them fuck?"

"The pictures—"

"You took them?"

"Yes, sir. I followed them."

"Why?"

"To give them to you, the instrument of God's wrath, the sword of His righteousness."

"For chrissake, you didn't even know I existed when you took those pictures," Gamrick flung back at him.

"Do not take the name of the Lord in vain," Hawkins intoned, glowing with fervor.

Gamrick was taken aback. Hawkins had switched their roles. But recovering quickly, he said, "Sailor, you address me as *sir,* understand?"

"Yes, sir."

"Why did you follow Anderson and Downs?" Gamrick asked.

"I prayed and God told me to provide His instrument of vengeance with proof of their abomination."

Gamrick rested his hands on the wooden crosspiece. Hawkins was sick, there wasn't any doubt about that. But was he sick enough to blow twenty-seven men away? "Did you know the woman in the photograph?" Gamrick asked, finding it difficult to look at Hawkins.

"No, sir."

Gamrick faced him. "How do you think the Lord responded to what you and that woman were doing?"

"The sins of the flesh were scourged from my soul," Hawkins said.

"What about the woman's soul?"

"She agreed to be scourged too," Hawkins answered.

Gamrick ran his hand over his chin and said, "Gunny, we'll go back to the base now."

"Yes, sir."

"Hawkins, we'll take you back to the ship. You are to say nothing about out conversation to anyone. Is that clear?"

"Yes, sir."

The three of them walked back to the jeep, and before they reached it, Hawkins asked, "Sir, am I confined to the ship?"

Gamrick was about to answer yes but stopped himself. He wasn't sure he had the authority to order him confined to the ship. "Not officially. But if I were you, I'd hold myself ready for more questioning."

"Yes, sir."

A short time later, Gorga pulled up at the entrance to the pier where the *Utah* was berthed.

Gamrick saw the telephone booth. It was just outside the gate. "You called me from there," he said, pointing at the booth.

"Yes, sir."

"Don't call me again," Gamrick said harshly, though he knew that by tomorrow Hawkins would probably be arrested and placed in the brig.

"No, sir. I won't," Hawkins said, climbing out of the jeep. He saluted Gamrick, who hesitated and unwillingly returned the courtesy.

"I'm in Norfolk," Gamrick said, speaking to Kate from a phone booth close to the heliport. "I want to see you. I'm on to something."

"Hint?"

"I'll spell it out when I see you," he said.

"I've come up with something too," she told him. With a quick laugh she added, "Two can play the same game."

"It's not a game," Gamrick answered. He was thinking more about his feelings concerning her than the gravity of what he had found.

"I didn't mean to make light of it," she said. "I could meet you—"

"I drove in," Gamrick told her, hoping she would suggest they meet at a place where they could have some degree of privacy—a place where he could take her in his arms and hold her.

For several moments neither of them spoke. Then Kate said, "Why don't you come here, to my place?"

Gamrick hesitated. He understood the unspoken invitation. He wanted to make love to her, but . . .

"Name the place and I'll be there," Kate said.

"There's an inn just this side of Gilbert's Corner, a few miles past Dulles Airport. I've passed it many times. It looks very pretty."

"You sure you didn't meet another woman there?" she teased.

"No, you're the first," he answered fervently.

"I believe you," Kate responded with equal passion.

"I should be there by fifteen-hundred," he said.

Kate repeated the time and added, "I'll be there. See you."

Gamrick clicked off. Minutes later he was aboard a helicopter on his way back to Washington. The flight was bumpy, and the pilot advised that a weather system was coming in.

It was more difficult to land than usual because of the strong cross winds, but the pilot managed to drop onto the pad after the third try.

Gamrick congratulated him and went directly to his Jeep, where he saw the metal box that Dimitri had dug up. Rather than leave it on the backseat any longer and risk the chance of forgetting it was there, he decided to bring up to his office and put it on his desk, where he'd see it the next morning as soon as he arrived.

The main office was deserted except for the OD. A Lieutenant Larson was now on duty.

"Anything interesting going on?" Gamrick asked, expecting the usual "nothing, sir." Weekend OD was a shit assignment even if it was rotated among three junior-grade officers.

"Several faxes came in for you and the admiral," Larson said. "They're on your desk."

Gamrick thanked him, went into his office, put the metal box on the side of the desk, and then picked up the faxes. The first, from the Virginia State Police, indicated that the body of a Hispanic male had been tentatively identified as Richard Cassado, the driver of the vehicle that had struck the cab.

The second fax came from the FBI. The fingerprints taken off the blue pickup that had followed him and those taken from the Dumpster and found on parts of the vehicle that had crashed into the main building at the Norfolk Naval Base matched those of Richard Cassado. It also gave Cassado's description and a list of prior convictions, most of which were connected to drug dealing.

The third fax was another from the Virginia State Police, and it simply said that the previous "but tentative" identification of the body as Richard Cassado had been "incorrect and further investigation would be need to make a positive identification."

Gamrick rubbed his chin. Richard Cassado—whoever he was and for whatever reason—had not only bird-dogged him but was also involved in several killings. And he might still be on the loose, and that was not a reassuring thought. It reminded him of the argument Folsim had made a few days before. *Too many accidents are being chalked up to coincidence* ... "Too damn many," he said aloud, putting the faxes down on the desk. But nothing in Cassado's rap sheet connected in any way to the military, or specifically to the Navy.

Gamrick arrived first and chose a booth in the tap room with a window view of the stream that eventually empties into the Potomac several miles away. The inn, a Georgian house, catered to overnight and weekend guests and provided excellent lunches and dinners for those individuals who had the leisure to appreciate authentic southern-style cooking and the money to pay for it.

The tap room was paneled with stained oak and illuminated only with candles on the table and oil lamps on the bar and an old-fashioned wheel chandelier suspended from the ceiling on thick ropes. The rough-cut floorboards were dusted with sawdust, and even the tables and chairs were made out of rough-cut wood.

Gamrick stared out of the rivulet-streaked window. It had started to rain while he had been driving. Then it had been no more than a shower. But in the last few minutes it had turned into a summer storm, complete with slashing streaks of lightning and tremendous rolls of thunder.

Gamrick tried to fit Cassado into a meaningful place and couldn't. Then Hawkins replaced Cassado, and he was sure Hawkins knew much more than he had already told him. Almost as quickly as Hawkins came into his thoughts, his grandson John became the center of his focus and increased his feeling of frustration, of impotence. And yet he was certain the boy was safe, though he knew that could be just wishful thinking on his part.

"A dime for your thoughts," Kate said.

Gamrick faced her and quickly stood.

"You looked so serious. I didn't have the heart to offer you the usual penny," she said.

Gamrick helped her off with her yellow nylon raincoat. She was dressed in a knee-length denim skirt and a white blouse open far enough down to expose the tops of her breasts.

"Put the coat there," she said, pointing to the bench opposite the one he had sat on. "I'll sit next to you."

He stepped aside to let her slide close to the window.

"Difficult driving," she commented, and as she looked around, she added, "Well, well, well!"

Gamrick chuckled and asked, "Does all that mean something?"

"It's charming," she answered.

"And the food is good too," he said with a straight face.

They looked at each other for a moment and began to laugh.

The waiter, a gray-headed black man with a soft voice, came to the booth and asked for their bar order.

"What are your drinking?" Kate asked.

"Bass ale."

"I'll have the same," she said.

"Bring a pitcher and some of the appetizers that are the specialties of the house," Gamrick told the waiter.

"My choice, sir?"

Gamrick nodded, and as soon as they were alone, Kate said, "You really did look deep in thought when I came in."

Gamrick admitted he had been.

"Before we exchange information, tell me if you have any word about your grandson," she said.

He shook his head. "Nothing."

"His picture will be on the tube starting tomorrow night," she told him.

"Thanks, and thank Bly. No, I'll do that myself," he answered, suddenly intensely aware of her. She was sitting so close to him, he could feel the softness of her thigh against his and the scent of her perfume.

"I'm glad you called me." Kate said.

"Glad professionally or—"

"I don't want to spell it out."

Gamrick nodded, but he would have enjoyed hearing she was there because of her feelings for him.

"Tell me what you found out," she said.

"Ah, you tell me, then I'll tell you."

"I'll flip you for it," Kate said, already digging in her bag for a coin.

Gamrick dug into his pocket and produced a quarter before she found her change purse. "Call," he said, flipping the coin in the air, catching it, and turning it over.

"Tails."

"Tails. You win," he said, smiling just as the waiter approached the table with a pitcher of ale and two iced glasses.

"I'll bring those appetizers out in a couple of minutes," the waiter said as he poured the ale. "Got shrimp, chicken and bits of chicken and some hot corn bread."

"Sounds wonderful," Kate commented.

"Be back soon," the waiter told them.

Gamrick raised his glass. He was about to toast their relationship, but she said, touching his glass with hers, "To the safe return of your grandson."

"To his safe return," Gamrick managed to say despite the sudden lump in his throat. She was a very special lady, a very special human being.

The waiter returned with appetizers, the sauces that went with them, a small loaf of hot corn bread, and a scoop of rich yellow butter for the bread.

"I haven't had lunch yet, and I didn't have much of a breakfast," Gamrick said.

"Well, this should get you started," the waiter said, smiling. "After this, you can really begin to eat."

Gamrick cut two slices of bread from the loaf while Kate put several pieces of each appetizer on a plate for him and then for herself.

"This morning I made the connection between Seaman First Class Donald Hawkins and several strange phone calls I had received," Gamrick began.

Kate nodded and commented, "Everything is delicious."

Gamrick said, "I had the admiral's OD trace the origin of the calls. One was made from a telephone booth just outside of the gate where the *Utah* is berthed, and the other came from a motel. I called the motel and a woman answered. I asked her to put Hawkins on the phone. She did.":

"Then you decided to pay Hawkins a visit," Kate said as she lifted the glass of ale to her lips.

Gamrick nodded and described what he and Gorga had found.

"That's sick," she commented, squirming. "Sick."

"Not to him," Gamrick said and related everything that Hawkins had told him.

"Do you think he was responsible for the explosion?" she asked.

Gamrick took a long drink of ale before he said, "Given his psychological state, I would say yes. But I'm not an expert. My considered opinion is that he knows much more about it than he has already told me."

"You don't really look like 'the instrument of God's vengeance,' " Kate said. "No, you look very much like a normal man to me."

"Normal in all ways," he said, looking straight at her. He sensed that the conversation could now easily veer in another direction.

"Yes, I know that," she responded, her voice low and throaty.

"Your turn," Gamrick said, putting his hand over hers.

"Some of the powder used to fire the shells was incorrectly stored."

Gamrick's brow furrowed. This was news to him. He removed his hand from hers. "I don't understand. That powder—"

"The story will be on the six o'clock news. It's a special."

"Kate, you're not just reporting a story. You're reaching out to the families, the wives and sweethearts of the men who were killed."

"The powder dates back to World War Two. It was stored on barges, and it was not properly ventilated. The temperatures went above those that are recommended by the Navy for the safe storage of the powder, and because of it the powder could have undergone changes that would have made it very unstable—susceptible to exploding prematurely under the right conditions." After a pause she added, "That's practically verbatim from Navy documents."

"Jesus!" Gamrick exclaimed.

"You could add Mary and Joseph to that because it could make the Navy culpable for the deaths of twenty-seven of its men, and not Anderson," Kate said.

"Where does the information come from?" Gamrick asked.

"The Navy's laboratories in Sandia. We're going to show several pages of the report on the tube."

Gamrick refilled his mug with ale. "Was all the powder aboard the ship bad or just some of it?"

Kate shook her head. "I don't know," she admitted.

"Could you find out?"

"I'll try." Then she said, "At least it's no longer an open-and-shut case. Even your boss can't claim that anymore."

"I wouldn't even try to guess what the admiral might do. Remember, there's pressure on him too—a lot more than we realize," Gamrick answered, becoming intensely aware of her again.

For a few moments neither of them spoke. Then Kate whispered, "What do you want from me, Clark?"

Gamrick's heart began to race. He took a deep breath before he said, "I want a loving relationship, a woman I can fully love and who can fully return my love."

"That's blunt enough," Kate responded.

"Too blunt for you?" Gamrick questioned.

Kate shook her head.

"This is an inn. There are rooms upstairs," he said.

Kate looked at the rain-splattered window. "It's not the way I thought it would happen." She faced him. "Talking about the murder of so many men and who's responsible for it one moment and the next being asked to make love."

Gamrick shrugged. " 'It's a world I never made,' " he quoted.

"I'm sure it would be a better place if you had," she said.

"It's lovely," Kate commented, facing Gamrick after looking around the room. It was on the second floor in a corner. It had two windows: one looked down on practically the same bit of landscape seen from the window in the tap room, while the second overlooked a lovely garden at the rear of the house. The furnishings mirrored the Georgian period, complete with a canopy bed and a brick fireplace built into one of the walls.

"You're lovely," Gamrick said, taking her in his arms and passionately kissing her on the lips.

She circled his neck with her arms. Placing one hand on the back of his head, she opened her mouth and gave him her tongue.

Gamrick gently squeezed one breast, then the other. He opened her blouse and kissed the top of each warm breast.

Kate unbottoned his shirt and pulled it out of his pants.

"Can you manage to unzip the skirt?" she asked.

"You better do it," Gamrick answered.

They stepped away from each other and quickly undressed.

Gamrick reached out and, drawing her close, pressed her naked body hard against his. "You're even more beautiful than I had imagined," he whispered.

She smiled, "Ah, so you imagined."

"Didn't you imagine me?"

"Yes, I imagined you," she answered, fondling his erect penis.

He kissed her again, and this time his hands moved all over her body, from her breasts to the wonderfully full convexity of her buttocks and finally to her warm, moist vaginal crevice.

She responded, opening her thighs for him and sliding the tips of her fingers over his scrotum.

Gamrick looked over at the bed. "We'd be more comfortable there," he said.

Together, he on one side and she on the other, they pulled back the bedspread and the summer comforter that was under it. He laughed and, gesturing toward the bed, said, "You first."

She nodded, climbed onto the bed and stretching out, she lifted her arms toward him.

Supporting his weight on his hands, Gamrick came down on top of her. "Your skin is red."

"The sex flush," she answered, fondling him again.

He kissed her again on the lips, then on the side of her neck, each nipple, the hollow of her stomach, and finally the lips of her vagina.

She began to moan and thrust toward his mouth. "I want to . . ."

"Do whatever you want," he said, stopping for a moment.

Kate moved around and circled his penis with her lips.

Gamrick gasped and used his tongue on her. The pleasure she gave him was intense. He moved his hands over her breasts, along the valley between the buttocks. He couldn't seem to hold enough of her, or feel enough of her.

Almost as if they had discussed it and had reached the decision, they moved away from each other, and she splayed her naked thighs for him to come between them and enter her.

He entered her gently.

Kate closed her eyes and gently fondled him. "It's good to have you inside me, Clark," she whispered.

He kissed her and said, "I have your scent all over me."

She smiled up at him.

"You taste good."

"You do too," she answered, answering his movements with her own.

Gamrick kissed her breasts, lingering to suck on each nipple for a few moments.

Kate arched toward him.

He quickened his movements.

"Yes," she whispered, her eyes closed. "Oh, yes!"

Gamrick closed his eyes too. He felt her hand under him, gently urging him, gently culling from him the fluid that would soon gush into her.

"Oh, Clark, Clark," Kate moaned.

He thrust harder.

Her hands were on his buttocks, pulling him into her.

He could feel her body tense under his, and for several moments she seemed to become as taut as a bow pulled to its limit. Then it snapped, imploded, and she loosed a wordless scream of delight. She shook. Her naked thighs locked around his back, while her fingers clawed it.

Momentarily conscious only of Kate's orgasmic frenzy, Gamrick felt the hot surge of his own passion course through him and burst free in an exquisite explosion of such intense pleasure that he felt himself passing through huge rivers of color and responded with an animal growl of elemental satisfaction.

Neither one moved.

Gamrick reveled in the softness of her body under his. Opening his eyes to look at her, he found her looking at him. He caressed the side of her face, then her hair and whispered, "I could easily fall in love with a woman like you."

She put her fingertips against his lips. "I *have* fallen in love with you," she said.

Gamrick rested his head on one of her breasts and gently held the other. He was experienced enough to know they were saying things engendered by the moment. But he also knew such moments were often the beginning of long and intense relationships. He fervently hoped this moment would be one of those special ones.

The rain had stopped before Gamrick and Kate left the inn, and he drove home slowly savoring memory of the hours he had spent with her, remembering the intimate spaces of her body as though each had been there for his pleasure. So intense was his preoccupation that he arrived home without really knowing how he had gotten there. The house loomed up in front of him, a darker mass against a star-studded night.

Gamrick checked the digital clock on the Jeep's control panel. It read 10:15:04. That Iris was asleep did not surprise him. She probably had watched TV for a while, had a few drinks, and then gone to bed. Her usual night. Punching the security code, he disarmed the house alarm, and as he started to go inside, he looked over his right shoulder toward the road and stopped. Where the path into the woods began, there was the barest glimmer of light . . . a flashlight. He shook his head. Phosphorescence, the ordinary garden variety that came from decaying matter or from certain kinds of fungi. Satisfied with this explanation, Gamrick opened the door and was greeted by Dimitri, who quickly indicated he had to go out.

"Okay, Dimi, your need is more important than mind," he said, running his hand over the dog's head. "But it has to be a quick one. No playing around. Understand?"

Gamrick reached for the flashlight that was always kept on a small table just inside the doorway when he suddenly remembered Cassado. "Better be safe than sorry, boy," he told Dimitri as he went into the den and got the 9mm Wayne had bought him. Gamrick chambered a round and said, "Now we can go." On the way out he picked up the flashlight.

Dimitri dashed ahead and found his favorite tree. He sniffed at several others and suddenly stopped. His ears went up and his tail curled. He was rigid.

Gamrick knew that stance—Dimitri was on full alert.

"Easy, boy," Gamrick said, reaching down to stroke the dog.

Dimitri uttered a low, angry growl. His ears were back now.

"Okay, Dim, it's just another squirrel or some other animal," he said softly.

The next instant Dimitri bolted toward the path leading into the woods.

Gamrick went after him. The growth alongside the path was still wet from the rain.

Suddenly a man shouted, "Get this fucking dog off me!"

Gamrick pushed the flashlight into his back pocket and, running into the woods, held the 9mm ready.

Dimitri began to howl.

"I'm getting the fuck out of here," a second man shouted.

Gamrick found Dimitri on the ground. He put the flashlight on, bent over him, and ran a hand over the animal's quivering body. The dog's flanks were wet with blood. He'd been slashed with a knife. "Easy, boy," Gamrick said and moved his hand over the animal's hind legs—they weren't injured. He tested the two front legs. Both had been smashed. "Goddamn son of a bitch!" Gamrick yelled.

Suddenly Dimitri stirred and, growling, tried to stand.

Gamrick dropped the flashlight and looked behind him just in time to see a man coming at him. He raised the 9mm, and with a quick squeeze of the trigger he

pulled off a round. The shot shattered the night still-
ness.

The man seemed to leap up and then fell backward.
Even as he fell, Gamrick squeezed off another
round.

The man crashed against a scrub pine.

Gamrick stood up and put the beam from the flashlight on the man. He recognized him. He was the short,
chunkily built officer he had seen at Cool's funeral—
the one who had looked uncomfortable in his uniform.
He held a trench knife in his left hand. Blood poured
out of a hole in his chest. He was dead.

Gamrick moved the beam from the man to Dimitri.
The dog had been slashed in several places. He too had
died. Gamrick bent down and caressed Dimitri's head.
He fought back the sob in his throat. Cradling the dog
in his arms, Gamrick started back to the house. Before
he reached the front door, Iris ran out.

"Thank God you're all right," she shouted. "The police are on their way."

"They killed Dimitri," he said tightly. "The fucking
bastards killed my dog!" Then, still holding Dimitri's
limp body, Gamrick sat on the steps in front of the
door and waited for the police to come.

Officers Lance and Richie came back to the house.
"No sign of the dead man," Richie said. "But there's
blood all over the place, and we found the knife. We'll
get a good set of prints off it."

"Are you sure the man was dead?" Lance asked.

Gamrick nodded. "I hit him twice. There wasn't
anything left of his chest." He was sitting on the step,
still holding Dimitri's body.

"That dog saved your life," Lance said.

Gamrick quietly said, "He gave the last full measure
of devotion."

"Do you want us to take him, Captain?" Richie
asked.

Gamrick let out a deep sigh. "No, I'll bury him my-self. He deserves that from me."

"Are you sure you didn't see a vehicle on the road after you came back to the house?" Richie asked.

"One didn't even go by," Iris responded. "I was out here with him all the time."

"Can you think of any reason why someone would be in the woods?" Lance asked.

Gamrick looked up at him. He was about to shake his head when he remembered the metal box Dimitri had dug up. He told the officers about it.

"You never mentioned it to me," Iris said.

Gamrick shrugged but didn't offer an excuse.

"Where is the box now?" Richie asked.

"My office. I was going to have out electronic's peo-ple go over it."

"Let us know what they find," Richie said. He then told them that investigators from the Galesville police department and from the state police would be there in the morning to make a further examination of the area.

"Any time," Gamrick answered.

"Captain, I hope you don't mind me saying this, but someone has you tagged," Richie said.

"I can handle it," Gamrick answered, more curtly than he had intended. But he did not want anything said that would alarm Iris any more than she already was. She was having difficulty enough coping with John being missing. She didn't need something else to worry about.

"Yes, sir," Richie answered.

"Iris, will you please get me a shovel?" Gamrick asked.

"You're not going to bury Dimitri now, are you? It's almost midnight."

Still holding Dimitri, Gamrick stood up. "The shovel, Iris," he said.

"We'll be in touch," Richie told him.

"I'm sorry I can't shake your hand. But thanks for coming out here," Gamrick said.

Richie touched the peak of his cap with his finger. "Good night, Mrs. Gamrick," he called, and motioning to Lance, he walked toward the patrol car.

While Iris watched, Gamrick buried Dimitri at the back of the house, under his favorite tree overlooking the cove. When he was finished, he went back into the house and into the kitchen, where he poured himself a double vodka and one for Iris.

"Aren't you going to say something?" she asked.

"There's nothing to say," Gamrick answered. "I lost a good buddy." He finished his drink, poured another, drank it in two long swallows, and said, "I'm going up to shower." He looked down at his shirt and pants. They were stained with Dimitri's blood. "I killed the motherfucker," he said. "I know I did, and if I ever find the other son of bitch, I'm going to kill him too."

"Clark—"

With a furious gesture he dismissed whatever she was going to say, hurried out of the kitchen, and up the steps to their bedroom and into the bathroom. There, he closed the door, turned on the shower, and sitting down on the side of the tub, he wept for Dimitri, for John, and for himself for having to weep . . .

Chapter 13

Folsim was already in the office when Gamrick arrived, and greeted him with "My God, Skipper, what the hell happened to you?"

Going behind his desk, Gamrick said, "Dimitri was killed last night by intruders."

Folsim gave him a quizzical look.

"My dog. I shot one of them, but the cops couldn't find the body."

"You're joking."

Gamrick shook his head. "I'm not joking," he said.

Folsim sat on the edge of the desk. "You killed one of them?"

Gamrick picked up the three faxes he had already read, handed them to Folsim, and said, "Here's something to make your morning too, and—"

His phone rang.

"Captain Gamrick here," he answered.

"Thank God you're all right," Kate said. "The night desk man at the station called last night and told me about the shooting. I wanted to phone you at home, but—"

"Yes, I understand," Gamrick said.

"Someone is close by?" she asked.

"You might say that," he answered.

"Can we meet for cocktails?"

"Yes."

"The Sea Sands?"

"That will be fine."

"Four."

"Yes."

"I love these short, staccato conversations." Kate laughed.

"So do I," Gamrick answered and put the phone down. He felt much better for having heard her voice, the soft lilt of her laughter, and for knowing she was concerned about him. It was hard for him not to think about her in that special way that a man thinks about a woman after he has made love to her and wants to make love to her again. . . .

"There must be a link somewhere between this Cassado guy and our investigation," Folsim said, putting the faxes on the desk.

"I recognized the guy I shot."

"Who the hell was he?"

"I don't his name, but I saw him at Cool's funeral. He was there with another man. Both were officers."

Folsim launched himself off the desk just as the phone rang again.

Gamrick answered it.

"Captain, this is Lieutenant Horace Cranshaw, Virginia State Police."

"Lieutenant, Commander Folsim will also be on the line," Gamrick said, motioning to Folsim to pick up the phone on his desk. "Okay, Lieutenant, please continue."

"We located the vehicle and the body of a man some ten miles west of your place," Cranshaw said. "The vehicle and the body had been set on fire. But we managed to get a thumb and forefinger of the dead man's right hand, and because we had recent faxes of a man named Richard Cassado, we were able to match his prints to those of the dead man and those on the knife that the Galesville police turned over to us. This time there is no doubt that you shot and killed Richard Cassado."

Gamrick sucked in his breath and slowly let it out before he asked, "Have your men gone over the ground around my house?"

"They're on their way out there," he said. "And we recovered a Navy radio-telephone signal device."

Gamrick glanced at the box on his desk. "Would you please describe it, Lieutenant?"

"About ten inches long and four wide. Inside there are various electronic modules. One of my men said that it can pick up incoming and outgoing calls from a distance up to five hundred feet and transmit them to a receiver up to ten miles away."

"I have one on my desk that my dog had dug up," Gamrick said. "I didn't know what it was."

"Cassado and another man, or other men, were probably attempting to bury another one when you interrupted—"

"My dog did the interrupting," Gamrick said, feeling a knot in his throat and immediately clearing it.

"We're going to need a written statement from you describing the entire incident. There will be an inquest, but it will be only a formality."

"How soon do you need my statement?" Gamrick asked.

"Two, three days from now will be fine," Cranshaw said. "There is no doubt in our judgment that Cassado was driving the truck at the time it struck the cab and that he was the man who followed you in the blue pickup truck."

"I don't have any doubt about that either," Gamrick answered.

"Because he was a former Navy electronics specialist, we also suspect that he might have been involved in the car bombing of the main building at the Norfolk Navy Base."

"Lieutenant, do you have his service number?" Folsim asked, entering the conversation for the first time.

"Sure do ... 6016649," he said, repeating the number. "He got a BCD for drug dealing. Spent three years in the Portsmouth Navy Prison."

"Not one of our best," Gamrick commented.

"What we can't figure out, Captain, is why he was on your tail," Crenshaw said.

Gamrick shrugged. He wasn't going to tell him that Hawkins had said the men aboard the *Utah* were using drugs, especially the men in turret number two. That was strictly Navy business, and the Navy would handle it in its own way.

"Our best guess is that Cassado and the other men who were with him are in some way tied to your board of inquiry," Crenshaw continued.

"If they are, we don't know about it," Gamrick answered. "But if we do happen find any link, I will ask permission to release the information to you, Lieutenant."

"That would be much appreciated."

"Thank you for the information you have given us," Gamrick said.

They said good-bye, and as soon as Crenshaw clicked off, Folsim let loose with a rebel yell. "Now, that's what I call having the pieces fall into place," he said, leaving his desk and planting himself on the edge of Gamrick's. "We got lucky this morning."

"Luckier than you think," Gamrick answered and quickly outlined what Hawkins had told him.

Folsim bolted off the desk and began to pace. Suddenly he stopped. "We have only Hawkins' word that he had permission to leave the turret."

"Right."

"Anderson had permission, and we have a record of it."

"Right again."

"Then we might have made a terrible mistake," Folsim said.

"Now, that seems like a very real possibility," Gamrick answered.

"Do you think that Hawkins is tied to Cassado?"

Gamrick ran his hand over his chin. "I don't know. He said the men were using drugs, and we found marijuana on him at the motel."

"Not conclusive but nonetheless interesting," Folsim commented, mimicking an English accent.

The phone rang. Gamrick picked it up and said, "Captain Gamrick here."

"Captain, the admiral asks that you report to his office immediately," Martins said.

"That 'immediately' sounds ominous," Gamrick responded.

"It might be. He's in a fury over something."

"I'm on my way," Gamrick said.

"What's happening?" Folsim questioned, following him halfway to the door.

Gamrick shrugged, paused, and facing Folsim, he said, "The admiral seems to be creating big waves, or is about to."

Folsim looked bewildered.

"Don't worry. I've been in heavy weather before," Gamrick said and left the office.

Russo was standing in front of his desk, waiting for him. They exchanged salutes. Then Russo said, "The Secretary of the Navy called me last night and demanded to know—and I am quoting him now—'how that damn TV woman obtained her information when I haven't even seen those test reports yet?' "

"Sir?" Gamrick questioned, and though Kate was the person referred to, he was not going to compromise her or his relationship with her by giving any indication he knew what the admiral was talking about.

Russo glared at him. "Did you watch the six o'clock or the eleven o'clock news?"

"No, sir. At six I was out, and at eleven—"

"Well, where the hell were you at eleven o'clock at night?" Russo questioned.

Gamrick took a deep breath, exhaled, and said, "That was just about the time I killed Richard Cassado, sir."

Russo did a double-take, pointed at the chair in front of the desk, and after telling Gamrick to sit, he went to

his own chair. "I read the three faxes that came in over
the weekend. Now, will you tell me how you found,
killed, and identified Cassado?"

"He found me. I killed him and the Virginia State
Police made a positive identification of the body."

While Russo did his ritual finger-drumming on the
desk, Gamrick told him what had happened at the
house on Sunday night.

"You're a lucky man to have had such a dog," Russo
said.

"Yes, sir, I am," Gamrick answered.

For a moment neither of them spoke. Then Gamrick
said, "Sir, there's a good possibility that Anderson is
innocent." And before Russo could answer, Gamrick
told him how he had identified Hawkins' voice as the
one of the "wrath of God" caller on the telephone and
the results of the interrogation that followed.

"Sunday was hardly a day of rest for you, was it,
Captain?" Russo said with an edge in voice and his
face very red.

"Sir, Hawkins—"

"I don't give a fiddler's fuck about Hawkins," Russo
answered. "I began by asking you a question to which
I got a strange but acceptable answer. Then you tell me
another strange and totally unacceptable story."

"Unacceptable—?"

"Unacceptable because you were acting without authorization, Captain. The investigation was over and
you knew it was over."

"Sir, with all due respect, there are loose ends—
there still are loose ends."

"Not for the Navy there aren't. We have our man.
We have his motive, and by the living God, we are going to have a court-martial. The investigation is over,
absolutely over. Do I make myself clear, Captain
Gamrick?"

Exerting tremendous self-discipline, Gamrick remained silent.

"Just how far did you bend the rules, Captain?" Russo questioned.

Tight-voiced, Gamrick responded, "I requisitioned a chopper, a jeep, and a Marine."

"Using authority that you no longer possessed?"

"Yes, sir."

"I intend to investigate this matter as—"

"Sir, again with all due respect to your rank and your years of dedicated service, you do not see the proverbial forest for the trees, and threatening me will not stop the truth—"

"Silence," Russo roared, slamming his hand down on the desk. "Keep absolutely silent, Captain. That's an order."

The two men glared at each other.

"Dismissed!" Russo rasped.

Gamrick stood up. For the first time in his thirty years of service, he disobeyed an order and did not move.

Russo looked up at him.

"If you won't get to the truth, I will," Gamrick said, and without either saluting or waiting for Russo to respond, he did a precise about-face and walked out of the office.

In a fury, Gamrick stopped at Martins' desk and said, "I'll be out for a while."

She studied him for a moment. "That bad?"

He nodded. "That bad and worse."

"Do you want to leave a number?"

"No . . . And thank God, I don't have a beeper," he said.

She nodded and whispered. "He soon gets over his tantrums."

Gamrick shrugged. "I don't give a damn if he does or doesn't," he answered, adding, "See you."

"See you," she echoed.

Gamrick left the office, went directly to his Jeep,

and drove to a park alongside the Potomac, where he parked and began to walk.

The sky was cloudless and the temperature and humidity comfortable. A slight onshore breeze made it even more pleasant.

That he had had a confrontation with Russo was almost a source of satisfaction, though he had never been insubordinate before. But he wasn't fighting for himself, he was fighting for another man's life—fighting for justice, which, in his opinion, was what he and the admiral were supposed to be doing. There wasn't any way for him to mend the relationship between himself and Russo. And, more to the point, he really didn't want to.

"The man is wrong," Gamrick said out loud, leaning on a railing and speaking to the river. "He knows it and he knows I know it."

A large yawl came into view. Under power and with only her mizzen set, she was heading downstream toward Chesapeake Bay. Watching her somehow brought Gamrick's whole life into focus, and he found it less than meaningful. More so now that he faced the reality of never getting his two stars, let alone of going beyond to the top position, the Chief of Naval Operations. Just as Russo had pulled strings to get him a new command, he would pull the same strings to deny him the opportunity. He would be forced to retire in grade; his naval career was over.

Gamrick grabbed hold of the railing, and rocking back and forth, he told himself that he wasn't going to let Russo roll over him. "I'm not going to move out of his way. I'm going to fight the bastard. I'm going to fight him. . . ."

Suddenly Gamrick knew exactly what he was going to do. It might mean that he would have to resign from the Navy, but under the circumstances that would have happened sooner than later. He returned to his car and drove straight to the Navy prison where Anderson was being held.

* * *

The interrogation room was small—furnished with a table, two chairs, and an unshielded electric bulb in a metal fixture that hung down from the ceiling on a length of chain.

Anderson did not look pleased to see him.

"Sit," Gamrick said.

Anderson obeyed. The young man was paler and thinner than he had been just a few days before.

"Tell me about the time you, Downs, and the woman were on the beach," Gamrick said, sitting down.

Anderson flushed. "How do you know about that?" he asked.

"I have photographs."

"Of Julie too?" Anderson asked. Before Gamrick could answer, he said, "It ain't right for you to look at her naked body."

Surprised by the answer, Gamrick covered it by changing the subject, and asked, "How are you being treated?"

Anderson nodded. "Good. I am finding my way back to God again with the help of the chaplain."

Gamrick said, "That will help you answer all of my questions truthfully."

"Yes . . . but tell me how you got photographs of us. We didn't have a camera. Where did you get them? Are you trying to trick me?" He stood up and leaned so close to Gamrick that the Marine guard started toward them.

"It's all right," Gamrick assured the Marine. "Everything is under control."

"Yes, sir," the Marine snapped.

"Sit, Paul, and tell me where and when those pictures were taken," Gamrick quietly demanded, though he already knew.

"Early this summer, at the nude beach in North Truro on Cape Cod. The three of us went up there for a few days. Gus's father had a house up there."

"Donald Hawkins took those pictures and sent them to me," Gamrick said.

"Of Julie too?"

"Yes," Gamrick answered. "Now, listen to me. For reasons I can't talk about now, I have a reasonable doubt that you are guilty."

Anderson asked, "Donald and you saw Julie naked?"

"That doesn't matter," Gamrick told him.

"Other men—"

"Anderson, it doesn't matter," Gamrick said, trying hard not to lose his patience. In a softer tone he said, "I don't think you're guilty."

"What does that mean to me?"

"It means I want to defend you," Gamrick said.

Anderson left the chair and began to pace, stopped, and looked questioningly at Gamrick.

"I want to be appointed as your defense counsel," Gamrick said.

"But you're not a lawyer."

"I am a lawyer."

"You're a submariner."

"And I'm a qualified lawyer. I can defend you. All you have to do is request me for your defense counsel. That's the first step," Gamrick said, knowing that regulations would prevent it from happening. But he was gambling on being able to go around the regulations.

"You put me here," Anderson said, sitting down again.

"Hell, Paul, I'm the only one you can trust. The Navy has punched out a one-way ticket for you."

"Will you give me some time to think about it?"

"Think about it, but don't take too long. I really want to help you," Gamrick said.

"You believe me?"

Gamrick hesitated. Anderson had had a legitimate reason to be out of the turret. He'd signed into a sick bay. And there wasn't any way he could have had a hand in any of the events since his arrest. The Navy needed a scapegoat and Anderson was it.

"Yes, I believe you," Gamrick said.

For several moments the two of the men were silent. Then Anderson said, "I can be executed, can't I?"

"You won't be," Gamrick said.

"But I can be?"

"Yes," Gamrick said in a low voice. "You can be."

Anderson stood up, walked to a corner of the room, stood there for several seconds, and came back to the table. "I'll ask for you, Captain Gamrick," he said.

"Good." Gamrick stood up and shook Anderson's hand. "We'll beat them. You'll be a free man."

"I'm counting on it, sir," Anderson said.

When Gamrick returned to his office, he found messages from Iris, Hal, and Kate. He wanted to call Kate first, but instead punched out his home phone number.

After four rings, Iris answered and asked him how he was feeling.

"I'm okay," he said, picking up a pen to doodle.

"Really?"

"Good enough to run the four-minute mile," he answered.

"Jeff phoned and wanted to know if there was anything he could do to help Hal," she said. "I told him there was nothing. But that Hal needed all the support he could get and to stay in touch with him. He said he would do it."

"That's about all any of us could do now," Gamrick answered. "I hope you didn't say anything about last night. He doesn't have to worry about me when he goes up in one of those flying blowtorches."

"Not a word."

"Good," he said, quickly adding, "I won't be home for dinner."

"Again?" she asked.

"I have work to do here," Gamrick answered, very much aware of the disappointment in her voice. He did not want to tell her what had happened between him and Russo—she had enough to worry about—but he also wanted to be with Kate for a few hours if it was possible.

"The Johnsons on the other side of the cove invited us over for dinner," she said.

"Sorry, but I really can't cut away," Gamrick lied.

"Try not to come home too late," Iris said before hanging up.

Gamrick clicked off and punched out Hal's number, who instantly recognized his voice.

"Any word from John?" Gamrick asked, beginning to doodle.

"None."

Gamrick tried to think of something supportive to say that wouldn't sound like a chiché, but he couldn't. Instead he asked, "How is Donna holding up?"

"Doing the best she can," Hal said. "Jeff called. He hadn't heard about John until he got back from his training exercise. This time his ship was in the Antarctic Ocean."

"That's no place to land and take off from a carrier," Gamrick said, remembering the many times he had deployed down there. "Even if you are running hundreds of feet under the surface, it's still a very dangerous place."

Hal changed the subject. "I want to send a gift to Mr. Bly and—"

"No need to," Gamrick answered.

"John's picture has been on the tube several times over the last couple of days."

"I'll take care of it," Gamrick said.

"Are you sure?"

"Yes. I'll do it."

"Thanks, Dad," Hal replied. Then he said, "I'm sorry about the way I acted the other night."

"It's forgotten," Gamrick said.

"I really hurt Mom."

"I'm sure she's forgiven you," Gamrick said. "She's very worried and—"

"Dad, she sounded as if she had a couple too many when I spoke to her earlier."

Gamrick didn't answer.

"She needs help," Hal said.

"One problem at a time, Hal. None of us can handle any more than that," Gamrick said, aware that he'd made two small drawings: one of a naked woman, the other of a man in a cage.

"Speaking about problems, how's your investigation going?" Hal asked.

"Going," Gamrick replied.

"That's not exactly a precise answer."

"Wasn't meant to be," Gamrick said, running several lines through his doodles.

"Listen, Dad, I have a class in five minutes. I'll call you as soon as I hear something," Hal said.

"Send my love to everyone," Gamrick told him, and as soon as he clicked off, he punched out Kate's number. Her secretary told him that she was out on an assignment, and he left a message for Kate to call him back. As soon as he put the phone down, Martins called and told him to report to Russo.

"Fair or foul weather?" Gamrick asked.

"Deadly calm," she answered.

Gamrick thanked her, put the phone down, and heading for the door, he realized he was about to play hardball with a man who was used to winning. But Clark was used to winning too, by outthinking his opponent. And he had already thought ahead—thought about doing the unthinkable, at least as far as Russo would be concerned, and that gave Gamrick a much harder ball than Russo imagined he had.

Russo gestured toward the coffee table, and that, Gamrick instantly realized, meant that this discussion would be considerably less formal. There was even a

carafe of coffee there, two mugs, and a plate with assorted cookies on it.

They sat opposite each other, and Russo poured coffee for them before he said, "This morning—well, I'd
like to think that we're professional enough to forget it
happened, Clark."

"I have no problem with that," Gamrick said, tasting
the coffee. It was hot and a bit too strong for his liking,
but out of courtesy he would manage to drink one
mug.

"This situation—that is, the board of inquiry—has
everyone uptight, especially since the issue of homosexuality is involved," Russo said.

Gamrick nodded. "Anderson appears to be either bisexual or heterosexual."

Russo bit into a cookie topped with chocolate and
chewed on it. "The Navy wants to be done with this
entire matter," he said after swallowing the cookie and
taking a sip of coffee.

Gamrick nodded. "So would I."

"Anderson—"

"Sir, even the Navy can't get a conviction on the evidence it has against him. Given Hawkins' statement
about the use of drugs—"

"As soon as he addressed the court, it will realize
that he is a very sick man," Russo said.

"Sir, Hawkins claims he had permission to leave the
turret, but we only have his word for it; whereas we
have a record of Anderson—"

"Yes, yes, I know that and I also know that one
could argue a tie between Cassado and the explosion
aboard the *Utah*. But the one man who stands to gain
the most from a material standpoint is still Anderson."

Gamrick nodded.

"The Navy sees that—"

"Sir, the issue of the bad powder can't be overlooked," Gamrick said. "More than one person had to
know it was aboard, had to shift enough of it where it
could do the most damage, and had to remove the red

X from at least three bags so they could be moved to gun number two in turret number two. If all that was done, it had to be done for a reason."

"I agree absolutely."

Gamrick looked at him questioningly. This was a one-eighty shift.

"The reason was two million dollars," Russo said, not even trying to conceal the note of triumph in his voice. Then he added, "You see, we really don't have any differences about this situation."

Gamrick put his mug on the coffee table, and in a low, precise tone he said, "The Navy wants to finish with this matter as soon as possible. It wants to avoid having to answer for still using powder from World War Two, and to do that it needs a scapegoat. Sir, Anderson deserves considerably better from us than he's getting, or is about to get."

Russo's brow furrowed. He stood up and went back to his desk.

Gamrick followed him.

Neither of them sat.

For several moments Russo stared out of the window behind the desk. then he faced Gamrick, and scrutinizing him, he said in a low, almost sad voice, "I've always prided myself on being a good judge of men, especially those assigned to work with me. But in your case, Captain, I was completely wrong."

Gamrick remained silent.

"I, of course, take full responsibility for my own mistakes. I thought you were a good team player—no, I really believed you were an excellent team player. Certainly until now your record shows that."

"Thank you, sir," Gamrick snapped out.

Russo's face became florid, and he glared at Gamrick. "But I overlooked something. I overlooked, or to be more accurate, I wasn't aware that you have a second and even a third calling that obviously makes you think that in this man's Navy you're something special, an officer with special—"

"Sir, my service record needs no apologies, and with all due respect, you do not have the right to criticize a particular aspect of my personal life."

"You interrogated Gunner's First Mate First Class Anderson this morning?"

"Yes, sir. I wanted to know more about those photographs of him, Downs, and the woman."

"Would you tell me why you wanted to know more about the photographs?"

"I wanted to know who the woman was. She will be critical to his defense."

"Defense?"

"Yes, sir. I asked Anderson to have me appointed his defense counsel."

"You did what?" Russo shouted.

The phone rang before Gamrick could respond.

"Admiral Russo here," he exploded into the phone and listened for several moments. Then he said, "Thank you, Captain," and put the phone down. "Seaman Third Class Hawkins was found floating not far from the *Utah* with a longshoreman's hook in the back of his skull."

Gamrick sucked in his breath and slowly let it out.

"Someone phoned the TV station and told them where to look for the body."

Gamrick said nothing. His prime witness had been murdered.

Russo squinted at him. "Any brilliant ideas, Captain?"

"None, sir."

Russo finally sat in the chair behind the desk and said, "There's no way on God's green earth that you will be permitted to defend Anderson."

"Sir, again with all due respect to you, I will—"

Russo leaped to his feet. "Are you threatening me, Captain?" he roared.

"Sir, you have the power—"

"No, Captain. This meeting is at an end. And off the

record, I will see to it that you never get another command again. Now get out of my office."

"I will take this entire matter public," Gamrick said with exaggerated calmness. "I will blow this fucking cover-up sky high."

"That is a threat, isn't it, Captain?"

Gamrick stood up. "And if that doesn't do it, I will resign and become Anderson's counsel." He too was on his feet now and even angrier than Russo. "The media would make the Navy look—"

"Blackmail, that what it is!" Russo shouted.

"No, sir, it is—"

"I don't give a flying fuck what you call it. To me it's blackmail."

Gamrick could feel the heat in his cheeks. He was sweating profusely. he had dice and they were still in the air.

"I'll make some phone calls and have the necessary orders cut," Russo said as if he was deflating. "It's against regulations, against the laws passed by Congress."

"I'm sure you can do it," Gamrick answered sharply. "It's a matter of how much you want to do it, sir."

"If I do it, I will do what I have to do to protect the Navy."

"And I will do what I have to do to protect a man's life," Gamrick answered, his eyes boring into Russo's.

"What if the strings won't be pulled because—"

"I will resign and defend him wearing civilian clothes. I will defend him in uniform or out of it," Gamrick said.

Russo uttered a deep sign and in a much softer tone said, "You had a chance to go to the top, and you threw it away for a man—not *even* a man! Would you at least tell me why?"

Gamrick rubbed his chin. He couldn't give a definite answer even to himself, let alone formulate one that Russo might understand.

"Clark, I really do want to understand," Russo said.

"Sir, the Navy has been my life for most of my life, but—"

"My God, man, you're throwing away everything for a nobody, for someone whose not worth a fraction of your own worth."

"He has a right to a fair trial," Gamrick answered in a low voice. "The Navy has already decided that he's guilty."

"Then, for the love of God, why are you willing to try to undo something that is already done? The case is open and shut."

"Because it would be worse for the Navy if after he was found guilty and perhaps executed, additional evidence came to light that proved him innocent."

"Don't tell me that you're trying to protect the Navy," Russo said, angry again.

"No. I can't make that claim," Gamrick answered evenly.

"Well, that's something."

"I am trying to get to the truth," Gamrick said.

"The 'truth' you're trying to get to, and for which you are willing to throw away thirty years of distinguished service, is already there. But for some perverse reason, or reasons, you refuse to acknowledge its presence."

Gamrick said, "We have an honest difference of opinion, sir."

"Is that all you have to say?" Russo bellowed.

"Yes, sir."

"Dismissed!" Russo growled.

"Yes, sir," Gamrick answered, saluting.

Russo did not return the courtesy.

Gamrick met Kate at the Sea Sands. She arrived a few minutes before him, and they stayed to have a drink before leaving and going to a cheap motel two miles down the road. He was thankful that she didn't ask questions about the previous night's incident, though she did say, "One of my staff people told me about what happened to Dimitri. I'm sorry. I know how much he meant to you."

"He was a good buddy," Gamrick answered.

On the way to the motel, neither of them spoke. But Gamrick hiked up her skirt and rested his hand against the inside of her bare thigh. He could smell her perfume, a subtle rose scent mixing with something else he couldn't define. But it conjured images of her naked body melding with his.

The motel room was a box with yellow walls, a door, and a window with a black pull-down shade. A shower curtain separated the bathroom from the rest of the room. But they were alone and it had a bed.

This time they stripped as soon as they were in the room, and as soon as they were naked, Gamrick eased Kate down onto the bed, kissing each of her bare breasts, then, in turn, he sucked each into his mouth.

"My, you're a hungry man," Kate chided.

"I want to love you."

"You are," she said, moving herself under him. "Come inside me. I need to feel you there."

Gamrick brought her to a quick, violent climax that heightened his own orgasmic pleasure moments later.

"I haven't come so quickly in years," Kate said, caressing the top of his head. "Maybe not since my college days."

Gamrick kissed her deeply on her mouth, finding her tongue with his. That he could want a woman so intensely was something he hadn't felt in years.

"You must have had some day," she commented when their mouths finally separated.

"Not one of my better ones," he said.

She put his hand on her breast.

"I am going to defend Anderson," Gamrick said, aware of her nipple against the palm of his hand. "But my star witness, the person who I thought—and still do think—is a more likely suspect than Anderson, has been found floating in the water with a longshoreman's hook in the back of his skull."

"Hawkins?"

"Hawkins," Gamrick answered.

"That's one hell of a ship!" she commented.

"It seems to be."

"But once you tell the court how deranged Hawkins was—"

"Attacking the credibility of a dead man will not do much for Anderson," Gamrick said.

"But just the fact that Hawkins was murdered should tell the court that someone was afraid of what he'd reveal."

"Anderson is on trial, not Hawkins."

"Whoever killed, or had Hawkins killed, knows—"

Gamrick shook his head. "Regardless of Hawkins' death, the case against Anderson is open and shut as far as the Navy is concerned."

Kate took hold of his free hand and kissed the back of it.

"There's more. When this is over, I'm going to turn in my papers."

"Resign?"

Gamrick nodded. "I had a discussion with Admiral Russo—"

"Discussion?" Kate questioned.

"It doesn't really matter what you call it. The upshot of it was that I no longer have a place in the Navy."

Kate gathered him into her arms and kissed him gently on his mouth. "You're quite a man," she said. "Quite a man!"

Gamrick laughed. "I was waiting for the opportune moment to say something similar to you."

"With a difference in gender, I hope?"

"A woman, a wonderful woman!" he exclaimed, kissing her breasts again.

"I know this is a strange time to bring this up, but I really don't know a thing about you," Kate said.

Gamrick drew away from her, and with mock dignity he said, "Ask me anything about myself, madam, and I will immediately answer those questions."

"What's wrong?" Kate asked.

In a poor imitation of a western drawl, he said, "Lady, come to think of it, I don't know a darn thing about you either. Ah don't even know where you hail from."

The two of them laughed, then Gamrick said, "The most important thing, the most interesting thing about me right now, is that you're here with me and I'm going to make love to you again."

"Really?"

"Really," Gamrick answered, and gently parting Kate's naked thighs he lowered his head between them and began kissing her gently . . . .

Virtually all of the lights in his house where on when Gamrick pulled into the driveway, and before he was out of the Jeep, the outside lights came on. The front door opened, and Iris called out, "I thought you'd never get home."

"I'm home," he answered, reaching into the back of the Jeep for his attaché case.

"People were all over the place most of the day, and the phone rang off the hook," Iris said when he reached the door and stepped inside the house.

Dutifully he kissed Iris's cheek, put the attaché case down in the hallway near the door, and walked into the kitchen. He missed Dimitri's always joyous greeting.

"How was your day?" Iris asked.

"Not the best I've ever had," he answered, taking a bottle of Molson ale out of the refrigerator. He did not want to tell her about his decision to defend Anderson and his discussion with Russo until a more opportune time. Now he was very tired, and she was somewhere between being overwrought and just this side of being pixilated.

Iris picked up a bottle of Stolichnaya and poured a generous amount into a glass over two ice cubes.

"I had to put up with all sorts of questions," she complained.

"I had a few myself to answer," Gamrick responded, drinking the ale directly from the bottle.

"That Kate Bannon had the night off, but her stand-in reported that another member of the *Utah*'s crew had been murdered."

Gamrick nodded and took another pull on the bottle.

"I wish you wouldn't drink that way. It's so common," Iris said.

"Sorry," Gamrick answered and poured the remaining ale into a glass.

"Two of the ship's crew said that they and some of the other men were beginning to believe that the ship was jinxed," Iris said.

"Sailors can be a superstitious lot. It comes from having to deal with—"

"Does this murder have anything to do with your investigation?" she asked after drinking most of the vodka in the glass.

"Yes. He—"

"You killed a man last night, didn't you?" she asked.

Gamrick nodded and wondered—even though she'd called the police—just how much she remembered about what had happened. "It's over," Gamrick said, not sure whether, indeed, it was, or if by saying it, he could convince himself and her.

Iris trembled.

He wanted to go to her and put his arm around her, or better still, take her in his arms to comfort her. But he couldn't—not so soon after he'd been with Kate.

"The house isn't the same without Dimitri," she commented.

"He certainly made his presence felt."

She agreed and got up to pour herself another drink.

"Before you do that, you better listen to what I have to say," Gamrick told her. For him to have waited for the opportune time would have been just way of avoiding the issue, avoiding whatever would follow. This had to be the opportune time.

She stopped and looked at him. "Something about John. I knew it. I could feel it in my bones."

"I am going to defend Anderson," Gamrick said.

That stopped her; her hand that held the bottle hovered in the air for several moments. Then she put the bottle down and said, "Is that all?"

Gamrick shook his head and related what had happened between him and Russo.

By the time he finished, Iris was pacing back and forth.

"I'm sorry—"

"Oh, no, you're not," she snapped and stopped pacing. "Never once did you think about me, of my future. I too had my dreams, the dreams of being an admiral's wife. Do you know what that means?"

"Iris, I couldn't—"

"I asked you if you know what it meant to me. You didn't. You didn't really care about that. I had to kiss the ass of one admiral's wife after another even though I wasn't in the fucking Navy. But I was in it by association because I was married to you."

She finished pouring herself another drink. "It was my father's money gave us the things your salary couldn't have. It was that money that made you a millionaire in your own right."

"Is this really necessary?" Gamrick asked, standing.

"You stopped my acting career. I could have been someone on the stage."

"Iris—"

"Don't 'Iris' me," she said after taking a huge swallow. "Tell me, Captain, just what are you going to do when you have to earn a living like most men, who don't use the military to hide in?"

"We should have had this out years ago," Gamrick answered. "Then maybe we'd be happier." He started out of the kitchen.

"What the fuck is that supposed to mean?" Iris screamed, hurling the glass after him.

Suddenly the phone began to ring.

Gamrick reached it before Iris and said, "Captain Gamrick here."

"Back off, Captain, if you ever want to see your grandson alive," a muffled voice on the other end said, then clicked off.

Iris looked at him questioningly.

"Nothing. Just a reminder from the OD," Gamrick lied and continued up the steps.

His thoughts a-whirl, Gamrick remained awake. The threat against John unnerved him in a way that he'd never before experienced. He couldn't think about anything else. He knew that many people in and out of the Navy wanted Anderson dead. But there was an enormous distance between wanting one person to die and being willing to kill another to get what they wanted. Or were they just trying to frighten him off? Stop him from defending Anderson. If the caller had John, he would have said so. Gamrick pursed his lips. He had to go with his intuition, his gut feelings. The call was a bluff; John was still free.

Sleep finally came to Gamrick when he forced himself not to think about the upcoming trial, or even his now all too murky future and allowed his mind to fill with the memory of Kate's naked body against his. . . .

Chapter 14

Late the following morning Gamrick was ordered to report to Russo again. That the admiral had not returned his salute the previous afternoon still rankled him, though he remembered having done the same thing out of pique a few days before.

Russo pointed at the chair in front of his desk and said, "I'll be brief, Captain. I have discussed your particular situation with the CNO and the Secretary. Neither is inclined to accept your conditions."

"Then I will resign, and the matter will no longer be under their jurisdiction," Gamrick answered without hesitation.

"There is a compromise solution," Russo continued. "Unless, of course, you have developed such a hard-nosed attitude that—"

"Sir, spare me your comments," Gamrick said.

Russo flushed and said, "I'll remember to do that, Captain. The compromise is this: we appoint Anderson's defense counsel, and we appoint you his assistant."

Gamrick leaned forward and said, "Only if I have the complete authority and I am permitted to address the court on behalf of my client."

"The Navy will never—"

"Sir, the Navy has already agreed. You are trying to get the best deal you can. I understand that."

"And your best deal is?" Russo said, still flushed.

"You may appoint whoever you want, but he will

be a classic figurehead. I will have complete authority."

"The Navy will never agree to put that on paper," Russo said.

Gamrick shrugged. "That is not my problem."

Russo stood up. "You are a hard-nosed bastard."

Gamrick nodded and said, "I suppose I am." Then he too stood up and asked, "Is there anything else, sir?"

"I'll confirm our agreement—"

"In this case Special Orders will do fine," Gamrick said, trying not to smile. He had won!

"There is one more matter for us to discuss," Russo said. "Your resignation."

"Win, lose, or draw, it will be on your desk the morning after the court renders its verdict," Gamrick answered.

"Just out of curiosity, Captain, what do you intend to do when you leave the Navy?" Russo questioned.

For a few moments Gamrick chuckled, then he said, "Excuse me, sir, but I suddenly realized the enormous truth in the expression 'What goes around comes around.' My father was a lawyer."

"A failed one, from the information in our data bank."

"A failed one? I think not. An unsuccessful one? Absolutely. But not failed, Admiral. I'm living proof that he did not fail."

Russo did not answer.

"There is one more thing, sir, that I must have," Gamrick said.

"Nothing—"

"Sir, I need the authority to continue the investigation," Gamrick said.

"Absolutely no."

"And retain Commander Folsim," Gamrick continued, purposefully ignoring the negative response.

"No, and that is final."

"Then, sir, we do not have a deal," Gamrick answered.

Russo said tightly, "I will have to speak to the CNO and the Secretary before I agree to that."

"I understand," Gamrick told him, but he knew Russo was just going through the motions; he'd be allowed to continue the investigation, and Folsim would remain assigned to him.

"Dismissed," Russo snapped.

Gamrick nodded and rendered the obligatory salute. This time Russo returned it.

Gamrick contained a smile, did a sharp about-face, and left the office.

Folsim was waiting when Gamrick returned to his desk and asked, "Are you or aren't you in deep shit?"

Gamrick sat in his swivel chair before he answered, "Let's say, Commander, I'm afloat in deep shit and I asked that you continue to be assigned to me."

"Skipper . . ." Folsim left his perch on the end of his desk and approached Gamrick's. "But the investigation is over."

Gamrick smiled at him.

"It isn't over?"

"Right, it isn't over," Gamrick answered. "Certainly you can request a transfer to a different assignment, but given there now seems to be some sort of a connection between the accidental death of your good friend Steve and our investigation into what happened aboard the *Utah,* I thought you'd like to fly this one down to the deck, so to speak."

Folsim scratched the top of his head.

"I'm going to push to defend Anderson," Gamrick said.

"Woo-ee, you're full of surprises this morning, Skipper," Folsim exclaimed. "You know it will never happen. The regs are against it."

"I could put up a much stronger defense if I had

you with me," Gamrick said, ignoring Folsim's negativism.

"Skipper, I don't know what kind of deal you cut with the admiral, but I do know that bright star of yours will become—or already is—very dull. I'm a top gun. When I leave this assignment, I'll be assigned to a carrier. I'll be the CAG [Carrier Air Group Commander]. Skipper—"

"There's no need for further explanation; I understand," Gamrick said.

"Jesus, your son is a pilot. Suppose he was in my position. What would you advise him to do?"

Gamrick left the chair and went to the window. Clouds were gathering in the southwest. A new weather system was coming in.

"I'm not even sure I understand why you're not just stepping back and letting the Navy have its way. You're worth a dozen Andersons," Folsim said.

Gamrick looked at him for several moments, then turned toward the window again. "Maybe that's the reason," he said in a low voice, "or at least, it's one of the reasons. I don't particularly like him, but he's caught in an enormous spider web partially because of his sexual behavior and partially because certain individuals in the Navy do not want to accept their responsibility for what happened aboard the *Utah*."

"After this is all over, the Navy will correct itself. It always does."

Gamrick nodded. "I understand that. But an innocent man may be put to death before it corrects itself." He faced Folsim again. "I'd understand if you decided to request a different assignment. I really would understand."

Folsim returned to his own desk. "I'll think about it," he said.

Gamrick was about to tell him to do that when the phone rang and he answered it.

"Do you remember me?" Kate asked.

"Certainly. I remember everything about you."

"Really."

"Absolutely."

"I could test you on that. I mean, there are some very private—"

"When it comes to discussing those places, it's best done one to one," Gamrick said.

"I kind of guessed you would have a unique approach to the subject matter at hand."

"The subject matter must always be at hand during that kind of discussion."

"You could have it at hand at one this afternoon if you're so inclined."

"Oh, I'm definitely inclined."

"My apartment at one," Kate said.

For a moment Gamrick hesitated. He remembered the voice of the man who had answered the phone the time he had called.

"Anything wrong?" Kate asked.

"Nothing," he lied.

She gave him the address and said, "If you don't watch out, I'm going to fall in love with you."

"Yes, I would say that's a distinct possibility on my part too."

She laughed and clicked off.

The moment Gamrick put the phone down, Folsim said, "I'll say this about you, Skipper, You're a hard-nosed bastard and so am I."

The two men looked at each other for several moments, then exploded with laughter.

Kate occupied an eight-room penthouse apartment on the top floor of a luxury apartment house near the center of the city, within walking distance of the TV station.

Kate greeted him at the door wearing nothing more than a diaphanous, white negligee. She took hold of his hand, led him inside, closed and locked the door, and facing him, put her arms around his neck.

He embraced her and opened his mouth to meet her tongue.

"Come," she said, taking hold of his hand. "The bedroom is this way."

"My, my, you're an impatient lady," he chided.

"*Au contraire,* I have been very patient," she answered.

The apartment was furnished the way Gamrick thought it would be. Nothing was ostentatious. There were books, magazines, and newspapers from every English-speaking country in the world on various coffee tables.

The bedroom was almost spartan with only a king-size bed, a blond wood night table on each side, and a metal sculptured lamp on each, a light wood dresser with a mirror above it on one wall, and several large black-and-white and color photographs of landscapes and two—one black and one color—of her nude.

While Gamrick undressed, Kate waited for him in bed, and when he finally joined her, she said, touching his erect phallus, "Now who's impatient?"

"He is," Gamrick answered blithely.

She laughed and, bending down, kissed it deeply.

This time they made love with deliberate slowness, taking time to enjoy the exquisite sensations flooding their bodies. And when they were finished, their naked bodies stayed together for a long time in the afterglow of the experience. Neither one spoke.

Gamrick savored the silence and the warmth of Kate's body against his. Somewhere he had read or heard that the time after making love was as important as the climax. That, he had always thought, might be a slight exaggeration. But not until this particular time with Kate had he ever felt its intense, ineffable beauty.

Gamrick didn't realize he had drifted into a light

sleep until he felt her lips against his ear. He opened his eyes and said, "I thought I was dreaming."

"I have to go to the station soon," Kate said.

He kissed gently on her lips. "And I have to get back to my office."

"You didn't say whether you—"

He put his finger across her lips. "Anderson will get a fair trial," he said.

She smiled and kissed him passionately on the lips.

"More of that and you'll never make it to the station and I won't go back to the office," Gamrick said.

"Same time tomorrow?" she asked.

"Maybe. I can't say for sure because I want to interview Anderson's girl, and she lives in New York. She's important to his defense."

"When will you know?" Kate asked.

"I hope sometime this evening. I'm going to call her then. I suspect she works."

Kate left the bed. "Will you phone me when you know?" she asked.

"Yes."

"If I'm not in, leave a message on the machine," she said. With a broad smile she added, "Now, if you don't think it's too untoward, I'd like to shower with you."

Gamrick stood up. "I was going to suggest the very same thing," he answered, putting his arm around her bare waist and escorting her into the bathroom.

That evening Gamrick phoned Julie Giodono, and only after a fair amount of cajoling did she agree to meet him. The next morning he flew to the Home Port Naval Station on Staten Island by helicopter and then was chauffeured to Julie's home on Endor Street.

The Giodono house was a two-story structure with a small, manicured plot of grass in front and a driveway with a green Toyota in the driveway.

Mr. Giodono, a short man in his early fifties, glared at him.

Gamrick identified himself.

"You guys don't have any reason to bother my daughter," he growled.

Gamrick answered, "Sir, this is a federal matter and concerns no one other than your daughter, Julie."

Suddenly a good-looking young man appeared behind his father. "Is this the man for Julie?" he asked.

Again Gamrick identified himself.

"My son Gregory. He's widd da Republican party here, an' if I have trouble—"

Gamrick glanced back at the chauffeur. He was no Sergeant Gorga. He was just a driver and he wasn't armed. . . . Sometimes just the display of a side arm could work miracles.

Gregory said, "You do not have the right—"

"If need be, I will get a federal order, and that will be very unpleasant for you and cause me to waste a great deal of time," Gamrick said.

"Yous wait out here," Mr. Giodono said, retreating inside but not completely closing the door.

In the time that it took Gamrick to shift his attaché case from one hand to the other, the door opened and Mr. Giodono said, "Julie will be right down."

Gamrick entered the house and was immediately in the living room, which was furnished with a large white sofa, a mirror that covered the entire wall behind it, two large chairs facing the sofa, a variety of dark wood end tables, and blue wall-to-wall carpet that flowed down into the dining room and up the steps to the second floor.

"My wife, Lorraine, is upstairs widd a headache," Mr. Giodono said. "I have coffee on da stove. You want a cup?"

"Yes, thank you," Gamrick answered, hoping that by drinking a cup of coffee with the man, some of the tension would ease.

"I ain't a rich man, but my kids got more than

most, an' Gregory here is in politics. My oldest, Vinny, is in films," Giodono said as he placed a cup of coffee in front of Gamrick. "Julie is goin' to cosmos school."

"Cosmetology school," his son corrected.

"That kind of school," Giodono said.

Not really knowing what kind of a response was wanted, Gamrick nodded.

"This is a good Catholic home. My kids do what's right."

"I'm sure they do," Gamrick said.

"This sailor took Julie—"

"Daddy, he's not interested in that," Julie said, entering the kitchen.

Gamrick stood up. She was a startlingly beautiful young woman with big sloe eyes, long black hair, and a well-developed body. Wearing tight black short shorts that seemed to boldly outline her vaginal lips and loose-fitting white T-shirt that fell away from her full breasts whenever she leaned forward, she blatantly advertised her sexuality.

"Thank you for meeting me," he said, shaking her hand.

"Paul is in big trouble, isn't he?" she asked.

"That bastard should rot—" Giodono began.

"Daddy, please don't start," Julie screeched. "I don't want to hear it."

"He left you widd a fuckin' kid, that's what he did!" Giodono shouted, now on his feet.

Tears started to pour out of Julie's eyes.

"White trash!" Giodono shouted. "You let white trash fuck you!"

Gregory moved his sister out of the kitchen.

"I gotta have government people here—"

"Pat, stop it!" a woman screamed. "Stop it!"

Gamrick was still standing.

"Dis is da man who came to see Julie," Giodono told her, breathing hard.

"Captain Gamrick," Gamrick said.

"I'm Julie's mother."

"Pleased to meet you," Gamrick replied, extending his hand.

She shook it and called Julie back into the room. "Now, everyone leave these two alone."

"Someone should be here—" Gregory began.

"Enough. Everyone, out of here," she ordered.

Reluctantly father and son left the kitchen and she followed. She dominated, of that there wasn't the slightest doubt.

"Please," Gamrick said, gesturing to one of the chairs at the table. He sat opposite her and in a quiet voice he said, "Paul never said anything about having fathered a child."

Julie shook her head and her eyes watered.

Gamrick said, "He needs your help, now."

"I don't know. Since my dad found out that I was pregnant and then I read about Paul—my life is all messed up."

"You go to school, don't you?"

"Naw, that's what he likes to tell people," she answered. "I was going to, but—well, I don't. I had a job in Manhattan for a while, but then my boss—well, we went out on a couple of dates and I—well, he expected I do it with him whenever he wanted it, so I left."

Gamrick said, "I want you to be a witness for Anderson. I want you to tell the court that you were lovers."

"Jesus, my father would kill me!" she exclaimed.

"If he's convicted, he could be executed," Gamrick said.

"My father would kill me. You saw what he's like."

Gamrick took a deep breath, exhaled, and reaching down, he opened his attaché case and took out the packet of pictures that Hawkins had taken. "I have these, Julie. They're enough to have you subpoenaed. I'm going to have to introduce them as evidence." And he handed the photographs to her.

"Oh, my God!" she wailed. "Where—"

"That doesn't matter. That's you, isn't it?"

"Yes, it's me," she said in a whisper. "If my father sees these, he'll beat the shit out of me. He'll kill me."

"Did he beat you when he found out about the baby?" Gamrick asked, taking a stab in the dark.

"Yes," she whispered.

"And the baby—"

"I lost it in the third month," she said, looking through tear-stained eyes at him.

"Paul is on trial for his life," Gamrick said. "You read about the insurance policy. You knew Downs. The Navy claims that Paul and Gus Downs were lovers."

Julie shook her head. "We were just fooling around."

"Julie, did you have sex with Downs?" Gamrick asked.

"The three of us slept together," she answered with childlike innocence.

"That's not what I asked," Gamrick said.

"Downs was never inside me. He liked to play with my breasts—and touch my cunt," she whispered.

"And what did you do with him?"

"Gave him head."

"But you did have sex with Anderson?" Gamrick questioned.

"Yes."

"And he didn't mind Downs touching you, or you giving Downs head?"

She shook her head. "Sometimes when I was doing Downs, he did me."

"Do you?" Gamrick asked, unfamiliar with the expression.

"You know, either fuck me or go down on me."

Gamrick rubbed his chin; Anderson was obviously bisexual and Downs wasn't, or he was and had an agreement with Anderson about—

"Gus really loved Paul," Julie said.

"Did you ever see them do more than just fool around?" Gamrick asked.

She played with the golden cross that hung between her breasts.

Gamrick repeated the question.

"Yeah, they fucked. Sometimes I'd join them," she whispered, looking straight at him. The look of innocence was gone now, and her eyes were bright with lust. Even her nipples became hard and her breathing quickened.

"The Navy is going to claim that Paul and Gus were lovers, they argued over something, and Paul killed him and all of the other men in the turret for the insurance money, for two million dollars," Gamrick said.

"They never argued," she said.

"Never?"

"Not even when Gus started to play with me and I didn't feel like having him do it. I told Paul to make him stop, and Paul said, 'He's my buddy. If he wants to play with you, that's okay with me. If you were his girl, he'd let me play with you anytime I wanted to.'"

"What did Gus say?" Gamrick asked.

"Yeah, he said, 'You're damn right, Paul. I'd let you diddle my woman anytime you wanted to'," Julie answered.

"Are you in love with Paul?" Gamrick asked.

Again she played with the cross before she said, "Yeah, I guess I am. He's really good in bed."

Gamrick nodded. More marriages were made there than in heaven.

"You got any more questions?" she asked.

"Only one—will you be a witness for the defense, for Paul?" Gamrick said, gathering the photographs together and putting them back into the attaché case.

"I need to think about it," she answered.

"Either you love him enough to be there, or you

don't love him at all. There isn't any middle place in this, Julie," Gamrick told her.

"I'll be there," she answered quietly.

"Good," Gamrick answered.

"Should I call my mother and—"

"Just one more question," Gamrick said, and before she could object, he asked, "Did you know a sailor named Donald Hawkins?"

She instantly paled. "No," she said. "I never knew no one like that."

"I thought you might have," Gamrick responded. She was lying, but this wasn't the time or the place to find out why. He'd wait until he had her on the witness stand to get the truth out of her.

"Can I call my mother and father back here?" she asked.

"Yes," Gamrick answered.

As soon as Giodono returned, he insisted that Gamrick have another cup of coffee and a piece of peach pie that he'd baked the previous evening. "I want to tell you that all of my children are good and especially Julie. We never had any trouble with her. . . ."

The second evening after Gamrick visited Julie, he and Iris were at dinner. They carried on a desultory conversation that creaked along like an old cart on a road full of ruts. More and more Gamrick was preoccupied with Anderson's forthcoming court-martial. So far he hadn't met the lawyer with whom he would work. But he had met McCafery, and the man was every bit the hardass he was reputed to be. And he saw Anderson, almost on a daily basis, who was more interested in his opinion of Julie's physicality than in the explanation of why he would not be the actual person defending him. He also had seen Kate both of the past afternoons, and when he wasn't thinking about the court-martial, he thought about her—relived their love-making, imagined the feel of her body, the scent of it and even the movement of her hands when she spoke. . . .

"Clark, I don't believe you heard a word I said," Iris complained, placing her knife and fork on the plate in front of her.

"I was thinking about the court-martial," he lied.

She made a moue and said, "Harry Jamerson has invited us over for dinner on Saturday night."

The name didn't immediately mean anything to Gamrick. Iris had so many friends, especially from the theater, whose names she bandied around almost all of the time that in Gamrick's head they all flowed together and meant absolutely nothing.

"He's a producer," Iris explained just as the phone rang.

Gamrick was closer to the phone and answered it. A man said, "We have your grandson. Back off, Captain. Back off or he's dead."

The line went dead.

Gamrick's hand trembled.

"What is it?" Iris questioned.

He put the phone down. It was the third call since he had visited Julie. . . .

"Will you tell me what's going on?" Iris demanded, her voice going almost to a scream.

"A threat on the boy's life," he said tightly.

"On John's life? Someone has John?" Now she was screaming. "Who is it? What did he say?" She bolted out of the chair, knocked over several glasses, and pulled the place setting and everything on it off the table.

Gamrick stood up. "No one has John," he said. "No one."

"How can you be sure?" Iris yelled. Pointing her finger at him, she shouted, "You care more for Anderson than you do for your own grandson."

"That's a dumb thing to say," he shouted.

"You're going to defend a man—put your entire life on the line—for a fucking queer!"

Gamrick threw up his hands. "You just don't fucking understand this whole thing, do you?"

"No, I don't. I never will and I never want to," she shrilled.

"Oh, that's really an intelligent, enlightened way of looking at something," he said mockingly.

"I'm sick of it . . . I'm sick of you."

"That's your problem. Maybe if you didn't drink so fucking much, you'd be able to understand—"

"I'm leaving you. I've had it. I don't want any more," she shouted, breathing hard, her face very red. "You've wrecked my life, and now you're about to sacrifice your grandson's life for—good God, I'm willing to bet you can't even tell me why you're doing it."

In a tight, angry whisper Gamrick answered, "Because I believe the man is innocent."

"So you're willing to trade his life for John's?" she fired back. "Have you told Hal what you're willing to do? After all, he's John's father."

"No, I haven't told Hal, and I'm not willing to trade one life for another."

"But that's what you'll be doing. The person on the phone—"

"No one has John," he said in the same tight whisper he'd used moments before.

"They said we'd never see him alive if you continued on the case, didn't they?" Iris shouted.

"They don't have him," Gamrick roared. "They don't fucking have him."

"Then why are they—"

"Because they want this case done with just the way the Navy does but for different reasons. They want Paul Anderson to take the fall. They don't have John, but if they can get me to believe they have him—well, they don't want me to defend Paul, or do anything that will help in his defense."

Iris walked to the door, speaking in a near monotone. "You're crazy, Clark. This case has made you crazy. You're not the same man I've known for thirty years. You can't see anything else but this trial. That's all right for you, but it's not for me. I'm leaving you."

Gamrick looked straight at her. This was a crossroads in their lives. "You do whatever you want to do," he answered. "I'm not going to stop you from going if that's what you want to do. And I'm not going to plead with you to stay either. The choice is yours, Iris."

For several moments neither of them moved. Then Gamrick said, "I'm going out. I won't be back until late."

"I won't be here," Iris told him.

Gamrick shrugged. "I repeat, the choice is yours," he said.

She nodded, turned, left the kitchen first, and went upstairs.

A few minutes later, Gamrick drove his Jeep out of the driveway, turned onto the road, and headed toward Galesville. Angry and frustrated, he floored the accelerator, and as he sped by a telephone booth, he realized how much he wanted to, needed to speak with Kate. He slowed, made a U-turn, and stopped at the phone booth. But just as he was about to dial Kate's private number, he changed his mind and phoned Hal instead.

"I called because something has come up that I want you to know about," Gamrick said after the usual greeting was over. "I've been receiving phone calls about John. The latest one came this evening."

Hal was silent, though he could hear his son's ragged breathing.

"The person says they have John," Gamrick said. "He wants me to drop the case against Anderson. But I don't believe they have John."

Again Hal was silent, and Gamrick heard his ragged

breathing before he said, "I don't believe them either, Dad. But you're the man who has to make the decision."

"You know I love John," Gamrick responded.

"Yes, all of us know that, Dad. But it's your call."

"And if—"

"Don't ask me to tell you that I won't blame you if you make the wrong call. I can't tell you how I will react. The only thing I can tell you is that I think they're bluffing and that you're the man who has to make the decision."

"I've got to do what I believe I should do."

"I know that, Dad. I really do know that, Dad," Hal answered.

Gamrick uttered a deep sigh.

"You've been making hard calls all your life, Dad."

"Thanks, Hal ... I'll be in touch," he said and clicked off before he gave some hint of the problem between him and Iris. His son had more than enough to worry about now.

Gamrick was about to leave the phone booth, changed his mind, and dialed Kate's private number.

A man answered, but before Gamrick hung up, Kate came on the line.

"I'm sorry—" He began but couldn't continue. He fought down the desire to ask who the man was.

"Are you all right?" Kate asked.

"I've been better. I want to see you."

"Now?"

"Now," he emphatically told her. "As soon as possible."

After a few moments of silence, Kate agreed. "The Sea Sands in an hour," she said.

"I'll be there," Gamrick answered, hung up, and completely drained, he slumped against the side of the booth. This was one of the very few times in his adult life that he had needed to be comforted, reassured by another person and, yes, even loved. . . .

Gamrick arrived at the Sea Sands before Kate and

chose a rear booth. Pete's wife saw him from behind the bar, and coming out to serve him personally, she greeted him warmly.

"Ms. Bannon will be joining me," he explained.

"Do you want to order now?"

"Two Stolis on the rocks," he answered.

"I'll send them over with one of the girls," she said.

"Where's Pete?" Gamrick asked.

"An allergy of some sort got him, so he took the night off," she explained.

Gamrick nodded sympathetically.

The drinks arrived at the table just as Kate walked into the door. As usual, she was stunningly dressed. This time in tight light blue pants and a matching blue blouse open at the neck. That he'd made love to her that afternoon seemed almost impossible, and yet as he looked at her, he realized how much of her body he knew, relished, and loved.

She spotted him and came straight to the table. "No, don't get up," she said, settling next to him in the booth and leaning close to kiss and be kissed.

"Stoli on the rocks," he offered, pointing at one of the glasses.

"That will do fine," she answered, picking up the glass and drinking. Then she said, "I think I was followed."

He looked at her questioningly.

"There was someone tailing me from the time I left the garage under my building."

Even as she spoke, another couple entered.

"Is this the first time?"

"Yes."

"Did you see the driver?"

"Not clearly."

"What kind of car?"

She shook her head. "Maybe a black or dark blue station wagon of some sort."

Gamrick shrugged. "A man sees a beautiful woman in a car alone on a secondary road—"

"No, Clark, he was behind me all the way from the city," she said.

"Only a couple came in. Are you sure he was alone?"

"The only thing I am sure of is that I was followed," she said, finishing the rest of her drink.

Gamrick did the same before he told her in fits of starts and stops about the threatening phone call he had received and the argument it had caused between him and Iris.

"My gut feeling is that whoever wants me to back off is bluffing," he said. "If they had John—well, if they had John they would have some proof they have him."

"You're a poker player, aren't you?" she asked, putting her hand over his.

"A damn good one. Most boat skippers are. We have to be. It comes with—I was going to say turf, but there isn't any where we play."

"I understand," Kate said, gently playing her fingers over his hand.

"I just needed to be with you," Gamrick told her.

Looking straight at him, she said, "Aren't you going to ask about . . ."

Gamrick pursed his lips, and turning his hand so that now he was holding hers, he answered in a low voice, "No, I don't own you, Kate. I didn't want to think about the other men in your life, though I knew they were there."

"Clark, I—"

He reached across the table with his other hand and put it against her mouth. "Listen," he said softly.

She nodded.

"There's twenty years between us. I consider myself lucky to have met and fallen in love with you before I became too old to enjoy the pleasure that you give me. I don't think I—no, I know I never really experienced the love of a woman before I met you—"

She started to interrupt.

"Please, let me finish; I've had several affairs. I told
you that. But I never wanted to be with any woman the
way I want to be with you. . . . I love you, Kate."

She kissed the back of his hand. "Would it mean
anything to you if I said I love you too?" she asked.

"It would mean a great deal," Gamrick said.

"I love you, Clark Gamrick," Kate told him. In a
passionate whisper, she added, "I do love you, Clark,
very, very much."

Gamrick admitted, "I needed to hear that, Kate. I really did." Then, smiling broadly, he said, "Let's order
something to eat. I'm suddenly very hungry."

"So am I," Kate answered, kissing the tips of his fingers.

When Gamrick returned home, he was surprised to
find Iris there. Neither of them mentioned the argument, but she said, "I'll sleep in the guest room."

"If that's what you want to do, do it," Gamrick answered and went into the den, where he began to re-
read the transcripts of the video interviews of the men
from the *Utah*. There was something missing from the
information the men had given, and that something had
killed the men in turret number two, killed Hawkins,
Wright, and Cool and now—whatever it was—it was
trying to kill him. . . .

Exhausted, Gamrick went upstairs, showered, and
climbed into bed. But that missing something nagged
him, keeping him awake. Aware of Iris's movements,
he heard her go into the guest room and close the
door.

Except for the usual night sounds, the house was
very quiet. Then, suddenly, without any reason, he began to sweat. His heart skipped a beat and began to
race.

"Goddamn," he swore. Leaving the bed, he went to
the window and looked out. A blacked-out station
wagon swung around the cul-de-sac, and the next instant his Jeep exploded, becoming a mass of flames.

The force of the explosion blew the window out in front of him, and shards of glass struck his face and bare arms.

"What happened?" Iris cried, rushing into the room.

"Call the fire department, then the police," Gamrick said calmly as he turned on the light.

"My God, you're bleeding. Your face—"

"Make those calls. I'll take care of myself," he said and went into the bathroom. The cuts looked worse than they were, and as he put antiseptic on them, he realized that the missing something had just sent him a clear message.

"I made the calls," Iris said from the open doorway.

"Thanks."

"I looked downstairs. The front door and several windows were blown out," she said.

"If the Jeep had been parked closer to the house, the damage would have been much more," he answered, cleaning one of the cuts on his face.

"Here, let me do that," Iris said, stepping into the bathroom.

He gave her the bottle of Lavcol and the bag of cotton balls.

"Are you sure there isn't any glass in the cuts?" Iris asked as she worked on them.

"I'm sure," Gamrick answered, knowing the situation between them had over the last few minutes changed.

The sudden scream of approaching fire engines startled the two of them.

"We better go down," Gamrick said.

"Do you know how it happened?"

"Yes. I was at the window a moment before the explosion. It's their way of telling me to drop the case."

"Their way?" Iris asked, her voice dry with fear.

Gamrick took hold of her hand. "I don't know who they are. But they killed twenty-seven men, killed

Wright, Cool, and Hawkins and they want the Navy to kill Anderson."

Her eyes wide with fear, Iris said nothing.

"Will you come downstairs with me?" Gamrick asked.

She nodded and managed to croak, "Yes."

"Thank you," Gamrick said, and still holding her hand, he led her out of the bathroom and down the stairs.

Chapter 15

The next morning Gamrick remembered the telephone-bugging system Dimitri had found and called the telephone company to check whether or not they had dispatched a work crew to his home within the last month. As he had expected, the answer was negative.

Then, just before noon, the chief fire inspector from the county in which he lived phoned to tell him his Jeep had been destroyed by a bazooka round and he had notified the local authorities in Graysville and the state police.

Gamrick thanked him and then phoned Lieutenant Martins to find out if he could see Russo sometime during the day.

"It would have be at seventeen-thirty," she said.

"Put me down," he answered.

"Done, sir," she told him.

Gamrick thanked her and turned his attention to Folsim. "My Jeep took a bazooka round last night," he said.

Folsim's jaw dropped open.

"Just a burned-out shell now," Gamrick said.

Folsim left his chair and perched himself on the end of Gamrick's desk. "Sir, pardon the expression, but we're in deep shit."

"I think you're right; we're in deep something, but what the fuck is it?"

Folsim got off the desk and began to pace, while Gamrick left the chair and stood in front of the window.

"Could some of the men hate Anderson so much they were willing to kill two men—?"

"Skipper, in the eyes of the men he killed twenty-seven shipmates," Folsim said.

"But did he?"

"As far as they're concerned, he did."

"All right, let's go on the assumption he did. How does that justify doing what they—whoever they may be—have done? They have killed two men and have tried to frighten me into giving up the case."

"I didn't say they were normal. I only said that they were angry, and angry men are capable of some very terrible actions."

Gamrick rubbed his chin. "Certainly, you're right about that but—and it's a big but—there's no guarantee I'm going to get an acquittal for Anderson. To add to that, they don't know I'm going to play a role in his defense. That information has not yet been made public. All they know is that I am the chief investigating officer."

Folsim stopped pacing. "Are trying to tell me that *they* could be from our side of the fence?"

"The Navy isn't the government. There was bad powder aboard the ship, and it shouldn't have been there. A dozen or more congressional committees are already howling for blood because that powder should not have been aboard. Heads will roll."

Folsim began to pace again, and without stopping he said, "So far, everything from the bazooka round to the dumptruck that struck the cab has been government property."

"Yes, it has been," Gamrick answered.

"All right, how does a guy like Cassado tie into a cover-up operation?" he asked, stopping a few feet from Gamrick.

"A hired gun. Any one of three or four agencies have been known to use them," Gamrick said. "Maybe that's why I haven't been killed."

"That just flew over me," Folsim said.

"If I were killed, that would cause another investigation to be started. No, it would be much better if I could be made to quit. Killing me would give them more problems."

"You think the—"

"I really don't know what to think," Gamrick said. "I just gave you one of two possible scenarios. The other you gave me—some of the men angry enough to make sure Anderson is convicted. But there is a third scenario; only I don't know what it is."

"Then how do you know it exists?" Folsim asked.

"Because it's the something which neither one of us can define," Gamrick answered. "I went over the transcripts of a dozen different men last night, and as I read each of them I had the distinct feeling all of them had left something out. There's a missing piece, or pieces."

"They lied?" Folsim asked.

Gamrick shook his head. "The sin of omission rather than the sin of commission."

"Could you have been reading into—?"

"Yes, I could have, but I don't think I was."

Folsim came back and perched on the edge of the desk again. "Skipper, maybe next time it won't be just a warning," he whispered, locking eyes with Gamrick.

"You can still request—"

Folsim shook his head. "You go the limit, I go the limit. I owe Steve an answer, and I owe myself one too."

Gamrick smiled. "You're a hard-nose bastard, Commander."

"Yeah, I know. It's the fault of the company I keep," Folsim answered with a deadpan expression.

The phone on Gamrick's desk rang.

Folsim answered it. "It's Ms. Bannon for you," he said, handing the phone to Gamrick.

"I thought it best to identify myself," Kate said as soon as Gamrick came on the line.

"Yes, it was," Gamrick answered.

"Are you okay?"

"Yes. I thought you'd ask that question. But we haven't had any decision on that yet."

"Can you come to my place this afternoon at about one?"

"Certainly. That's a very good idea. Thank you very much," Gamrick replied.

Kate laughed. "You do have a way with words, Captain."

"Thank you for calling, Ms. Bannon," Gamrick said and replaced the phone in its cradle.

"Did you know her first husband was a fighter jock like me?" Folsim asked.

For a moment Gamrick didn't realize he was talking about Kate.

But when Folsim explained, "He punched out on a routine training mission up around Greenland."

Gamrick said, "I know nothing about her."

"She has that rare combination of beauty and intelligence," Folsim said.

Gamrick agreed.

"Between the two of us, the admiral has more than a passing interest in her," Folsim said, winking broadly.

Gamrick hoped the sudden rush of heat he felt didn't show in his face, and he purposefully opened the drawer on the side away from Folsim, pretending to look for something in it.

The phone rang again. But this time it was Folsim's, and as soon as he answered, Gamrick straightened up. The idea of Kate and Russo having any sort of relationship other than a professional one was enough to destroy whatever small remnant of well-being he had left.

Kate pulled into the motel parking lot right behind Gamrick, and within a matter of minutes their naked bodies melded into a unity of violently exquisite movement and delicious sensual pleasure that brought them to the mystical mountain peak of orgasmic ecstasy.

"Why so wild today?" Kate asked, playing her fingers through his hair.

"Sometimes I get that way," Gamrick answered. "Did you mind?"

"I'd ask for a repeat performance—if that's the right word—but I'm too exhausted now. Maybe later."

Gamrick laughed and squeezed her breast. "That can't happen at the snap of one's fingers," he said, snapping his fingers to accent his statement. "It comes—hell, I don't know where it come from. Lust, I guess."

"Ah, so you really do lust after me, or is it for me?"

"For, after, and around you if you want the absolute truth," Gamrick said.

She smiled and said, "That's the kind of talk every woman wants to hear."

"And what do you think every man wants to hear from every woman?"

Kate slowly slid her hand down his chest and stomach to his penis. "That he's the best cocksman in the entire world, that being fucked by him is the best she's ever been fucked."

"And what about this particular man?" Gamrick asked.

Kate moved out of his embrace and began licking his now turgid penis, only to pause long enough to say, "In this situation, with this particular man, a woman's actions are more important than what she might tell him."

Giving himself up to the galvanic tendrils of pleasure moving through his body, Gamrick lifted her up over him and, looking up at her vagina, pressed his lips against it while she went back to moving her tongue over his penis, but this time she held it in her mouth. The bad feelings he had about her and Russo miraculously vanished. She was with him and that was all that really mattered.

* * *

Gamrick was in Russo's office at precisely 1730. He stood at attention in front of his desk.

Russo looked up at him and pointed at the chair. "You may sit, Captain."

"Yes, sir," Gamrick snapped.

"If you hadn't requested this appointment, I would have," Russo said.

Gamrick remained silent. Even before he'd entered the office, he decided to maintain whatever standard of formality or informality Russo would set. Now he would not speak until Russo gave him permission to.

"I assume you had a particular reason for requesting this meeting," Russo said.

"Yes, sir," Gamrick snapped again.

Russo began to drum on the top of the desk with the fingers of his right hand. "Will you please state your reason?" he asked.

"Sir, over the last two weeks several attempts have been made to kill me."

"What the hell are you talking about?" Russo exploded.

"Sir, last night my Jeep was destroyed by a bazooka shell," Gamrick said in a level voice. "Prior to that I was forced to kill a man who was attempting to kill me. And prior to that incident the cab—"

"Spare me your recapitulation, Captain," Russo said, now standing behind his desk chair and resting his elbows on the top of its high back. "Just tell me what you want."

"Navy authorization to keep a weapon on my person for self-protection, sir," Gamrick answered.

"I didn't realize you cared a tinker's damn for Navy authorization, since in the past you've certainly acted without it."

"Yes, sir, I did," Gamrick said. "But the circumstances are different. I am asking authorization to carry a sidearm to protect my life."

"Are you sure you are not in the grip of your own

imagination about this matter, as you are about other matters?"

"Sir, I did have to kill a man who was attempting to kill me and did inflict such a terrible wound on my dog that I was forced to destroy the animal myself."

Russo sat again. "With what kind of weapon do you intend to protect yourself?"

"A 9mm automatic," Gamrick answered.

"You're really not taking any chances, are you?"

"No, sir," he answered. "There's no cure for being dead."

Russo glared at him but said, "I will have Lieutenant Martins prepare the authorization papers."

"Thank you, sir," Gamrick answered.

Russo ignored him and said, "Now to Navy matters."

"Yes, sir," Gamrick snapped instantly, seething with anger.

"I have appointed Lieutenant J.G. Jacob Harkowitz defense counsel. You will meet with him oh-nine-hundred tomorrow and assist him in preparing his defense of Seaman First Class Paul Anderson."

"Sir—"

"You have questions, Captain?" Russo asked.

"Yes, sir."

"I'll anticipate your first question and explain that Lieutenant J.G. Jacob Harkowitz is a qualified attorney. He has been on staff here for his entire term of service. In another three months he will leave the Navy with the rank of lieutenant, having repaid the United States government for subsidizing his legal education. He is obviously not Navy, not one of us."

"Sir, would you explain your last statement?" Gamrick asked.

Russo began to drum on the top of the desk again. "He is not a professional officer."

"Oh, I thought you meant he didn't observe the same holidays like Christmas and Easter," Gamrick said as guilelessly as he could.

"That too," Russo growled.

Gamrick nodded.

"Any other questions, Captain?"

"Just one."

"As long as it is just one," Russo said.

"Aren't you throwing meat to the lion?"

"And just what is that supposed to mean?" Russo boomed.

"Sir, I apologize. It was a rhetorical question, and therefore the answer must be given by me. It is, of course, yes," Gamrick said.

"Captain, this meeting is at an end," Russo said with undisguised anger in his voice.

"Yes, sir," Gamrick answered. He stood up and saluted.

Russo hesitated a moment or two, then returned the courtesy.

Wayne's Rolls was parked in the cul-de-sac when Gamrick came home. He hadn't made any plans with Iris about having dinner home or at a restaurant. After the firemen had left last night, she had returned to the guest room.

Wayne came out of the house before Gamrick was out of the Lincoln and greeted him with "I hear tell you've been having all sorts of adventures."

They shook hands, and Monique and Iris came out of the doorway together. Both were wearing short shorts and polo shirts.

"I thought you intended to stay down—"

"It seems all the action is up here, so I came back," Wayne laughed.

Gamrick greeted Monique with a kiss on each cheek and Iris with a nod. He saw no reason to be hypocritical about their relationship. Despite her concern while taking care of his cuts, she had chosen to return to the guest room.

"I was sorry to hear about Dimitri," Wayne said,

putting his arm around Gamrick's shoulder. "He was one hell of a good friend."

"Thanks," Gamrick said. "He was one of a kind."

"I had the door and the windows repaired," Iris told him as he stepped inside the house.

"I suggest we go for dinner to that seafood house that Clark likes so much," Monique said.

"Great idea!" Wayne responded. "What about it, sis? Clark?"

"I'm willing," Iris answered in an almost tearful voice that made Gamrick realize that she'd been crying.

"Clark, you haven't said yes or no," Monique commented.

"I'll go. Just give me a half hour or so to shower," he said.

"Good. Sis, you call and make the reservations," Wayne said.

Iris immediately went to the telephone.

"I'll be ready as soon as I can," Gamrick said.

"Don't rush," Monique replied. "I want to change, and I'm sure Iris does too."

As soon as Gamrick saw Wayne he had realized, his brother-in-law hadn't just left Hilton Head because he got tired of it; he left because Iris had called him and he was here to make right again what Iris thought was wrong. Just when and how Wayne would broach the subject of his defection from the ranks of levelheaded men was impossible for him to guess. But how much his brother drank would be a good barometer. If he drank a lot, the man-to-man conversation would be put off until tomorrow evening, or the one after that. If he hardly drank, then it would be tonight.

Gamrick was right. Wayne limited his drinking to a couple of martinis; then, after dinner, when everyone was in the Rolls on the way to the house, Wayne made his opening gambit.

"Sis tells me you've done a one-eighty. You're going to be a civilian sooner than later," he said.

"As soon as the court-martial is over, I'll submit my resignation," Gamrick answered.

"Without ever reaching flag rank?"

"The bottom line is that I have violated the rules—no, that's not completely right. The Navy is attempting to violate the rules, and I am going to try to stop them. Ergo, I am violating the rules by their standards."

"What the fuck do you care—"

"The bottom line is that I do care about what is just and what is unjust. Anderson has been convicted before the court-martial has begun."

"You know the Navy. Things might get fucked up for a while, but sooner or later they get straightened out."

"That won't wash," Gamrick said.

They reached the house and as they walked toward it, Wayne said, "You put in thirty years. You were awarded the Navy Cross. You're not just anyone."

"Neither is Paul Anderson."

"For god's sakes, he's a fucking fag; he's not even a man!" Wayne exploded as they went through the door.

Gamrick faced him and said, "If you were to be judged by your sexual behavior or by your drinking habits, Wayne, how would you fare?"

Wayne flushed.

"But *he* didn't kill all those men," Monique said in her husband's defense.

"So far, no one has proved that Anderson did it either," Gamrick answered, moving into the living room and turning on some of the lights.

"Just what the fuck are you doing to your life?" Wayne growled angrily.

"I'm making an attempt—probably last time I'll ever really be able to make one—to account for it," Gamrick answered.

"What about the past thirty years?"

"What about them?"

"They count for something."

"Certainly they do. They were obviously a long preparation for what is now happening. The bottom line is that I will continue to defend Anderson because I do believe in the right I swore to defend with my life if it ever came to that, and several times it came damn close. Now, if you'll excuse me I have a hard day ahead of me tomorrow and I'm very tired."

"What about your marriage?" Monique asked.

Gamrick almost laughed. That question coming from her was ludicrous, especially after she had tried to seduce him the last time she was here.

"What about your marriage?" Wayne echoed. "And what about John?"

"Nothing about my marriage. It's on the rocks," Gamrick snapped.

Iris began to sniffle.

"Iris drinks too much and I am beginning to drink too much, and I won't follow her down the primrose path of self-destruction from cirrhosis of the liver or from an alcohol-saturated brain, which by the way, Wayne, you are well on the way to risk having both conditions."

"Ah, so now you're Captain Fix-it," Wayne answered angrily.

"I noticed that you haven't explained why you chose to put John's life on the line," Monique challenged.

"No. And I don't intend to explain it. This discussion is over," Gamrick said just as sharply. "I understand your concern, but the best thing Wayne and you can do is to do nothing. Iris and I will solve our problems, and whatever solutions we arrive at, they will be the ones—"

"You leave the Navy now and you can forget about a position with the company," Wayne said.

Iris gasped. she was about to speak, but Gamrick waved her silent and said, his voice now menacingly flat, "Don't threaten me, Wayne. Don't ever threaten me."

"And just what the fuck do you think you're going to be able to do when you're a civilian again?"

Gamrick suddenly felt lightheaded—filled with a kind of schoolboy joyfulness that schoolboys are too young to appreciate when they experience it. "I'm going to hang out my shingle and practice law. I'm going to be a lawyer. Probably a public defender because I certainly won't need money to live after I dump the half a million shares of company stock that I personally own."

Wayne blanched.

"You didn't know I own that much, did you?" Gamrick asked.

"You wouldn't do that," Wayne said dryly.

Gamrick didn't answer.

"That would drive the price of the stock down. It would give our competitors the opportunity to buy—"

"I know exactly what it will do," Gamrick said harshly.

No one spoke and the ticking of the clock on the mantel became sledgehammer blows until Gamrick said, "Good night." He turned and started to walk out of the room.

"You've changed, Clark," Iris called after him. "You're not the same man I married and lived for the past twenty-five years."

Gamrick stopped and faced her. "Maybe, just maybe, I'm really me for the first time in my adult life. Maybe, just maybe, the other Clark Gamrick existed because he had to. He had made a choice and had lived with that choice. But now—now he has been given a second chance to become his real self, and he isn't going to make the mistake of letting it slip away."

"And where do I fit in this epiphany of yours?" she wept. "Where is my second chance?"

Though Gamrick felt sorry for her, he shrugged and said, "It's not for me to give you a second chance, Iris. It's for you to find it and take it, if you really want it."

She shook her head and said, "I thought we had a

good marriage. I thought we"—she began to sob but managed to blurt out—"loved one another."

Gamrick rubbed his chin and in a quiet voice he responded, "I thought so too."

As he left the room, he heard Monique say, "He's got to be involved with another woman."

Gamrick was too far away to hear what Wayne answered, but he could guess.

Lieutenant Jacob Harkowitz reported to Gamrick the following morning at 0900 and to his surprise Harkowitz was very different from what he had imagined. He was a strikingly handsome, tall, blond, blue-eyed young man with muscles that could come only from assiduous attention to a regime of body-building exercises.

Gamrick invited Harkowitz to sit in the chair next to his desk and said, "There's nothing personal in what I am about to say."

"In the Navy nothing ever is personal, is it, sir?" Harkowitz responded.

Taken aback for a moment, Gamrick still decided to let Harkowitz know exactly where he fitted. "You've been dumped on me, Lieutenant, because the Navy—"

"Sir, the case was up for grabs and I grabbed it," Harkowitz said.

"Explain."

"Word got around that the admiral was looking for a lower-grade short-timer to defend Seaman First Class Paul Anderson."

"Nothing official?"

Harkowitz smiled. "There are ways and there are ways. This way didn't leave a paper trail."

Gamrick rested his elbows on the table. "Why did you grab the case?"

"Sir, may I be frank?" Harkowitz asked, his blue eyes suddenly lighting up with mischief.

Gamrick nodded.

"You've been dubbed the 'Crusader Rabbit.'"

Gamrick started. He hadn't heard that and resented it. "So you thought you'd come along and have some fun. Cartoon characters are supposed to be funny, aren't they, Lieutenant?"

"Sir, unless someone gives a damn about Anderson, he's going to wind up dead or in prison for the rest of his life."

There was a passion in Harkowitz's voice that tore Gamrick away from his bout with self-pity and brought him back to the reality of the interview. "Go on," he said.

"I've been following the case ... nothing official. Just in the newspapers and on the tube. The only TV person who has some hold on the reality of it is Kate Bannon."

"It would seem that way," Gamrick answered evasively.

For several moments neither one spoke. Then Harkowitz said, "I'm out in six months. I can win this case, and if I do, when I get out I'll have the biggest law firms in the country running after me."

"So there's a strong personal motive too, isn't there, Lieutenant?" Gamrick said sarcastically, rubbing his right thumb and the finger next to it together. "Money, money, money makes the world go round."

"You asked me to be frank, sir," Harkowitz answered without hesitation.

"So I did, Lieutenant, so I did," Gamrick answered.

"Sir, with all due respect, to Captain McCafery—"

"Ah, so you know about him?" Gamrick questioned.

"Yes, sir. It's hard not to know about a man who is called the 'Shark of the Courtroom,' or 'Hardass McCafery.' "

"And you think you can best him?"

Harkowitz smiled. "Bring him down and make him cry mama," he said with a straight face and laughter in his eyes.

Gamrick too suppressed a smile and asked, "You don't think much of yourself, do you?"

"Sir, I'm the best," Harkowitz answered.

"How many cases have you won?" Gamrick asked.

"None, sir."

"How many times have you been involved in a court-martial?"

"Never, sir."

"That makes your claim with regard to your professional ability somewhat extravagant, wouldn't you say?" Gamrick responded.

"Only, sir, if you look at what might commonly be called the dark side of it."

Gamrick hesitated a moment, then exploded with laughter, and Folsim—who was sitting at his desk a few feet away pretending to be deeply absorbed in some papers but listening intently—joined him and called out, "He's got balls. That much I'll say for him."

Harkowitz looked at Folsim and then back at Gamrick, and without so much as the hint of smile appearing on his face, he said, "I've got balls, a good-size dick, and what's more important, I have smarts." Then suddenly his tone shifted and he said, "I'm not a professional officer and I'm a Jew. I'm not a member of the club and I never will be, in the Navy or out of it. For the last four years I've been pushing papers around, writing briefs for other officers. I ate shit because I had to. Now—well, now—"

"You want Captain McCafery to 'eat shit,' as you just so eloquently put it," Folsim said, speaking for the first time since the interview began.

"No, sir, that's not my style. I want to show how good I am."

Gamrick leaned back in to his swivel chair. He could fight Russo on his choice of counsel and probably win. But it could turn out to be a Pyrrhic victory at best. He would just turn around and assign someone else who wouldn't have experience and who would lack Harkowitz's brashness, his self-confidence, qualities needed by any fighter in the ring or in the courtroom. Come to think of it, even in a damn submarine. . . .

"You're on, Harkowitz," Gamrick said.

"Sir, thank you."

"Don't thank me until you know the conditions, and then don't thank me until we've won an acquittal for Anderson."

"Yes, sir," Harkowitz answered.

"The conditions are as follows: everything that I say to you or you hear said between myself and Commander Folsim—"

"That's me," Folsim said from his desk. "But you may call me Bob in unofficial situations."

"Yes, sir—I mean Bob."

Gamrick said, "You treat everything you hear or that is said by me or Bob as top secret."

"Yes, sir."

"You can stop the 'sir' routine. Here you use my given name, Clark, or my surname, Gamrick. I don't give a damn which."

Harkowitz nodded.

"Second, you don't discuss the case with anyone, not your girlfriend, your mother, father, or your God."

"On that last one . . . does he have more control over what we discuss than I?" Harkowitz asked, deadpan.

Gamrick glanced over at Folsim. "As a bonus Russo gave us a complete package: a lawyer and a comedian," he commented, keeping his face as expressionless as Harkowitz's. Then he said, "I will tell you exactly what to say in the courtroom. You're my mouthpiece in every sense of the word."

Harkowitz looked as if he was about to object, but Folsim cut him short. "We don't want any fuck-ups," he told him.

And Gamrick added, "You can take the glory. I want the acquittal, and I won't get it if you try to tear McCafery apart. He devours guys like you for breakfast, lunch, and dinner."

"I—"

"That's the deal. You either buy all of it or you don't get any of it," Gamrick said in a hard but not angry tone.

Harkowitz nodded and said, "I'm the *happy* owner of a Gamrick one-of-a-kind deal." This time there was enough of a smile on his face to make Gamrick and Folsim laugh.

The opening day for Anderson's court-martial was set for the Wednesday after the Labor Day weekend, September 8. That gave Gamrick and Harkowitz two weeks to prepare their case. Gamrick found that Harkowitz, like himself, had a photographic memory, enabling him to absorb enormous amounts of information and also, like himself, convert that information to logical trains of thought.

On the steamy Friday afternoon before the Labor Day weekend, Gamrick and Harkowitz walked out to the parking lot together. Folsim had left earlier in the day, and Gamrick planned to spend the weekend sailing the *Snark* on the Chesapeake, possibly taking it out to sea for a while.

Neither of them spoke until they were clear of the building, and then Harkowitz said, "I've been thinking about that missing piece that keeps coming up."

"I'm listening," Gamrick said, and though Harkowitz was younger than Hal, he accepted him as a professional equal because of the particular situation.

"Suppose the people who have been trying to kill you have only been trying to scare you?"

Gamrick stopped and said, "The dead men and the two men I killed might just indicate the opposite."

"Neither Harry or Steve were supposed to die."

"Go on."

"Hawkins was killed because he was a wild card, and a wild card was too damn risky to be allowed to live," Harkowitz said.

"So far, I don't see—"

"Just suppose everything was done to frighten you?"

"I've already supposed that," Gamrick said, starting to walk again. "Remember, my grandson's life was threatened."

"I haven't forgotten. But it was made to keep going. Not to abandon ship but to stay with it—to save it, salvage it, if you will?"

Gamrick stopped again. "Are you trying to tell me that everything that happened was for my benefit?"

"Something like that," Harkowitz said.

"You're going to have to be more specific. Let's get into my car and out of this steam bath," Gamrick said.

Harkowitz shook his head. "There could be roaches in your car or mine, for that matter. I'll explain what I think here. From Hawkins we know that something weird had been going on aboard the *Utah,* and it's a good guess that drugs were involved."

"Okay, we know that."

"Anderson and Downs are players. The stakes are two mil. That's enough to buy protection and still have a lot of fun money left over."

"I can't even begin to guess where you're going with your line of reasoning—that is, if you want to call it reasoning," Gamrick said, taking off his cap and wiping his forehead with a handkerchief.

"Anderson agrees to take the fall on condition that he's protected, goes free."

"Come on, that means that Downs—"

"Is still alive," Harkowitz said.

"No way. There are still three unidentified bodies, and one of them has to be Downs. Besides, how does that account for my role and—"

"You're the patsy," Harkowitz said, looking straight at Gamrick.

"You've been working too hard," Gamrick answered.

"Listen, Clark, bad powder was taken aboard. That just doesn't happen. It was made to happen. Then the bad powder is sent to a specific gun in a specific turret."

"If I'm reading you right, you're saying that there is a chain of command in what happened."

"Something like that," Harkowitz admitted.

"And how did I become involved?"

"Probably by a quirk of fate," Harkowitz said.

"Shit, man, that's no answer!" Gamrick answered in his best imitation of a southern accent.

"You were there. You had the right profile."

"Then Russo—"

"Not him. He's flashy but straight. No, someone with his—or more than his power—picked you," Harkowitz said. "Admiral Russo is basically a by-the-book man. You weren't going by the book, and whoever picked or suggested you *knew* that you wouldn't, that you'd fight to prove Anderson innocent."

"This is a hell of a time to tell me that you don't believe he's innocent," Gamrick responded.

"Oh, I believe he's innocent of setting off the explosion," Harkowitz said, then quickly added, "but I also believe he's not innocent about some other things."

"Maybe not. But that's not the issue."

"Clark, I'd be willing to bet my life that he knows exactly what the missing piece is—or to put it more precisely, who it is."

Gamrick now wiped his face. There was no doubt that Harkowitz had done a tremendous amount of thinking about this, and as wild as his ideas seemed they were worth exploring.

"Why don't you come sailing with me this weekend?" Gamrick suggested. "It would give us time to talk this over and see whether or not your thesis is really meaningful."

"I've never been aboard a sailboat," Harkowitz said.

"Come, then."

After a moment's thought, Harkowitz said, "Follow me to my place. I'll pick up some clothes, then I'll follow you."

"I'd agree to anything to get out of this damn heat," Gamrick said.

* * *

Wayne came out of the house as soon as Gamrick pulled into the cul-de-sac. He was somewhat taken aback to see Harkowitz.

Gamrick introduced them and said, "Jacob and I are going out on the *Snark* for a few days. Take Iris to New York with you."

They trooped into the house with Gamrick leading.

"I thought you would want to continue the conversation that we were having last night," Wayne said.

Gamrick shook his head. "As far as I am concerned, the matter is not up for discussion." He motioned Harkowitz to follow him out to the rear deck and down to the *Snark*.

Once on board, Harkowitz said, "My keen sensitivity tells me that your brother-in-law is pissed at you."

"Stand by on the forward line while I take the stern," Gamrick said, ignoring the comment. He had no intentions of discussing his private life with Harkowitz—or anyone else, for that matter. "Let go bow lines," Gamrick ordered.

"Let go bow lines," Harkowitz repeated.

The *Snark* began to drift away from the dock.

Gamrick went down to the cockpit, started the engine, put the screw in reverse, and eased out into the middle of the cove. "From here on, we move entirely by sail. You can help or not as you please," Gamrick said.

"I'm a quick learner. Show me what to do or tell me, and I'll do it," Harkowitz replied.

"Good. Take the wrapping off the mainsail," Gamrick said, pointing to the laced canvas covering.

By the time they reached the mouth of the cove, the mainsail was up and Harkowitz was at the electric winch, ready to set the foresail at Gamrick's command, which came loud and clear the moment they were in the expanse of the Chesapeake.

The *Snark* heeled to the port the instant the foresail was up and moved briskly on a port tack.

Harkowitz returned to the cockpit, sat opposite Gamrick, and said, "This is a hell of a lot better than working."

Gamrick grinned. "Now, but you might change your mind later."

Harkowitz raised his eyebrows. "Listen, Skipper, I'm a guest. Guests don't work, not even where I come from."

"Where the hell do you come from?"

"You mean you haven't looked at my jacket yet?" Harkowitz asked.

"Dereliction of duty, I'm afraid," Gamrick answered, giving the helm a two-spoke turn to the starboard.

"Upper West Side of Manhattan. My dad is in shrimp. Buys and sells them by the carload. Made tons of money after failing at everything else."

"So you're the bright light of the family?"

"Yes. North Carolina—the whole route."

"And the Navy?"

"NROTC."

Gamrick nodded and said, "How good a cook are you?"

"Odd that you asked. I was wondering the same thing about you," Harkowitz laughed. Then he added, "I've been told by several different women that my cooking is better than theirs."

"A judgment probably based on their hope to get more than a good roll in the hay from you," Gamrick commented.

"Skipper, I may be young, but as Hamlet said, 'when the wind is southerly, I know a hawk from a handsaw.' "

Gamrick laughed. He appreciated any man who could quote from Shakespeare. "The galley is fully equipped. There's meat in the freezer, and the closets have everything else you will need. Just ring the bell when dinner is ready."

Using the microwave oven, Harkowitz made delicious meat balls and spaghetti. And later, after the table was cleared and the dishes washed, Gamrick and he sat in the cockpit, enjoying the deepening pink sky in the west and the already dark sky in the east, where Venus was the brightest object in the sky.

"Are we going to sail all night?" Harkowitz asked.

"About another half hour and then we'll be anchoring for the night at a place called Tracy's Landing," Gamrick answered. "Tomorrow we'll head farther down the bay and maybe make it out to the ocean; or if we don't, we'll tie up at the dock of an old friend of mine in Virginia Beach."

Neither one spoke until Harkowitz said, "There's a yacht behind us."

"Astern of us," Gamrick corrected, looking behind them. A very large, well-lit yacht was almost directly behind them.

"I hope they see us," Harkowitz said.

Gamrick reached into the storage space under the transom and brought out a pair of infra-red field glasses. "Take the helm," he said, moving away from it and training the glasses on the yacht. "The *Sea Devil,* out of Wilmington, North Carolina. She's oceangoing, all right," Gamrick said, replacing the glasses and taking the helm again.

Almost to the minute, a half hour later, the lights of Tracy's Landing appeared ahead on their starbaord side. Gamrick ordered the sails winched down and tied. Then he switched on the *Snark*'s diesel and headed her into the protected anchorage while the *Sea Devil* continued on her way down toward the mouth of the bay.

There were at least a dozen boats riding at anchor, and as Gamrick eased the *Snark* into the cove, the skippers of the boats they passed called out their welcomes.

"Do you know any of them?" Harkowitz asked.

"Sure, most. But casually. They recognized the *Snark,"* Gamrick answered.

Soon they were moored, and Gamrick said, "I'm tired. I'll see you in the morning about oh-six-hundred."

"This is your show," Harkowitz answered.

Gamrick went below, showered, and climbing into the bed in the master bedroom, he fell asleep almost immediately but not before he conjured images of Kate's naked body into his thoughts for him to enjoy. . . .

Gamrick was awake long before the darkness vanished and went for a swim before making eggs, bacon, and coffee for breakfast. Morning finally came with a copper-colored sky in the east.

Gamrick waited until Harkowitz was busy eating his eggs before he said, "The beautiful sky in the east means that we'll probably get some bad weather in the next twenty-four hours, and that means we won't be going out to the ocean."

"Anything you say, Skipper," Harkowitz answered.

"We'll head for Tangier Island. We'll be there by late afternoon."

Harkowitz nodded, and in less than fifteen minutes, they were underway, using the diesel to get them out of the cove.

"It doesn't look like we'll have that bad weather you predicted," Harkowitz said.

"Red sky in the morning, sailor take warning," Gamrick answered. "It's almost always true."

As soon as they were out of the cove, Gamrick ordered the sails set and beat against the wind, which came out of the southeast more strongly than the wind the previous afternoon.

For several hours they discussed the case, and finally Gamrick said, "If I understand your theory correctly, someone for some unknown reason wanted me to be chief investigator, and—"

"Hold it right there," Harkowitz said.

"Okay, I'm holding it."

"He knew you would bulldog it through, even to

making the unheard-of request that you represent Anderson at the court-martial, which the regs specifically forbid, though I imagine in certain circumstances the ranking court officer could circumvent."

Gamrick rubbed his chin. The only one who came close to Harkowitz's description was Kate. She had actually given him the idea of representing Anderson. But her motive was the same as his—justice for someone who was being tried because of his sexual preference rather than his connection to the crime. . . .

"You've come up with a name," Harkowitz said. "I can see it in your eyes."

"Nothing," Gamrick lied.

"Think, Skipper. There must be someone."

"Let's get back to what I was saying," Gamrick said.

"We're back."

"That someone influenced Russo. That makes him a patsy"—he hated that word—"like me."

"Not exactly. A patsy in the sense his behavior was predicted and someone used without him realizing what was happening. Russo would have gone after Anderson just on the basis of his sexual orientation, and since we already defined him as a by-the-book officer, he would do what the book says he should."

Gamrick studied the young man in the cockpit next to him. Not two months before, if he had heard a young officer speak the way Harkowitz spoke about a senior officer, he would have been infuriated and probably sought to discipline him, and now? He had changed. But he still wasn't sure whether it was a change for the better. "I agree with that," Gamrick said.

"Clark, what about Downs?"

"He's dead."

Harkowitz shrugged. "Not until one of those unidentified bodies is identified as his do we know that, do we?"

"Everyone was killed."

Harkowitz shook his head.

"Okay, one missing piece," Gamrick said.

"The second one is more important," Harkowitz said. "Once we have it, we have the reason for everything that happened aboard the *Utah*."

"And does the mighty Harkowitz have any ideas?"

"Skipper, we're going to have to drag it out of the witnesses at the trial, but we will get it. We'll get it, and our man will walk out of that courtroom a free man."

"If you have nothing else, Jacob, you have a super-abundance of confidence," Gamrick said. "Now, stand by to shift the sails, we're going over to a port tack. The wind has freshened and the weather will turn dirty very soon."

Harkowitz looked up at the blue sky. There was nothing to indicate a change in the weather.

"Counselor, trust me," Gamrick said.

"Have I any choice out here?"

"None," Gamrick said.

They changed their tack twice in the next hour, and by the time they finished the second maneuver, word came over the shortwave from the local national weather station warning all small craft to head for a sheltered harbor. Gamrick tuned it to the Coast Guard frequency.

"Storm warnings are going up from Cape May, New Jersey, south to Cape Hatteras, North Carolina. All small craft are advised at this time to seek shelter. Winds up to thirty-five miles an hour are expected with higher gusts to sixty."

"We should just beat it," Gamrick said.

"Jesus, look at those clouds. Where did they come from?" Harkowitz asked, pointing at the sky above the mouth of the bay.

"A squall line," Gamrick answered. "Time to take in all our sail and let the diesel do what it's there to do." After tying down the helm, he manned the winch for the mainsail, while Harkowitz was at the other. At his command both sails were brought down almost simultaneously. Quickly they secured the booms, reefed and tied the sails. By the time they were back in the cockpit, the *Snark* was pitching and rolling violently.

Gamrick started up the diesel, and in a few minutes they had gathered headway. Though the wind was much stronger and there was considerable spray from the four- to five-feet waves, Gamrick put up the weather shield, which protected them from the wind and spray.

During the next hour of heavy weather, Gamrick had little to do but hold a steady course and keep his eye on the radar. There were several ships around them, all running for the safe harbor at Tangier Island.

"Does this happen often at sea?" Harkowitz asked.

Gamrick nodded and said, "But I'm usually under it deep enough if it's bad not to feel it."

The squall broke over them just as the island came in sight. Lightning and thunder tore the sky apart, and when they reached the marina, the best space they could get was at the public dock.

"This is a strange place," Gamrick said when they went below to change into dry clothes. They had decided to spend the night ashore, at the Island Inn, the only hotel there. "Almost everyone here and in Crisfield, the town, on the mainland looks alike. More inbreeding, I guess, than most other places along the bay and the nearby coast."

"Isn't this one of the few places the locals speak a form of Elizabethan English?" Harkowitz said.

"Here and in certain towns in the Great Smoky Mountains."

"Have you ever heard them?"

Gamrick nodded. "Now and then when they didn't realize that an outsider was near."

They packed whatever they needed for the night in shoulder bags and were ready to leave the *Snark* when Harkowitz looked out of the port side port hole. "Isn't that the *Sea Devil*?"

Gamrick came alongside him and looked. "Yes. She's at the refueling dock."

"You mean she'll go out again?"

Gamrick shrugged. "She's built to take a lot more than this," he said.

"You know what I could go for now," Harkowitz said as they unzipped the cockpit's canvas cover and stepped out into the slashing rain and wind. "A hot bowl of soup."

"Hot soup would certainly be welcome. You can get excellent she crab soup here. That town Crisfield I mentioned is the crab capital of the world."

"Now, that is a distinction worthy of pride." Harkowitz laughed as they walked down the length of the pier onto Main Street. A few minutes later, they registered at the hotel and were lucky enough to get the last available room, with double beds and its own bathroom.

"Let's get rid of these shoulder bags," Gamrick suggested, "then get some of that good she crab soup."

Their room was on the third floor at the far end of the corridor. As soon as they were in it, Gamrick unzipped his bag and took out two guns: his 9mm and a snub-nose .38, which he handed to Harkowtiz.

"No way, Skipper. I hate guns and—"

"It's not a gift, Lieutenant, it's an order," Gamrick said in his sternest voice. "Flick the safety off if you have to fire it."

"This is a hell of a time to pull rank on me," Harkowitz groused.

"Take it," Gamrick snapped, putting the 9mm in his belt behind his back so it would be covered by the jacket he wore under his raingear.

Harkowitz did the same. "And I thought this weekend would be a fun time."

Gamrick said, "The one thing you don't want is a 'fun time.'"

Harkowitz placed the .38 in his belt just the way

Gamrick had. "I happen to accidentally shoot my ass off, I am going to hold you personally responsible."

"You do that," Gamrick answered, grinning. Looking at his watch, he said, "It's a bit too late for that hot soup, but early enough for a couple of drinks."

"Shit, I forgot my camera!" Harkowitz exclaimed. "You travel with your firepower, I travel with my camera."

"There's a bar on Main Street just up from the public dock. We'll go down there together. You go back to the *Snark,* and I'll wait for you at the bar."

"Good, but don't shoot anyone until I arrive. I wouldn't want to miss the fun," Harkowitz said.

"I'm not laughing," Gamrick replied, and the two of them left the room.

Outside, the combination of wind and rain were as brutal as before. The only difference now was that the cloud cover was so dense and black it seemed as if it were deep twilight rather than early evening.

When they reached the bar, Gamrick pointed at the swinging weather-beaten shingle. "Ale House," he said reading the words. "I'll be in the Ale House. You think you can remember that?"

"Not if I stand here much longer," Harkowitz said.

"Good," Gamrick answered, turned, and went inside, where the pungent odor of beer and damp sawdust on the floor was pervasive. He went straight to the bar, claimed an unoccupied stool, and sat down, resting his feet on the brass pipe that ran the length of the bar's bottom.

The barkeep—a round-faced, bald-headed man with porcine eyes and a frayed white dish rag on his shoulder—asked him what he was drinking.

"Stoli, if you have it," Gamrick answered.

"Only carry American drink. None of that foreign shit," the man answered.

"Then give me the best American shit you have," Gamrick answered.

The man's round head gave a slight bounce to the

right, and for the barest moment he looked at Gamrick with an expression of total loathing, but the next instant he smiled and said, "You wouldn't care to try some stuff made not a dozen miles from here by a friend of mine on the mainland?"

Gamrick knew he was being set up for a shot of moonshine, white lightning, or whatever else it was called around the bay area.

"If you'd like something more—"

The thunderous roar of a powerful explosion cut him off and sent several bottles on the shelf behind the bar crashing to the floor.

Gamrick ran into the street and looked down toward the public dock. Where the *Snark* had been, there was now a burning hulk. Too stunned to move, he watched her burn. Despite the rain, she burned quickly. Only the mast was left sticking out of the water like the trunk of a dead tree.

Chapter 16

Gamrick walked slowly down Main Street toward the public dock. The island's volunteer firefighters and their one old hoser were already there. The two on-duty policemen were also there, and he could see, despite the wind-driven rain, a Coast Guard launch just coming into the harbor.

When he reached the wreck and made his way through the crowd of people, Gamrick identified himself as the owner of the burned-out boat to the policemen.

"I saw it go up," an old man said. "Boom, and it was gone in sheets of fire."

"Anyone on board?" one of the cops asked.

For a moment Gamrick hesitated, then he nodded and said, "Lieutenant J.G. Jacob Harkowitz, USN."

"Are you—"

"Captain Clark Gamrick, USN," Gamrick said, taking out his wallet and showing them his ID card.

"We're going to need a statement," one of the officers said.

Gamrick nodded.

The Coast Guard launch tied up close to where the *Snark* had been. A red-faced, burly master chief came ashore. "That sucker is finished," he proclaimed.

"We thought you'd see it that way, Luke," one of the cops said.

"And where the fuck is the proud owner?" Luke asked.

"That man over there," he said, pointing at Gamrick,

who had moved away from the cops to look down at the charred and broken remains of his handiwork.

Luke said something that sounded familiar, like English, but Gamrick couldn't understand it.

The two cops laughed.

Gamrick slowly faced them. It was their laughter that brought him to a fury. "I'm the proud owner," he said, hissing out the words.

"When was the last time your boat was inspected?" Luke asked.

"At the beginning of June," Gamrick said.

"Have you proof of ownership?" Luke asked, obviously enjoying his role.

Speaking in a hard, deliberate tone, Gamrick said, "I want a diver to go down and look for my friend's body and examine the wreck."

"You boys didn't tell me about a body," Luke said, looking over his right shoulder at the two cops.

"You didn't ask. Besides, that's police business," one of them answered.

The other agreed.

Luke faced Gamrick again. "Did you say you wanted a diver?"

"Can you read, mister?" Gamrick said, pushing his flipped-open wallet close to Luke's face.

"Yes, sir."

"Good, then you understand who I am and where I'm coming from." Gamrick was breathing hard. He seldom pulled rank the way he just had, but sometimes the situation would force him, and this was one of those situations.

"Yes, sir."

"A diver, now. You tell your buddies over there," Gamrick said, hiking his thumb toward the two cops, who were less than a yard away, "not to touch anything. The FBI will be down here first thing in the morning."

"Yes, sir."

"And tell them whatever statement I make will be

made in the presence of an FBI agent and an officer from the NCIS."

"Yes, sir."

Gamrick took a deep breath, and suddenly realizing that something was wrong, he looked over his right shoulder at the fueling dock. The *Sea Devil* was gone. He faced Luke again. "I want everything the Coast Guard has on the *Sea Devil*, out of Wilmington, North Carolina, and I want it two hours ago."

"Sir, that might be difficult to get on Saturday—"

"I told you what I wanted, Chief. What I don't want is excuses."

"No, sir."

"Good. You will be able to find me in the hotel, or in a bar. But find me you will."

"Yes, sir," Luke answered, saluting.

Gamrick snapped a return salute and strode off, the crowd magically parting for him. He walked up Main Street back to the hotel and went to his room to phone Russo, who would then have to decide how to proceed.

The door was slightly ajar. . . . His heart began to race. He reached around to his back, under his raingear, and sliding the 9mm out from his belt, he flicked the safety off. With the gun securely in his hands and his finger on the trigger, he took a deep breath and kicked the door open.

Harkowitz was sitting up in one of the beds, pointing the .38 at him.

Gamrick lowered the 9mm, put the safety on, and said, "You're dead." Then he took out his handkerchief and wiped the sweat off his face.

"I thought it was—"

"Put the fucking gun down," Gamrick said, suddenly feeling exhausted. He reached back and closed the door.

Harkowitz lowered the .38 and said, "Aren't you going to ask me what happened?"

Gamrick nodded. "Give me a few moments. I didn't

expect to see you here," he said, dropping onto one of the chairs in the room.

"Someone is coming," Harkowitz said.

Gamrick heard the approaching footfalls too and knew it couldn't be Luke. He'd been followed. . . .

"Kill the light on the deck," he ordered, already standing with 9mm in his hand, the safety off. His instincts told him the hunter was there for the kill. Rivulets of sweat poured down his face and back. Kneeling, he pointed his weapon at the door and whispered, "Stay on the deck."

Harkowitz didn't answer.

Gamrick gulped for air and slowly released it. Images raced through his brain: his sons, grandchildren, Iris, Kate—Kate, naked in his embrace . . . Kate so close, so close that he couldn't see—

The door burst open and fire from a small submachine gun chewed up the bed, shattering the room's silence.

A hulking figure was silhouetted against the dim light of the hallway.

With deliberate slowness Gamrick sucked in air and held it until he had squeezed off two rounds.

The chatter of the submachine gun combined with the explosive noise made by the two rounds.

A scream came from the figure in the doorway. Then throwing up its arms, it staggered backward, dropping the submachine gun.

Gamrick fired two more rounds.

The figure slammed into the wall on the opposite side of the narrow hallway, bounced off it, twisted, and fell face up just outside of the room.

Gamrick stood up. "Turn on the lights," he said in a steady voice. He walked to the door and looked at the dead man. He had seen him at Cool's funeral; he had been with Cassado on the far side of the room.

Gamrick and Harkowitz were seated in front of Admiral Russo. It was Sunday, the day after the shooting, and Russo had already made it clear he resented having to be in the office on the Sunday of the Labor Day weekend.

"Weekends seem to be troublesome for you, Captain," Russo said, drumming his fingers nervously on the desk. "You know this means another board."

"Yes, sir," Gamrick answered.

"I ordered you here because—"

"Sir," Harkowitz began, but Russo glowered at him and said, "The only reason you're here, Lieutenant, is because you were stupid enough to go sailing with—"

Gamrick was on his feet. "With all due respect, sir, I was the target of an assassination attempt. My sailboat was set on fire, and you act as if I did something wrong by defending myself."

Russo looked up at him and growled, "You're still in the Navy, Captain, remember that."

"Even that doesn't prevent you from having some understanding of the situation," Gamrick answered, sitting.

Russo leaned back into his swivel chair. "Someday you could have been the CNO, or perhaps the Chief of the Joint Chiefs of Staff, but for some perversity on your part, you blew it all away, *Captain.*"

Gamrick didn't answer. Those goals no longer interested him.

"You don't seem to understand that the Navy wants—"

"Sir, it is not a question of what the Navy wants," Gamrick interrupted, and before Russo could speak, he said, "Anderson is on trial because the Navy needs a scapegoat, and because of his alleged sexual behavior, he's it."

"For god's sakes, Captain, you're the one who brought the pictures of him and Downs to me," Russo exploded. "That's hard evidence of—"

"Of his sexual behavior."

"Listen to me, after the trial the entire crew of the *Utah* will be dispersed throughout other ships, and that will be the end of it," Russo responded.

Harkowitz said, "I saw that man aboard the *Snark,* and I was with Captain Gamrick when he came to the room. Those acts—"

"I told you why you're here, Lieutenant," Russo snapped.

Gamrick shook his head.

"And what is that supposed to mean?" Russo questioned, leaning forward and drumming on the desk.

"I'm going to say something that is off the record," Gamrick told him.

"Go ahead."

"You're more than just a bright man, you're a very clever man, or you would not be behind that desk. I'm sure you've run the facts of this case through your mind as many times as I have, and I'm sure that you see what I, Lieutenant Harkowitz, and Commander Folsim see."

"I see what is best for the Navy," Russo answered.

"Then let me spell out what we see."

Russo uttered a weary sigh.

"I'll begin by telling you the man I killed was at Lieutenant Cool's funeral with Richard Cassado. Cassado is the man who killed my dog, attacked me, and who I killed."

Russo stopped drumming his fingers on the desk. "Are you certain?" he asked.

"Lieutenant Martins can identify him from the photographs the police took of the body. She was at the funeral with me."

"I didn't know she was there," Russo admitted.

Gamrick shrugged. He did not want to get off track. "Now to the questions: who suggested that I lead the investigation?"

Russo looked at him quizzically.

"I came out of left field. You only knew I was on your staff. You had no idea who I was or what I could do. Someone had to suggest my name to you."

"Two men did: the Secretary of the Navy, John Howard, and Senator Dobbs," Russo answered.

Gamrick smiled. "The Secretary of the Navy has access to my jacket—my profile."

"Yes."

"Did you ever ask either of them why they recommended me?"

Russo flushed. "I assumed they had their reasons," he said.

"They certainly did."

"Where is all this leading?"

Gamrick said, "One more question, sir. Do either of them own an ocean-going yacht?"

"The senator does."

"The *Sea Devil,* right?"

"Yes."

"The *Sea Devil* followed us to Tangier Island. It tied up at the refueling dock just long enough to drop the hit man off."

"You can't prove that."

"Only because the man is dead," Gamrick said facetiously.

"Captain, you're swimming in very dangerous waters," Russo commented, drumming on the table harder than he had before.

"I spoiled someone's master plan," Gamrick said. "I was chosen to investigate Anderson because I had the right profile: I'd bulldog the situation and eventually wind up where I am now—his defense counsel. But something happened that wasn't supposed to. I pressed Hawkins, and he told me about some of the things that had gone on aboard the *Utah.*"

"You said he was sick," Russo counted.

"Yes, but not so sick that he would not have delivered under the pressure of examination."

"I'm trying to get rid of one disaster, and you're trying to create another," Russo said.

"Sir, it has already been created," Gamrick answered.

"Do you intend to go after Dobbs and Howard?"

"If there wasn't a connection between them and

what happened aboard the *Utah*, I wouldn't be here and we wouldn't be having this conversation," Gamrick said.

"I take that to mean that you will," Russo responded.

"I will do whatever I have to do within the bounds of the law to win Anderson's freedom."

Russo took several moments before he said, "This conversation never took place."

"Never," Gamrick responded.

"Absolutely never," Harkowitz said.

"To protect Folsim, I'm going to have new orders for him on Tuesday morning," Russo explained.

"I didn't think so when I first met him, but he's a damn good man," Gamrick said.

"He's going to marry my niece," Russo said.

"All the more reason to protect him," Gamrick responded.

"And who will protect the two of you?"

Gamrick looked at Harkowitz and said, "I remember having read or heard that 'God looks after fools, drunkards, and the United States.' I guess we'll have to be satisfied with that, sir."

Russo smiled. "I made a mistake about you, Captain. I thought you were Navy, and you're not."

"I made the same mistake myself, but it took almost thirty years to find out. You were faster at finding me out than I was."

"Now, that's a compliment I never expected," Russo said, "but let me give you one in return. After I realized I made a mistake about you, I thought you were a crank, a nut job."

"That's hardly a compliment, sir," Gamrick said.

"Now I have to change that view too. You're one hell of a man, Captain. One hell of a man!"

Gamrick nodded and said, "Coming from you, sir, that's certainly a compliment."

* * *

Gamrick had called Kate from his office before he met with Russo, and now that the meeting was over, he sent Harkowitz home and he went to her apartment.

She greeted him at the door wearing a black lace negligee with nothing underneath it.

As soon as he was inside the apartment, he took her in his arms and kissed her passionately.

She eagerly responded.

Within a matter of minutes they were in bed.

"You don't waste time," she laughed, kissing the side of his face.

"Not with you," Gamrick answered, savoring the warm taste of her breasts.

Caressing his penis, she said, "I think I'd like it inside me."

"I was hoping you'd say that," Gamrick answered, maneuvering her over him. "You're the rider now." He placed his palms over her breasts.

She began to make a small circular motion with her bottom and at the same time reached under his scrotum to caress him.

Gamrick closed his eyes. The rhythmic contractions deep inside her felt like dozens of pairs of lips moving along the length of his penis.

She quickened her movements, put her head down on his chest, and her hands on his shoulders. Each time she thrust down, he thrust up.

"Soon," she whispered. "Oh soon!" And she moved faster.

Reaching under Kate, he gently caressed her.

She put her mouth on his shoulder, and the next instant her body tensed. She bit him on his shoulder, and with her body shuddering she climaxed.

Gamrick pushed deep into her and in a moment of ecstasy grabbed hold of her breasts and squeezed them just hard enough to make her cry out in pain. The next instant he let go of them and placing his hands on the sides of her head, he brought her face close to his and kissed her on the lips.

Moments later she rolled off him and settled at his side.

He put his arm around her, and resting his hand on her bare breast, he said, "I had some trouble over the last thirty-six hours."

"Is that why you grabbed hold of me the way you did?" Kate asked.

Gamrick told her what happened.

"My God!" She was trembling. "My God!" she said again and pressed her hand on his. "Maybe it's time to seriously think about—"

"I have thought about it, and I have some clues."

"What are they?"

Suddenly Gamrick remembered his thoughts about just before the would-be assassin had thrown open the door and begun firing. He let go of her breast and pushed himself up against the back of the bed. How much and with whom is she involved? Has she—

"What's wrong?" Kate asked, sitting alongside him.

He took hold of her hands. "I need to know your role," he said quietly.

"I don't know what you mean by 'my role.'"

"Kate, you urged me to do something to help Anderson," he said, tightening his grip.

"You're hurting me," she said.

He let go of her and said, "You knew about the powder. How?"

"You know I can't tell who told me about it," she answered.

Gamrick rubbed his chin and realized that he'd almost made a terrible mistake. He'd allowed suspicion and insecurity to take control of his reason.

"You come here, make love to me, and then—"

"I'm sorry, Kate," Gamrick interrupted. "These last few weeks have been very difficult. I still don't know where John is, my marriage is a shambles, and several people have tried to kill me. And—" he hesitated.

"And what?" she asked.

"And I want you for myself," he said, realizing that jealousy was at the heart of his suspicions.

Gently Kate touched the side of his face. "I love you, Clark," she said in a low, throaty voice. "If I didn't, you wouldn't be here now."

"It's just that—"

She put her finger across his lips and said, "I have to accept the fact you make love to Iris."

Gamrick answered, "It's not the same."

"It's not the same for either of us, Clark," Kate said. "We have what we have, and what we have is worth keeping."

Gamrick put his arms around her, and pressing her naked body against his, he whispered, "Yes, it's worth keeping."

Chapter 17

A legal yeoman read aloud each of the four charges and their accompanying specifications against Anderson. Under the Uniform Code of Military Justice, he was being charged with the destruction of government property, Article 108; improper hazarding of a vessel, Article 110; murder and voluntary manslaughter, articles 118 and 119.

Listening to the monotone drone of the yeoman's voice and seated between Harkowitz and Anderson, Gamrick felt constricted.

During the time it took to read the charges and specifications and have Harkowitz enter a plea of not guilty to each, Gamrick studied the five members of the court. Rear Admiral Joseph Edwards was the ranking officer. The other four were senior-grade captains. He did not know any of them personally, but he and Harkowitz had studied their service records over the last two days. Edwards, Burk, Croft, and Davies were surface men. Captains Henry and Moon were former jet jocks. All of them had seen service in Vietnam. Edwards' son, a riverine officer, had been killed there. Except for their uniforms and their short haircuts, they looked like any other assemblage of men. Croft and Davies ran to corpulency, while Edwards and the other three were lean from either working at it or from genetic makeup. Expressionless, each of the men listened intently to the yeoman's reading.

Gamrick tuned the yeoman's voice out and listened to his own internal one, which was laying out a plan to enable him to take a more active role in Anderson's defense. He looked at Captain McCafery at the table on the opposite side of the courtroom and tried to decide if the ability of the man was equal to his reputation. Anal retentive, perhaps? A hardass? Might be if he sensed he could get away with it . . . Gamrick glanced at Harkowitz. Very sharp but not yet sharp enough to duel it out with McCafery.

Suddenly Gamrick realized that Edwards had adjourned the court until 1300. He leaned close to Harkowitz. "Did I miss anything important?" he asked.

Harkowitz gave him a questioning look.

"Wool gathering," he answered. "You know how it is when you're having fun."

Two Marine guards came to escort Anderson back to his cell.

"Those court members looked as if they were recently embalmed," Harkowitz said on the way out of the courtroom.

"That's not a kind remark," Gamrick responded.

"Not kind perhaps. But absolutely true," Harkowitz answered.

As soon as they stepped out of the courtroom, they had to push their way through a crowd of TV people, and every time a microphone was shoved in their face they said, almost in unison, "No comment."

At lunch McCafery, carrying a tray with salad and a bottle of apple juice on it, came over to their table and asked if he could join them.

"Certainly," Gamrick said, gesturing to the empty chair next to him. "I don't see why we can't be civilized about having an adversarial relationship."

McCafery laughed.

"But before any relationship can start, introductions are in order," Gamrick said and immediately introduced himself, shook McCafery's hand, which had a firmer grip than he had suspected, then introduced Harkowitz, who also shook McCafery's hand. "That done," Gamrick continued, "we can go on to enjoy a long—and I hope not always adversarial—relationship."

This time McCafery didn't laugh; he smiled, showing two rows of very white teeth. He was a tall, proud-looking man with chiseled features, a leonine head of black hair, dark gray eyes, and long tapering fingers you'd find on a pianist's hands.

"Well, the morning was certainly exciting," Gamrick commented.

"Yes, I noticed that you were there more in body than in spirit," McCafery said.

"That's only an impression," Harkowitz said. "He does that to screen his intense acuity."

"Interesting that you should use the word acuity," Gamrick responded, "because at this very moment that sense of acuity tells me that our guest has come bearing gifts."

McCafery's brow knitted, then he said, "Not a gift so much as a way to put an end to a very disagreeable situation."

"We're listening," Harkowitz told him.

Gamrick waved his right hand, put down his corned beef sandwich, drank some beer before he said, "Any offer of anything less than dismissal of all charges is totally unacceptable and would be a terrible way to start our newly established adversarial relationship."

McCafery looked as if he had just discovered he'd been eating turds.

Gamrick smiled at him. He had unhorsed him, if momentarily, and was enjoying every moment of it.

"You're gambling with the man's life," McCafery said gravely.

"No, Captain, I am sure that I will be able to keep his life, while you, sir, are gambling that you will be able to take it."

"Gentlemen," McCafery said, standing, "in any situation our relationship would have been short-lived." And he left the table.

Gamrick lifted his glass and drank the rest of the beer.

"Did you take some special pill this morning?" Harkowitz asked.

Gamrick stood his head.

"It would not have hurt to listen to his offer, and it might have helped," Harkowitz said.

"I made him angry," Gamrick answered.

"Yes, that would be an accurate description of his emotional state when he left the table," Harkowitz said.

"Don't try to imitate me," Gamrick told him.

"I would never be equal to the task," Harkowitz replied.

Gamrick waved his comment away and said, "He was going to offer us the mercy of the court if we pleaded guilty on all counts, and that would put Anderson away for life. That's not much of a gift, even from someone who isn't a Greek."

"How could you be so damn sure?"

"Because that's what I would have offered if I were in his place. Had we taken it, he would have come out of this trial with accolades. He made his try, and he will try again as the evidence begins to go against him. The one thing he can't offer is Anderson's acquittal. That's something we'll have to fight for and win for him."

"My God, Captain, you almost sounded as if you were inspired," Harkowitz commented with a grin.

"Don't you believe it. It was only the combination of corned beef and beer talking," Gamrick answered, with a sly smile back.

McCafery gave his opening statement, in which he hammered away on the combination of Anderson's homosexual relationship and venality which resulted in the death of twenty-seven men. He concluded, "The government will prove that Seaman First Class Paul Anderson is guilty of all charges and specifications."

When Harkowitz's turn came, he stood up and read a prepared statement asserting Anderson's innocence of all charges and specifications. "The Navy had been misled into the dark and murky passageways of an individual's sexual behavior because of the political value this court-martial appears to have."

Both statements were mercifully brief, and after a ten-minute recess the trial started.

Gamrick scribbled a note to Harkowitz, who read it, gave him a strange look, and received a sharp whispered order, "Do it." He stood up and said, "If it please the court, I request that all trial procedure be conducted by my colleague, Captain Clark Gamrick."

"Objection," McCafery roared before Edwards could answer and was on his feet approaching the members of the court.

"Sir, the court should be aware of the circumstances of my appointment as Seaman First Class Paul Anderson's defense counsel," Harkowitz said.

"He is the—" McCafery began.

"Captain McCafery, permit me to hear what the defense counselor is saying," Edwards said in an even tone.

"Yes, sir," McCafery answered.

"Sir, this case was put for grabs and I grabbed it," Harkowitz said.

"Will you explain to the court how you were appointed the defense counselor for the accused?" Edwards said.

"Yes, sir," Harkowitz said and gave a full explanation.

Edwards listened intently, then said, "Captain Gamrick, your presence here as adviser to the defense counselor is without precedent, and the court was asked to permit it because of the extraordinary nature of the case."

Gamrick stood up. "Sir, it is neither the defense counselor's intention nor mine to establish new precedents for the Navy court-martial procedures."

"Then what is your objective, sir?"

"To give the accused the best possible defense. Captain McCafery is an experienced courtroom warrior. My colleague's youth alone prevents anyone from making that claim, and this, other than appearing in a traffic court, is my first time in a court of law."

"Objection," McCafery shouted, again on his feet. "Captain Gamrick is attempting to influence the court to permit legal status when such status, by the actions of the NCIS, have already been denied."

"My only intention, Captain, is to serve justice," Gamrick flung back.

"Justice is not the issue here."

"If justice is not the issue, then the Navy should not waste taxpayer money with this trial and execute the accused," Gamrick answered.

"The court will vote, and it will remain in session while its members vote," Edwards said.

Gamrick sat, and gesturing to Harkowitz to do the same, he said, "No matter which way the vote goes, we've scored a few points."

Harkowitz didn't answer, and Gamrick didn't attempt to continue the conversation. Instead he allowed his thoughts to drift to Kate. Thinking about her both calmed and aroused him simultaneously. He couldn't help himself. When he thought about her, he was like an eighteen-year-old again. . . . Eighteen might be pushing it a bit—certainly not more than twenty. She—

Edwards cleared his throat and said, "The court will allow Captain Gamrick the right of cross-examination, but the court directs the court recorder to show that this decision has been made because of the unusual circumstances surrounding the choice of the defense counselor, which in due course will be the subject of an investigation by a board of inquiry, and the unusual nature of the crime for which the accused is being tried. The court does not want its actions to be interpreted as an attempt to create a precedent. Its actions are based solely on the case before it."

Withholding a grin of victory, Gamrick kept his face expressionless.

McCafery put three witnesses on the stand—men from the other gun turrets—who indicated the friendship between Anderson and Downs was exclusionary.

Neither Gamrick nor Harkowitz cross-examined, but they reserved the right to recall each of the witnesses at any time during the trial.

At 1600 Edwards adjourned the day's proceedings and set the start for the following day at 0900.

Gamrick and Harkowitz made their way through the crowd of press and TV people. Kate was there too, but she was off on one side talking into a camcorder.

She saw him, flashed a big smile, but never missed a beat.

Outside, Harkowitz stopped short and said, "Okay, you scored some brownie points, but you did it by making me look stupid."

"So that's what nibbling at your craw," Gamrick answered.

"Nibbling is not exactly what it feels like."

"Had I told you what I intended to do, we would have discussed it. Had we discussed it, you might have responded negatively, just as you are doing now—not that you don't have good cause. But I didn't have time. The idea came to me while listening to the yeoman read the charges and specifications."

"We could have discussed it at lunch," Harkowitz said petulantly as he began to walk again.

"With McCafery there?"

"Okay, you did it. You won your point. Next time—"

"I will discuss strategy with you before I execute it," Gamrick said. "Now, can we go somewhere for a cold drink and something to eat?"

Harkowitz smiled. "I was wondering when you'd ask."

* * *

The next morning Gamrick recalled one of McCafery's three previous witnesses, a huge man, Gunner's Mate Nicholas Drosses, to the witness stand.

"Remember, you are still under oath," Gamrick said.

"Yes, sir," Drosses answered.

"Do you have a special friend on ship?" Gamrick questioned.

"Objection," McCafery said.

"On what grounds?" Gamrick asked.

"The word special has insulting connotations to my witness."

"Will you define your use of the word special for the court, Captain?"

"Yes, sir," Gamrick answered. "A buddy with whom the witness goes on shore leave, talks to, plays cards—in other words, a best friend, a special friend."

"Yes, sir," Drosses volunteered.

"And you spend most of your free time with him, even go on double dates—"

"Objection!" McCafery said. "The counselor is leading the witness."

"Sustained. Captain, will you tell the court what your ultimate objective is with this witness?"

"Sir, Gunner's Mate Nicholas Drosses has a buddy, a best friend. The Navy encourages the buddy system—all of the services encourage it—yet Captain McCafery saw fit to make it seem unusual and peculiar when that same buddy system, best friend, or even special friend was the relationship between Seaman First Class Paul Anderson and Seaman First Class Gus Downs."

McCafery said, "In an effort to spare the court a parade of witnesses who will attest to the fact that they have best friends, I will concede that the relationship between the accused and the deceased—"

"Objection!" Gamrick said. "Neither one of the three remaining bodies has been positively identified as the body Seaman First Class Gus Downs."

"One of them must be," McCafery snapped.

"Objection sustained," Edwards said. "Rephrase your statement, Captain."

McCafery glared at Gamrick and said, "The government will acknowledge the exclusionary nature of the buddy system, but it will place in evidence these photographs, which clearly show that in the relationship between Seaman First Class Paul Anderson and Seaman First Class Gus Downs the exclusionary nature of their friendship went far beyond the bounds of normal behavior between male friends."

"Mark the photographs as exhibit one," Edwards said, taking them from McCafery's hand.

Gamrick whispered to Harkowitz to watch the faces of the members of the court.

"To a man they're expressionless," Harkowitz answered.

When the photographs were finally handed to a yeoman, who marked them, McCafery said, "Those photographs clearly show the true nature of the relationship between the accused and Seaman First Class Downs. They were homosexual lovers."

"Objection," Gamrick called out.

"Overruled," Edwards said, sternly adding, "A old Chinese proverb states, 'A picture is worth a thousand words.' Those photographs are worth many thousands of words."

"Sir, there is a woman in three of those photographs," Gamrick said, now standing.

"Captain—"

"With all due respect to the court, the fact that there is a woman sexually involved with the accused and only the accused should indicate the possibility that the accused could be bisexual."

"Objection," McCafery said. "The court has already overruled on the contents of the photographs."

"Captain Gamrick, would you please explain to the court what difference it would make whether the accused's sexual behavior is labeled homosexual or bisexual, since in each the element of homosexuality exists?" Edwards asked, the tone of his voice clearly showing his annoyance.

"I will, sir, when the woman in the photographs is before the court as a witness for the defense. But in your own words that a picture is worth a thousand words, there are several that clearly show the accused having intercourse with a woman."

Edwards ran his fingers through his hair. "The court will expect a further explanation when the woman for the defense is presented to the court. But in the meantime let the record show the photographs show the accused involved in bisexual behavior."

McCafery paraded out several other witnesses, some of whom were ship-design experts who testified that a bomb placed anywhere in the portion of number two turret where the explosion had taken place would have disastrous consequences.

It was Harkowitz's turn to question the witnesses, which he did only to establish the fact that the explosion could have been caused by a sudden electrical fire, or even a mishandling of the powder.

McCafery objected, asserting, "The findings of pyrotechnical experts clearly indicate there was a primary explosion." And he introduced the chemical analysis of the explosion's residue as evidence.

"No further questions," Harkowitz said and reserved the right to recall the various witnesses.

McCafery called Navy psychiatrist Commander William C. Bliss, who had examined Anderson, to the stand. He testified that Anderson was indeed a homosexual.

"Would you say that the accused would not have sexual relations with a woman?" Harkowitz asked.

"A woman would not be his choice for a sexual partner," Bliss said confidently.

"Under all circumstances?" Harkowitz asked.

"Objection!" McCafery called. "The court knows where the counselor is leading the witness."

"Sustained," Edwards said.

"Could you, Commander, explain to the court a homosexual's reaction to a woman's genitalia?" Harkowitz asked.

"In most situations it would be one of extreme disgust and often fear."

"You're certain of that?"

"Yes."

"Then Seaman First Class Paul Anderson should, according to you, be unable to have intercourse with a woman?"

"It would be highly unlikely."

Harkowitz went to the table where the photographs had been placed, picked them up, and handing them to Bliss, he asked, "Can you identify the man in each of these photographs?"

Bliss flushed and stammered, "Certainly, it's Seaman First Class Paul Anderson."

"Is he in this courtroom?"

"Yes, he is sitting at the table there," he said, pointing at Anderson.

"In each of the photographs, does the accused look as if he's extremely disgusted or in any way afraid of having coitus with the woman?"

"No," Bliss whispered.

"Does he look as if he's enjoying himself?" Harkowitz asked.

A ripple of laughter skidded through the courtroom. Even Gamrick smiled.

"Objection," McCafery shouted, obviously not amused. "The counselor is attempting to have the witness define the emotional state of the accused at the time the photographs were taken."

"Sustained," Edwards said.

"I have no further questions," Harkowitz responded.

"Does the prosecution have additional witnesses?" Edwards asked.

"No, sir, the prosecution rests its case," McCafery said.

"Will the defense be ready to present its case this afternoon?" Edwards asked.

"Yes, sir," Harkowitz answered.

Edwards adjourned the court for lunch and set a return time for 1300.

As soon as the court was back in session and Edwards asked the defense to present its case, Gamrick stood up and said, "With the court's permission I would like to relate a series of events with regard to the photographs that have been put in evidence by the prosecution."

"Objection," McCafery said. "The photographs do not need any explanation."

"They do not, but how you came by them does," Gamrick snapped before Edwards could speak.

"Sir, the counselor for the defense is trying to divert the court from the single issue—namely, the accused's motive for killing his lover."

Edwards studied Gamrick and McCafery for several moments before he said, "Make your statement brief, Captain."

Gamrick began, "The photographs were mailed to me by Seaman Third Class Donald Hawkins. And by his own admission he'd taken them when the accused, Gus Downs, and Ms. Julie Giodono were on a nude beach in Truro, Massachusetts." Gamrick went on to describe the phone calls that Hawkins had made to him. When he finished, he thanked the court for the opportunity to address it, and then he called his first witness, Marine Sergeant Vincent Gorga, to the stand.

"Sergeant Gorga, will you tell the court exactly what took place when we arrived at the motel room where Hawkins was staying?"

"On Captain Gamrick's orders, I broke the door down and we entered the room. Hawkins and the woman were naked. Hawkins was on the floor, and the woman was about to strike him with a whip. He'd already had several cuts on his back from it."

"Objection," McCafery called. "The witness does not know that the alleged cuts on Seaman Third Class Donald Hawkins' back were made by the whip he saw."

"Sustained."

"Sergeant Gorga, will you tell the court what you heard Seaman Donald Hawkins tell me?"

"That he was being punished for his sins and that the woman would have been punished for her sins if we hadn't arrived."

"What sin was he talking about?" Gamrick questioned.

"Having sex," Gorga answered.

"Objection," McCafery said. "How could the Sergeant be sure that he meant that?"

"Because he used the word fucking, sir," Gorga answered.

Again a ripple of laughter went through the courtroom.

"Sergeant, will you tell the court what Seaman Third Class Donald Hawkins said about the men aboard the *Utah* and specifically the men who manned gun number two in turret number two."

"Claimed they were all Satanists ... that he alone wasn't, that they worshiped the Devil and he was forced to sleep with a cross in his hand to protect himself."

"Did he admit to using drugs of any kind?" Gamrick asked.

"Yes, sir. I found marijuana—in his bag. He said he bought it from one of the other crewmen on the ship."

"Objections," McCafery offered. "We only have Sergeant Gorga's testimony as to what Seaman Third Class Donald Hawkins said or did not say."

"I will take the witness stand and substantiate the sergeant's response," Gamrick said.

"Captain Gamrick, the court does not understand what bearing Seaman Donald Hawkins's sexual behavior has on the guilt or innocence of the accused. The man is dead," Edwards said.

"The fact that the man is dead has a bearing on the trial," Gamrick responded, glancing at Anderson, whose sudden start indicated he had not known Hawkins was dead.

"Will you please clarify that statement for the court?"

"I am not prepared to make a further clarification at this time," Gamrick answered.

"The court will expect one before this trial is over. Seaman Third Class Donald Hawkins is not on trial, and because of his untimely death, the court will not tolerate any attempt on the part of the defense to vilify the man."

"It is not the defense's intent to vilify the man, only to show that his behavior was suspect."

"Suspect for what?" McCafery demanded to know.

"For killing twenty-seven men," Gamrick fired back.

In an instant the courtroom exploded with exclamations of surprise and dismay, forcing Edwards to rap his gavel several times before the spectators were quiet again. Then looking straight at Gamrick, he said, "Unless you are prepared to show the court hard evidence that corroborates your allegation about Seaman Third Class Donald Hawkins, you will refrain from mentioning his name again during these proceedings. The personal side of the deceased's life has no visible bearing on the guilt or innocence of the accused."

"With all due respect to the court, the deceased hated the accused, and he hated the twenty-seven men who died in the explosion."

"Are you really suggesting that Hawkins was responsible for the death of those men?" McCafery questioned.

"I am suggesting that he had a very strong motive," Gamrick said quietly.

"Captain Gamrick, I must caution you about making unsubstantiated statements," Edwards said.

"Sir, the very fact that Seaman Third Class Donald Hawkins was murdered, coupled to the information about him that was given here today, has to suggest something to the court about—"

"Objection," McCafery shouted, his face very red. "The counselor is attempting to put a dead man on trial."

"I am trying to prevent the accused from being made a scapegoat," Gamrick answered.

Edwards again cautioned Gamrick not to make unsubstantiated statements.

"And what kind of statement will be made, sir, about this court if it finds an innocent man guilty?" Gamrick questioned.

Edwards said, "This court is adjourned until oh-nine-hundred tomorrow morning. Captain Gamrick, I want you in my office immediately."

"Yes, sir," Gamrick answered.

Within a matter of minutes Gamrick was in Edwards' office, where the admiral, pointing his finger at him, said, "You have overstepped your role, Captain, and I demand that you present a written apology to the court."

"Sir, I am there to defend the accused. He is on trial for his life. I will do everything I can to prevent him from being the Navy's scapegoat."

Edwards flushed. "If Hawkins was the man who set the explosion, tell me why he was killed'?" he asked tightly.

"I cannot answer that. But there is a great deal of evidence to indicate Hawkins had more than one reason to want twenty-seven men dead."

"Unless you can prove that Hawkins actually placed a bomb in the turret, the accused will be found guilty."

"Sir, my client is innocent," Gamrick responded.

"Dismissed!" Edwards said.

They saluted each other, and Gamrick left the room knowing that he'd pushed Edwards too far.

Before the trial began the next morning, Gamrick had breakfast with Kate in a diner not far from where they had spent the night together at a small motel in Virginia Beach. Because Gamrick's thoughts were already involved with the events of the day yet to come, he listened to Kate more than he spoke. To have made love to her just a short while before and to be sitting opposite from her now gave him an enormous sense of well-being—a kind of inner warmth. He reached across the table and squeezed her hand.

"Did you mean what you said before?" Kate asked, looking at him over a fork on which a piece of egg and sausage was speared.

From the throaty sound of her voice, he knew exactly to what she was referring. "Yes, I want to marry you," he answered.

She nodded.

"There's twenty-odd years between us, but—"

"When?" she asked.

"It will take awhile to arrange a divorce," Gamrick answered.

Kate said, "I didn't intend to fall in love with you, Clark. I wanted to go to bed with you, and as long as it would last, it would last."

"There's more between us than just what happens in bed," he said.

"Yes, there is. I'll marry you because I love you."

Gamrick laughed. "That is a good answer and a good reason," he said. Bringing the back of her hand to his lips, he whispered, "I love you, Kate."

She leaned slightly forward and also whispered, "If we had more time, I'd take you back to the room and show you how much."

Gamrick felt a sudden burst of heat in his groin.

"Another time, my love. Now I have to do battle with the forces of darkness."

This time she kissed the back of his hand.

The courtroom was silent as Julie Giodono took the stand. She looked smaller than Gamrick had remembered and even more frightened than when he had seen her. Dressed demurely in a simple black suit with a white blouse, there scarcely seemed to be any connection between her and the nude woman in the photographs.

After she gave her name and address, Gamrick produced the three photographs of her and Anderson having coitus and asked, "Are these photographs of you, Ms. Giodono?"

"Yes," she answered, flushed.

"And will you identify by name the man with whom you had coitus?"

She looked at him questioningly and said, "I don't understand."

"Coitus means sex."

"Oh! Paul Anderson," she answered.

"Is he in this room?" Gamrick answered.

She pointed at Anderson.

"Now, Ms. Giodono, will you tell the court where you were when these pictures were taken?"

"The beach in North Truro, Massachusetts, about two mônths ago. A few days before the explosion on the *Utah*."

"These documents are being entered in evidence. They confirm the place, give the exact location in terms of latitude and longitude, and they also give the exact date and time. They were prepared by the Naval Photographic Laboratory," Gamrick said.

The documents were accepted and marked as evidence.

"According to the same analysis, the photographs were taken with a telephoto lens from a distance of four to five hundred yards at an angle of thirty degrees," Gamrick explained.

"Will the counselor reach the point of statement?" Edwards said.

"The photographs—the three that Ms. Giodono has in her hand—and the others were taken by Seaman Third Class Donald Hawkins."

"Objection," McCafery stormed. "The court only has your statement that he admitted to having taken them."

"Sustained."

"Your witness," Gamrick said, looking at McCafery.

"Ms. Giodono, why were you naked in the presence of two men, one of whom was your sexual partner?" McCafery asked, moving close to the witness stand. Before she could answer, he said, "Isn't it true that you were there to have sex with both men?"

"Objection," Gamrick shouted, leaping out of his chair. "The prosecution is leading the witness."

"Sustained. Restate the question," Edwards said.

"Do you consider having sex a private act?"

"Yes."

"Then why did you allow Seaman First Class Anderson to have sex with you in the presence of another man?" McCafery asked.

"We were drunk," she said softly.

"But you knew what he was doing?"

"Yes," she mumbled.

"You did say yes, Ms. Giodono?"

"Objection," Gamrick said. "The counselor is badgering the witness."

"Sustained."

"Now, Ms. Giodono, I want you to remember you are under oath before you answer my next question. Did you also have sex with Seaman First Class Paul Anderson and with Seaman First Class Gus Downs separately?"

"Yes," she said in a whisper.

"Louder, Ms. Giodono," McCafery demanded.

"Yes," she answered. "Yes." Then she went limp and her head dropped forward, looking more like a battered rag doll than a young woman.

"I haven't any more questions at this time, but I reserve the right to continue the cross-examination should I deem it necessary," McCafery said.

Gamrick stood up and approached the witness stand. "Ms. Giodono, will you please explain to the court why you had sexual relations with Gus Downs?"

"He threatened to do something terrible to Paul if I didn't," she answered.

"Will you tell the court what Gus Downs threatened to do?" Gamrick asked.

Before Ms. Giodono could answer, McCafery called, "Objection. The testimony cannot be substantiated."

"Sustained."

"Did Seaman First Class Gus Downs enjoy having sex with you?"

"Objection," McCafery said. "The defense is asking the witness to make a judgment."

"Sustained."

"Will you tell the court what happened after Seaman First Class Downs had sex with you?" Gamrick asked.

"He vomited and said he couldn't understand why Paul enjoyed doing it with me," she answered.

"Objection," McCafery called again. "This is all hearsay. The court has no way of authenticating what the witness said."

"Ms. Giodono has just given the court an example of a homosexual's reaction to having sex with a woman. Commander Bliss, whose testimony is already on record, stated that some homosexuals would be 'disgusted and frightened of a woman's genitalia.' Gus Downs vomited. That certainly must indicate disgust," Gamrick said.

"Objection overruled," Edwards said.

"Did Seaman First Class Downs ever tell you that he and Downs were lovers?"

"No, sir."

"Who told you about their relationship?" Gamrick asked.

"Paul did," she answered softly.

"Please, Ms. Giodono, louder."

"Paul told me that he and Gus were lovers."

"Will you please tell the court when and why he told you?" Gamrick asked, facing McCafery.

"The night he asked me to marry him. He was going back to his ship."

"Excuse the interruption," Gamrick said. "But that was seventy-two hours before the explosion occurred aboard the *Utah*." Then turning to Ms. Giodono, he asked her to continue.

"Paul asked me to marry him," she said, looking at Anderson. "Then he said that he and Gus did things together—did things that a man and woman did."

"The things you did with Paul?" Gamrick pressed.

"Yes," she answered in a barely audible voice.

"Now tell the court what Downs said he would do if Paul married you," Gamrick asked.

Ms. Giodono shifted her position several times, looked at Anderson, whose head was bowed, then at Gamrick, who nodded and said, "Tell the court."

"Gus said he'd show the pictures of us to Paul."

"And how did Gus get the pictures of you having sex with him?"

"Another sailor took them," she said.

Gamrick handed her a picture of Hawkins. "Is this the man?"

"Yes."

"Let the record show that Ms. Giodono identified Seaman Third Class Donald Hawkins as the man who photographed her and Seaman First Class Gus Downs while they were having coitus," Gamrick said, placing the photograph of Hawkins on the table where the other photographs were.

"Ms. Giodono, where and when were the photographs of you and Downs taken?" Gamrick asked.

"That same weekend when the three of us were staying in North Truro," she answered.

"Did Downs make you do anything else?"

"Gus said I had to have sex with Hawkins too, or he'd show Paul the pictures," she answered.

"Did Downs take pictures of you and Hawkins while you were having sex?"

"Yes."

"Why did you agree to having sex with both men at the same time?" Gamrick asked.

"Because Gus said he'd hurt Paul," she said, her voice now choked with emotion.

"Objection!" McCafery called. "This is all hearsay. The defense should at least be able to produce the alleged photographs."

"Ms. Giodono, will you please give me the photographs that you showed me earlier this morning?" Gamrick said.

Ms. Giodono opened her bag and handed an envelope to Gamrick, who in turn passed the envelope to Edwards, who examined them and passed them to the member of the court to his right.

After all of the members of the court had looked at the photographs, they were entered as an evidential exhibit.

"Ms. Giodono, will you tell the court how Downs made you aware of the photographs that have just been entered as evidence?"

"Gus sent them to me. He wrote a note saying that he had a set of the same pictures and that if I went through with the marriage to Paul, he'd show them to him."

"Objection," McCafery called. "The witness has not produced the note."

"Ms. Giodono, will you please give me the note?" Gamrick asked.

"Objection overruled," Edwards said as he accepted the note from Gamrick's hand.

"Even after Seaman First Class Anderson told you

that he was involved in a homosexual relationship with Seaman First Class Downs, you agreed to marry him?"

"Yes," she answered. "I love him."

"One more question, Ms. Giodono. Will you tell the court how Seaman Third Class Hawkins reacted to having sex with you?"

She became even more flushed than she had been, and in a whisper she said, "He seemed to like it, but he wanted me to beat him with a belt afterward. He said God wanted him to purge his sins. I didn't know what he was talking about."

"Did you beat him?"

"Yes, he said I had to do it or God would punish me for being a whore," she whispered.

"Objection," McCafery roared, leaping to his feet. "The defense counselor expects the court to take this witness's word because he has produced several photographs of doubtful origin."

Edwards ran his fingers through his hair several times before he said, "Objection sustained."

"Your witness," Gamrick said, moving back to his place behind the table.

"Ms. Giodono, did you find that having sex with several different men, and at various times in front of other men, increased your sexual excitement?" McCafery asked.

"Objection," Gamrick said. "Ms. Giodono's sexual tastes are not at issue."

McCafery answered, "I am attempting to establish the moral character of the witness and thereby give the court the opportunity to see through the defense's obfuscation of the real issue in front of the court."

"Sustained."

"A simple yes or no, please, Ms. Giodono?" McCafery demanded in a harsh tone.

"Yes," she answered, nodding. "I never did it like that before."

"Then you did not object to Seaman First Class

Downs' suggestion that he and another man have sexual relations with you?"

Gamrick leaped to his feet again and shouted, "Objection!"

"Overruled," Edwards snapped. "The witness will answer the question."

"No," she whispered.

"Did you enjoy the attentions of—"

"No, I did it because of what Gus said he would do to Paul," she cried. "I love Paul."

"You never discouraged either Seaman First Class Gus Downs or Seaman Third Class Donald Hawkins. You fucked both men, didn't you?"

Edwards instantly rapped his gavel.

"I apologize to the court," McCafery quickly said. "My zeal to have this witness tell the truth got the better of my discretion."

"The court accepts your apology," Edwards said and adjourned the trial until 0900 the next morning.

Despite the slip on McCafery's part, Gamrick realized that his most important witness had been discredited. As he and Harkowitz left the courtroom, McCafery joined them and said, "You gave it your best shot and missed the target. The problem was, you had two bad guys: Downs and Hawkins. Most of Ms. Giodono's testimony seemed to prove that Downs blew himself up and that Hawkins was just a weirdo."

"It's not over until it's over," Gamrick answered, knowing that McCafery was right. He took hold of Harkowitz's arm and made an abrupt right turn, leaving McCafery to continue walking alone.

Chapter 18

Depressed and exhausted, Gamrick spent a few hours with Kate in her apartment. He chastised himself for having divided the court's attention between Hawkins and Downs.

"You did the best you could," Kate said.

"My best wasn't good enough. I thought I would have it locked up when I put Julie on the stand. I knew that McCafery would try to break her down, but I didn't think she'd come out looking like—"

"You didn't think she'd come out of it looking like Miss Innocence, did you?" Kate asked, leaving the bed and walking naked across the floor to get her negligee.

"It was all so crystal clear in my mind before McCafery began to question her," Gamrick said.

Kate returned to the bed and sat on the edge close to him. "You wanted it to be crystal clear. If I had been McCafery, I would have done the same thing. I would have tried to show the court that she enjoyed what was happening to her. Otherwise she wouldn't have allowed Hawkins to photograph her and Downs and then let Hawkins fuck her. That, in my opinion, is what turned the court against her."

Gamrick nodded and said, "She never mentioned that she had had sex with Hawkins."

"She was probably too ashamed to, but under cross-examination—well, it's a tough spot to be in. . . . But so far McCafery is ahead on points."

"Too many points," Gamrick answered, putting his arms around her and easing her down next to him.

"If I had known you wanted—"

"I just want to hold you," he said. "I'm too damn tired to do anything else. Besides, I have to drive back to the house and make sure everything there is all right. I haven't been home since the Labor Day weekend."

"You'll go after dinner. I'll cook something for the two of us. I really don't feel like going out."

"Oh?"

She shrugged, and it gave Gamrick pleasure to see her breast move. He smiled.

"And what's that all about?" she asked.

He put his hand on her breasts and said, "These. They're beautiful, exquisitely wonderful."

"I'm glad you think so," she answered, "because I think you're exquisitely wonderful. All of you is exquisitely wonderful."

"Ah, then no part of me is better than—"

She put her hand on his penis. "This is the key to that special place where magic lives."

Gamrick laughed and hugged her tightly. "No wonder why so many millions of people love you."

She gave him a quizzical look.

"Because, my love, all of them know you possess 'that special place where magic lives.'"

"I didn't know it was that obvious."

"Obvious it is not. But there's just enough of a hint of it visible to make you every man's dream and every woman's goal."

"What a wonderful line, Captain," she chided. "No wonder I'm here in bed with you wearing nothing but a flimsy negligee and you have one hand on my breast and the other on my crotch. I knew there must be a reason for it."

"You said something about dinner," he reminded her.

"If you insist."

"I'm starved," he said, sucking the breast nearest to him into his mouth.

"If you're that hungry I better make something to eat. How about a western omelette and some french fries?"

He let go of her breast and said, "It sounds good, sounds very good."

When Gamrick arrived home, he found the red signal light blinking, and he pressed the Play button in order to hear the tape.

"Dad, John is safe," Hal said. "He's with Jeff. Call as soon as you can."

A sudden surge of energy rushed through Gamrick. "I knew it," he shouted. "I knew it." And he began to laugh. Moments later, he dialed Hal's number.

Before the first ring was finished, Hal answered.

Without any preliminaries Gamrick said, "Now, tell me what's going on."

Hal laughed and said, "Jeff phoned about an hour ago to say that John arrived five minutes before."

"Just like that?"

"Jeff took the family out shopping, and when he returned John was there. Jeff says he looks good, a bit tired and probably a few pounds thinner than when he had left, but otherwise fine. We're going to fly out there and pick him up the day after tomorrow. Mom is coming with us."

"Good, good! I can't even begin to tell you—"

"I know, Dad," Hal said gently.

"Just wait until I see that son of yours, I'm going to—"

"You know all you're going to do is sweep him up into your arms and hug him. Hell, Dad, he did what you did."

"Only—"

"Only, he's your grandson. That's the real *only*."

"I guess you're right," Gamrick answered, feeling fatigue begin to seep through his body again. "Let me speak to Mom for a few minutes."

Iris came on the phone and said, "Well, you were right all the time, Clark."

"That doesn't matter. That he's safe and sound it all that really matters. Give him a big hug and a kiss for me."

"I will."

"I think you should stay with Hal until the court-martial is over," Gamrick said.

Iris hesitated, then answered, "Yes, if that's what you want."

"That's what I want," Gamrick said.

Again there was a pause before Iris asked, "How is it going?"

"Today was a very hard one."

"You sound done in," she commented.

"That's what I am," Gamrick responded.

"Try to get a good night's sleep and good luck for tomorrow," Iris said with an obvious quaver in her voice and clicked off.

Gamrick put the phone down, aware that Iris had fought back tears. Uttering a loud sigh, he said aloud, "Iris, we're a problem that's going to have to have a solution." Then he dialed Kate's private number to tell her about John.

"Hello," a man answered.

Gamrick slammed down the phone. Furious, he paced back and forth several times. That she was with another man after he had left her made him angry with himself for loving her the way he did. He stopped pacing, went to the bar cart, poured a double vodka, and quickly drank it. Then he poured the same amount again, held the glass up, looked at it. Then shaking his head, he carried the glass into the kitchen and dumped the vodka into the sink.

After a fitful night of sleep, Gamrick awakened with something less than a bright and eager attitude. He tried to phone Kate, but even her answering machine didn't answer.

At 0800 he met with Harkowitz at a luncheonette a short distance from the heliport for breakfast and outlined the day's strategy, which was to keep hammering on the idea that Hawkins had the motive and at least the same opportunity to place a bomb as Anderson, and was mentally sick enough to have done it. And—other than his version—there wasn't any reason for him to have left the turret.

"He still isn't our missing piece," Harkowitz said, raising a cup of coffee to his lips.

Gamrick didn't say anything.

"I gave the situation a great deal of thought," Harkowitz said. "Hawkins was bananas but not smart enough. Anderson is smart, very smart."

"Hawkins might have been stupid enough to do it. Crimes are not necessarily committed by smart criminals. The fact that so many of them get caught is proof that they're not so smart."

"And some of them don't get caught. The missing man is in that small percentage that doesn't get caught."

Gamrick thought about that for a bit, but it was hard for him to concentrate because he couldn't help thinking about Kate. He knew he was being foolish, juvenile, and probably overreacting, but he loved her and—

"Are you all right?" Harkowitz asked.

"Yes ... Yes, listen, you go on ahead. I want to make a phone call before we board the whirly bird," Gamrick answered.

"Sure. But what do you think about what I said?"

"Unless we come up with that missing piece, or pieces, Anderson is a dead man."

"Maybe we should put him on the stand?" Harkowitz suggested.

"And give that shark McCafery a chance to tear him to pieces? No, thank you," Gamrick responded.

"He certainly did that to Ms. Giodono," Harkowitz commented.

"He did indeed," Gamrick said. "I'll get the check and make my phone call."

"See you, Skipper," Harkowitz answered.

Gamrick dropped a ten-dollar bill on the table, which was more than enough to cover their breakfasts and the tip. Then he went to the phone booth and dialed Kate's number again. This time the phone company's automatic answering machine came on the line and said, "The number you are calling is out of service." The recorded sound of a woman speaking made him even more angry, and after slamming the phone back on its hook, he left the phone booth and hurried to the heliport.

Minutes later, the helicopter landed in the Norfolk Naval Base, and there was a car waiting for Gamrick and Harkowitz to take them to the building where the trial was being held.

"Are you really sure you're all right?" Harkowitz asked as soon as they were seated in the rear of the car.

Gamrick's impulse was to tell him to worry about himself, but the look on Harkowitz's face was enough to stop him. He was truly concerned. "Tired," Gamrick said. "My grandson, John, finally turned up after being missing for almost a month."

Harkowitz's jaw dropped. "The boy that's been on TV is your grandson?"

Gamrick nodded.

"But how could you concentrate with that on your mind?" Harkowitz questioned.

Gamrick didn't respond immediately. The years of being in the military had left their mark. The success of a mission took precedence over everything else, including his own feelings, which were now in a turmoil over Kate. . . .

"Okay, I'll take a rain check on that answer," Harkowitz said as the driver stopped the vehicle.

* * *

As soon as Gamrick and Harkowitz entered the courtroom, a Marine guard told them to report to Admiral Edwards' office.

"Now, what the hell do you think this is about?" Harkowitz asked.

"Whatever it is, it is obviously important enough for him to have us meet with him," Gamrick answered as they went to the back of the courtroom.

"Maybe McCafery hauled up the white flag?" Harkowitz suggested.

"No such luck," Gamrick responded, lowering his voice as he knocked on the admiral's door.

"Come," Edwards called out.

Moments later Gamrick and Harkowitz were inside the office and saluting. Gamrick said, "Captain Gamrick and Lieutenant Harkowitz reporting as ordered, sir." McCafery was already there, seated on one of the three chairs set up in front of the admiral's desk.

Looking up at them, Edwards returned the salute and said, gesturing to the two empty chairs, "Please sit down, gentlemen." He waited a moment until they were seated. "I asked Captain McCafery to be present so that neither of you has more information than the other."

Gamrick nodded.

Edwards continued, "The man you shot and killed in the hotel in Tangier Island, Captain Gamrick, has been positively identified as Lieutenant Carl Fusco, ammunition officer aboard the *Utah,* assigned to the magazine that fed powder to all of turret number two's guns."

Gamrick started out of his chair and immediately stopped himself. But Harkowitz made a very distinct whistling sound.

"I was informed that your Jeep was destroyed by a bazooka round," Edwards said.

"Yes, sir, it was."

"Lieutenant Fusco would have had access to such

ordnance, and if he didn't have direct access, he probably knew individuals who had."

"Yes, sir," Gamrick answered. "But he came off Senator Dobbs's *Sea Devil.*"

Edwards' brow wrinkled. "Can you prove that?"

"Only if members of the crew or the senator's guests were—"

"Captain, again you are in grave danger of making a wild statement and this time it's about a United States senator," Edwards said.

"Sir, there was very heavy weather that afternoon. The island ferry had stopped running. No other boats came into the harbor after I did except the *Sea Devil,* and she went to the fuel dock directly across from where I was moored at the public dock."

"Sir, I saw the lieutenant on Captain Gamrick's boat," Harkowitz offered.

"May I give you a word of advice, Captain Gamrick?" McCafery said.

"I'm listening," Gamrick answered.

"If you attempt to muddy this case any more than you already have, I will file a formal complaint against you and Lieutenant Harkowitz."

"That sounds more like a threat than advice," Gamrick said calmly, though he was very angry.

"Captain, I admire your courage and I even admire your zeal, but don't open a can of snakes unless you are prepared to have your own and the lives of people you love opened to public scrutiny."

Gamrick flushed. *The son of a bitch knows about Kate. He's investigated me—or he has ties leading back to Dobbs too. . . .*

"I must caution you, Captain Gamrick, and you, Lieutenant Harkowitz, about making any wild accusations in court. The consequences for the two of you and for the accused could be very grave," Edwards said, looking first at Gamrick and then at Harkowitz. After a momentary pause he added, "I have sent a team of experts to the *Snark* to determine what caused her to explode into flames."

"The Coast Guard has already determined that she was set on fire and that Lieutenant Fusco was the arsonist."

"The lieutenant's roll is hearsay—"

"For chrissakes, Captain, I saw the man do it," Harkowitz said.

"What reason would he have had—"

Gamrick whirled toward McCafery. "I killed him because he was trying to kill the two of us. I didn't kill him or Cassado for sport. They were trying to kill me. To kill me, he would first have to get to me. To make that easier, he tried to limit my movements. Now do you see it, Captain, or would you like a fucking diagram?"

McCafery paled. His lower lip trembled. He stood up, and in a tight voice he challenged, "I'm willing to take you on, Captain, anywhere, anytime. Just name the fucking time and place, and I'll be there. Now, Admiral, I request permission to be excused from this meeting."

Edwards studied him for a moment before he said, "I will excuse you, Captain, when this meeting is officially over."

"Yes, sir," he answered, sitting again.

"I just might take you up on that challenge, McCafery," Gamrick said.

"Gentlemen, unless this bickering stops, I will have no recourse but to officially reprimand the two of you," Edwards said. "What should concern us is the trial. Now, let's get on with it."

"Sir, I request an adjournment until tomorrow, when I hope to have new evidence for the court," Gamrick said.

"Another delaying tactic," McCafery said. "Sir, this court-martial could be over before lunch."

"A man's life is at stake. A few more hours won't

matter if the prosecution is so sure that the court will find the accused guilty," Gamrick said.

"It's not inconceivable that a certain group of men hold Captain Gamrick responsible for Hawkins' death and are out to get him," McCafery said, speaking to Edwards.

"I'll grant your request, Captain, but with yet another caution," Edwards said.

"Sir?"

"Don't let your zeal overrun your sense of reality. Be sure that the evidence you introduce in court tomorrow is hard evidence."

"Yes, sir," Gamrick answered.

Gamrick, Harkowitz, and Anderson were in a small room in the base brig. Anderson sat at one end of a rectangular table. Harkowitz occupied the chair to his left, while Gamrick stood behind the chair at Anderson's right.

"I need straight answers, Paul," Gamrick said calmly. "Answers that will give you your freedom."

"Yes, sir," Anderson said.

"Over the Labor Day weekend I shot and killed Lieutenant Carl Fusco," Gamrick said.

Anderson stiffened.

"He tried to kill me and Lieutenant Harkowitz," Gamrick said.

"What was going on aboard the *Utah*?" Harkowitz asked.

Anderson shook his head. "Nothing," he whispered.

"Nothing brings nothing. But your 'nothing' has killed four men. Two of my men, two of the men that were in some way connected to your 'nothing' and Hawkins."

"How was Hawkins killed?" Anderson asked, going pale.

"He was found near the *Utah* floating face down with the back of his skull crushed in," Harkowitz said.

Anderson squeezed his hands together, and looking

straight at Gamrick, he said in a tight voice, "If I tell
you—"

Harkowitz looked as if he was about to speak, but
Gamrick shook his head, then touched his arm to be
sure he did not.

"I can't," Anderson said, shaking his head. "I can't,"
he sobbed. "Even if they can't get at me, they'll get
Julie."

"You're on trial for your life," Gamrick exploded.

Anderson covered his face with his hands.

"Who the hell are you afraid of?" Gamrick pressed.
"For god's sakes, you don't have any chance of
beating—"

"This is the way it has to be," Anderson said, dropping his hands and looked up at him with tears stream-
ing down his face.

Gamrick nodded. For you, but not for me. . . . Then
uttering a deep sigh, he answered, "I can't help you if
you don't want me to."

Anderson folded his arms on the table, and cradling
his head in them, he wept.

For several moments Gamrick watched him. Then
putting his hand on Anderson's heaving shoulder, he
said in a soft voice, "We'll find some way of getting
you out of this."

Anderson looked up at him. "It wasn't supposed to
go like this," he wept. "It wasn't supposed to."

"What wasn't supposed to go like this?" Gamrick
asked.

But Anderson buried his face in his arms again.

"Paul, tell me what wasn't supposed to go like this?"

"Who set you up?" Harkowitz asked.

"Paul—"

"No . . . no . . . you don't understand," Anderson
cried, suddenly lifting his head. "You don't understand."

"We want to understand," Harkowitz said.

"You can't," Anderson wept. "You can't."

"Paul, unless you tell us—" Gamrick began.

"I can't tell you. Don't you understand they'll kill Julie? They'll kill her the way they killed Hawkins. Maybe even worse."

Gamrick nodded, signaled Harkowitz that they were finished, and squeezing Anderson's shoulder, he said, "Remember, Paul, we're on your side." Then he went to the door, opened it, and told the Marine guard they were finished with the prisoner.

"That wasn't very successful," Harkowitz commented as they walked out of the brig into the bright sunshine of a wonderful September day.

"But what the hell did he mean when he said, 'It wasn't supposed to go this way?' " Gamrick questioned.

"Maybe he meant his life or his relationship to Downs?" Harkowitz answered.

Gamrick shrugged.

"Well, Skipper, now what do we do?" Harkowitz asked.

"First we have lunch. For some reason I'm hungry. Then we'll go back to our office in D. C. and read as many transcriptions of the tapes as we can. Maybe we'll get lucky."

"I wouldn't bet on it," Harkowitz answered.

They lunched in the OC, flew back to Washington, and spend several hours reading transcripts made from the tapes.

At eighteen-hundred, Gamrick said, "Pack it in, Counselor. The only thing I've gleaned from the two dozen or so transcripts I read—"

"Let me tell you something," Harkowitz said.

"I'm listening."

"The interviewees were holding back. Essentially all of them gave the same answers, often using the same words."

"Yes. It's the same reaction I and the other men on the board of inquiry had when the investigation started," Gamrick said.

"They're afraid of something, though."

"The same thing or persons that Anderson is afraid of," Gamrick said.

"I'd bet on it," Harkowitz responded. "But how do we find out what it is?"

"We could pick a dozen men and—no, damn it! We'll put Anderson on the witness stand. We'll make him tell us."

Harkowitz stood up and paced the length of the room several times before he stopped and said, "McCafery will devour him. But—"

"I'm counting on that *but,*" Gamrick responded. "Maybe between Hardass McCafery and two of us, we'll break Paul down. . . . Maybe he'll realize that his life is worth saving."

By the time Gamrick ate, drove home, and entered the house, it was 2000. He switched on the light and had started to go upstairs when the phone rang.

He went into the den, picked up the phone, and said, "Captain Gamrick here."

A man said, "Let Anderson take the fall, or you'll never see your lady friend again. To prove we're playing hardball, talk to her."

"Clark, help me!" Kate cried.

"Kate?"

Coming back on the phone, the man said, "The ball is in your court."

"You harm—"

The line went dead.

Gamrick's hands trembled so violently he dropped the phone. He felt as if his brain had suddenly turned to gray mush. His lips quivered and finally he screamed, "Kate . . . Kate . . . Kate."

The sound of his own voice frightened him, and he lurched to the chair behind the desk and dropped onto it. To stop himself from shaking, he gripped the chair arms. "Think," he told himself. "Think." The next instant he bolted from the chair, ran out of the house, and getting in the car, he switched on the ignition. The moment he heard the engine, he switched it off and slumped over the steering wheel.

Several minutes passed before Gamrick had enough strength to walk back to the house and phone the Washington police and then the FBI. But no matter what Gamrick told them, neither organization would act unless the person had been missing for twenty-four hours.

Gamrick sat at his desk, staring out the window at the cove. He blinked back tears and said aloud, "I love you, Kate . . . I love you."

Hours later, Gamrick climbed into bed, but sleep, despite his desperate need for it, eluded him. With his hands behind his head, he stared at the ceiling. He had been between a rock and a hard place more than once, but this was different. Now someone else was there with him. And he whispered Kate's name into the darkness as if by doing it, he could conjure her to him.

When the gray light of dawn began to flow across the window, Gamrick slipped into a light, restless sleep that was torn away from him by the slashing ring of the phone.

The man on the other end said, "There's a small package outside your door." Then he clicked off.

Gamrick slipped on a bathrobe, raced down the stairs, and unlocking the door, he threw it open. The package was on the ground directly in front of him. Wrapped in ordinary brown paper, it was the size of box used to hold a diamond ring.

He picked it up, retreated into the house, and went into the kitchen. His hands trembled and his heart raced. That it might be an explosive device entered his mind, and he ran cold water over it for several minutes before he tore the soggy wrapping paper away from a small metal box with a hinged top.

Gamrick moved to the kitchen table and placed the

box on it. Now he could hear the booming of his heart, and his hands were still trembling. "Easy," he said aloud. "Easy, Clark." And he slowly opened the box, and seeing two bloodstained nipples, he screamed, "Oh God, no . . . No!" He staggered backward. The room spun. He grabbed onto the sink and vomited.

Even as Gamrick fought to gain control of himself, the phone rang again.

The man said, "Next time you'll get her cunt."

Gamrick tried to speak, but before he could, the man said, "Remember, the next time you get her cunt." Then he clicked off.

Pushing himself to function, Gamrick began his daily routine of shaving and showering. Everything he did seemed to be done in slow motion.

On the way out of the house, Gamrick closed the metal box, and as he put it into his pocket, the phone rang again. Afraid to answer it, he let it ring four times before he picked it up.

Iris was on the other end. "I didn't wake you, did I?"

"No, I was on my way out," he answered.

"Are you all right?"

"Yes . . . yes, I'm fine. Just tired."

"I had an awful dream that you were hurt and needed help," Iris said.

Gamrick was struck by the irony of the moment, and swallowed hard, he reassured her that he was fine.

"I've been doing some thinking about our future," Iris said, "and in a way I'm glad that you're going to be your own man. I think we'll do just fine, Clark. Don't you?"

Gamrick wanted to tell her that he was having great difficulty living through each minute, but he said, "Yes, we'll do just fine."

"I'm happy that you think so too," she responded.

"Iris, I must get to court on time," he said.

"Yes ... yes ... Good luck, and I love you."

"I know you do," he answered, but he couldn't bring himself to tell that he loved her. He put the phone back in its cradle and left the house.

Chapter 19

Anderson took the stand and was sworn in. He sat very straight and looked at Gamrick and only at Gamrick, who asked him to identify himself to the court.

"Seaman First Class Paul Anderson."

"Now, Paul—"

"Objection to the use of the man's given name," McCafery said.

"It was an attempt to put the man as much at ease as possible in these surroundings and under these conditions," Gamrick explained.

"Objection overruled," Edwards said.

"If it please the court, the defense will not attempt to establish where Seaman First Class Anderson was at the time of the explosion. The defense acknowledges that he was not in the *Utah*'s number two turret and was, in fact, in the ship's sick bay at the time. To prove this, the defense enters into evidence the log of the attending physician, Commander William C. Hasse. The log notes the arrival of the accused by name a full three minutes before the explosion took place."

"Mark Commander William C. Hasse's medical log appropriately," Edwards ordered.

"Now, Paul, would you tell the court what your relationship to Seaman Third Class Donald Hawkins was?" Gamrick asked.

"Objection," McCafery called. "The accused's relation to anyone other than Seaman First Class Gus Downs is not of any consequence. The prosecution admits that the accused did not kill Seamen Third Class Hawkins."

"It is important for the court to understand the particular conditions—the interpersonal relations that existed on the *Utah* before it can rule judiciously on the guilt or innocence of the accused."

"Objection overruled. Proceed, Captain Gamrick," Edwards said. "I am extremely interested in finding the logical end to your line of questioning."

Gamrick almost did a double-take. The statement was another warning without actually giving one. "Paul, would you tell the court what your relationship was to Seaman Third Class Donald Hawkins?"

"We were not friends," Anderson answered.

"What was his nickname?" Gamrick asked.

"The Preacher."

"Who gave him that name?"

Anderson hesitated.

"You did, didn't you?" Gamrick said.

"No, sir. Gus did," Anderson answered.

"And that's what the men called him—the Preacher?"

"Yes, sir."

Gamrick moved away from Anderson, faced him, and asked, "Did you ever torment—tease him?"

"Not in the way that the other men did," Anderson said.

Gamrick nodded. He could tell from the way Anderson answered that he was more relaxed now. Even his posture had become less rigid.

"Did Gus ever torment him?"

"Yes, sir."

"Would you say that Hawkins had good reason to kill every man—?"

"Objection," McCafery shouted, leaping to his feet. "The counselor is leading the witness to a conclusion that would be nothing more than speculation."

"Objection sustained," Edwards said, looking dourly

at Gamrick. "Captain, please remember that Seaman Third Class Hawkins is not on trial here."

"Yes, sir," Gamrick answered. Then, moving close to Anderson again, he said, "Paul, now tell the court what really was going on aboard the *Utah*."

"Objection," McCafery called. "The man is on trial because the court knows about the accused's relationship—"

"With all due respect to the court," Gamrick said, turning to face its members, "the court knows only what certain individuals want it to know about what happened aboard the *Utah*."

Edwards ran his fingers through his hair and whispered some to the officers on either side of him. Then, he said, "Objection overruled. The defense will repeat the question to the accused."

Gamrick nodded and repeated the question.

Anderson shook his head.

"Paul, you must answer the question."

"I can't," Anderson said, becoming rigid again. "I can't."

Gamrick took the small metal box out of his pocket, and clearing his voice several times beforehand, he said, "I ask the court's permission to show the accused the contents of this box."

"Objection," McCafery shouted, on his feet again. "The item must be given to the court as evidence before it can be shown to the accused."

Again clearing his throat before he spoke, Gamrick said, "The contents of the box are not evidential, yet they have—or to be more accurate—should have a direct bearing on the last question I asked the witness."

"May the court and the prosecution view the contents of the box before it is shown to the witness?" Edwards asked.

Gamrick hesitated. Then he said, "Sir, it is necessary for my purpose to have the witness view the contents of the box before anyone else."

"Objection," McCafery called. "The box and its

contents can not have the importance that defense will have the court believe."

"Lieutenant Harkowitz, do you know what is in the box?" Edwards asked.

Harkowitz stood up and answered, "No, sir. I did not even know of its existence until Captain Gamrick produced it."

"Thank you, Lieutenant. Objection overruled," Edwards said. "But before you resume, Captain, please define your purpose."

"It is as it was from the beginning of this court-martial—to elicit the truth."

"Proceed," Edwards said.

Suddenly Gamrick became aware of the enormous weight of the silence that filled the room. He moved very close to Anderson and locked eyes with him. With a quick movement he opened the box and pushed it in front of Anderson. "Tell the court what you see," Gamrick said. "Tell—"

Anderson uttered a wordless scream and shrank back in the chair, holding his hands out in front of him as if he would push away the box.

"Tell the court what you see," Gamrick ordered, his voice tight with emotion.

Anderson went pale. His eyes were wide with fear.

"Tell them," Gamrick hissed in low, deadly tone.

"Nipples," Anderson cried out. "A woman's bloody nipples!"

Pandemonium erupted. While everyone seemed to be shouting at the same time, Gamrick stood very still. Much as he tried, he couldn't prevent tears from running out of his eyes, and used a handkerchief to wipe them away.

Edwards rapped his gavel several times, and above the noise in the courtroom he bellowed, "Order in the court. Order in the court."

The noise level diminished, then ceased altogether.

"Another outburst like that and I clear the court," Edward growled. He waited until everyone was silent before he turned his attention to Gamrick. "Captain, the court frowns on dramatic gestures."

"Yes, sir, I am aware of that," Gamrick answered.

"Then, sir, you will explain your actions here and now," Edwards ordered.

Gamrick closed the box but continued to hold it in his right hand as he explained in a low, emotionally choked voice, his close relationship with Ms. Kate Bannon and the events of the previous night and early that morning.

"Objection," McCafery said. "The captain's personal life has no bearing on this case."

"I intend to prove that there is a connection to what happened to Ms. Kate Bannon and this case."

"Objection overruled," Edwards said.

Gamrick faced Anderson again. "Anderson, why weren't you and Downs accepted by the other men?"

"We know why!" McCafery snapped out.

Gamrick whirled around and looked straight at McCafery. "You're too quick, Captain . . . too quick even for—"

Edwards rapped his gavel and said, "Captain McCafery, control your outbursts, and Captain Gamrick, control your temper. Another outburst from you, Captain McCafery, and you will be charged with contempt. That applies to you as well, Captain Gamrick."

Both men answered, "Yes, sir."

Gamrick repeated the question. "Why weren't you and Downs accepted by the other men?"

"We were not interested in the same things," Anderson answered, nervously rubbing his hands together.

"Tell the court what those things were," Gamrick pressed.

Anderson shook his head.

"Paul, you're on trial for your life," Gamrick said. "Sooner or later it will come out."

"Drugs," Anderson whispered.

"Louder," Gamrick roared, now more confident than ever that he had a chance to win Anderson's freedom.

"Drugs," Anderson repeated, saying it loud enough for everyone in the courtroom to hear.

McCafery leaped to his feet. "Objection. There isn't any way to prove the validity of that statement."

Gamrick held out the metal box and said, "I intend to prove the connection between this box and the problem that existed aboard the *Utah*."

"Objection overruled," Edwards said. Looking at Gamrick, he added, "The court understands your emotional state, Captain, but it will not countenance a line of questioning which will only confuse the issue. The court has allowed you considerable latitude, but it must now restrict you to keeping to the purpose of this trial."

"Sir, the defense appreciates the degree of latitude that the court has extended to it," Gamrick said. "Its purpose is no different from the court's. It is seeking the truth."

"Continue," Edwards responded.

"Paul, would you say that most of the men in turret number two, and those particularly who manned gun number two, were users?"

"No, sir," Anderson answered.

Gamrick was taken aback, and he took several steps away from the witness box. Once again he was aware of the absolute silence in the courtroom. "Paul," he said, moving close again, "if they weren't users, what were they?"

Anderson began to fidget. He rocked back and forth.

"Answer the question," Edwards ordered.

"Transporters, sir, carriers," Anderson said in a barely audible voice.

"Louder," Gamrick snapped.

"Carriers."

"Objection," McCafery called. "This is hearsay."

"Objection overruled," Edwards said. "The court

would like to hear the defense's line of questioning without interruption."

"Paul, would you define—explain what a 'carrier' did for the court?" Gamrick asked.

"They moved drugs from foreign ports of call to the States."

"How did they move the drugs?"

"In condoms. The carriers swallow the condoms and bring drugs aboard that way. They stored the drugs in a safe place after they came out of the body. Then they would bring them ashore in condoms. That way they—the drugs—couldn't be detected."

"The condoms were swallowed?"

"Yes, sir."

"Once to get the drugs aboard, once to get them off the ship?" Gamrick asked.

"Yes, sir."

"What drugs?"

"Coke mainly, but anything else that could be powdered," Anderson said.

Gamrick moved to the table where Harkowitz sat, turned to the members of the court, and said, "If it please the court, I'd like a moment to consult with Lieutenant Harkowitz."

"The court will remain in session while Captain Gamrick and Lieutenant Harkowitz confer," Edwards declared.

Gamrick bent close to Harkowitz and said, "Hawkins had told me about the drug users, but never mentioned the smugglers."

"Do you think it will do any good to follow this angle?"

"I don't see any other way now. I'll go the distance," Gamrick responded. Straightening up, he addressed the court and said, "The defense is ready to continue." He walked slowly back to the witness box. "Paul, was the explosion aboard the *Utah* in any way related to the transporters?"

"Yes, sir."

Gamrick nodded and in a quiet voice said, "Paul, tell the court who killed the men in turret number two."

Anderson shook his head. "I can't," he cried. "I can't."

"You've gone this far, now go to the end. Tell the court who killed the men in turret number two."

Weeping, Anderson covered his face with his hands.

"Who killed them?" Gamrick roared.

Anderson dropped his hands and shouted, "The other men . . . the men who cut the nipples off Miss Bannon, the men who killed the investigators. The men who burned your boat and who tried to kill you."

McCafery was on his feet and came out from behind the table. "Objection . . . objection . . . objection . . . Not one word of the witness's testimony can be proven."

In a fury Gamrick shouted, "Then why was this done?" He thrust the metal box at McCafery. "Tell me, why this was done?"

Edwards rapped his gavel for order and said, "Each of you will have a written apology to this court at oh-nine-hundred tomorrow morning. Is that understood?"

"Yes, sir," Gamrick answered.

"Captain McCafery?" Edwards questioned.

"Yes, sir."

"Is the defense finished questioning the witness?" Edwards asked.

"No, sir."

"Continue, Captain Gamrick, but note that the court reserves the right to rule on the prosecution's objections at the conclusion of your questioning."

Gamrick moved close to Anderson again and asked, "Do you know what caused the explosion in turret number two?"

"I can only guess."

"Objection. The witness admits that he is only making a guess."

Edwards again spoke to the officer to his right and

Irving Greenfield

then to one of his left before he said, "Objection over-ruled."

"Would you tell the court what your guess is?" Gamrick asked.

"Everyone in the gun crews and in the magazine knew we had several hundred bags of bad powder aboard, that powder was marked with a red X and removed to another section of the magazine."

"Is there a record of the number of bags marked with a red X?" Gamrick questioned.

"I don't know, sir."

"Are you saying that one or more bags of unstable powder was deliberately supplied to number two gun."

"Yes, sir."

Gamrick heard the low murmur of disbelief that rose and fell like the wind caught under the eaves of a house. He glanced up at Edwards and saw an almost imperceptible nod.

"Paul, if the bags were marked with a red X, why were they fired?" Gamrick asked, facing the witness.

"I can't answer that. But before I was taken off the ship, I heard that either the red Xs had been removed from some of the bags, or the men saw the red X but the order to fire came and they had no choice. They had to fire."

Gamrick went to the desk and picked up several pieces of a paper, including a news clipping. "These Xeroxed copies of pages from the *Utah*'s log give the dates and the exact number of powder bags taken aboard. Here are several documents from the Navy's research laboratory indicating that those bags marked with a red X aboard the *Utah* did contain highly unstable powder. And last, a newspaper clipping that appeared in the *Washington Post,* dated ten days after the explosion, suggests that the explosion might have been caused by the mishandling of highly unstable powder."

"Mark the evidence appropriately," Edwards said.

Gamrick stepped back to the witness box. "I have a few more questions, Paul."

"Yes, sir."

"Did Seaman Third Class Hawkins obtain his drugs from someone in the gun crew?" Gamrick asked.

"Yes."

"Do you know the name of that person?"

"Lieutenant Carl Fusco," Anderson said. "Fusco controlled one group of carriers."

"Then, there were two groups of carriers aboard the *Utah*?"

"Yes, sir."

"Did they cooperate with each other?"

"No, sir. The men from one would often fight the men from the other group for control."

"The other transporters, the competing group, were in turret number two, weren't they?"

"More than half of them made up the crew for gun number two," Anderson said.

"Would you say that Seaman Third Class Hawkins knew about the drug war aboard the ship?"

"All of the men knew."

"How was the code of silence enforced?" Gamrick asked.

"By threats—sometimes by beating a man."

"You told me that the same 'they' who tried to kill me killed Hawkins?"

"Yes, sir."

"They killed him to keep him silent?"

"Yes, sir," Anderson answered.

"Objection," McCafery called. "The defense is leading the witness to conclusions that cannot be substantiated."

"Sustained," Edwards said.

"Did the ship's officers know about the drug war?"

"Some of them were involved," Anderson said.

Gamrick moved back to the table, faced the court, and said, "I am finished with the witness."

Edwards nodded and asked, "Does the prosecution wish to cross-examine the witness."

"Not at this time, but the prosecution reserves the

right to call the witness back to the stand should it
deem it necessary," McCafery said.

"The court acknowledges the prosecution's right to
recall the witness," Edwards answered. "This court is
adjourned until oh-nine-hundred tomorrow. Captain
Gamrick and Lieutenant Harkowitz, please report to
my office."

"Yes, sir," Gamrick responded.

"Trouble?" Harkowitz asked.

Gamrick shrugged. "In this man's navy you never
know," he answered, gathering his papers into an
attaché case.

"You know, you were damn good," Harkowitz said
as they walked out of the courtroom and into a crowd
of waiting reporters.

"I have no comment," Gamrick answered, when
pressed to make one about the fallout from the trial.

"Do you have anything to say about your relationship to Kate Bannon?" another reporter asked.

"We were very good friends. I admired her very
much," Gamrick said and pushed his way through
them and into the corridor that was restricted to anyone
other than authorized personnel.

Gamrick knocked on the admiral's door.

"Come," Edwards called out.

"Captain Gamrick and Lieutenant Harkowitz reporting as ordered," Gamrick said, saluting.

Edwards returned the salute, and gesturing to the
two chairs in front of the desk, he said, "Please sit,
gentlemen. I'd offer you something to drink, but this is
only my temporary office while the trial is in progress. . . . Well, Captain, you realize that the events that
took place in the courtroom this morning will undoubt-
edly have an enormous impact on the lives of several
different individuals."

"Yes, sir," Gamrick answered.

"I think at least a half-dozen different investigations
will result from the testimony given," Edwards said.

"Sir, Paul Anderson's sexual conduct was being tried, not his guilt or innocence—"

Edwards held up his hand. "Captain, save that for your summation. The reason for asking you to report to my office is to ask you to reconsider your resignation. If you decide to stay, I will see that you have a permanent appointment with NCIS."

"Sir, I appreciate your offer, but I no longer have any interest in continuing my naval career. Because of my experience on the board of inquiry and at this trial, I have found another identity inside me, one that needs to come out and function in a different environment."

Edwards smiled. "I had the feeling that you would refuse, but I wanted to make the offer anyway."

"Thank you, sir," Gamrick answered.

"And as for you, Lieutenant Harkowitz, you could do worse, but not much better, if you teamed up with Captain Gamrick once you're discharged," Edwards said.

Harkowitz grinned and said, "Thank you for making the recommendation, sir."

Edwards shook hands with both of them, and said, "This trial will probably be the high point of my career as a chief officer of the court." Then he escorted them to the door and said, "I have one question, Captain, before you leave."

"Sir?"

"Do you deny that Anderson is a homosexual?"

"No, sir. The testimony given by his fiancée and the photographs prove that he is at least bisexual. I only defended him against the charge of having killed twenty-seven of his shipmates in order to collect the money from an insurance policy."

Edwards accepted the explanation with a nod.

Gamrick and Harkowitz exchanged salutes with Edwards, and Gamrick, opening the door, led the way out of the office.

"Well, well," Harkowitz said as soon as they were out of the building, "the admiral had a great idea."

"Law partners?" Gamrick asked, knowing it would be that.

"Yes."

"You draw up the papers and I'll sign them," Gamrick answered.

Harkowitz stopped short.

Gamrick continued to walk and called out, "Just don't stand there. Come and let's consummate this odd relationship over lunch."

Harkowitz caught up to him and said, "I'm buying."

"You bet you are," Gamrick answered.

The night was the worst time for Gamrick. When he came home, there were messages from Iris, Hal, and Jeff on the answering machine, but he did not want to speak to anyone. He was tired, and though he was sure Kate had been killed, he hoped that her death had been swift.

He sat in his study and looked at the closed metal box that he had placed on the desk in front of him. Sure that his true relationship with Kate would surface, he wasn't prepared to apologize for having loved her to anyone, including Iris.

From time to time he left the chair to pour another vodka for himself. When he felt a certain emotional numbness, he heaved himself out of the chair, climbed the steps, managed to shower, and eventually got into bed and slept.

The ringing of the phone woke him, and pulling himself up, he answered it.

"This is William Bly," the voice on the other end said.

Gamrick was suddenly wide awake.

"Kate's naked body was found early this morning off the bridle path in Rockhill Park," Bly said.

"Jesus Christ!" Gamrick exclaimed.

"They mutilated her," Bly said, almost sobbing. "They—"

Gamrick cleared his throat before he asked, "Does she have any family?"

"None."

"I'll take care of everything that has to be done," Gamrick said, his voice cracking before he reached the end of the sentence.

"I'll see you soon," Bly said and clicked off.

Gamrick put the phone down and rubbed the tears out of his eyes, forced himself out of bed, and managed to do all of the things necessary to get out of the house.

The moment he opened the car he saw the box. It was on the seat next to the driver's. Unable to move, he stared at the box for several minutes. There was no doubt in his mind what was inside the box.

Finally he picked up the box and opened it. Kate's bloody pubis and vaginal lips were inside with a note that read: "This was taken from her while she was still alive."

Gamrick closed the box, put it back on the seat next to him, and clamping his jaws together so tightly that pain shot up both side of his face, he turned on the ignition and slowly moved out of the cul-de-sac. When he had gained the roadway and gone only a short distance, he pulled over to the side of the road, stopped the car, and tightly griping the steering wheel with both hands, he lowered his head and wept. . . .

Besieged by reporters when he entered the building, he pushed his way through them repeating over and over again, "No comment."

Edwards called the court into session promptly at 0900 and asked, "Does the prosecution wish to cross-examine the accused?"

"No, sir. The government rests its case against Seaman First Class Paul Anderson."

"Does the prosecution want to make a closing statement?" Edwards asked.

"Yes, sir," McCafery said, coming out from behind

the desk. "The defense has not proven that the accused is innocent. The defense has indeed shown that if the accused were innocent, he would have died in the explosion with those shipmates who did perish. The accused is here today in this courtroom because he had knowledge of what was going to happen. The guilt or innocence of the accused will be decided here today, but there is no doubt that Seaman First Class Paul Anderson is either guilty as charged because he had prior knowledge and committed the sin of omission by now informing the proper authority, or he was part of the plot to kill the men who manned gun number two in turret number two aboard the battleship *Utah*."

Edwards waited until McCafery was seated again before he asked Gamrick if he was ready to make his summation.

"Yes, sir," Gamrick answered, moving into the open space between the tables, the dais where the members of the court sat, and the empty witness box. He took several moments before he said, "First, I want to thank the court for the courtesy and latitude that they extended to me, my colleague, Lieutenant Harkowitz, and the accused Seaman First Class Paul Anderson." He paused a moment before continuing. "The prosecution would have you believe that the deaths of two of my officers, Commander Steve Wright and Lieutenant Harry Cool, just happened. He would also have you believe that Kate Bannon's mutilated body, which was found earlier this morning, is not in any way connected to this case. That the accused single-handedly set off an explosion that killed all of the men who manned gun number two in turret number two aboard the *Utah*. That Lieutenant Carl Fusco, who attempted to kill me and Lieutenant Harkowitz, had no connection with this case, or that my presence here was the result of happenstance rather than a cold, calculated decision made by Senator Dobbs and the Secretary of Navy, John Howard. He would even have you believe that the death of Seaman Third Class Donald Hawkins was the result of something beyond the scope of this case. But none of the aforementioned situations are beyond the scope of this trial because they are all connected to it, connected to the men who gave the orders to destroy the men in turret number two. The accused had no hand whatsoever in the murders of Commander Wright, Lieutenant Harry Cool, Seaman Third Class Donald Hawkins, or Ms. Kate Bannon. Nor did he have any role in the attempt to murder me and Lieutenant Harkowitz because he was already incarcerated, awaiting this trial. The prosecution claims that he was guilty of the sin of omission, or of complicity. He cites the fact that Seaman First Class Paul Anderson is here in the court as proof of one or the other of his assertions. But the ship's medical records show that he continually suffered from sinusitis, and, as anyone who has ever been in a gun turret will testify, after several rounds are fired, fumes build up even with the exhaust system going.

"The accused did not abandon his battle station. He asked for and obtained permission to go to the sick bay.

"What, then, is he guilty of? He is guilty of so-called deviant sexual behavior, and it is this issue that prosecution attempted to have tried in this court—and, I might add, for very political reasons, since the issue of allowing homosexuals to serve in the military is far from settled. The accused is innocent of all charges and specifications that were placed before this court."

Gamrick nodded at the conclusion of his statement to Edwards, who said, "The court will now vote on the charges and specifications against Seaman First Class Paul Anderson. This court will remain in session until the court reaches a verdict."

"Not a bad summation," Harkowitz whispered to Gamrick when he returned to his seat.

Gamrick remained silent. He had done everything he could to win the case. Now it was up to the five members of the court to make the final determination. And he was having great difficulty keeping Kate out of his thoughts. He needed to place the parts of her that were sent to him in a final resting place, but not in the grave . . . in the sea . . . "In the sea," he whispered.

"What?" Harkowitz asked.

"I said, we'll see," Gamrick said.

Harkowitz shot him a quizzical look but did not pursue it.

Ten minutes later, the members of the court returned, and Edwards rapped the gavel. "The court finds the accused not guilty of all charges and specifications—"

The bubble broke and cheers erupted in the courtroom.

Edwards rapped his gavel three times and called, "Order in the court room . . . order in the court room." When it was quiet again, he said, "The court recommends that Seaman First Class Paul Anderson accept an immediate discharge from the United States Navy for homosexual behavior in accordance with Article 21 of the Uniform Code of Military Justice, which specifies the terms and conditions of such a discharge." Then he rapped the gavel three times and said, "This court is now adjourned."

McCafery came over to the table where Gamrick and Harkowitz were gathering their papers. He shook hands with them and said, "You put up a hell of a fight, but he's guilty."

Gamrick said, "It's over, Captain."

McCafery nodded. "Justice is truly blind, but truth, Gamrick, is a double-edged sword." And without waiting for an answer, he walked away.

"I wouldn't exactly call him a good loser," Harkowitz commented.

Gamrick shrugged, and together they left the courtroom only, once again, to face a very large and eager group of reporters, all of whom wanted a statement.

"Other than to tell you that Lieutenant Harkowitz

and I will be leaving the Navy, we have nothing else to say," Gamrick said.

"What have you to say about Kate—?"

"Nothing more than I had said in court," Gamrick answered and began pushing his way through the group. When he and Harkowitz were finally outside, he said, "I will meet you later. But now I have personal business to take care of."

"Give me a time and a place," Harkowitz said.

"The Chowder Hut. It's down on the waterfront. I'll be there around seventeen-hundred."

"Are you sure you will be all right?" Harkowitz asked.

"I'll be fine," Gamrick answered. "Believe me, I'll be fine." He turned and walked toward the car that would take him to the heliport.

On the way to rent a small powerboat, he stopped at a bait shop and bought a half-dozen eight-ounce sinkers and the best-grade nylon fishing line available. He took the sinker, line, and the two boxes that had been sent to him, boarded the boat, and headed out into the Potomac. When he reached the bay, just off the mouth of the river, he cut the engine and carefully tied several of the sinkers to the box he'd received that morning and one to the smaller box that had come the previous morning. Then he sat down on the rear thwart of the rocking boat, and holding each of the boxes on his lap, he said, "I know I'm responsible for your death. But I couldn't undo what I had already done. I wanted you for my wife, Kate . . . for my wife, Kate. Not a sad memory that will be with me for the rest of my life. . . ."

He dropped the smaller of the two boxes into the sunlit waters first. It sank immediately. Then he dropped the larger box into the water. It remained on the surface for a few moments, then it too sank.

Gamrick moved forward, vented the gas line, and turned on the ignition. The engine sputtered, then caught. He took hold of the small wheel and made a hundred-and-eighty-degree turn.

Kate's funeral took place three days later. There were fifty people at the graveside despite the first, cold mizzling rain of autumn.

Gamrick was alone. Iris, after reading about his affair with Kate and listening to TV commentators talk about it, had asked for a divorce, which he would not contest. His sons, Jeff and Hal, tried to convince him not to act hastily. But he said he would go with whatever she wanted.

The priest had given a brief eulogy in the chapel, and two of Kate's TV colleagues had also eulogized her.

The priest recited the last few prayers in Latin. Then her casket was lowered into the grave, and Gamrick knew that unlike Hamlet, who leaped into the grave and clutched Ophilia to his breast, proclaiming his love for her, he could only stand mute and accept the awful weight of guilt for her death.

The thud of the first spade full of earth struck the top of the casket. Gamrick winced as though he had been struck. One by one the mourners added their shovel full of earth until his turn came. He hesitated. Tears filled his eyes. Then he pushed the spade into the soft, dark earth, and standing over the grave he slowly tilted the spade down, allowing the earth to slide off and gently fall on the casket. Then a sudden anger gripped him, and he thrust the shovel into the mound of earth that would eventually be used to fill the grave. . . .

Epilogue

Gamrick and Harkowitz became law partners specializing in criminal law. They opened a luxurious office in Washington, D.C., and quickly became two of the most sought-after lawyers in the business.

Three months after Gamrick left the Navy, Senator Dobbs, Secretary of the Navy John Howard and several of *Utah*'s ranking officers were charged with drug trafficking and awaited trial.

Gamrick grew a beard, which came in gray. He saw his sons and grandchildren frequently. He never saw Iris and lived alone in the house on the cove. He gave some thought to building another ocean-going sailboat, but satisfied his desire for sailing by taking out a small catboat.

He went to the office every day and sometimes even on Saturday and Sunday. He often went to Kate's grave, put flowers on it, and would spend hours sitting on a stone bench which he had put there for that purpose.

Despite Harkowitz's efforts to involve him in a social life, he eschewed it and preferred to be alone, read and listen to music.

Almost a year after the court-martial, Gamrick stopped at the office on a Saturday night on the way home from an evening at the Kennedy Center and, picking up the mail that had been delivered earlier that day, saw a letter addressed to him. It had been mailed from Hawaii. He switched on the light, sat at his desk, opened the envelope, and removed two folded pieces

of paper. Scotch-taped to one was a color photograph
of Anderson, Julie, and Downs. The three were naked.

Gamrick stared at the photograph. His lips trembled.
Then, suddenly bolting up, he shouted, "Downs ...
Downs ... Downs." Still standing, he unfolded the
second sheet of paper and read:

"We're a family now. It cost a million dollars to
make it happen. But the second million makes everything a lot easier. I was afraid it was all over when you
got to Hawkins. Then the drug guys became real nervous. They wanted me to take the fall, but you got me
off. Hardass McCafery was right: I knew but didn't
tell. Gus knew but didn't tell. Julie knew but didn't
tell. Gus was never in the turret. There are more places
to hide aboard a battleship—"

Gamrick stopped reading. He let the paper fall to the
floor, and dropping to his knees, he covered his face
with his hands and softly but uncontrollably sobbed.
Truth's double-edged sword had struck a mortal blow.

By the year 2000, 2 out of 3 Americans could be illiterate.

It's true.

Today, 75 million adults...about one American in three, can't read adequately. And by the year 2000, U.S. News & World Report envisions an America with a literacy rate of only 30%.

Before that America comes to be, you can stop it...by joining the fight against illiteracy today.

Call the Coalition for Literacy at toll-free **1-800-228-8813** and volunteer.

Volunteer Against Illiteracy.
The only degree you need is a degree of caring.